What people are saying about …

THE FEAST OF SAINT BERTIE

"Popa's novel showed me that the simple life can be a spiritual feast—and a chance to help others. A riveting read that taught me much about myself."

DiAnn Mills, author of *When the Nile Runs Red* and *Awaken My Heart,* speaker, and teacher

"A story-feast from the get-go! *The Feast of Saint Bertie* is a surprising, engaging, and unique novel that will challenge readers to rethink what it means to be a Christ-follower in today's crazy, materialistic culture. With vivid characters, unconventional settings, and a beautifully unfolding plot, this book is the kind that stays with you—like the fond memory of a great meal."

Mary E. DeMuth, author of Christy Award–nominated *Watching the Tree Limbs*

"*The Feast of Saint Bertie* is a gripping journey through one woman's loss, which leads to the discovery of all that was missing. Kathleen Popa serves up a rich and tender story with characters that are alive and compelling. From the first mesmerizing scene to the final page, *The Feast of Saint Bertie* is sustenance for heart, spirit, and soul, a story you will long remember."

Sharon K. Souza, author of *Every Good and Perfect Gift*

THE FEAST OF

SAINT BERTIE

THE FEAST OF
SAINT BERTIE

a novel

KATHLEEN POPA

David C Cook®

transforming lives together

THE FEAST OF SAINT BERTIE
Published by David C. Cook
4050 Lee Vance View
Colorado Springs, CO 80918 U.S.A.

David C. Cook Distribution Canada
55 Woodslee Avenue, Paris, Ontario, Canada N3L 3E5

David C. Cook U.K., Kingsway Communications
Eastbourne, East Sussex BN23 6NT, England

David C. Cook and the graphic circle C logo
are registered trademarks of Cook Communications Ministries.

This story is a work of fiction. All characters and events are the product of
the author's imagination. Any resemblance to any person, living or dead, is coincidental.

All Scripture quotations are taken from the Revised Standard Version
Bible, copyright 1952 [2nd edition, 1971], Division of Christian
Education of the National Council of the Churches of Christ in the
United States of America. Used by permission. All rights reserved.

The quote on page 214 is from *The Story of a Soul (L'Histoire d'une Âme):
The Autobiography of St. Thérèse of Lisieux With Additional Writings
and Sayings of St. Thérèse, by Thérèse, de Lisieux, Saint, 1873–1897,*
trans. by Thomas N. Taylor (Thomas Nimmo), 1873–1963.

LCCN 2008931907
ISBN 978-1-4347-9987-6

© 2008 Kathleen Popa
Published in association with Janet Kobobel Grant, Books & Such
Literary Agency, 4788 Carissa Ave., Santa Rosa, CA 95405

The Team: Don Pape, Nicci Jordan Hubert,
Amy Kiechlin, Jack Campbell, and Karen Athen
Cover Photos: Corbis; and iStockPhoto

Printed in the United States of America
First Edition 2008

1 2 3 4 5 6 7 8 9 10

062608

FOR NOAH AND ALEX, MY TWO BOYS

ACKNOWLEDGMENTS

I am deeply grateful to my dear friend Sharon K. Souza, who insisted on reading chapter after chapter of this novel as I wrote it, even after learning that the story would hit painfully close to her personal sorrow. Sharon, my heart broke with yours. Thank you for helping to make this a better book.

Janet Kobobel Grant, I'm glad that you are my agent, and my friend. Thank you for understanding the stories I want to tell, and for your wisdom and help in finding those stories a home.

Don Pape, I'm delighted to publish a second novel with David C. Cook. Thank you for your faith and support in making it happen. Nicci Hubert, I loved working with you. Thank you for seeing what the story needed when I didn't. You made me a better writer. John Hamilton, thank you for a beautiful cover design. Ingrid Beck, Amy Kiechlin, Jack Campbell, Karen Athen, and everybody at David C. Cook, thank you for your excellent work.

Gayle Roper, James Scott Bell, and the members of Gayle's 2006 Fiction Mentoring Clinic, thank you all for your help, advice, and encouragement in this project.

Steve Campbell, Dan Lockwood, Jeff Weber, Scott Daugherty, Peggy Durfey, Ingrid Salomonson, Dave Coon, and Jill Lee-Jones, thank you all for your excellent technical advice.

Irene Spaulding, my sister, thank you for proofreading the manuscript one last time before I sent it off to the publisher.

Margaret Conner (Mom), thank you for encouraging me

every day of my life. Time and experience have taught me the depth of your wisdom and love.

Alex, Noah, and Julia, thank you for making life and motherhood a joy.

George, thank you for bringing coffee and sometimes breakfast to my desk, for loving me when I am at my most neurotic, for saying I'm beautiful when I am not, for helping me persevere when the writing is hard. I am blessed to be your wife.

PROLOGUE

They're just decorations, these candles. You don't need anything to pray. Truly, it is best to come with nothing—only yourself.

Just one of the things I've learned.

But this sweet night of jubilation in my mountain retreat, in my small cell, made of stone—okay, cinder block—calls for a bit of ceremony. I think of the woman I was when I came here, all I feared and all I prayed for—and all I've been given. Silk and velvet wouldn't be out of place. Frankincense and myrrh would fit right in. But I have made my vow, and candles seem best.

I start with just one candle, then add another, and another till I have five. I line them up in a row on the floor. I sprinkle crushed rose petals about and breathe in their fragrance and the sweet smell of cinnamon rolls. I fetch the pomegranate I plucked from the tree down the road and run my fingers over its aged flesh. I split it open and squeeze the juice into a cup to serve as my communion wine. I set the cup beside the candles.

I slip my shoes off, kneel, and close my eyes.

Prayer can be such sweetness. I begin alone, or so it often seems, and that's frightening at first, but I follow the path and wear it clean, and it grows familiar. And then I find myself in the best of company.

No words this time. I don't always need them. Tonight, there's only love, which is joy, which is thanksgiving.

I open my eyes and begin my communion supper. I pull the plate before me, and lift the cinnamon roll in two hands.

"This is my body broken for you," I recite.

When I pull the roll apart, it unwinds, dripping sweet molten butter and spice, dropping raisins and walnuts. I place a bite inside my mouth and chew. Savor.

I lift the cup. "This is my blood which was poured out for you. The blood of the new and everlasting covenant." I hold it to my lips and drink.

It's been a year now since I came. I gaze at the candles and think how lovely they are, flickering in a fiery tarantella, like the dance I witnessed at the ocean's edge when my friends kicked stars back into the sky. It was the same night I danced my own sort of reel behind closed eyes, when the saints of ages took me in at last as one of their own.

CHAPTER 1

Fire is a lovely thing, I've always thought. Always loved the chrysanthemum orange of it, the way it reaches.

Even that April day when it flared through my house as though the framework were made of wax. I watched from Suzanne's lawn, still in my funeral black. I didn't wear a veil; no one does anymore, though I do see wisdom in them. A funeral is such a public affair for such private pain. Of all times when a woman shouldn't worry how she looks ...

But the fire wafted black smoke, and it seemed the house I'd shared with Larry wore its own veil while it burned inside.

The sun had begun to set so I moved closer to the fire for warmth, but Suzanne pulled me back.

"There's nothing you can do, Bertie," she said, not understanding. She pulled my head to her shoulder, and for a moment, it felt good to leave it there.

But I pulled away. I knew I had to stand full on my own two feet. I also knew that once I told Suzanne what I intended to do, she'd try to stop me. And I was so easily stopped in those days.

But didn't the fire seem like an omen, a divine nod of approval? There'd be no house to set in order, no hospital bed or wheelchair to return to the Parkinson's Center. No hesitation, and no turning back. I could actually go through with it.

No matter what Suzanne thought.

And the woman does think. On overdrive. She'd spent the entire ride to the funeral drilling me yet again about Garrett, my son who had dropped off the face of the earth sometime in the past four months. Had I called his ex-girlfriend? Had I tried his cell phone? Had I spoken personally to the head of human resources where he works—or used to work?

Could Suzanne really think I hadn't done everything possible to reach my son? It was me, sitting day by day beside his father's wheelchair, as he curled into himself like a wilted rosebud and wept that mewling cry his disease had left him. When the nurse came by for her daily rounds, I used *my* free time to drive to Garrett's apartment, knock on his door, slip notes in his mailbox, make calls that rolled into voice mail. The day Larry entered the hospital, again, with pneumonia—*was it only a week ago?*—I tried one last desperate time to bring Garrett to his father's deathbed.

Both his land line and cell phone had been disconnected. I had learned that he quit showing up for work without warning, and he'd abandoned his apartment with three months rent left unpaid. His girlfriend had broken up with him a year ago, and the reason she told me: his outbursts and anger …

What was a fire compared with my missing son? My mind halted at the thought of all I'd lost. This house was the least of it. I could let it go.

The fire truck hunkered across the street near our gingko tree. Voices sputtered from the radio—to no one, I guess, as no one seemed to listen. The occasional whiff of smoke caught in my breath, but most of it ascended skyward. A gush of water arced from where two firemen squatted in yellow suits, to the top of the pyre that was my home.

I slipped a hand into my shoulder bag and roamed my fingers over the contents: the torn spine of a paperback book, the snapped closure of a small Bible, and the embossed leather of a journal.

"All shall be well, and all shall be well" ... I whispered the words beneath my breath.

A fireman with his gloves off carried a clipboard across the street and glanced over the scattered watchers till his eyes found mine. "Roberta Denys?"

"Yes?" I shook his hand.

"I'm Fire Marshal Matthew Huong with the Saratoga Fire Department. Do you remember me?"

Should I? I tried to place him.

"I used to attend your church. You watched my daughter in the nursery. I'm very sorry about your husband."

Suzanne stepped forward. "I remember you, Matthew. I'm Suzanne Keyes. We were both in the Christmas play one year."

"Of course." He shook her hand, then turned to me. "May we speak privately?"

To my relief and distress, Suzanne stepped back. I followed him a distance away.

"It's been quite a day for you, Roberta. I'm sorry. It's good there's no wind. A fire like this can endanger the homes around it, but we're going to keep it contained."

I nodded.

"Now there was just you and your husband living in the house, is that correct? No children or other family members?"

"No, just the two of us. Our son lives, um, on his own."

"Do you know what caused the fire?"

I had no idea. "I turned off the heater before I left—or at least that's what I generally—"

"—can't very well attend the funeral if he doesn't know his father's dead." It was Suzanne's whisper, back behind my right shoulder.

I turned and caught the eye of the woman beside her, a new neighbor I'd barely met once. I scowled at Suzanne and she stopped.

Matthew cleared his throat, and I gave him my last shred of attention.

"I'm speaking a little out of school here, but I don't want you to be in danger. We'd normally wait to tell you this after the investigation, but we've already found clear evidence of arson. I can't specify what kind of evidence, but one of your neighbors, uh, Carroll ..." He glanced at his clipboard.

"Graham."

"Yes, Carroll Graham said she saw someone running from your backyard, a man, she thinks, but he wore a hood, and she couldn't describe him. Because it happened during the funeral, it's possible the arsonist could have known that you were away."

Arson.

The word floated between us, opaque and undefined. I did try to focus, but my mind offered all the wrong pictures: Larry's withered body in a coffin. A flurry of rose petals ...

"Do you have any idea who might have set the fire? Was anyone missing from the funeral?"

I pushed my glasses up my nose. My hands were trembling, so I folded my arms to keep them still.

Arson.

"I'm sorry," said Matthew. "I'm sure you're overwhelmed, with a funeral and a fire in the same day."

I motioned over my shoulder. "Would you mind if Suzanne—"

"Go ahead."

I reached a hand and she was back beside me, clutching my arm with her acrylic nails.

"Roberta, was anybody angry with you or your husband? Maybe a disgruntled employee ..."

Suzanne frowned. "Larry resigned his position six years ago."

He wrote a note on his clipboard. "Six years ... And Mr. Denys was CEO at ..."

"ConjuTech," I said.

"You'd be surprised how long some folks remember. Perhaps neighbors, relatives—"

"Nope." Suzanne pinched the word off with her lips.

He looked at me. "Even an angry driver on the road, someone who displayed road rage."

"No," I said. "Nobody I can think of."

"Did you disable your security? The alarm did not go off."

Suzanne gave a firm shake of the head. "Not possible."

"The system was only used for the main house," I explained. "And I've hardly been in there in ... months."

"Years," Suzanne corrected.

I caught the familiar tension in her voice, and cringed. But she was right. "Years. We moved into the guest apartment after Larry's diagnosis." I pointed to the small extension opposite the garage. Flames curled outward from several windows along the outer wall.

All shall be well …

Matthew pulled a card from his clipboard and handed it to me. "Thanks, Roberta. I think we're done for now. Please call if you think of anything that might help the investigation."

"I will."

"Do you have someplace to stay tonight?"

"She'll stay with me," Suzanne said.

I looked at her.

"In Amber's room. She's been married two years."

"I know that, Suzanne. I went to the wedding."

"And wasn't it nice of you to come?"

Matthew looked from me to her, and back again. "Do you have a cell phone where we can reach you?"

I gave the number to him, and he walked away.

Half of the people milling about were strangers: teenagers in soccer uniforms, a woman in a business suit. A young man in an Oakland Raiders cap like Garrett used to wear. For just an instant I thought it was him.

But it wasn't.

I'd never liked Suzanne's way of fixing her gaze on me, like there was some message that I should decipher. "What?" I asked.

"Nothing."

"Suzanne, what?"

"I just think you'd better find your son."

What could I say?

I looked back toward the house. A fireman walked through my front door with an ax in his hands. The left front corner of my bedroom collapsed.

I slipped my fingers back into my purse, clutched the spines of my books like they were the hand of God, and whispered the words of Julian of Norwich to my soul:

"All shall be well, and all shall be well, and all manner of things shall be well."

———

And for a short while I almost had myself convinced.

I went home with Suzanne, made my calls to the insurance people—well, Suzanne called them, and I answered questions. But we got through it.

Then, before she could bring up Garrett or any of the ways I'd failed her as a friend, I shut myself up in Amber's room.

I lay in the dark for three hours, retching wide-mouthed like some tragic actress in a silent film. One sniffle, I knew, and she'd be back at my side, clucking, commiserating, taking charge of everything. Even my tears.

So much for Julian of Norwich.

You think you're all right when these things happen. At first, there's this silent fog that softens the edges of things, makes them beautiful really. Mysterious.

Anyway, wasn't it better this way? Larry out of his wheelchair at last, out of that withered body of his?

Oh, but God! I did ache for him! Grief thrashed inside me with such violence, I curled into myself and held a pillow to my open mouth.

Desperate, I wiped the palms of my hands across my eyes, kicked the covers off, and stood. The floor was thickly carpeted over con-crete, but I walked softly all the same. I eased open the door and peered into the living room.

The television was on. Suzanne sat cross-legged before the cof-fee table, working on her laptop. I'd forgotten. The woman hardly sleeps. And she'd lost half a day's work following me around.

I pulled the door shut and released the knob. As soon as I turned around, I realized my solution: the window, large and low to the floor.

I slipped into the bathrobe Suzanne had lent me and pulled back the sheers. I squeezed the latch till I felt it release, then drew the window to the side.

Once it was open, I leaned out and drew a deep breath of cool air. Just beneath the ledge there grew a juniper bush. I took care, stepping out, to fit first one bare foot, and then the other into the narrow space between the shrub and the wall. But my nightgown caught on the branches, and when I stepped away I tore a slit in the fabric as long as my hand.

Suzanne's lawn was wet and cold under my bare feet. I crept to her gazebo and sat on the glider, pulling my feet up and tucking the bathrobe around them. The night sky hovered low, pink from the street lamps and hazy from the smoke that drifted from my gutted home across the street.

In the morning, I'd pay Suzanne for the torn nightgown. I doubted it would merit a footnote once I started telling her my plans. Not that they were big plans; they weren't. But to Suzanne, for whom living large was a life's vocation …

Well, you see, I meant to live small.

CHAPTER 2

Huddled up in the cold air, I couldn't cry anymore. And I wanted to. I wanted to release the sorrow, but it settled into my stomach like a rock.

I tried to remember Larry's face. Not the wax-doll face in the casket, but the face he used to turn to me when he lifted his chin and smiled. Like we'd never met, and he'd only just spotted me and liked what he saw.

How long had it been since he'd done that? Eighteen months, I guessed, since he'd lost the ability to lift his head, and a year since his eyes had clamped shut. And, no, that curled-in version of Larry was not the one I wanted to remember.

I sat on the glider, wanting only the smile he gave me on our second wedding day.

Just a month past his diagnosis, we'd gone to Alaska. "While I still can," said Larry, and I agreed. We found a secluded lake that day, half iced over, frosty blue. Our second wedding had no guests, reception, or fancy clothes. Just a white sprig of yarrow he'd placed in my hair.

He'd settled himself on the ground, his back to a rock, and laid his cane to the side. He invited me to sit beside him. I did, and we sat silent for a long time, just taking in that still blue expanse. At last he touched my hand, and asked, "What will we do with the rest of my life?"

Then, despite all those perfunctory years of marriage, I did a reckless thing. I wailed. "I want you back," I said. And the way he raised his eyebrows, I understood, because we'd never left each other. We had only left ourselves. "I want *me* back," I continued. "We used to have time to talk about our thoughts and ideas, about the things we read, and now we have so little …"

I felt like a train careening out of control, talking like this, but I was telling him the truth. In our courtship and the first six months of marriage, we'd had nothing but time for each other. Then Garrett came along and changed all of our plans, and Larry set about making a living. And no one can doubt he did a first-class job of it. He built ConjuTech to a respectable size; we put Garrett through Stanford and built our house. But we hadn't talked in that old way in decades, and time was running out. Still, the books he read were all about business now, and I didn't begin to know what went on in his head.

He fixed his blue eyes on mine, and said nothing. I took a deep breath, and summed it up: "I just want us back." I'd leave it there.

But what would he do with that? Would he give me that level executive eye he'd developed over the years? Put a reprimand in my file for excess emotion? What would he do?

Incredibly, he covered his eyes with his hand, and wept. "Me, too." I took his other hand, and he wove his fingers into mine. "Me, too," he said again.

I scooted closer, and we held each other and talked till we came to an understanding, or perhaps just till we ran out of words.

At last he grabbed his cane and started to stand, and I got up to help him. We faced each other, and like the beaded hippy he'd once been, he plucked that stalk of yarrow, and tucked it in my hair. Then he straightened himself and cleared his throat. He took my left hand and pulled from it the two-carat diamond "success" ring he'd presented to me seventeen years before to replace my twenty-five dollar silver wedding band.

Why did he take my ring? What was he telling me? Had I misunderstood?

He put it in his pocket, and pulled out in its place … the silver band.

"You planned this," I said.

"Is it okay?"

Oh, yes. Yes it was okay. It was the dream I'd never acknowledged come true. I'd missed the silver band and all it represented. The diamond had never felt right. "Yes," I said, weeping again. "Yes."

So there, by that glacial blue lake, we made our promises again with only a fish rippling the water to witness. We kissed, and then he broke away and hobbled through the forest as fast as he could with that cane, which was faster than I would have imagined. I followed behind, laughing. *What in the world?* When we reached the road, he flagged down a passing car.

And who should the driver turn out to be but a priest!

Larry handed him our camera, explaining, babbling, that we were newlyweds, and would he please, if it wasn't a bother, would he please snap the picture. So, bewildered and in a hurry, the priest took just one snapshot, but it was a good one. Me laughing, looking prettier than I actually am, and Larry handsome with his long silver hair and those celestial blue eyes.

A great picture.

I rocked myself in Suzanne's glider and smiled, remembering. I should get the snapshot enlarged, I thought, I should …

My pictures! I clapped a hand to my mouth and moaned.

And then I found the way I would cry that night, the one realization that would wrench my grief into the open air.

CHAPTER 3

Well, but there was a chance, wasn't there, that some of the pictures had survived? Couldn't there be a corner someplace the fire had missed?

We'd kept most of our photos in archive boxes on a shelf in the family room.

Some—the best of them—were in the guest apartment. We'd moved there the very day we returned from Alaska. It was a way of simplifying, and a way of going back.

And we'd pinned that snapshot over our bed.

I eased my feet onto the grass, then started for my home. In the dim light of the street lamp, the house looked almost like nothing had happened, like I could walk through the door and drown my sorrows in a cup of tea. My tea, in my cup, in my own guest apartment. I tucked myself for a moment behind Suzanne's jasmine trellis—hiding, I guess, from anyone who might drive by and catch me there in Suzanne's torn nightclothes.

But no one did. I heard the traffic on Quito Road and the distant roar of the highway. But here, all was quiet.

I slipped out from the jasmine and walked to the street. The pavement was warmer than the grass had been, and I stepped from one foot to the other, to dry them. Then I crossed to the other side.

The minute I stepped foot on my own lawn, the basset hound next door began to bark. I stepped back, but he bellowed like a foghorn.

I knew what he wanted. Larry used to give him dog biscuits through the hole in the fence, and later it was me, poking them through to please Larry. But the biscuits were all burnt now, and the racket was going to wake the neighborhood.

I walked through my gate, across to the fence, and crouched at the hole. "Wainwright!"

He quieted. I heard his dog tags jingle as he loped across his yard. "Only me, Wainwright. See?"

I slipped my hand in. He licked it, and I stroked his nose. When I stepped away, he scratched at the fence, but I'd won his silence. I turned to the house.

The yellow police-barrier tape forbade my entry. From behind the tape, I tried to peer through our bedroom window, but all was dark inside. Of course, the glass was coated with soot, I should have known.

When I turned away, I saw something white against the dark grass, over near the hydrangea. I walked across the lawn, beyond the yellow tape, and picked it up.

It was a collector card, bent in the middle. In the dark, I couldn't see the image, but it was a Magic the Gathering card. The oddest memories lie near the surface—the moment I touched it, I felt myself back in my family room some twenty years prior, picking up Garrett's cards off the floor. I held it to my nose and closed my eyes. It still smelled like the palm of a young boy's hand.

When I opened my eyes, I saw there were more, scattered under the bush. Dutifully as ever, I bent to pick them up.

When I reached for the last one, my hand brushed something hard with slots. Garrett's Rubik's Cube.

I groped further under the bush, and found his old Hacky Sack, and a Koosh Ball. Things we'd kept in a box on Garrett's old dresser.

What in the world?

Well. The firemen might have carried things out of the house. For who knew what reason.

I walked to our bench beneath the arbor to rest, and gave that yellow tape my full attention.

Arson.

Someone had burned my house down. I almost laughed. Someone that angry—how could I not know who it was? But I didn't know. I had no idea. It didn't matter, though. I had no problem walking away from all this.

All but the pictures. In the morning, I'd call the fire marshal and ask when—

The gate squeaked open.

I tucked myself into the arbor's shadow and held my breath.

"Bertie?"

"Suzanne!" I scolded, desperate to mask my embarrassment. "You scared me!"

"What are you doing here?"

"It's my home." A lame answer, but it would have to do.

"Do you have any idea what time it is?"

"How'd you know I was here?"

"Carroll called me."

"It was me, Roberta," came Carroll's voice over the fence. "Wainwright woke me up, and I thought it might be a burglar or … someone. I saw a guy running away from your house, did they tell you that?"

"Yes, they told me."

"Do they suspect foul play?"

"They seem to."

"I wish I'd gotten a good look. I'd just driven up, and I saw him run around the corner. It was only a second, and I didn't think much about it till I saw the smoke. I think it was a man."

"Thank you for talking to them."

"You okay?"

"I'm fine, Carroll. Sorry for the noise." Carroll retreated back into her home, and I lowered my voice to a whisper. "What'd you think, Suzanne, that you'd just confront the arsonist by yourself?"

"I saw you weren't in your room, Bertie. I knew it was you, not him. What are you doing here? It's a crime scene."

"I just …" I shook my head.

"C'mon. Let's go back. You don't even have shoes on. And don't touch anything!"

I tucked the cards and toys into the pocket of my bathrobe, and followed her home.

When we got there, she made us some tea. "You could have used the door."

"You would have stopped me."

"Come in here." She lead the way to the living room and settled on the couch.

I sat beside her. "You've redecorated." Her white living room had been painted blue and fitted with beige leather furniture.

She leaned over to the glass table, retrieved her laptop, and perched it on her knees.

I really was tired, and if she wanted me to admire her Web site …

But she didn't. She opened a file, and there, right on top, was a picture of Larry. It was one of his best, a headshot taken years before, the day ConjuTech went public. He'd thought to send it in to the *Mercury News*, but instead he'd gone with another one, more formal. But this one showed him amused and handsome, just a bit unkempt. This was the one I would have picked.

"Suzanne …" I tried to tell her what it meant to me, but one more word and my voice would break. I brushed my tears away.

Below that picture, she had one of Garrett, standing next to her daughter, Amber, on their first day at nursery school.

"We always thought they'd get married," Suzanne said. She scrolled down.

There were, I guess, a hundred pictures or more, some I didn't even know she had: of our wedding, of Garrett's first day home from the hospital.

And the last one, by some miracle, was of Larry in his flannel shirt, and me with yarrow in my hair, radiant beside that lake in Alaska.

I wiped my face with the palm of my hand. "This is what I was looking for over there."

"I was going to put nice little graphics around them, but—"

"No need."

She pushed the button to eject the CD from her laptop, and handed it to me.

"Suzanne?"

"What?"

I pulled the bathrobe away from my leg and showed her the tear in the nightgown. "I accidentally—"

"Go to bed, Bertie," she said. "I really don't care."

So that's what I did. I gave her a hug and thanked her again, returned to Amber's room, and shut the door. I set my CD of pictures on the dresser, pulled out Garrett's trading cards and toys, and set them beside it. Then I thought better, gathered Garrett's things in two hands, and stuffed them deep into my handbag.

I went to bed, and whispered the words again.

"All shall be well, and all shall be well ... "

CHAPTER 4

I woke to the kind of music I can describe only as a sonic laxative, a burbling soup of synthesizers and wind chimes and something like troubled gastric juice that I'd long since thought I'd heard the last of.

But I heard it now, so loud the headboard rattled against the wall.

An unearthly voice whispered between the notes. I rolled to my back and sat up, searching the walls for speakers, till I saw the panel in the ceiling, painted ice blue to blend with the rest of the room. Almost directly overhead.

"Suzanne!" I couldn't hear my own voice.

I put on my borrowed bathrobe, cupped my hands to my ears, and escaped into the hall. The volume was quieter there, and I shut the door on the problem. Still, the house rang with noise. The television chattered the morning news to an empty living room. I switched it off. "Suzanne!"

She marched out of her bedroom, toweling her hair. "What's wrong?"

"Where's the switch in Amber's room?"

"What switch?"

"The music switch." I walked, and she followed. The doorknob trembled under my hand when I turned it and pushed open the door.

"Oh!" She crossed the floor, reached behind the desk, and the music was gone—at least in this room. "I don't know how that happened." She turbaned the towel around her head. "The crisis is over. Stop wringing your hands."

I stuffed them in my pockets.

"It's nice music, don't you think?"

"Interesting."

"It's got subliminal messages woven through, scientifically designed to help you feel confident and competent. Do you feel confident and competent?"

"Not really."

"Well. I'll have you know, I've sold two houses since I started listening to this. Come on. If we hurry, we can have breakfast together."

I followed her to the kitchen, which she'd painted the color of wheat and tiled with granite. "Have you changed every room in this house?"

"Only the ones Charlie was in."

"What time is it?"

"Six o'clock. But I need to go in early. The phone's been ringing off the hook this morning. I hope you didn't hear that. You like oatmeal?"

I already knew better than to answer—she meant for me to say yes. "What's wrong at the office?"

"A feng shui problem." She dumped two packets of instant

oatmeal into two bowls, carried them to the refrigerator, and decanted hot water from the door.

"Feng shui?"

Her cell phone trebled the 1812 overture. She pulled it from her pocket and flipped it open.

"Hi." She fetched a spoon from the drawer, and stirred my oatmeal. "You're kidding me! He really won't sign?" Suzanne paced the floor. "Well, look. We've got till this afternoon to talk him down. Hold him off a few hours. And call Moretti; tell him I want to meet with him this afternoon. No, wait. I've got a showing at three. See if you can get him in at eleven. Bye." She flipped the phone shut and dropped it in her pocket, then retrieved her oatmeal and took a bite.

"You've got to go," I said.

"No, no. I still have …" She glanced at her watch. "Ten minutes. Guy's got a buyer for his house, but the buyer's Taiwanese, and he won't sign as long as there's a concrete planter across from the back door." She shrugged. "Supposedly, it's bad luck. But the seller calls it silly superstition and would rather lose the sale, evidently, than back down."

I nodded.

"I've handled his type before." Suzanne straightened her posture and took one of her cleansing breaths. "Confident and competent." She passed her teeth over an acrylic thumbnail, then looked at me and shook her head. "You're holding that bowl the way you hold your hands, like it's your life rope or something. Loosen up."

"Suzanne, I'm a new widow. Give me at least a day."

"I'll be generous. Two days. And then we're going to get you a place to live, and a job."

"A job?"

"I know you don't need the money. But you need the diversion. You've spent the past six years holed up over there with Larry. It's time you joined the living."

I dropped my spoon back into the bowl. "Larry was alive, Suzanne. The whole time I was with him."

Her cell phone rang, and she pulled it from her pocket. "What?" She dumped the rest of her oatmeal down the garbage disposal. "Fine. When's he want to meet? No, that's too early. I need time to—" She bit her thumbnail, leaned into the living room and looked at the television, which I'd turned off. "Well, what's the traffic report say?" She pushed her forehead against the doorjamb. "Fine then, I'll take the 101. Bye."

She snapped her phone shut, and picked up exactly where we'd left off. "I know Larry was alive, Bertie. But don't you want something to do now?"

"No. I mean, I don't want a job. I have something else in mind."

"They have a list of volunteer opportunities at the church office—"

"Not that, either."

"Well, what then?"

"You don't have time to hear it."

"How much time can it take?"

"I've got a plan, Suzanne. Later, when you've got time, we'll sit down and—"

"I think you'd better tell me now."

I crossed my arms. "I'm going to move onto my Skyline property."

"Oh." She shrugged and pulled two cups from the cupboard. "That we can manage. But you'll still need a place to stay while they build a house up there. That'll take several months." She handed me my coffee. "Come to think of it, that would make two building projects, counting your little problem across the street. That's an awful lot to load on your plate—are you sure?"

"No, no building projects."

"What do you mean? You've got to at least rebuild—"

"Do you remember that man who wanted to buy my house two years ago, and I wouldn't sell?"

"Vaguely. I don't remember his name."

"It's Steve Travalla. I've got his card in my purse, and I'll give it to you. I want you to call him up and offer him my property."

"What, the mountain property?"

"No. I'm going to live there, remember? My property here. He wanted it for spec housing. He was going to tear my house down, anyway—"

"Bertie, no. You can't sell now, of all times. Without a house on the lot, I can't get near the price—"

"I don't care." I tightened my fingers around my cup. "I don't care about the money."

"Fine, you don't care about the money." She checked her watch. "Let's talk in my room. I need to get dressed." Before she finished the sentence, she was halfway there. I followed.

Her bed was strewn with papers and files. "Did you sleep at all?" I asked.

"Sleep's overrated." She stepped into her closet and turned on the light.

I sat on the window seat.

"Okay, so you don't have anyplace to live up on Skyline," she called from the closet. "Unless you plan to pitch a tent."

"I don't need to. I own a small building there."

She stood in the doorway, buttoning her shirt. "What building?"

"Halfway up the hill. You remember? It's that little cinder-block—"

"Shed." She finished for me. "It's a shed. You can't be serious."

I smiled.

"You're going to live in that shed, on that dirt floor."

I clasped my hands, and pressed one thumb along the palm to my wrist. "It doesn't have a dirt floor."

"You're insane." She looked me in the eye and bit her thumbnail.

"Larry wouldn't think so."

"Larry thought you should live in a shed?"

"Larry understood my spiritual needs."

"Spiritual needs." She rolled her eyes. "Spiritual needs, fine. But why would you—?"

"That's *definitely* more than you've got time to hear."

She checked her watch. "Give me the short version." She pulled the towel from her head and fingered her hair into place.

I felt a prickle of sweat beneath my arms and looked away to catch my breath.

"Just anytime you feel ready." She checked her watch again.

"I had a vision."

"I didn't hear, Bertie. You had a what?"

"A vision. Actually—three."

I heard a sound like splitting sticks, and she cursed. Her acrylic nail had broken lengthwise, and half of it lay at her feet. Her cell phone rang, and she flicked it out of her pocket. "Cammie, what?" She retrieved her broken nail. "Well, he's a half hour early. Why should he expect—tell him I'm on my way. Tell him the traffic's heavy and I might be late." She snapped the phone shut.

"There is no short version of the story, Suzy. And you need to get going."

"Wait, wait." She bridged a hand across her forehead and squeezed her temples. "You had ... *visions*. You were over there having *visions*, and they told you to go live in a shed."

"No, I was eighteen the last time, and no one told me to—"

"Bertie, stop!" She took a breath, and paced the next question, like she was teaching a slow learner. "Where does your son fit in all this?"

"I don't know where Garrett is."

"Exactly."

"He's a grown man—"

"Who might very well have burned your house down yesterday."

If she'd slapped me, I'd have felt it less. "What?" I couldn't breathe.

"I'm sorry, so sorry. I shouldn't bring this up now. But don't you see it? He disappeared when his father was dying. I don't know what's up with that, but it's not the act of a ..."

I finally took a breath and shuddered.

Suzanne sat beside me. "Bertie." She took my hand. "I'm not saying he did it; I don't know."

I pulled away. "Okay, so something's obviously up with him. It doesn't mean he burned my house down."

"Of course not. It's just that every time Garrett acts up, he always sets something on fire."

"That's not fair! And it's not—"

"Remember when he burned your doghouse down?"

"We didn't even have a dog anymore; it was a harmless prank. And he was what? Eleven? In fact, Amber was involved, as I recall. Maybe she's the culprit."

"And the time he got suspended from Stanford for—"

"Burning his roommate's undershorts in the shower stall. Oh, that proves it." I attempted a laugh and failed. I desperately did not want to cry, but there it was.

Because I'd just remembered two incidents the all-knowing Suzanne knew nothing about. One was the shouting match Garrett had with Larry in the garage, maybe a week before the diagnosis. The other was Garrett at fifteen, fuming over something I'd said, lighting a match to my photograph in the bathroom sink. He was angry that day. It was no prank.

Had I missed the signs somehow? Had my son become a monster, and I just never knew?

"No." Suzanne pulled my head to her shoulder. "No, it doesn't prove anything."

I wrapped my arms around her and clung there, more in an effort to bind myself to the mast than because of any sort of affection for this longtime friend, who'd just whipped up a storm in my mind. Where was my son? What was happening to Garrett? "You're right," I whispered. "I can't go anywhere till I find him."

"You can stay here," she offered. "As long as you want."

I didn't want.

Her cell phone rang again. Without bothering to answer, she hugged me once more and rushed out the door.

CHAPTER 5

If I'd tried to stand, I would have fallen over. Trembling, I lifted my coffee cup from the window ledge and parted the curtain, watching as Suzanne's Escalade cannonballed out of the driveway.

She was gone. The "confident and competent" music had played itself out, leaving only the ticking of the wall clock. That, and the thrashing waves inside my head.

Garrett used to say he hated me. Not always, but often enough. The day he burned my picture, he said a lot of things.

But so what? When a child says that, he means, "I hate being grounded," or "I hate when you tell me no," or whatever. Right? Lots of kids say that to their parents, and they grow up to be doctors, or teachers, or, in Garrett's case, an engineering manager.

Not an arsonist.

I leaned my head back and gazed at my home across the street. Soot stains fanned from my windows and trailed up the plaster. A hole had been hacked through the side wall, and a pile of boards and debris lay beside it. The daylilies were trampled.

But my wild rose climbed the fence as though nothing had happened. It had grown to magnificent proportions over the years, and that was a miracle, considering Garrett had once ground it to a shred with his mountain bike.

Why was I only remembering the negative? There were good memories of Garrett too. There was the time we brought him home from the hospital. There were mornings at Gymboree. There was ...

So little. So little to remember.

Or was I just tired? The morning, the week had sapped the life from me, and I couldn't think at all.

A white mail truck pulled up outside the window. A blue-uniformed postman stepped out of the driver's seat, walked around the truck, and placed a fistful of envelopes into the box near Suzanne's drive.

He turned, and paused to study the remains of my house. After a long moment, he crossed the street, opened my mailbox, and slipped the mail inside.

He returned to his truck and moved on.

It did no good to sit in Suzanne's window, torturing myself. The sooner I found Garrett, the sooner I'd know he was all right.

I roused myself from the window seat and returned to Amber's room to dress in a castoff T-shirt and jeans.

I'd spoken on the phone with human resources at Vector Empowerment where Garrett worked, but I hadn't actually visited his department. Surely he'd made a friend or two there. Someone would know where he was.

I grabbed my purse and stepped out the front door.

I took one more look at my house across the street and breathed a long sigh. The rosebush was intact, the lawn freshly mowed, and in the middle, my house sat ruined and desolate. I shook my head, then crossed the street to retrieve my mail.

There was a catalog from Horchow. An electric bill. And an envelope from Bill Nolan, our attorney. Something about the estate, probably. I put the envelopes into my purse, walked to my car in Suzanne's driveway, and got in. What did Bill want? I thought things were taken care of for now. I retrieved his letter and opened it.

Inside was an envelope with my name on the front. The upper-left corner bore a return address:

From Larry

In heaven

Someone's terrible joke?

No. It was his handwriting: the trembled strokes, the lines pressed hard into the paper. Just the way he'd written after the Parkinson's diagnosis, sitting in his recliner with a lap desk, scrawling last-minute notes to his office at ConjuTech before he resigned.

I tore it open, and read:

To my beautiful wife, Roberta:

I hope it's not too great a shock, finding my letter in the mailbox at this particular juncture. My reasoning is simple: I've never wanted you to face anything alone, and your first year as a widow is something to face. So I mean to go through it with you in the only way I can. This is my last gift to you, Bertie: 52 letters which Bill has agreed to send at the rate of one per week, beginning the day of my funeral.

By the way, how was the funeral? Not too depressing, I hope. I hope there were lots of funny stories, and the music wasn't too bad. I hope nobody said "dust to dust"—what's the point of that, anyway? Mostly, I hope you and Garrett found reasons to smile.

I'm sure my brother came, and unless something drastic happens before you receive this letter, I'm just as sure he left right after—a plane to catch, right? Important business to attend to, no doubt.

I'm no one to talk, I know. I didn't build ConjuTech by meditating in my prayer closet, but at least I knew what a prayer closet was when Dr. Carter delivered the diagnosis.

Rich has no idea. All that bluster is just his escape from the voices in his head. Please, Bertie, when you've recovered, look him up. Tell him it was me, from the grave, who sent you, to tell him what the voices are trying to say. That should mess his head up a bit.

I also want you to talk to Garrett. Over the past several months it's become clear to us both that he's angry with me, but I just reacted, just yelled back. I think we might have resolved it eventually if I'd tried to listen and if I hadn't gotten sick. Now that I'm terminal, he doesn't seem to think we should talk about it. Just put on the good face for the dying, right? I wish I could break through, but I don't hold out much hope.

So, Bertie, please, when you can, tell him everything I did was done in love, whether he understands or not.

I think I've let you down in one important way. I've always known about that spiritual longing of yours. I fell in love with you the day you told me about the nun you met when you were twelve, who said she was married to Jesus. "You can do that?" you asked. Right there you knew what you wanted to be when you grew up. Of course, your mother deadpanned, "You can't be a nun; you're a Protestant."

The day you told me this, I wondered if you'd lower your sights and marry me.

Those visions of yours: God doesn't hand them out for entertainment. He knew you wanted Him. But life took over, and I let it. Things have been great between us these past months, but it's all been about me and my illness, and the future holds little hope that this will change.

I'm so sorry, Bertie. I want to encourage you, now that I'm gone: Follow those visions, wherever they lead. I don't know what that means, but I think you do. Don't hold back. Do what it takes to find your way.

And don't let Suzanne talk you out of it.

I love you, Bertie. I'll write more next week.

Good-bye for now.

Love,

Larry

CHAPTER 6

A knock sounded on the driver's side window and I spun to face it.

There was my gardener, bent at the waist, his leathered face peering so earnestly, I wanted to hide. I'd been crying; I was a soggy mess, and I'd forgotten to call him about the fire.

I fumbled with the letter and stuffed it in my purse, then swiped my palms across my face and rolled down the window.

"You okay, Mrs. Denys?"

"Victor, I'm sorry. I should have called you."

He reached in his pocket and handed me a rumpled pack of tissues. "It's all I have, but … lucky for you, I have allergies."

"Yes." I managed a chuckle and blew my nose.

He motioned toward my house. "A fire? What happened?"

"I don't know. They say it was arson."

"Arson!"

"Apparently someone broke into my house and poured gasoline … Did you see anything unusual yesterday when you did the yard?"

"No, nothing. But how terrible."

His breath caught just a little, and I realized his concern was not only for me. How could it be? Victor had worked for us four full mornings a week for the past ten years. We had to be at least a third of his income, maybe half. "I'm going to rebuild, Victor."

But was I?

"Somebody will rebuild," I said. "We'll still need landscaping."

Victor nodded.

"Why don't you just do the front yard today? Would that be okay?"

"Of course. I'm so sorry about your husband, Mrs. Denys. And your house." Victor headed back to his truck, and I started the car.

I'd barely pulled into the street before he was there again, signaling me from the curb. I rolled down the passenger window. "Yes?"

"I just remembered something. A couple weeks ago. I noticed the curtains had been opened on the back window in the corner." He pointed. "I think they were closed before."

Garrett's old bedroom. *Garrett's* bedroom!

I forced myself to smile as if Victor's comment meant nothing. "Oh, that would have been me. I went in there to do some cleaning, and I thought I'd open some windows and air the place out. I meant to close all the curtains when I was done, but I guess I missed those."

Victor nodded and returned to his work.

Of course I'd lied. I didn't know what, if anything, the curtains could mean, but I didn't want to discuss it with him. And I didn't want him to discuss it with anyone.

I pulled back into the street and rounded the corner.

Suddenly my breath came in gulps and spasms. I forced myself to slow down, to focus on the yelp of my crying, not the chatter in my head.

I needed to pull over, preferably someplace quiet, but everywhere I looked there was a gardener mowing a lawn, or a pool-service van pulling up a drive. Two women power-walked by, their bent arms pumping like boxers in the ring. I spotted a willow tree at the end of a cul-de-sac, its long strands brushing the pavement. I maneuvered into its curtained shade and cut the ignition.

Breathe slow, I told myself.

I grabbed Larry's letter from my purse and caressed it as if it were Larry himself. "Don't let Suzanne talk you out of it." How had he known?

Slower, slower. Inhale, exhale.

A ray of sunlight pierced through the hanging branches of the willow. I leaned back and closed my eyes.

For just a moment I dozed, but in my sleep I saw, of all things, the face of my father, turning to regard me over the top of his Thunderbird. He winked at me. It might have seemed like every other time he called me his princess and tossed me a wink, except that this time he forgot to smile. I was eleven, and I felt the weight of the moment down the center of my chest, in my heartbeat, in the catch of my breath. A business trip, he said, but his business trips had gotten so long. The last one had been six months. This one would last the rest of my childhood. A year later we got the divorce papers. No one told me. I found them in the bathroom on the back of the toilet, marking the place in my mother's copy of *The Feminine Mystique*. I didn't understand most of the typed document, but the word *divorce* was clear enough.

That was my first major episode. I had knocked the plaster fish off the wall to get my mother's attention, since I couldn't catch my breath to speak. The next moment, she shook me by the shoulders, yelling, "Slow it down, Roberta! Right this minute!"

How I survived that, I don't know. I don't remember much past finding the papers, except that the next morning when I trudged past the empty field on my way to junior high school, feeling like nobody's princess at all, I was brought short by a gust of rose-scented wind that tingled against my face and arms like ginger ale.

I lifted my head and found myself in a flurry of pink rose petals, spiraling around each other in a light so clean it might have flared through cut crystal.

It wasn't simply a gust of wind through someone's rosebush, because there were no rosebushes … just a broad open field. More than that, the light and the tingle in the air settled into me like a kind of quiet, like love.

The only person at Vector Empowerment who would talk with me was Winton Tanaka, another manager in Garrett's department. The receptionist gave me a visitor badge to clip to my lapel and asked me to wait. Which I did. For thirty minutes.

The lobby was impressive, and I'd seen my share of corporate lobbies. I'd designed Larry's first, back in 1989, in a small office park in Sunnyvale. Of course that one measured eighteen feet by twelve, and "designing" it meant painting the walls taupe and hanging track lights from the ceiling grid to highlight the aluminum corporate logo.

When ConjuTech moved into a larger building, Larry and his partner hired a professional decorator, and she did a fine job.

But this place. Windows two-and-a-half stories high on three sides, translucent white, like rice paper. The diffused light effected a pristine sense of aloof simplicity. In the center stood a twelve-foot sculpture of the company's spiral logo, etched and iridescent, as if cut from a massive silicon wafer.

Surrounding the sculpture were four gray sofas as square and solid as concrete. The receptionist behind her brushed-metal desk urged me to take a seat, but I declined.

I checked my watch.

A door opened, and a young Asian man stepped out. "Mrs. Denys?"

I took a step toward him. He crossed the room to shake my hand. "I'm Winton Tanaka. Sorry to have kept you waiting. I had four fires to put out before lunch this morning, instead of the usual three."

Fire, fire everywhere. "I understand."

"I'm very sorry about your husband. I used to work for him, you know."

"Did you?"

"Anyway, I only have a half hour. Do you mind if we talk in the company cafeteria? You need lunch, right?"

"Sure." I forced a polite smile.

He slid his card through the reader and opened the door. I followed.

We entered a hall lined with gray flannel cubicles, as high as Winton's head. Around the next corner, the cubicles were shorter, so that I could see over the tops to the laminate desks strewn or stacked with papers. Most of the chairs were empty, most of the computer

monitors switched to floating or dancing screensavers. We heard
a collective shout of voices, and Winton smiled over his shoulder.
"Come on, I'll show you something."

We turned another corner and entered a sunlit lounge with a
coffee bar and a microwave. To my left, several workers clustered
around a young woman seated at a computer station. The monitor showed two humanoid figures formed of cylinders and spheres,
locked in slow-motion combat.

"It's called Toribash," said Winton. "The blue guy's VEC, and
the red one's some fool at Microsoft. It's our Friday incentive: The rep
who ships the most orders gets to play, and the rest get to watch."

Microsoft thrust a kick to VEC's shoulder, and the figure's
blue arm detached, flew to the side trailing red droplets, bounced
twice and landed at Microsoft's feet. No matter. VEC already had
Microsoft's neck locked in its remaining arm. To the delight of all
watchers, the head severed, and VEC gave it a kick that propelled
it high into the air. Before Microsoft could recover, VEC delivered
a punch to the gut and sent the opponent sprawling to the mat in a
spew of scarlet rain. The small audience leaped and cheered.

"Very bloody." I looked toward the door. None of this had anything to do with Garrett, and Winton had said he had just a half
hour.

He took the hint and led me out.

The sign by the double door read, "VEC Cafeteria." We entered
and got in line at the metal steamer table, where three white-coated
chefs served beef medallions with goat cheese and thyme, or salmon
on beds of lemon balm.

"Nice," I said, taking in the indigo walls, the cubist paintings, the recessed lights, and paper lanterns. The linen cloths, the single iris on each table. "Very nice."

"The company likes to keep us *in* the building," he said. "We have our own fitness center and laundry service on campus. We have a day care with closed-circuit cameras so you can watch your kid grow up on your monitor. Oh, and if he gets the measles, we've even got a sick-child-care facility."

"You're kidding."

"Hey, it's either that or we don't hire moms. Just like ConjuTech or any other company in the valley, VEC expects a lot from its employees. But in return, we give them important, exciting work to do, and a very nice cage to do it in." All this he said with a dimpled grin that looked just like Larry's.

"Order anything but the calamari," he said as the line moved forward. "I had it yesterday, and it was rubbery."

I ordered the salmon and pulled my wallet from my purse.

"I'll get this," he said, and placed a hand on my wrist.

The more I looked, the more he reminded me of my husband. The ponytail was just like Larry's, only black instead of blond. He wore the same black corduroy pants Larry favored, the same blue button-down shirt with a pen in the pocket.

Winton took his plate of tortellini and led the way to a window table. I paused to watch him. Amazing. He *walked* like Larry: relaxed, muscular, with a casual dignity that took me back to the student union in college where I'd met my husband years before.

Larry had stridden across the room that day, directly to my table. Without so much as a hello, he bent to tip the book I was reading for a glance at the cover. "Thomas Merton," he said, nodding his approval. Such a simple gesture it was—one tilt of the chin, and a dimpled smile—and I thought I could live for a nod like that.

Nobody I knew read Thomas Merton, and nobody I cared about understood why I did, or why I didn't treat my visions with Pepto Bismol, or why I was obsessed with things I couldn't prove. But this luminous man with the air of a saint sat down to discuss the book with me, and before he stood up again, I thought I could live for him.

And for thirty-five years, I did.

Winton set his plate on the table and looked at me. I crossed the room to join him. By this time I had maybe fifteen minutes. "You worked with my son?" I got right to the point.

"I did. When I heard he'd gotten the position, I was excited. Having worked at ConjuTech, and knowing that Garrett was … well." He leaned forward. "Larry Denys was my guru."

"Your guru!" I flashed the smile I'd given out at countless company parties, to numberless groupies who told me my husband was …

"Just a brilliant man," Winton continued. "The whole concept behind ConjuTech. He didn't just build a better mousetrap. He discovered a vital economic purpose for mice and an elegant way to package them. ConjuTech revolutionized the way the Silicon Valley would change the world. He completely jumped the curve, and he made it work by attracting the best of the best to work for him. And the drive and intensity he inspired was just … unprecedented. Your husband was a brilliant man. Everything I know, I learned from him."

"I believe you."

"One thing he taught me was that anybody with a brain and a

work ethic can make it big in this valley." He tapped the table with his finger. "That's why I took the job here. A few years ago, VEC was a young start-up that was destined to succeed. A good idea and angel investors double parked at the curb. I wanted to get in on that, to know just a little bit what it was like to be Larry Denys."

"And now you've got an idea of your own." I knew it was coming. I'd heard it before.

There it was, the conspiratorial wink.

Time was running out. "Winton," I began.

"You want to know about Garrett." He sighed. He started to speak, then sighed again. "Garrett's just not like his dad. He's reclusive, and he gets these moods. Really, I can't believe he's your husband's son."

I pushed my plate away. "I can assure you, he is."

"Sorry. I didn't mean … How much did he tell you about what happened?"

"Nothing."

"I don't even know how much I should tell you. He … he let his lead engineer skate for a year."

"Skate?"

"He finally found one he got along with. He fired Vijay Patel, one of the best we ever had, and then two others just quit. Finally he finds one he likes, and things seem to go well. But the guy turns in bogus reports month after month, and Garrett never checks them out. And the thing is, VEC announced the launch of what promised to be our flagship product. And all the while there were major, major obstacles. By the time we found out … We fired the engineer, and we …" He looked at me and looked away. "We fired Garrett."

A silence hung between us, till Winton cleared his throat.

"Not everyone's cut out for the Silicon Valley. Not everybody has the vision, or the passion, or whatever it is." He shrugged. "Where's Garrett now?"

"I don't know. I'd hoped you could tell me."

"You don't know where he is? He didn't … he didn't go to the funeral?"

"Unless he caught it on the news, he doesn't know Larry's dead."

"Well." Winton turned in his chair. "What about his girlfriend, she must know—"

"Garrett had a girlfriend?"

"You didn't know about Eloise? She works in Fremont, at Sun Microsystems."

"No, I didn't know," I said, breathing a half sigh of relief. Garrett might have moved in with her. It might be as simple as that.

Winton pulled out his Palm Pilot and a business card. "I don't remember her last name, but there can't be more than one Eloise in her department." He wrote the number on the back of his card.

The half hour was up, but I had what I needed. Winton walked me out. Or rather, I led the way, and he kept up. Once we got to the lobby and he took his leave, I quickened my step. Outside, I jogged to my car, rushed inside, and flipped open my cell phone.

Then I stopped myself. Before I dialed the number I dropped my head to the steering wheel and whispered. "*All shall be well, and all shall be—please*," I begged. "Please, please, please, let Eloise tell me where to find Garrett."

CHAPTER 7

Glory to God for answered prayer. When I called Eloise's office, her coworker said she was in Portugal with her boyfriend. No wonder I couldn't find Garrett. He was out of the country.

Lightheaded with relief, I drove up the mountain. Traffic had slowed, and I was stopped near the Cats Restaurant on Highway 17. I settled back into my seat and turned to admire the restaurant's patchwork of stone, brick, and shingle.

It had been built into the hillside, generations before. The hill's stone core formed the back interior wall. The roadhouse had served in early times as a stagecoach stopover, and later as a speakeasy. Even, some say, as a bordello. A thousand stories had woven themselves into this place, sad stories, and scandalous. Romances too, one would hope, but who knew? The Cats was a wizened bohemian dozing in the afternoon as if nothing had happened.

Larry and I once fancied our own story had woven its strands in with all the rest in the tavern's dark corners. Of course, in those early days our scandals were the quieter type, subtly fashioned of the books we bent our heads over, grasping our coffee cups, stroking each other's feet with bare toes beneath the table. It was the thoughts we had devised together, and the questions we asked in secret that bred a luxuriance that had nothing to do with money, and a passion that lasted … well, for a time.

I looked away.

I would not surrender the blessedness of this moment. The breeze blew warm through my open window, and I was so grateful to at last have an idea where my son was, so wondrously grateful, I could cry. He was in Lisbon, beautiful, romantic Lisbon, with a girlfriend. My son was fine.

And now there was work to do. Before evening, the sleeping bag and books and other necessities I'd bought and piled into my backseat that afternoon would all be arranged in their places on the concrete floor of my new home.

Or was Suzanne right, that the floor was dirt? At the moment, I really didn't care.

I opened my sunroof, and let the light pour over me like honey, sweet, sweet light and the hot smell of flint from the mountain. This time of year, the Santa Cruz Mountains always smelled like an enormous match had been struck. Like God had started some cosmic furnace, right here where the slag of my old life would burn away.

I was more than ready. There had been a time, years before, when my prayers had been sumptuous things, deep whispered dialogues in the dark. Not every time, but often enough. If every prayer had been that way, I might have noticed when things changed. But I didn't notice. I only knew that it had been years since my prayers had been anything but a monologue with nobody there.

Thomas Merton once said that to be alone was to be with God. I prayed it was true and hoped my prayers were heard. In that kind of solitude, I would be less lonely than I had been in quite some time.

My cell phone rang. Suzanne again. She was behind me somewhere on this road.

"I'm stopped," she said.

"So am I. Anything about it on the radio?"

"Yep. It's just a truck stalled near the Idylwild turnoff. Not *at* the turnoff, mind you, or he could get off the road."

"There's no hurry."

"Huh."

Everything was a hurry for Suzanne.

"Tell me again," she said, "just where in Europe this son of yours has gone."

"Lisbon, with a girl named Eloise."

"You don't think it's strange that Garrett ran off to Europe when his father was dying?"

"I do think it's strange that Garrett ran off to Europe. This girl must have pulled some major heartstrings; you know how he hates to fly. But his father had been dying for six years. He'll be home in a week. For heaven's sake, Suzy, why don't you just write down all your questions and I'll ask him."

She was silent so long I wondered if she'd hung up. "What sort of toilet facilities is this shed of yours going to have?" she asked finally. "I'm starting to need one."

"There's a little store just up the road from my property. It's got bathrooms."

"Really? That's your plan?"

"Sure, why not?"

"Fine. It's fine … for most of the time. But what if you have to go to the bathroom at four in the morning?"

"I sleep at four in the morning." I smacked my forehead with the butt of my hand, glad Suzanne couldn't see. My answer was true as far as it went. But it went only two hours. Six o'clock. I always woke up at six o'clock, and when I did ...

"That's bogus."

"What?"

"When you wake up in the morning, you have to pee. What are you going to do?"

"I'll pee in the forest."

"You're comfortable with that?"

"Of course." I smacked my head, and smacked it again.

"Who'd have ever thought?"

"Listen," I said, pulling forward with the traffic. "We're starting to move. I'm hanging up."

"See you at the cloister," she sang.

CHAPTER 8

I flipped the phone shut and slam-dunked it onto the passenger seat, glad to be rid of Suzanne for the moment. This woman was not the friend I needed at that moment, but she was the one I had. Faithful to a fault, sticking with me through thick and thin, like she always did, whether I wanted her to or not.

Ah, but … there was a time when I did want her to, when I needed her to stick by me, and she did. Once upon a time, this woman was exactly the friend I needed.

We met in 1980 when Larry invited Charlie Keyes, his buddy from National Semiconductor, to our apartment to sign the papers for their new start-up, ConjuTech. Charlie brought his wife, Suzanne, with him. She carried their daughter, Amber, on her hip, and he brought the champagne.

The two men were drunk with optimism that night. I was the only one who seemed to understand that we were jumping off a cliff.

Little Garrett had the flu, so I pulled the bentwood rocker to the kitchen table where they'd spread the papers. With my son on my lap, I rocked a staccato beat with that chair, asking, "You're going to quit your job? You're going to quit your *job?*" My father had worked at IBM for thirty years before he retired. He had bought a twenty-eight-foot sailboat the family never used, he had gambled too much in Reno once, he'd *left* us, but he had never quit his job. It might have been fine if it was just Larry and me, but we had Garrett to think of, and a stack of bills on the kitchen counter.

Suzanne wrapped her hand around mine, pulled me to my feet, sick child and all, and led me to the living room. To this day I don't remember exactly what she said. She explained the Silicon Valley mindset to me, or tried. She explained what Larry and Charlie were going to accomplish with ConjuTech. Don't ask me how, but she knew.

More to the point, she showed me the venture capitalist's check. Of course, Larry had told me about it, but Suzanne explained that part of the check was for salaries. Our husbands' salaries for a full year.

Someone should have mentioned that before.

Of course, as Larry and Charlie's vision for ConjuTech expanded, the salaries they allowed themselves diminished to about half. "Just enough for necessities," Larry said, but his idea of necessities did not include medical insurance or a minimally warm house on winter nights.

Mine did, and so did Suzanne's. My solution was to insist on a raise, but she had another idea. She invited me for dinner one night while the guys worked late. She sat me down at the table with Garrett and Amber, disappeared into the kitchen, and returned with an enormous stainless steel pan of chicken gruyere. An enormous pan, big enough to serve fifty.

I pointed out there were four of us, and two were children, who didn't eat much and preferred spaghetti.

"If I shop in the right places," she said, "I can make this for one dollar eighty cents a serving."

"Okay ..."

"We can sell it for six dollars a serving."

"We?"

And so began La Pêche Blanche, the catering service Suzanne and I started together.

Well, she said we started it together. I remember dragging my feet. What kind of sense did it make, to bolster a *large* struggling start-up business, by creating a *small* struggling start-up business?

Only, we never did struggle, Suzanne and I. At least not financially. We turned a good profit at our very first event and never looked back for fifteen years.

The only struggle was the one behind my navel, every time I made a cold call. I hated it. I hated asking the receptionist if I could speak with the person in charge of company events. I hated it when she said yes. I hated shaking the hand of the brisk young woman who gave me ten minutes, standing there in the waiting room. I hated filling those ten minutes with words, talking very, very fast, explaining that our service was the best, our food was the best, and our prices extremely ... not cheap, uh, *competitive*, was the word Suzanne said to use.

Serving the actual food was easier, but leaving Garrett in day care was its own kind of heartache, and in truth, I hated it all.

Again, enter Suzanne. She taught me how to make eye contact, how to stand straight, how to smile and give a good handshake. She taught me how to look positive and calm when my insides were on spin cycle. What was Suzanne's new mantra? "Confident and competent." She taught me how to fake it. And I had to fake it every time.

I quit the day I realized neither my insurance bill nor ConjuTech needed La Pêche Blanche. Not Suzanne. She carried on alone till she realized she could make more money in real estate. A good thing too, since Charlie thought up a new idea and backed out of ConjuTech at exactly the wrong moment, just before it transformed itself from a success into a legend. My guess was that Suzanne had ended up the better breadwinner.

The traffic slowed again, just as I came into view of the Lexington Reservoir. The sun slipped one blinding ray beneath the lowest edge of my visor. I turned out of its path onto Black Road and let out a breath of tired air, glad to be off the highway. Driving uphill, I took my time accelerating. An Audi TT I'd never even seen gunned its engine at my rear bumper and immediately pulled to the side and raced to get around me. I cringed at the haze of condemnation the driver left in his wake.

I knew the feeling very well. And I'd long since learned to wish it a lovely life and go my own way.

The hill leveled out, and I turned onto the road where I would live. And there, not perhaps three hundred feet from my property was the little store I remembered: a barn-red two-story building with a porch and a single gas pump in front. A tangle of wild roses draped itself around the post that supported a hanging wooden sign:

Mountain Pantry General Store
Groceries, Books, Videos,
Baked Goods
& Gas

The minute I parked in front of my property and opened the car door, I realized it was easily a full ten degrees cooler on the mountain.

An old set of stone stairs led the way up the embankment. I climbed till I found myself in a circle of redwoods. I stepped off the path onto a spongy mat of needles and leaves. How deep did they go? How many decades or centuries lay casually layered beneath my feet?

I paused in the center, dropped my head back, and gazed upward. The trees moved in unison, in a wind I didn't feel, but I caught the whispered hush, and swayed in communion, and closed my eyes.

I climbed past the little shed toward the top of the hill where Larry and I had planned to build a timber mansion. It was the affluent thing, to live in a grand home on this beautiful mountain. It only added a half hour to the commute, and Larry and I could afford it.

But I had reasons for living here that had nothing to do with affluence. I worked my way around a fallen redwood, overgrown with ferns and stretching flat-capped mushrooms. A few more steps up the bank, and there was the ridge that looked out over a shallow tree-lined canyon, which stretched for miles westward. The gilded shimmer in the far distance was the Pacific Ocean.

I heard the motor of Suzanne's Escalade and returned to the path down the hill to meet her. She parked behind my car and opened the door.

"It's cold up here!" She tramped up the stairs, rubbing her arms, then stopped on the path in my circle of trees.

"Listen to the wind," I urged. "Isn't it beautiful?"

"Prime mountain property." She started up the stairs again. "Let's see this hermitage of yours."

"That could be its name," I said, following. "The Hermitage."

"When I went to Italy after my divorce, I stayed at a spa called The Hermitage."

"This isn't a spa. This is serious."

"I see that."

We'd come to the warped wooden door of my shed. Suzanne pulled on the rusted latch. It whined like a cornered cat.

Inside, I wandered the small ten-by-twelve-foot room, flicking down cobwebs, kicking at the dirt on the floor. The *concrete* floor, I noted—Suzanne had been wrong. Still, it was a dark place. There was a window on the left wall: one small, desolate pane of glass, cracked in the corner, crusted on the outside with dirt and bits of rotting leaves.

And beside the window stood my friend, with her arms crossed, eyeing me over the tops of her glasses.

"I'll clean it up," I said. "Light some candles—"

"Oh, Bertie."

"I'll be fine here."

"You'll be all alone."

"There are neighbors."

"The door's no good. You can't lock it. What if someone attacks you?"

"I've got my cell phone."

"Oh, that's safe. Are you going to hit him with it?"

"Who's going to attack me? Who'll believe anybody lives in this thing?"

Suzanne chuckled. "Good point."

An amber glow from the doorway suddenly glanced across her

cheek and warmed the back wall. I leaned out the door. "The sun's going down," I said.

"Let's get to work, then." She headed down to the cars, and I followed.

While I pulled the bags from my backseat, she opened her Escalade's rear door and rummaged through a large Rubbermaid box. "What are you doing?" I asked.

"Just getting … a few … necessaries." She emerged with a can of Raid, a roll of paper towels, a bottle of Windex, and a three-foot-long broom. She yanked the handle, and it expanded to full size. "A realtor's got to be prepared."

I hadn't even thought of a broom. I stood back and watched, amazed at this woman. The entire history of our friendship, it had always been the same: One moment, I'd feel desperate to free myself from the steely, controlling grip of her manicured hands, and the next, I'd be overwhelmed by her loyalty, her devotion. Her knack for always having the very thing I needed.

"At least you can get food." She motioned toward the Mountain Pantry.

"I brought food."

"Oh yeah? Like what?"

"Tuna fish, baked beans …"

"Forgive me if I don't stay for dinner."

I climbed the hill behind her, dropped my bags outside the door, and pitched in. Within minutes, the place was clean. "What would I do without you?" I asked, and then cringed. I could hear her very thoughts. *You managed fine for six years. You managed fine the day Charlie left …*

"Let's get you set up," she said.

I stepped outside, gathered my bags, and hauled them in.

Suzanne chuckled.

"What?"

She pointed to the bags. "Nordstrom's!"

"So?" I pulled out the shoes I'd bought that afternoon and set them neatly in the corner.

She started cackling, so hard she fell sideways. "Stuart Weitzmans?"

I turned and set my hands on my hips. "It's a good brand. They're comfortable."

She slid down the wall to the floor, laughing like an asthmatic chicken. *Ack, ack, ack.* "What kind ... of *nun* ... shops at Nordstrom's?"

"They're good quality," I argued. But there she was, *ack, ack, ack,* and I started to laugh. "They'll last longer."

She wiped tears away, struggling to compose herself. "Show me what you got from Pottery Barn."

"No."

She sniffled and wiped her eyes again. "Really. I won't laugh."

"You're laughing now." And so was I.

"Come on."

I sat beside her and reached for the bag, knowing everything inside was boxed and wrapped in tissue. Nice tissue, royal blue. Suddenly I wanted to hide my face.

Suzanne took the bag from my hands, pulled out a box, and opened it. She pushed back the tissue, then lifted the bowl inside to the dim light from the window. It glowed in her hands. Earth brown, but the proudest brown you ever saw. The glaze shimmered like the purple on a California poppy.

"One bowl. Very Zen." She smiled and leaned to the side to look me square in the face. "How long since you've been to Wal-Mart?"

I didn't want to talk to this woman. The answer was never. Back when Larry and I were young would-be missionaries, we shopped at Kmart on occasion, when we could afford to. But there was no Wal-Mart. A very long time ago. "It's just stuff," I said.

Sighing, she wrapped an arm around my neck, and I leaned in.

"My daughter's first day of college was easier than this," she said. "Remember that day? You with Garrett and me with Amber, and all that rain. We just knew they'd be engaged by the time they graduated. If Amber hadn't miscarried, we'd be grandmothers together. Do you remember?"

Amber's miscarriage was something I preferred not to remember. I looked away. "Then you'd never have gotten rid of me."

"I'm not getting rid of you. And you won't get rid of me, either, no matter where you move."

"I know, Suzy."

"You ever going to tell me about those visions of yours?"

My mind flashed a memory of the leather skin of a pomegranate, splitting open to reveal seeds like rubies, a scent like snowfall, and a feeling, a rapturous feeling of ...

"Suzanne," I said. "When you pray, do you ever feel that you're getting anywhere?"

"Sure. Business is good. Houses are selling. Amber and Roger are happy."

"I don't mean that. I mean, do you ever feel that you're intimate with God, like the love affair in the Song of Solomon?"

"The Song of Solomon?" She frowned at me. "A love affair?"

I could see she had serious concerns for my sanity. "I just mean, do you feel that God is there?"

"Of course He's there. I don't question it, Bertie. I just talk to Him, tell Him what I want. I heard this lecture awhile ago, about living a more powerful life through prayer. It was very good. I've got it on tape someplace. I could loan it to you."

"Where would I plug it in?" My shed had no electricity.

"Bertie, are you sure you want to do this?"

"I'm sure, Suzy."

"Okay." She pulled away and rubbed her arms. "I'll bet you didn't think to buy a coat."

I hadn't. She knew me so well. "I'll be fine."

"It's getting very dark." She stood.

I looked up at her and realized she was going to leave. I hurried to my feet. We faced each other, and I used every trick she'd ever taught me to fake a smile. Confident and competent.

"Light a candle before I go."

I picked up the lighter I'd set beside a cluster of candles on the floor, and lit them all. The shed took on the gothic glow of a small chapel.

"That's better," she said. In the candlelight I saw brimming tears in her eyes. She hugged me and walked out the door.

I stood on my threshold and watched her go, as the last saffron glimmer of sunset disappeared behind the redwood-shrouded horizon.

CHAPTER 9

When she drove away, I stepped back inside, pulled the door shut, and turned to face the cinder-block walls. They almost seemed to press toward me. The structure was small, ten feet by twelve, built to keep garden equipment for some house that no longer existed. Everything smelled of soil.

How old was the roof? Without stretching, I touched the ceiling to test its wooden slats. They yielded to my touch and released a powder of debris. I sputtered and flailed at my face and hair. When I opened my eyes, I glimpsed a spider racing across the floor, darting into a chink between two bricks. I felt a tickle and flailed at my neck and head, then fetched a brush from my purse and tore it, again and again, through my hair. But still, my skin crawled. I pulled off my T-shirt and shook it out, inspected it, and put it back on.

I looked up and saw the last several legs of a millipede disappearing between two boards.

I walked circles along the walls, shuddering, imagining squirming things behind every crack in the plaster, every dark corner, every layer of rotting wood. How was I going to sleep in this place?

Suzanne's can of Raid stood at the ready against the wall. I snatched it up and started spraying in the corner. Immediately a beetle dropped from the ceiling, directly into one of my new shoes.

I stopped spraying and replaced the lid on the can. I didn't want to cause a shower of writhing insects in the fading light, in my new cloister, on my first night of contemplative bliss. It crossed my mind that perhaps I hadn't properly thought things through.

My cell phone protruded from a pocket in my purse. I stared at it a long moment, considering … then took the shoe to the door and dumped the dying bug outside.

I paused there, breathless, stunned at the utter absence of light. I'd seen the pink night sky of the city. I'd seen the shadows in a house with the blinds drawn at night. But I'd never seen darkness, black darkness like this. The wind that hushes so softly through the tree-tops in daylight acquires a voice at nightfall. The breathing, wordless voice of something immense.

I looked upward. The tops of the redwoods fringed a deep night sky and a scatter of stars. But such stars! Such piercing, glacial stars, such distilled light. In darkness like this, I diminished to nothing at all.

I back-stepped and shut myself inside.

It was cold. I wished I'd brought a coat. I wished for a coat so badly, I started to cry. The tears gained momentum, and I doubled into myself, sobbing for that coat, till I surprised myself by wailing the name—*Larry!*—and then I knew the real reason I wept and there was no stopping.

After a time, I grew weak. I ate a half can of baked beans, cold, then changed into the heavy flannel nightgown I'd bought. I layered on the black sweater, and two pairs of socks. I inspected my sleeping bag for insects, then cocooned myself inside. Leaning

over, I blew out all but one of the candles, then lay back against
the hard floor.

In the light of the single flame, my shadow rocked like a boat
against the wall. I closed my eyes.

Hardly more than two weeks ago, I'd rolled Larry's wheelchair to the bedroom in our apartment. I'd slipped an arm
behind his back and another under his legs, and, light as he
was, I'd hoisted him into bed. I'd undressed him as I'd once
undressed our son, then gently slipped his pajama pants over his
legs, and buttoned the shirt over his shriveled chest. I'd crawled
in beside him, pulled up the covers and turned out the light.
Then, pretending all was as it had been in the beginning, I'd
stroked his hair back and kissed his forehead, kissed the downy
spot between his eyebrows, kissed the tip of his nose, and then
his lips. My husband.

A chill seeped through my sleeping bag from the concrete floor.

Outside I heard the wind and the crack of wood. Trees did that,
I told myself. I wondered, though: Did they fall, sometimes, when
they'd cracked clear through? My property was littered, here and
there, with fallen logs.

A rustle sounded outside my door, and I held my breath to listen. It quieted, and I relaxed. Then I heard it again. I reached for my
purse and drew the cell phone into the sleeping bag with me. I flipped
it open and poised my finger over Suzanne's speed-dial number.

Was I ready to back out so soon? I didn't know if I could face
her down a second time. I shut the phone and listened. Nothing.
Silence, and the sound of my own ragged breath.

Inhale, I told myself. *Exhale*.

I closed my eyes and tried to sleep. There would be sounds in a forest, all kinds of sounds you didn't hear in Saratoga.

I heard footsteps on dried leaves and whimpered. They paused, and started again.

Were they footsteps? The noise could have been a gust of wind, or a rabbit … right?

I closed my eyes, then heard the footsteps again. It was no rabbit. I stood, lifted my candle, and walked across the room. I nudged the door open a crack and saw something large and white before my feet. I lowered the candle for a better look. It was a plastic bag, with a note clipped to the closure:

Didn't want to wake you, but you'll need this. —Suzanne

I pulled the bag inside. She'd brought me a coat!

Was she still here? With the candle in my hand, I dashed outside. "Suzanne!"

No answer. Wearing only socks, I took several steps down the stairs to the road. "Suzanne!"

How could she have gone so quickly?

The redwoods loomed around me, seeming almost to breathe in the flicker of my candle flame. Everywhere, I heard cracks and rustles, a flap of broad wings.

I was alone. Trembling at the realization, I turned to run back for the closed-in safety of the shed—and found myself face to muzzle with a buck deer. I let out a cry, and he stiffened in place.

He lowered his broad velvet brow, and considered me with eyes like black marbles. I felt the huffs of his warm breath against my throat. Dark as it was, I saw only his face, his mouth clenched to a line beneath a black snout. In my candlelight, his horns threw a flickering shadow like trees behind him. Slowly, he turned to the side, then, swaying forward with each step, he stalked into the night.

I rushed inside and pulled the door, hard. It wailed like a dying demon against the threshold, but I tugged until it wedged tight.

I put on my coat, then climbed into my sleeping bag and zipped it shut. Something rustled outside. I pressed my hands to my ears and my face to my pillow, and closed my eyes.

———

I awoke in darkness. Disoriented, I stroked my fingertips against the concrete floor beside me and remembered where I was.

I had to use the bathroom.

Oh, Lord. Could it wait until daylight?

I shifted, considering. But no, it couldn't.

The candle had gone out. Where was my flashlight? I'd left it beside the dishes against the wall. I rolled over and groped my fingers along the floor, and found my bowl, my cup, and … There it was, my flashlight. I lifted it and pressed the switch. It threw pale, circular shadows, like echoes on the walls.

I got to my feet and slipped into my shoes, then remembered the buck. Did I really have to do this? I pressed my knees together to block the growing insistence.

All right then. I gave the door a good shove, and it squalled open. I stopped to listen, but all was silent outside.

I stepped out and moved my flashlight in a half circle. It bounced off the tree trunks and threw shadows everywhere. I didn't want to leave my urine next to the shed, but what if I got lost?

I heard the soft hush of wind and felt my own breath flutter like moths from my chest.

I spotted a break in the trees and stepped closer to investigate. There was something like a path, and a small moonlit clearing up the hill. I set out in small, timid steps.

When I got to the clearing, I found that it lay near the canyon. Beyond the edge stretched miles of trees, silver in the moonlight. I positioned the flashlight the way I'd come, to show the way back. Then, desperate, I stepped off the path, lifted my nightgown, and squatted.

When I finished what I'd set out to do, I returned to the clearing and gazed across the canyon and then at the familiar face of the moon. Such a constant, gentle light it shone. The stars gleamed unhindered, as though they were all that had ever existed, and their exquisite light pierced me to the heart.

I glimpsed an orange light through the trees. A campfire? I walked further for a better look. A broad cluster of red candles flickered in a leafless patch of ground beside the canyon's ridge, and a figure hunched beside them.

I looked behind me. My flashlight still pointed downhill toward home. I crept further into the trees, till I saw that the figure beside the candles was a woman. She covered her face with her hands and wept.

I wondered, *Should I do something? Perhaps go to her? Or would I only frighten her if I tried?* I stepped out of a beam of moonlight, into shadow.

The woman snuffled and dried her tears, then stood. She picked up a candle, carried it a distance away and set it down. She did likewise with the others until she'd created a circle, maybe five feet in diameter. Near the place where the candles had been, she picked up a broom. She moved to the circle, lifted her skirt, and stepped inside.

She started to sweep the ground. She followed the circumference, back-stepping and pulling the broom along, in an ever-tightening circle. When she got to the center, she stopped, and tossed the broom beyond the candles.

She faced the canyon and the full moon, snuffled, and wiped her eyes.

Her hair was dark. A breeze caught a strand of it, and lifted it above her shoulder.

She pulled up the hem of her top, and tugged the waist of her skirt down, to expose her middle. She was pregnant! Her belly shone white and full as an answering moon.

With spread fingers she stroked the taut skin, in circles that started up the sides, across under her breasts, and down the middle. She began to sway.

Was she singing? I heard sounds, like words, but very faint.

She lifted her arms, and moved as if to stroke the sky. She sobbed and dropped her hands to wipe her face.

Then she lifted them again, and, in a voice full of command and supplication, she wailed a single name:

"Diana!"

CHAPTER 10

I heard Larry call my name. "Bertie."

Just calmly, like he'd never been sick, like he was sitting right beside me. I reached out in my sleep to touch a husband who wasn't there. My fingers brushed the granular concrete floor. I opened my eyes.

Daylight seeped through the gaps around the door. I rolled over in shadow and took one full, painful breath to spread my ribs, then held my watch to the pale light and squinted. It was eight o'clock.

Everything was one shade of gray or another.

And everything smelled like old dirt. As if I'd been buried. For just a moment, I bawled against my open hand and drew my knees to my middle. Then I pushed the hair from my face and stopped.

This wouldn't do. I was already late waking up. I took a full breath that hurt somewhat less than the first had and gathered myself. It was only the grief of a new widow.

How long had I been outside the night before? It might have been a half hour or five hours, who could tell? I'd stayed till the woman extinguished her candles, gathered them in a basket, and padded away barefoot. By the tree-shaded moonlight, nothing more.

I thought of the woman's pregnant moon of a belly, carried high and all in front, the way I'd carried Garrett. I remembered the soft curve of Amber's belly, the day we saw her off to visit a friend in Hawaii. Barely three months along.

After she and Garrett broke the news, Suzanne gave me exactly one day to recover from the shock before she turned up at my door and set out her detailed plan for making a proper impression.

"On who?" I asked.

"The baby!" Spoken as though even I should have known as much.

"I don't think the baby's going to expect much, Suzy. Just love."

"Exactly! And I know where to find it. Get your purse."

She drove me straight to Scotts Valley and turned up a wooded country road.

"Where are we going?" I asked.

"Don't you remember Max Stein? We catered an exhibition for him in Palo Alto. Remember that chair—"

I swiveled in my seat and pointed. "The furniture guy!"

"Yes. The furniture guy!"

Max Stein was an amazing artist, whose medium happened to be hardwood. I remembered the most elegant mix of ebony and mahogany and maple, layered in stripes like geologic strata, formed in rounded organic shapes as if they'd grown in some enchanted place in the forest. Beautiful, beautiful chairs, tables … and baby cradles. And that was the idea. Our grandchild would begin life in nothing less. Of course, it would be a custom piece, and of course, he had other projects and couldn't start right away.

"No problem," said Suzanne, writing out the check for the deposit. "You have six months."

When Garrett arrived home from school that day, he barely stopped pacing to look at Max's brochure. What he wanted to know was how his father had proposed to me.

"He just asked."

"*How* did he ask?"

"Like this: 'Will. You. Marry. Me?'"

"That's it?"

"It seemed romantic at the time."

He pressed his palms to his eyes and groaned.

For all the tension over how we would manage things, get the kids through college, and help them care for the baby, it was a golden time. I'd never seen Garrett so beside himself with happiness.

So when Amber called from Hawaii to say she'd miscarried, of course he took it very hard and cried into my lap for nearly an hour while I fingered his hair and wept my own tears. It was understandable that Garrett fell behind in his schoolwork. Amber did the same and lost an alarming amount of weight. It was hardly a surprise that Garrett became withdrawn for a while, spent hours, whole weekends alone in his room. What did surprise me was that six months later, when I thought he was better, I learned he'd broken it off with Amber. He wouldn't tell me why. He'd hardly let Larry ask the question. It's sad, but tragedy can tear couples apart, even after years of marriage. What chance did Garrett and Amber have, as young as they were?

A month after that, I found Garrett sitting at his computer, gazing at a photo of a twelve-week-old fetus, tracing the outlines of a child he'd never know. So silent.

But that was a long time ago. Garrett was now in warm, sunlit

Portugal with this Eloise. Perhaps there would be a wedding, and perhaps there would be a grandchild yet.

I pressed my face into the pillow of my sleeping bag. The air on my neck was cold. To think that this dark, bug-infested hovel was home. Why hadn't I slept in my car? It never occurred to me. The thought of those leather seats! Heated leather seats if I turned the ignition on a few minutes. Even homeless people live in cars sometimes, don't they?

I already knew the answer; Suzanne didn't have to tell me everything. No homeless person ever lived in a Lexus.

Besides, I wasn't homeless. This was something I'd chosen.

I tried to recall the vision, the first one, with the rose petals. But it seemed, at best, a second-rate memory, something no longer mine.

If it ever was a vision. Maybe I'd made it all up, the whole spiritual thing. It had been so long ago, and I had been so young. Maybe I'd done something foolish, coming here to this place. I cocked an eye toward the rotting ceiling, and certainly, I felt like a fool.

Still, I had thought things out. The visions may have happened long ago, but they were real enough at the time. Real enough to carry me through, and real enough to change everything I wanted. By the time I met Larry, I knew I wanted a life unlike any I'd ever seen, nothing like my mother's or my father's. And however much I loved him, I wanted a life nothing, nothing like my brother's.

This was my chosen lifestyle. I'd come here with a plan, and I'd best get to it. If Suzanne found me weeping on the floor, she'd hoist me over her shoulder and carry me out of here. I could at least open the door and lighten the shadows a bit. Groaning, I got up on all fours and arched my back, crackling the vertebrae apart one by one.

I unzipped the sleeping bag, and the morning chill washed in. I stood as fast as my back would allow, bundled up in the coat Suzanne gave me, then stepped into my Stuart Weitzmans.

The shoes were cold. I puffed warm air into my cupped hands and held them to my face. I crossed the room and opened the door.

And stopped short.

Light—warm light the color of whiskey—descended in shafts through the trees. A june beetle traversed a rock covered with moss like spilled velvet. A chipmunk skittered across the brown mat of needles, up a sequoia and around to the other side of the trunk. A dove someplace chanted a tranquil call: "Oh ho! Too, hoo, hoo."

Everything was golden. I choked back a cry, a surge of some emotion like joy, maybe, or relief. Or of recollection: remembering why I'd come. A tear rolled down my cheek and onto my neck. I caught it with the palm of my hand.

Eager to wander, I ducked inside, stripped down to my cold gooseflesh and hurried into the clothes I'd bought myself. Simple, appropriate clothes: black pants, black shirt, black sweater. *Nice weave*, I thought, passing a hand over the merino wool that had already started to warm against my skin. The tags still hung by a safety pin under the arm. I glimpsed the price and shook my head. I unfastened the tags, tore them in bits, and dropped them in the trash bag—the Nordstrom bag made of heavy paper with tote handles—I could just hear Suzanne's "ack, ack." I turned it around, but the logo was on both sides. I decided to replace it with another. I pulled out the plastic one my sleeping bag had come in, stuffed the Nordstrom bag inside, and propped the whole thing against the wall. The side of this bag read "North Face." I rubbed my temples, turned away, and walked to the door.

Back when all this had seemed like such a good idea, I'd sketched out a little schedule based on the ancient rule of Saint Benedict. An *horarium*, as it's called in convents and monasteries. Of course, my mother was right: I am a Baptist, so I hadn't written in lauds, matins, or complines. In my book they would just be prayers.

But the beauty of it! I could almost hear the Silicon Valley din, the rushing cars, the droning voices of the radios and televisions and computers, the beeping and ringing and buzzing of phones and cell phones and clocks and Palm Pilot alarms, I could hear it all suction into the vacuum …

… of this silence.

"Oh ho! Too, hoo, hoo."

I was so hungry for this.

I fetched my purse and retrieved the leather journal inside—don't ask what I paid for that, but it was so monastically lovely—and opened to the first page:

Midnight – Prayer, then sleep

3AM – Prayer, then back to sleep

6AM – Rise and dress, prayer, reading, meditation

9AM – Prayer, work

Noon – Prayer, lunch, rest, reading

3PM – Prayer, work

6PM – Prayer, dinner, free time

9PM – Prayer, bed

It glowed, it was so simple. One dulcet chime of my new wristwatch every third hour.

Wristwatches that chime. Again, don't ask, but the tone was perfect.

Only I hadn't yet set the chimes. So I'd forgotten to pray at three o'clock. I had gotten up, probably at about the right time, gazed at the moonlight, and watched that pregnant girl do whatever it was she was doing. For a first night, that would have to suffice.

I brushed my teeth with water from a bottle, then pulled out my Bible and the instructions for my watch. And my glasses—the instructions were written in fine print.

I climbed to the top of the hill and sat on a sunlit rock. I peered at the instructions and read: "To select the first chime, while holding down button A, press button B until it beeps once."

I did this.

Only it beeped twice. I held it down again till it beeped three times, four times … and then it gave a long beep and a short beep. It was talking Morse code now. What did that mean?

I peered at the instructions. Nothing about long and short beeps. I gave it another try and lapsed into deep meditation, just reading the instructions and pushing the buttons.

So went the morning, till my watch read ten thirty (the jeweler had set the time), and I'd accomplished absolutely nothing. I hadn't figured out the chimes, and I hadn't prayed. Frustrated, I snapped the watch back on, stuffed the instructions in my pocket, and glanced about. The forest stretched for miles across the canyon. From my vantage, everything was chartreuse with sunlight.

In the mornings, this would be my place to pray.

I tried kneeling, but the sticks and pebbles bit into my knees. I got back up on my rock, then closed my eyes.

"God," I began. I cleared my throat.

"Lord," I corrected, thinking it the better word, a title, rather than a mere fact of existence. "Thank You for helping me find Garrett. Please help me talk to him when he gets home."

I swallowed.

"Thank You for all those years with Larry." The sound of his name from my own lips almost undid me. I took a breath and started again: "You know why I'm here. Please show me what to do."

Silence, and the sound of a car on the road below.

"Please," I whispered. "Please."

Okay, that was awkwardly brief, but I'd done my prayers. I whispered a quick "Amen."

I opened my Bible at random, and this is what I read:

> *"I know a man in Christ who fourteen years ago was caught up to the third heaven—whether in the body or out of the body I do not know, God knows.*
>
> *"And I know that this man was caught up into Paradise— whether in the body or out of the body I do not know, God knows—and he heard things that cannot be told, which man may not utter."*

Poor Paul. Cut him a little slack.

After an experience like that, you stammer. You say things like "cannot be told" and "I do not know." You repeat yourself, and then you stammer.

I know.

Not that I've gone to the third heaven. My visions were simpler than that; maybe I went to the second or even the first heaven. Or maybe only just outside the door.

But that's all. No further away than just outside the door. Which was good, for one who had always attended the quieter brands of churches.

Larry's aunt Blythe had visions all the time, at her Foursquare church in Sebastopol. She used to tell me about them when she came with Larry's parents for Thanksgiving.

You'd think she knew about my own visions, the way she talked on, and talked on, but Larry swore he never told her. Maybe it was only because I enjoyed her stories so much. But every year she had a fresh batch, and we would wash dishes or wander the backyard together.

"God was heavy in the church last Sunday," she announced once in the arbor behind my house. "Thick as water," she confided, folding her hand into mine. "Silent and holy, and we all just waved like sea kelp in the current, and the Spirit brooded over the waters like the first day of creation."

God knows.

And that was the least sensational of her stories; there were no angels in this one, and no falling—literally "falling under the Spirit's power" or any of the other things she described that made me afraid to go to church with her and allow her people to "lay hands" on me so that all moderation would slip from my body like a ghost.

But I could be kelp. I had been kelp, once, and I knew exactly what she meant. Thomas Merton had his kelp moments. Teresa of Ávila had visions that would startle Blythe into the sorts of ecstasies that would keep her talking straight through her funeral into the grave.

Teresa of Ávila was the queen of visions. One lasted fully two years. *Two years* in which she swam in the unseen presence of God, every moment of every day, every place she went.

I'd come to this shed for that kind of vision.

Or just one more moment like kelp.

CHAPTER 11

I stood to stretch.

Through the stand of trees to my left, I'd seen the woman the night before. I walked to the place where she had been. Her circle was still there, the rocks, leaves, and needles cleared to the perimeter, the spiral pattern brushed in fine lines by the broom straws. One set of footprints led out from the center, beyond the clearing, downhill toward the road.

I followed her direction with my eyes, wondering. Where had she come from? I remembered the sound of her weeping, a child-like cry, a cry to break your heart. She hadn't leaped into the canyon, and that was a relief. Though the slope was so gradual, she'd have scratched herself on the hillside brush probably, nothing more.

Where had she gone? To a steeper ridge? Perhaps I should have talked to her when I had the chance; but at the time it hadn't seemed the thing to do.

I hoped she was all right.

I continued along the canyon until the trail disappeared. The road had fallen silent. The morning rush to the highway had tapered off, and the quiet made me feel as if I were cloistered from the world.

I made my way across the slope taking care not to step or slide into poison oak.

The hill leveled out, and I found another path, bordered in redwood two-by-fours. A distance away, I saw a house, a hacienda with a tile roof and a broad veranda on the side facing the canyon. And an addition …

No—not an addition, but a tar-paper house going up right next door. *Right* next door. Close enough that the occupants could see into each other's windows, could hear each other's conversations if the windows were open. Perhaps the second house provided in-law quarters, but if so, they were good sized. Still, Suzanne would have pushed for something more marketable, more … distant.

A bald man emerged from the far side of the hacienda, pulling a hose toward a garden patch. Suddenly I felt like I'd been spying on him, but he hadn't yet seen me. I back-stepped out of sight, and turned to go.

My cell phone rang.

Wincing, I flipped it open, and walked as fast as I could away from the property.

"Yes?" I whispered.

"Roberta?"

"Vernon!" It was the financial manager we'd hired when Larry could no longer handle our investments. "How are you?"

"Better question: How are you? I heard about your fire."

Should I have told him? Something about his voice said yes, I should have. "I was just about to call you. When you'd had a chance to drink your coffee."

"I'm on my third cup. Are you all right?"

"Of course I'm all right. I was at the funeral when it happened, so I … you know. Who told you about the fire?" It would be just like Suzanne.

"I read the paper."

There was that tone again.

"And Suzanne called me. Are you safe? Could someone danger-ous know where you are?"

"No. I don't think anyone would come looking for me here."

"Okay …"

I didn't want to go into where "here" was.

"So what would you like to do?" he asked.

"Do?"

"We should probably get together."

"Why? There's nothing to do, Vernon. I'm not supposed to do anything, not while they investigate."

"There are still things to think about. I don't want to pressure you so soon after Larry's death, but what if we made an appoint-ment? We could set it a week or two out."

I pressed a hand to my head.

"Do you have your planner with you?"

I'd thrown it away, and the fire had burnt the trash can. "I'm not ready yet. Not even for that."

"Fine. Where are you staying?"

I cringed. "In the Santa Cruz Mountains."

"Do you have an address?"

I had no idea what it was. "Not yet."

"A number besides your cell phone?"

"My cell phone will work fine. Use that."

"Okay. Give me a call."

When he hung up, I dropped the phone back into my pocket. And it rang again. An unlisted number.

"Hello?"

"Roberta? This is Sam."

Sam Greenman, one of Larry's friends from church—a contractor.

"I heard about your house fire. Are you all right?"

"Yes, I'm fine." I softened my voice. "Thanks for asking."

"I imagine you're planning to rebuild. Have you thought who you'd like to handle the project?"

"I thought I'd let the embers cool before I made any decisions, Sam." Definitely not the tone I'd meant to take, but it did get him off the phone. Which was good, since another contractor and a tax accountant were lined up behind him.

———

I'd just gotten back to my prayer rock when I heard the Nokia song— for the fifth time that morning. I yanked the phone from my pocket, flipped it open, and fumbled. It slid down the hill and rang a second time. Without thinking, I darted after it, then slipped on the mat of pine needles, landing on my backside, and slid till my foot jammed on a rock. The cell phone rang its third and final time.

My foot! I pulled it toward myself and massaged beneath my ankle, groaning. It didn't seem broken, but it hurt to touch.

I grabbed the branch of a nearby bush to pull myself up to my good foot. I tried my weight on the other one.

I limped one step. And another. The second step hurt more than the first, and the third was worse than the second. But I retrieved my phone and made my way back to the shed.

My water bottle was still as cold as an ice pack. I sat in the doorway and propped it on top of my foot.

I was hungry.

I'd written in my journal an eating regimen for my new, simpler lifestyle. Nothing sweet or fatty, and by necessity, nothing that took much cooking. Shelf-stable foods seemed best, and whatever fresh fruits and vegetables I could find at the Mountain Pantry. The idea was to clear the clutter from my life, and from my mind.

I opened a can of tuna and scooped out a forkful. I wished now I'd skipped the more expensive solid albacore in spring water and gone instead for the mushier type. Eaten alone, it stuck in my throat like pressboard. Still hungry but gagging, I set the can aside.

All in all, my first morning on the mountain was a disappointment. I sat on my doorstep and listened while the breeze brushed the tops of the trees.

Within the hour my foot improved. I tried my weight on it. It wasn't too bad.

And I had things to do. I didn't want to spend another night without a toilet, not to mention another morning crouching behind the shed where no one could see from the road, or, I hoped, from anyplace else.

I should get more batteries for the flashlight. And I had to do something about those bugs in the roof. I fetched my coin purse, stuffed it in my pants pocket, and set out.

⌒

The sun slanted in shafts between the trees, brightening the ferns along the road. I walked around a corner, and there was the red clapboard house with a gas pump—the Mountain Pantry. On the side wall, it had an exterior entrance to a public restroom. That would come in handy. If I found some sort of makeshift bedpan with a lid, I could empty it there.

Up the road opposite the store, I saw a man with a dog. As he drew near, I realized he was the bald man I had seen that morning at the hacienda. I smiled and tried to appear as though I had not been spying through the trees.

I smelled cinnamon—hot cinnamon and yeast. Perhaps I'd made a mistake, walking to the store on a nearly empty stomach. Whatever was cooking inside definitely didn't fit my new simplified regimen.

When the man reached the store, he started to tie the dog's leash around one of the posts, but the minute he loosened his grip, the dog bounded my direction and halted. You could draw a ten-foot level line from the set of the dog's jaw to the soft center of my belly. I raised a protective hand. The dog spread his legs and trained on me the bold gaze of an armed soldier.

I froze.

"Che Che!" shouted the man, but the dog held position. The man trotted up and grabbed his leash. "Sorry!" I relaxed only a little and kept my distance.

"He's very protective."

"He's beautiful." I had to force a smile, but I'd told the truth.

Bears and lions and ravenous wolves are beautiful, and so was this
dog. "What is he?"

"He's an Akita. My ex-wife's. She and her new husband are in
Colorado till tomorrow." He tied Che Che to the post, and knotted
the leash a second time.

A voice pierced the screen door. "Russ! You keep that dog away
from Cotton!"

"Don't worry! I already fed him!" Russ winked at me and shook
my hand. "Now you know *my* name." His smile traced magnetic
lines around his face. He needed a shave.

"I'm Roberta Denys."

"Oh." His tone of voice made clear that he'd made the connection between me and my better-known late husband. Thankfully, he
made nothing of it. I'd never much liked being recognized by strangers. "You're limping. Are you hurt?"

"It's nothing too bad. I slipped on the hill by my house—"

"Your house?"

"Yes. I just moved in yesterday."

He smiled, as though he expected more.

"Just down the road a bit.

He looked the direction I pointed, squinting. "Huh. I've never
seen—"

"It's a very small house."

"Ah."

We walked in together.

"You got a lady friend?" The girl inside leaned over the counter,
petting a white cat next to the cash register.

"A new neighbor. She's got a small house down the road a bit, a very small house, she says. Just moved in yesterday." He opened the glass refrigerator door, pulled out a quart of milk, and turned to the small rack of DVDs.

"India Moon." She held out her fingers like she meant me to kiss them. A purple rose tattoo wound its way from the top of her pinkie, past her elbow, and under the folded sleeve of her T-shirt.

I shook her hand. "Roberta Denys."

A small glass display revealed the source of the sweet aroma: a dozen large cinnamon rolls, glistening with brown syrup. I went weak at the sight of them.

"Down the road, huh? What house is that?"

"Well, it's just before the bend. You've probably never noticed it."

"Nothing escapes India," Russ muttered. He put a DVD back on the rack and picked up another.

"You're limping."

"Yes. I—"

She pulled something from under the counter. "Try this."

I stared at the packet.

"Pito Pito," she said. "A natural analgesic. It's a tea—they use it all the time in the Philippines. First one's free. Try it."

"Thank you."

"How else can I help you?"

"I just need a few things. Uh, some batteries—"

"What size?"

"C."

She pulled a packet off the rack behind her. "How many?"

"Just two for now."

She slapped the packet on the counter and then fingered the pendant around her neck, a metallic blue disk with a silver figure of a woman.

"Do you have candles?" I asked.

"Sure, right against the wall over there."

I gathered five or six white emergency candles from the display and set them beside the batteries, then found a lidded plastic bucket that would do for a bedpan, and another for a sink. I thought through my mental checklist. "Do you have a bug bomb or something?"

"A what?" India leaned across the counter with the same look I'd gotten from Che Che.

"I've got a bug problem, and I—"

"You want me to help you commit insecticide?"

Russ chuckled.

"I guess that sums it up, yes. My ceiling is crawling with spiders and—"

"You could try a repellent."

"You mean like Off! or something?"

"There are several natural repellents. Spiders hate lemon juice, did you know that?"

"You want me to use lemon juice?"

"No, lemons are out of season. I don't import, and I don't carry the bottled stuff."

"Heaven forbid," murmured Russ.

"I do carry lavender oil. And tea tree oil. Both excellent natural repellents, though I think you'd like the smell of the lavender better."

I'd not made myself clear. "I've got a *very big* bug problem."

She crossed her arms and leaned against the shelf behind her.

"I really don't think—" I stopped.

She was pregnant.

I took in her face, the brown eyes and high cheek bones. The low, rounded hairline. Her hair pulled to a braid behind.

Her long dark hair.

The same girl.

"I … Sure … I'll take the lavender oil."

"Good choice." She scratched her belly. "Will that be all?"

———

That would be all. I paid for my purchases and limped toward home. I'd gone too far, tried too much. Each step demanded progressively more from me. By the time I reached the foot of my hill, I wanted to sit and wallow in misery for a while. But where? On the road? There were still the steps to climb.

So I climbed. One slow step at a time, with no rail to lean on. Halfway up, I heard my cell phone again. It would just have to wait. I took a step, and it rang again. Another step, and another ring. Another step and silence.

When I arrived at my shed, I dropped the buckets, grabbed the doorjamb, and collapsed onto the threshold. I pulled my shoe off and moaned. Once my foot quieted, I remembered my stomach. I reached for my half-eaten can of tuna, and pried open the lid.

And dropped the can.

Curled intimately around a fat lump of fish was a red centipede. I kicked the can away with my good foot, then examined the top of the doorjamb. No bugs there, and none around me on the floor.

Hadn't I promised myself a good wallow? I sniffled against my wrist and rubbed my foot, allowing the tears to flow down my cheeks unhindered.

My cell phone rang.

I reached inside to fetch it from my purse, flipped it open and read the small screen. "Hi, Suzanne."

"There you are. I've been trying to call. I was afraid maybe you'd taken a vow against telephones."

"It's an idea." I sniffled.

"Are you crying?"

"No. Just a runny nose."

"You're getting sick already."

"I am not—"

"I'm not surprised; it was freezing last night. Did you get the coat I brought you?"

"I did. That was very kind of you, Suzy. Thank you."

"How'd you sleep last night?"

"Fine. Just fine."

"I'll bet."

I turned the phone away, and sniffled over my shoulder.

"Bertie, I had to come back to the house this morning to grab a copy of my résumé."

"Your résumé? Why?"

"Something very exciting is happening. I got word that our manager is leaving. Which means they'll be needing a new one."

"That's wonderful."

"It's lucrative, that's what it is, if I get the job. And I've got a good chance; I'm the hardest working, most productive agent in the office."

I had no doubt.

"But that's not what I called about."

"Oh?"

"My housekeeper was there when I got home, and she told me she had found something interesting when she cleaned Amber's room. And I thought you might know a little bit about it."

"What's that?"

"A Magic the Gathering card." Her voice was pure, undiluted accusation.

I took a swift breath.

"Sticking out from behind the dresser."

"Sorry, Suzanne. I don't collect them."

"Neither does Amber, never did. Bertie, did you go into your house the night before last?"

"No. I didn't."

"Well then, did you take something you found around the house someplace?"

"Nooo ..." I used to speak to my mother in the same tone, a childish expression that screamed guilt. I bit my nail.

"Do you have any idea how illegal that is?"

"How illegal what is? Considering that *if* I had taken something, I would have taken it from my own yard. Outside the yellow tape."

She sighed. "Look, I don't blame you. Better you discuss with Garrett the gibberish on the back, than that the police should draw their own conclusions. Augh! What am I saying? You didn't hear me say that."

Gibberish? "What—?"

I heard her secretary call her name. "I gotta go," she said.

I flipped the phone shut. "What gibberish?"

"That's all I get from those things too."

Startled, I turned toward the voice on the stairway. It was Russ. "Umm … hi …"

"Gibberish. Humans survived for thousands of years without cell phones, you know. Just because we have more ways to talk to each other doesn't mean we have more to say."

"I'm starting to think I could do without mine."

He set two small paper bags down beside me. I smelled cinnamon.

"Seriously? This is the place?" He squinted at my hut.

"This is it."

"Why?"

I couldn't think of any answer but the truth. "It's a religious discipline I'm trying."

He raised his eyebrows. "That's unusual."

"I suppose it is."

"Well, you'll fit right in here. The mountain is full of unusual people."

"Like you?"

"No, I'm just the caretaker. Let's see these bugs of yours. May I?"

"Please." I moved to the side.

He stepped one foot in, raised a hand, and pushed on the ceiling, then leaped out while the debris fell to the floor. "You don't need a bug spray. You need a roof."

"I thought a bug spray would be easier to come by just now."

"You're right. It is." He squatted to open one of his bags and pulled out an orange can. "My private stash."

"A bug bomb!" You'd think he'd given me roses, the way I squealed.

"It says it'll kill anything, but I'm not sure in this place."

"Well, as I failed to bring a new roof with me, I'm grateful for whatever you can offer. Truly."

"How's that foot of yours?"

"Just fine. Thank you."

He knelt before me. "Do you mind?" Without waiting for an answer, he took my foot in his hands. "I'm not a doctor, but I know a little. I'm a massage therapist."

"A massage therapist." A very forward massage therapist.

He pushed against the side. "It hurts there?"

"Yes." I winced.

He slowly pressed with his thumbs. "A slight sprain. You should stay off of it."

"I am staying off of it. Well—I am now."

He sat on the ground beside the door and leaned on the cinder-block wall of the shed, then opened his second bag and pulled out a thermos.

"What's that?"

"Two cups of coffee." He pulled out the mugs and poured them full. "And ..." He reached back in the bag. "India's finest."

The scent of spice overtook me. He retrieved the cinnamon rolls and they bent in his hand under their own weight.

"Just coffee, thanks."

"Are you dieting, too?"

"Something like that."

"You and my ex-wife." He took a bite, drawing honeyed strings of caramel as he pulled away.

I swallowed. "India's an interesting girl."

"That she is. A witch, you know."

"A ..."

"Witch. She casts spells. No pointy hat, as far as I've seen, but her cat's named for Cotton Mather. But as long as she works her magic on these ..." He lifted the cinnamon roll. "... she can do whatever she wants. I just hope that store of hers pulls in enough money once the baby comes."

"The father ...?"

"... is her secret."

"Oh. Very mysterious."

He took another bite, and I could almost taste it as if it were my own. "Wasn't me," he said, his eyebrows raised. He'd caught me staring.

"No. Of course not."

"I'm a fine, upstanding man."

"Are you now?" He'd made me laugh, and he'd meant to. His smile lines shot like sunrays from his eyes.

"Now and forever, yes I am." He finished his cinnamon roll and licked his fingers. "Actually, she used to have a boyfriend, part of a coven that met up here. Black hair and a pierced tongue. He bought her that tattoo, and my guess is he also—"

"Got her pregnant."

"Right. Now here's the deal: You can't be here after we set off the bug bomb. So why not stay at my place tonight?"

"*Your* place?" Just that quick, he'd gotten to the point.

"I'll fix you a nice dinner, the best steak you ever tasted. You can rest your foot by the fire. Maybe soak in the hot tub."

What would I tell him? That my husband was still warm in his grave? But he knew that already, didn't he? "No, thank you," I said, in as forbidding a voice as I could muster.

He gave me a long look.

"I can set it off myself. I'll just sit right out here. With the door shut. I'll be fine."

"Have it your way." He gathered the thermos and two empty mugs and simply walked away, the fine, upstanding man who'd just hit on a new widow.

I sat there with the orange bug bomb in my hand. I'd have to take the food and water out of the shed, and my clothes. Everything, really, with my sore foot, and he'd left me here.

A cool breeze circled round the white bag he'd set by the wall, and lifted the scent of cinnamon to my nose. I groaned, thinking of all I'd said no to. A fire. A warm meal. The swirling waters of a hot tub. "He probably is the father," I muttered. "Poor India."

My stomach grumbled its own complaint.

I had some sugarless mints that might help. I rummaged around the bottom of my purse but failed to find them. I pulled out my checkbook and tried again. I pulled out my makeup bag, my coin purse … and one of the Magic the Gathering cards I had found in our yard the night of the fire.

I studied the picture: a dark beast with the arms and legs of at least four creatures. Ominously titled "Call to the Grave." A worn crease across the middle.

Garrett had loved these things.

I turned the card over, and froze. I'd never noticed that night in the darkness. Four thick black words were scrawled in magic marker over the printed copy: "Death is the end."

I drew in a sharp breath, leaned against the doorjamb, and tried to breathe. What hadn't I known about my son?

I reached inside Russ's white bag and pulled out the cinnamon roll. I wiped my tears and sniffled, then pulled a bite free and chewed. Mixed with my tears, it tasted like plaster in my mouth.

CHAPTER 12

I couldn't sleep that night. I did pray, though—about that witch girl, India, and the baby she carried. More accurately, my mind paced circles around that ceremony she performed beneath the moon: Did she do that every night?

I tried to pray about Garrett. When did he write those words on the back of his card? Probably when he was young, on one of those times when we'd argued over heaven knows what? Whether he could go see *Alien*, maybe something trivial as that.

Or perhaps he'd done it more recently.

Before I thought very far that direction, my mind would flit back to India, like a child who would rather do anything but the homework before her—or like a mother who would rather search anywhere but the darkest corners of her son's mind.

Which was crazy. Garrett was fine; he was with this Eloise in Europe.

Death is the end. What had he meant by that?

I wondered if India was out there now. I had no idea where I was.

To escape the torture of my own thoughts, I pulled myself from the floor to one leg, and tested my foot. It was good enough. I slipped into my shoes, pulled on my coat, and stepped outside.

The forest was as dark as the night before, but I remembered the path. Stray leaves and needles crackled on the steps under my feet. I limped to the top of the moonlit hill.

There was the light of her circle fire. A few soft footsteps through the trees, and I found a place to watch.

She stroked her belly like a crystal ball, and whispered—perhaps an incantation, or a prayer. I couldn't hear the words, only the sorrow.

When she finished, she back-stepped to the edge of the circle, lifted her skirt, and stepped over the candles. I thought she would blow them out, but she proceeded to the edge of the canyon and lowered herself to the ground. She sat for I don't know how long. A half hour? An hour? I grew sleepy and cold. I wanted to go back, but how could I without drawing attention? She'd settled into a stillness quieter than breath.

Should I have risked moving? Slowly, I pulled my knees to myself, braced against the tree behind me, and pushed forward to a squat—which shot a sharp twinge through my foot. I collapsed backward, and a twig cracked beneath me.

I looked up at her in time to see her turn her head in my direction. I froze in the awkward leg-up position of one who'd just fallen. The candlelight cast a halo around her hair, around the curved pear of her belly, but her face was obscured. She let out a shudder and rose, then scuttled about to blow out the candles and leave them where they stood. In a moment, she was gone.

I trembled, chilled by the feeling that there'd been a presence in the dark between the two of us, and now India had left me to face it alone.

An absurd feeling, but still I got to my feet, and slipped out of the shadow, back into the moonlit clearing—and turned my sore foot on a rock. I yelped, but resumed my pace, and hobbled down the hill, back to my candlelit shed.

I slipped out of my shoes, pulled off the coat, and crawled into my sleeping bag. And lay there, watching the shadows dance on the wall.

I couldn't sleep.

CHAPTER 13

The next morning my prayers were haunted by the memory of Garrett's card. Both cards. Among the several I'd stuffed in my purse the night of the fire, I'd found one more scrawled with the same sentiment. What did he mean by "Death is the end"? Maybe nothing. It could very well be the title of a song he liked—I'd heard worse, and it certainly fit the music he listened to.

Still, Suzanne's suggestion that my own son would do me violence ate at my insides like acid. I needed to confirm that Garrett was all right. I called Sun Microsystems and got Eloise's last name from a coworker: Pavia.

I only had to call three Pavias from the phone book before an accented voice on the other end of the line said, "Eloise? She's out of the country."

"Yes. She's with my son in Portugal."

"Oohh!" I heard the smile in her voice. She said something in Spanish away from the phone, then returned. "Your son is a nice boy."

Well, but of course he was, and what a comfort to hear her say it. I almost laughed. "Thank you. Thank you very much. I wonder if you might know where they're staying. I have something urgent to discuss with him—"

"Oh. Oh my."

"No, no, everything's fine—well not fine, but … there's just something I need to tell him."

And that easily she gave me the number of the hotel room in Lisbon where my son was staying with Eloise.

I checked my watch. It was nine o'clock. So it would be perhaps one a.m. in Lisbon. Best to let them sleep.

———

"A nice boy," she'd said.

Not the brooding, verbally abusive, erratic near-lunatic his last girlfriend—was it Christy?—had called him. Christy said he threw tantrums. She said he spent whole days in bed and didn't answer the phone. She told me I'd raised a "lazy, self-sorry pile of sludge." Her exact words. No wonder Garrett broke off with her. But Eloise's mother said he was a nice boy. And I'd been worried …

Garrett had gone through bad patches, like any other kid. I had no idea when he'd written on his collector card, but it was hard to imagine a grown man doing such a thing. This grown man was off in Lisbon with a young woman, very likely a much nicer young woman than Christy. It wasn't the chaste arrangement I would have wanted for him, but my son was no lunatic.

I was the one who was crazy, for letting Suzanne get to me like this, causing me to suspect my son of a crime against his own parents. There were serious, real-life matters to think about. I didn't have to make one up.

I still had to tell Garrett about his father, and that wasn't a call I looked forward to. In fact, now that I thought of it, the worst, most heartless way I could imagine to do that would be to tell him over the phone, and ruin his vacation when his father was buried already, and there was nothing he could do. Suzanne was a good friend, but I wasn't going to buy into her irrational suspicions and mishandle this whole thing. I would wait till I could be there to hold Garrett when he cried.

It was time for nine o'clock prayers. I knelt, and adjusted my knees to avoid a rough patch in the concrete. I leaned forward and laid my hands on the floor, slid them along the cold surface, and laid my forehead on top. Thus kneeling half prostrate for emphasis, thus demonstrating the seriousness of my intent, I prayed for Garrett and Eloise's safe return from Lisbon. I prayed for grace in breaking the bad news to Garrett. I prayed—*please!*—that God would join me in this little shed …

For forty-five seconds I prayed, until I heard a light knock at my door.

"Yes?" I voiced the question to the concrete.

"You're kidding. This is where you live?" It was India.

When I opened the door, she stood before me in saffron orange from head to toe. An orange embroidered tunic, a full orange skirt over bare legs, orange socks and orange Chinese slippers. She'd braided her hair into at least twenty long dark cords and gathered them in an orange band so they cascaded down the back of her head. A shaft of sunlight ricocheted off all that color and cast a golden glow into my shadowed home.

"Russ said you lived in a very small house." She gazed from my sleeping bag to the cinder-block walls behind me. "This isn't a house; it's a …"

"Gardener's shed."

"It takes all kinds."

I let her in.

She circled the room, sniffing, and I cringed. Could she smell the evidence of my mass insecticide?

"I brought you some more lavender oil. In case you need it." She held out the bottle, and pressed the tips of her fingers to her nose.

I limped across the room and accepted her gift. "Thank you."

"How's your foot?"

"Getting better, thanks."

"Did you try the Pito Pito?"

I'd forgotten all about it. "I ... I don't yet have a way to heat water."

She glanced around again, and zeroed in on the "kitchen," which consisted of a cluster of canned foods and bottled water stacked near the dishes on the floor. "My gosh. You don't have a way to heat yourself. What will you do when it gets really cold?"

"I suppose I have a few months to figure that out." So many things that seemed like obvious necessities to everyone else had hardly crossed my mind. I offered an embarrassed smile.

"And is this what you eat?" She picked up a can of baked beans, exposing a small beetle that rushed for cover. Unfazed, she turned the can and frowned at the list of ingredients.

Why did this girl intimidate me? How old was she, anyway? Twenty-two maybe, no more.

She set the can down. "I'll tell you what we're going to do right now." She picked up a bottle of water, and unscrewed the top. "Where is the Pito Pito tea bag?"

I retrieved it from my purse and handed it over. She removed the bag from its wrapper, folded it in half, and poked it in the bottle, then opened the door and marched out. I watched as she climbed the hill and set the bottle on a sunny patch of ground. She returned. "Give it a few minutes, and you'll have your tea."

"Smart thinking."

She sat on the floor, and I joined her.

"So why are you doing this?" She propped her elbows on her knees and leaned forward. "Russ told me who your husband was. You're not poor."

"No, not poor. It's … an experiment, I guess."

"To prove …?"

"Not to prove anything. It's a religious thing. A kind of … simplicity of life."

"Oh. What religion are you?"

"Christian."

She nodded, as though she wanted me to tell more.

"You don't hear about it much these days, but from the earliest time of the church, there have been people who wanted to dedicate themselves fully to God. To live simply, to have nothing, to *value* nothing but Him."

"Nothing? Don't you have family?"

"Yes, I have a son. But I meant material things."

"So you're going to be like Saint Francis. Are we going to find you naked in a field of flowers one day?"

"Naked?"

"Like Graham Faulkner … don't look so surprised! I know my stuff. At least once a year my mom and granny used to prop a bowl of popcorn on the couch between them and watch *Brother Sun, Sister Moon,* with Granny tweezing nose hairs and mom doing her macramé. Granny was a devout Catholic; she had all the beads and crosses. Mom just liked Graham Faulkner. *All* of Graham Faulkner."

I laughed. "You get Donovan to bring his guitar and serenade me, and I'll do the naked thing."

"Mom had the CD."

"Did she get rid of it?"

"She died last year. Breast cancer."

"Oh, I'm sorry."

"Ah well." She leaned back and looked around. "So what do you do here?"

"I pray, study the Bible. Or at least that's the plan. I'm still not on schedule."

"What schedule?"

She really seemed interested. I fetched my horarium and showed her. "It's a kind of—"

"Three a.m.? You get up at three a.m.?"

"Not exactly, not yet. I can't get the alarms to work on my watch."

"But why three?"

"I think your Granny might know why. The idea is to pray every third hour, so you're never far from God."

"I'd think God would want you to get some sleep."

"It's not so bad. I go back to sleep when I'm done. And anyway—" I stopped myself. I'd started to say that India had been up pretty early herself. But I wasn't supposed to know that. "I'm still trying to get my watch to work. Right now, the alarms aren't working."

"Well, when you get them to work, why don't you set one for eight o'clock Saturday night?"

"Why?"

"I'm having a party at my place. A jam session. Everyone's bringing their instruments if they have them, and food. But you wouldn't have to bring anything."

"I really thought I'd just be quiet up here."

"It might help, you know."

"Help what?"

"Well, you know, with your husband gone."

"You mean it would soften my grieving process."

"It might."

"That's nice of you, India, but I'm fine. It's just that—"

"It's not in your aquarium." She nodded.

"Horarium."

"Ararium."

"I just want to be quiet."

"So, I don't guess you'd want to drive into town tomorrow about nine thirty."

"Why do you ask?"

"I need a ride. To see my midwife in San Jose. Her back's out, so she can't drive, and my truck is totally falling apart. Right now it needs a carburetor, and I can't afford another one for at least a couple weeks, so it's not like I can just wait." She chewed a fingernail.

My stomach turned as I said it: "Sure, I can drive you." The last place I wanted to go was back into the noise and traffic.

But she smiled like the morning sun and I felt glad I hadn't refused. "Thank you," she said. "I missed seeing her last month because the clutch was out. Are you sure it's all right?"

"I'm sure. It's no problem."

She sat up straighter. "Okay, so you pray and study the Bible. You're probably done already. Now what?"

"When I finish I'll do some work. Fix up this place, that sort of thing. It's very nice here. I love to pray on top of the hill there, where I can see the canyon—" I stopped myself again, but it was too late.

She pressed a hand to her mouth, and sucked in her breath.

Oh, Lord. "Is something wrong?" I didn't really have to ask.

"What about your three-a.m. prayers? Do you go up the hill for those too?"

How stupid could I have been? There was no good way to tell her that I was the watcher she'd heard in the dark. But I didn't have to tell her; she already knew.

"I have my own beliefs, Roberta, and I'm not ashamed of them. But some things … some things are just—"

"No, it's not like—" I clutched my hands together.

She rushed out the door and slammed it shut, leaving me in shadow.

A moment later the door opened a crack, to allow one final shaft of saffron light. Her hand flicked in and set the bottle of tea on the floor. "Forget the drive to town. I can wait."

The door shut, and she was gone.

Spying. That was the word for what I'd done. I'd intruded on a private moment of India's. What had I been thinking? The first time was an accident, though I'd stayed too long even then.

But I had been worried about her, up there on the hill amid

her candles and moonlight, wailing to the night sky. Something was wrong. Still, I should have talked to her, not just watched from the shadows.

I leaned over and grabbed the tea she'd left for me, and held it to my forehead. My face felt hot, and my stomach had clenched itself into a fist. I twisted the cap off the bottle and took a sip. It tasted like smoke, and it hurt going down, like swallowed rocks.

How would I face her again? I couldn't just find another store to shop in, not unless I wanted to leave my peaceful cloister to drive down into the valley every time I needed to buy apples and carrots.

Or empty my toilet bucket.

Besides, this young woman with her tattoos and candles, who gave me lavender for my bugs and Pito Pito for my sore foot, who brewed the tea since I hadn't bothered to brew it myself, this pregnant little girl went up on that hill where she thought no one would see, at an hour so early she thought no one would hear—was it every morning?—and *wept!*

Someone ought to care about that. I would find some way to apologize. And then perhaps I could find a way to help.

Ah, but what way? I couldn't just stop in at the store and say, "Tell me all about it, dear." Her trouble almost certainly had to do with the father of that baby, and I already knew—by way of the local gossip—that she preferred to keep his black-haired, tongue-pierced identity a secret. I couldn't just barge in and ask. Especially after this morning.

I held a hand to my headache and let out a long breath. I'd have to find a way.

Maybe if I finished my nine o'clock prayers—it was now nine

thirty—something would come to me. I leaned over and placed my hands on the floor, and rested my forehead on top of them, overwhelmed with the sudden desire to escape into sleep.

I heard a loud noise outside, a sound of slapping wood. A knock sounded at the door.

I swallowed. "Yes?"

"I'm here to see a lady about a roof." It was Russ.

I found him standing with a bundle of green canvas slung under his arm, a tool belt over his jeans, and a pile of boards behind him. "Roberta Denys, I'd like you to meet my father-in-law, Boyd Farber."

A small older man with white hair and thick glasses leaned forward to shake my hand, and I obliged.

"What's all this?"

"First …" Russ opened the green bundle into an umbrella chair and set it on the ground. "I brought you some furniture."

"Oh no, really, it's—"

"A housewarming gift. Boyd here thinks you've got the right idea. He grew up in a log cabin in Illinois."

When Boyd grinned, his teeth came out to shine. They were too large for his mouth, and his glasses made his eyes look enormous. I had a feeling if I squinted I'd see a ten-year-old boy.

"It wasn't a log cabin," he said. "But it was small. People didn't used to need as much."

"That's the idea. I'm trying to need less," I said.

"To lighten your bags."

"What?"

"People spend too much time packing for the lives they think

they want. By the time they've got it all rounded up, they're out of
time, and they're too old to carry the luggage."

I looked from the pile of wood to Russ.

"We're going to build you a new roof."

"A roof? No, no. You can't—"

"Sure we can. Where do you want your stuff? We don't want it
getting dirty." Already he was in my hut, picking up my dishes, my
bottled water—and the nightgown I'd dropped to the floor when I'd
gotten dressed.

I snatched it away and rescued my toilet bucket—and my pride.
He set my dishes and water on a bed of needles several yards from
the hut and returned.

"Russ, please, this isn't necessary."

"Oh, but it is." He thumped the roof and dodged the debris,
proving his point. He gathered my canned goods into one arm. "You
can sit out of the way and keep us company. Or you can limp up to
my place. The deck has a nice view."

And then there'd be dinner and the hot tub. He'd tried this before.

I looked to Boyd, who'd already gathered my books. He stood
reading the spine of the red one. "*The Practice of the Presence of God.*"
He shrugged. "Practice makes perfect?"

What was Russ doing with a father-in-law anyway? "Didn't you
say you were divorced?"

"He got custody of me." Boyd walked by, and I snatched my
books from his arms.

Russ reached for a board. I set my foot on the pile just in time to
stop him. I didn't want any obligations to this massage therapist with
a hot tub. "This really isn't necessary. I came here to live simply."

"Fine. A bug-free dwelling might be a little simpler than what you've got. If it'll make you feel better, you can bake us some cookies. I like chocolate chip."

"I don't have an oven."

"So use mine."

There he went again.

Something crashed behind me, and I turned. Boyd had climbed six rungs up a ladder and pierced a crowbar through my tiny roof. "Argument settled."

I think I whimpered.

With no effort at all he jabbed two more holes. Russ picked up the umbrella chair and took my hand. He led me to a sunny spot a distance off where the hillside leveled out. "Let me be a neighbor, will you? Just sit here. It's a small roof. It won't take any time—we'll be done by afternoon."

So much for my prayers. I could limp to the top of the hill out of earshot, but my foot was very sore after the second mishap. Besides, for the moment, I'd lost all desire to go there, even in daylight.

The chair felt good. Since I'd arrived on this mountain I'd only sat on rocks and concrete, and my back had already begun to feel sore. I was fifty years old, a latecomer to the simple life.

Why not spend the time on my wristwatch, try to figure out the chimes? The instructions hadn't been much help. Maybe I could figure it out by messing with it.

I pushed two buttons and the watch beeped. That was what I wanted, right? What did the instructions say to do after that? Something about pushing button A once for every hour … The next prayer time was at six o'clock. Which was button A? I pushed the top one eighteen times to get to the eighteenth hour of the day. Then I pushed what I assumed was button B, and the watch *chimed*! Evidently I'd done something right.

Boyd glanced my way. "What's that?"

"Sorry, didn't mean to startle you. It's just my watch."

Now what? I tried pushing button A again. One long and two short beeps. What did that mean? I pushed the other one to set the nine o'clock hour, but nothing happened. I tried once more. It let out a continuous beep, long and unnecessarily loud.

Boyd turned again, and squinted. I gave up and put the watch back on my wrist.

The two men worked together as if they fixed roofs all the time. In a short while they had taken the original roof completely off. They spoke quietly, lifted a one-by-four to the roof with Russ on one side of the hut and Boyd on the other. I watched as Russ penciled off a cut line on the board, and the two men took it back down, braced it against the stack of lumber, and sawed it off.

My cell phone emitted a plaintive chirp and drew yet another glance from Boyd. I pulled it from my pocket and cringed. That was another thing I'd failed to consider, that my phone would need charging. I had both a car charger and a wall charger in my glove compartment, but no electricity in my shed. I could use the car, or I could ask someone for the use of their electric outlet. Russ, or India? Oh dear. The car was the better choice.

Later I would take a drive. For now, the sun shone warm on my shoulders, and I closed my eyes.

CHAPTER 14

A woman's voice woke me. "… in a few months when I've lost this fat …"

"You're not fat." I heard Russ's answer, followed by a mechanical clack.

"Well he's right either way. It wouldn't hurt me to do more sit-ups."

I opened my eyes. The roof was on—already!—and Russ was up his ladder with a staple gun, fastening tar paper.

A woman in shorts stood in my doorway, sweeping. The sun had warmed me clear through, and I gazed at this woman the way you squint at people on the beach when you've just opened your eyes.

She wasn't fat. Her legs were muscular as horses'. Her bare arms showed the slightest curve of biceps. "Just to get rid of my tummy," she said.

"You tell your Svengali, women have tummies." Russ bent away from the roof to look her in the eye. "Maybe it's not a real woman he wants. He could get himself a Barbie doll; she'd fit in his pocket, right where he wanted her."

"Be nice."

"I am nice." Russ spotted me. "Hello there."

"You're done already." I pushed myself up from the chair.

He descended the ladder. "All but the shingles. This should keep you dry and hopefully bugless for tonight."

The woman propped her broom against the wall. "I'm Brenda."

"My ex-wife," said Russ. "Brenda, this is Roberta."

"Russ tells me my dog scared you yesterday. I'm so sorry."

"Oh, it was nothing."

"He's friendlier than he looks. My husband takes him to obedience school, but he hasn't quite learned his manners."

Russ snorted. "Don't hold your breath."

"I meant the dog."

He grinned.

"It was sweet of you to help." I glanced around. "Where's Boyd?"

"Dad naps in the afternoon." She looked again at my hut. "Russ says you plan to live here."

"I do live here."

"I understand it's a religious thing?"

"Something like that."

"How so?" She seemed interested, but I didn't feel like explaining myself. Something about her expression made me feel like a specimen in a museum.

"Really, I just came for the solitude."

"Oh. Are you part of a group, or an order or something?"

"No."

"Are you Catholic? My cousin is a Capuchin nun. She says God called her to a life of silence, celibacy, and poverty. That means she can't talk, can't have sex, and can't go shopping. Is there anything worse for a woman?"

I smiled. But I remembered the nun I'd met when I was twelve, and sensed a kindred spirit in this cousin of Brenda's. "How is she?"

"Oh, she's fine. She sent me a picture, and she looks good, if you like her outfit. You know, black on black with accents of white. These Catholics with their Capuchins and these Anglicans with their Primates. So cute, like little monkeys."

I searched for some other topic to discuss, and just that moment, a new topic charged down the hill behind me. I heard a rustle of pine needles and turned. There stood the very dog we'd been talking about only a moment before. He glared at me with that same look I'd seen on the road, only this time he growled. Thankfully, he was on a short leash, held by a blond man in creased khakis.

"No!" The man jerked the leash. The dog softened his stance and whined at Brenda.

"What are you doing?" The man frowned. "I've been looking for you."

She touched a hand to her throat. "I didn't realize. I'm sorry."

"She's been helping me," said Russ.

"Helping you do what?"

"I'm putting a roof on for Roberta." He nodded my way.

The man looked at me and smiled, then turned on his blue-eyed charm. "It's a pleasure to meet you. My name is Gil."

I shook his hand.

"Is this your property?"

"It is."

"We're neighbors then. I live next door to Russ."

Immediately I remembered the house that sat in the lap of Russ's hacienda.

"Do you plan to build here?"

"No."

He looked at my hut.

"She's doing a religious thing like Nancy," said Brenda.

"Yes, it's similar," I said. "Although not exactly; I'm not Catholic or a nun."

"Good for you," said Gil. "So is this a meditation thing?"

"Well, sort of—"

"I know this woman in San Francisco, this fashion model who spent three months in the Mojave Desert with a teacher and a small group of people, last year. The teacher taught her to access certain universal principles to free herself of the effects of childhood trauma, and to block the thoughts within herself that attract future trauma. When she returned, she found she had begun to attract more of the good things in life to herself. She had double the modeling assignments, and at higher pay."

"How nice."

"If you'd like to meet her, just let me know."

"Uh, Gil," said Russ. He winked at me, and I did feel grateful to be rescued from the turn the conversation had taken. "Brenda was going to help me sort out her dad's medicine," he said. "Can't you walk Che Che by yourself?"

"It's Che," said Gil.

"That's what I said."

"Just Che."

Russ smiled.

"We have to go into the office. What's wrong with Boyd's medicine?"

"New prescriptions."

"You can't sort them out yourself?"

"No, it's too many, and too many times. What's so important? You were going to rest a day after your trip."

"She's not resting anyway. We've got paperwork to do."

"I'm sorry, Russ." She touched his arm.

"I need your help."

She looked from her ex to her husband and almost groaned.

Russ let out a long breath, then pulled a pencil and a gum wrapper from his pocket. "Can you remember what I gave him this afternoon?"

"Yes. I can write it down for you."

"Then tonight you come over and help me sort out the rest."

"Okay."

"Great!" Gil patted Russ's shoulder and turned to Brenda. "I'll get the car and pick you up."

My watch chimed. Loudly. The three of them turned their attention to me.

"Is that your cell phone?" asked Brenda.

"No. My watch alarm."

"If you have an appointment someplace, maybe we could drop you off."

"No. I'm just trying to figure out how to make it work."

"It sounds like a church bell. Is it part of what you're doing here?"

"Sort of." My face grew hot. She waited—they all waited for me to go on. "It's to remind me of prayer time."

"Prayer time." Gil gave me a long look. "Okay, then. I'll go get the car."

Brenda sat on my chair, held Russ's gum wrapper to her knee, then slowly wrote out two long words and pointed.

"This is the large blue pill. He takes that in …" She checked her watch. "A half hour. This is the tiny white one. He takes that in two hours." She wrote the times. "He doesn't need any more till after dinner. I'll be back in time."

Two folds in Russ's cheeks set a gentle smile in parentheses. "You'll make a good nurse one day. When are you going to finish your schooling?"

She looked away, then caught my eye and sprang from the chair. "I took your seat."

"Don't be silly. I've sat long enough."

She glanced down at the road. No one there yet. "Let's have coffee sometime; you can tell me about what you're doing. Do you have family nearby?"

"I have a son. He's on vacation."

A horn sounded from the road, where Gil waited in a sparkling black Lamborghini convertible. He gunned the motor. "Take you for a ride, Russ. Tomorrow!"

"I gotta go," said Brenda. Russ kissed her on the cheek, and she ran down the hill.

"Good luck with your convent!" Gil honked again, and the two were off.

Russ shook his head and set to cleaning up. Careful to keep pressure off my foot, I bent to gather scraps of wood. "They live next door to you?"

"Yep. She and I owned two lots when we were married. We were going to put in a large garden on the second, put in some herbs and vegetables, some roses for Brenda. After the divorce, she wanted to be there for her dad, and her dad wouldn't live with Gil. Boyd and I get on just fine. So this was their solution. Gil's solution."

"Gil's? And you don't mind?"

"Mind? What's minding got to do with anything?" He brushed the dirt off the front of his jeans. "Gil and I used to be business partners. We had a little spa in Los Gatos. When Brenda left me to marry him—let's see, not quite a year ago?—I managed to extricate myself from the business. I have my own little practice now, and he's just opened up his fifth tanning salon in the Bay Area. He's got a good head for finance."

"And he's comfortable living next door to you?"

"Sure. He thinks I'm enlightened. He thinks I still like him."

CHAPTER 15

When Russ had trudged halfway to the crest, I forced the door shut. It squawked.

"That door's the next thing I'll fix." His voice came muffled and distant.

"It's fine." I wasn't sure he'd heard.

One more repair project like the one we'd had that day, and Gil might put his universal principles and that good head for finance to work, maybe cage me in and sell tickets. "Yessir, folks, once the moneyed wife of Silicon Valley wonder boy Larry Denys, the she-hermit has given herself to lonely solitude, squalid deprivation, and a sexless life of prayer."

Only there was faint chance of solitude with neighbors like these.

And my little shed was pristine now, without a bug to be found. The small, cracked window had been polished to let in more light. My belongings had been dusted off and arranged along the wall. The place smelled of new lumber, and when I looked up, I saw nothing but smooth, clean wood.

And I had a chair.

This could hardly be called squalid deprivation.

The glazed finish of my bowl and plate glowed in the candle-light, and the silver gleamed beside them on a woven linen napkin. I was still a moneyed wife.

A moneyed widow.

As to celibacy, Larry and I had been sexless for some time before his death. But we hadn't been touchless. I sagged into the chair at the remembered texture of his skin, the whispering moisture of his lips beneath mine, the flutter of his hand on the small of my back. *Oh, Larry.* I stroked my fingertips along my arms for comfort—small comfort—and rolled down to my bed on the floor. My husband was gone.

And that life of prayer? It didn't exist. I had missed most of my scheduled times because I got interrupted, or distracted. And it hardly mattered. My prayers still seemed to go nowhere. But Teresa of Ávila and Julian of Norwich, they never nurtured such excuses.

Julian lived through the Bubonic Plague—three separate epidemics. There was no telling who she'd lost, but she'd be a statistical anomaly if she didn't suffer enough grief to put mine to shame. Far from resenting her suffering, she asked for more. And God obliged her, with pain, crippling illness, and near death. And there she was with her *All shall be well and all shall be well, and all manner of things shall be well.*

Safe to assume her prayers didn't echo off the stone walls of her cell, like mine. When Julian prayed, God crouched beside her, to catch every whispered word with His kiss. She'd left her writings; it was there for anyone to read. She knew the texture of God's skin.

I woke the next morning with a plan fully formed. The words "moneyed widow" had played in my head all night like a bad song, but by daybreak I knew what to do.

My watch said it was only seven; there was still time. I scrambled out of my sleeping bag and grabbed my purse. My cell phone—where was it?

I lifted out my cosmetic bag. One more time I'd wear makeup, and then I would throw it away. I pushed my calendar to the side and rifled again through my purse. Where was my cell phone? I glanced around the room. There it was in the corner. I dropped my purse and grabbed the phone, scrolled down my directory to find Vernon's number, and dialed. The call rolled into voicemail. "This is Vernon Brown at SVS Financial. I'm sorry I missed your—"

I punched the pound sign to skip the greeting. "Vernon, this is Roberta. I hope you've still got time available around ten or so, because I want to take you up on that appointment. If that's not a good time, call me and we'll reschedule." I tapped my foot, thinking. "But please make it ten o'clock if at all possible."

I hung up, then grabbed my purse, slipped on my shoes and left.

The windows of India's store were dark. The hand-lettered sign propped in the window read "Sorry I missed you! Come back when the sun's up."

But it was up—although barely. The light filtered in pale shafts through the trees.

Where did India live? I retreated down the steps back to the gas pump, to look around. The Mountain Pantry was a two-story building, with eyelet curtains wafting from the upper windows. Did India live up there? I walked to the side, where I found a set of wooden

stairs leading to a plank deck. I climbed the stairs and knocked on
the sliding glass door.

Inside I saw an orange couch turned away from me, and behind
that, three stools at a breakfast bar that separated the main room
from a galley kitchen.

I knocked again. A dark head of hair appeared over the back of
the couch; dark eyes squinted my direction, then dropped out of sight
again. This was going to be awkward. But if she'd just listen to me ...
I knocked again.

India stood and caught her balance, hitched up her pajama
pants, and straightened her T-shirt over her belly. She pushed her
hair off her face, walked to the door, and slid it open. "Miss me last
night? I wasn't in the mood for an audience."

"I didn't go."

"Well, I don't do daylight performances."

"I'm sorry, India. I didn't mean to spy on you, and I won't do it
again. I just wondered if you were all right."

She pushed her hair back again. "Is that all?"

"No."

She waited.

I felt so awkward, standing under her cold gaze. "I want to drive
you to see your midwife."

"I already canceled."

"Can you call her back?"

"It's fine. I'm fine."

"Please. I want to do this for you."

She stepped aside and let me in. "Why do you want to do this
for me?"

"For heaven's sake, India, be mad at me if you want, but leave your baby out of it. You need to see this midwife of yours. Or a doctor. Do you have one?"

"I don't have insurance. The lady I'm seeing is very good."

"Then call her. Please."

For just a moment she rested a hand on her belly. Then she fetched her phone and a worn business card from the breakfast bar, and returned. She pushed aside the rumpled blanket on the couch and sat, then squinted at the card, punched a number into the phone, and waited. "Marsha? Is your nine thirty open? Yeah, things changed. I can come. See you." She pressed the Off button, and dropped the phone to her lap. "You don't have to worry about me." But her eyes had already started to glisten with new tears. She looked away.

Why was she crying? What was she doing at night on the canyon's edge? There wasn't a single question that came to mind that I could ask, not with her spring wound tight as it was.

"Did you drink your tea?"

I nodded. "It tastes like smoke."

"But how's your foot?"

"Better." I lied. I didn't want to talk about the second injury. She squared her shoulders.

"Thank you, India." I stood. "We'll leave here at nine."

———

I left Vernon's office the way I'd meant to, like it was just a normal visit. I proceeded to the waiting room, said hi to Cathy at the desk, and asked about her little boy. She showed me the latest pictures, and

I said her son was darling, a little angel. Then I wished her a wonder-ful day, and left.

Vernon had questioned me—strongly—about my decision, asked if I was sure, and wouldn't I like to think about this? I told him I had thought it out thoroughly, and yes, I was sure. I tried to explain why, but he only muttered something about religious cults. I didn't expect he would understand.

On my way back to pick up India, feeling a powerful sense of relief, I stopped at the bank, then went to the Delta Queen Car Wash in Campbell. I let them clean the road dust off the Lexus in the big paddle boat that disguised the brushes and water jets inside. It made me late, doing this, and my cell phone rang while I sat on a park bench feeding popcorn to the ducks in the pond. I checked to make sure it wasn't Vernon, saw that it was India, and let it ring. I was late, but she'd have to wait.

When I pulled in the driveway of Marsha's nouveau-Mediterranean, India rushed out the front door and down the walk like she meant to run me over. "It's not a social call, you know. It only took a half hour, not even. You could have waited."

"I had an appointment of my own."

"Oh. Where?" She reached for the passenger door.

"Wait. Don't get in." I opened my door and got out.

"I didn't leave anyone to open the store. I'm going to be late."

"So? How much business do you get in the mornings?"

"It's my living."

"Well, come on then." I walked to her side, and held out the keys.

"You want me to drive?"

I nodded. "It's your car. You drive."

"My car?"

I smiled.

"What do you mean?"

"I'll explain while you're driving."

Slowly, she took the keys. I got in. India walked to the driver's side, opened the door, and squeezed her belly in behind the wheel.

"Sorry. I forgot to move the seat back."

She did it herself, and stretched the seatbelt around her middle. "I don't understand."

"You put that long key into the rectangular hole. That's the ignition—"

"You know what I mean. I'm doing okay, Roberta. You don't need to feel … I don't need this." She started the car and pulled onto the street.

"India, you're not seeing this right. When you gave me the Pito Pito, was it because you felt sorry for me?"

"Yes!"

"You did?"

"The way you hobbled around like a cripple or something. And then I saw where you lived—I thought *I* lived in a tuna can."

"Well, that's the point. It's what I want, India."

"Why?"

"Saint Francis, remember? How he renounced his wealth?"

"Yesss …"

"Well, I'm renouncing this car. And I need your help."

"My help?"

"For much the same reason. I don't want so much *stuff*. I don't want my life to be about what I own."

She looked at me so long we started bumping along the dots on the center line. I almost grabbed the wheel, but she returned her attention to the road. And drove in silence for several minutes.

I finally asked, "So will you take the car?"

The corners of her mouth turned ever so slightly upward. "Okay."

"It's okay?"

"Yeah." She smiled for real, now.

"Good." I opened my purse and pulled out the pink slip. Happily, Larry had kept it in a safe deposit box, and not at home, so it had been spared from the fire. I made a small flourish before signing it over to her, then stopped. "Is your name really India?"

"Better write that out to Prudencia MacBride."

"My. That's a long way from India Moon."

"I think my mom was on something when she named me; I don't know what she was thinking. How do you shorten Prudencia—and you have to shorten a name like that. But you end up with Prudence, which"—she patted her belly—"I have none of, or Prude, or Dense. Mom went to India in the wild days of her youth; I was probably conceived in India, so ..."

"And Moon is your—"

"Made that up too."

"What's wrong with MacBride?"

"If you knew my dad, you'd know what's wrong."

I leaned back and gazed at the pond to my right that was actually part of the Lexington Reservoir. Our turn onto Black Road was just ahead.

And then … it was just past.

"Let's go for a ride." India smiled.

"What about the store?"

"I don't get much business in the mornings." She opened the sunroof.

My cell phone rang. I flipped it open and checked. Suzanne. I flipped it shut.

"Who was that?"

"Wrong number."

"You didn't steal the car did you?"

"No."

"Just checking."

She raised both hands out the sunroof. "Whooo!" Just as I reached across to control the car, she dropped her hands and retook the steering wheel. She looked and acted like a young girl with a new car.

"You drive safely, young lady, or I'll take it back."

"Yes, Mother."

Still, I'd done a good thing, and I felt like a celebratory drive myself.

She took me all the way to Santa Cruz, then looped the car around town a few times while she found the Bose stereo system and the heated seats. She played with the automatic windows like they were a new invention. She finally cut the ignition under the lighthouse. I suggested we get out and walk around, look at the ocean.

"And leave my car? We can watch it right here." She lowered the back of her seat and folded her arms beneath her head, then with great effort, propped her feet on the dashboard. A large wave hit the rock before us, and water exploded twenty feet in the air.

"You're really serious about what you're doing, Roberta. I respect that. A lot of people aren't serious about anything."

"What are you serious about?"

"You mean, what was I doing on the ridge with my candles?"

I blushed. "It's none of my business."

"No. But you just gave me a Lexus."

"It's a gift. You don't have to explain yourself."

"Aren't you just a little bit curious?"

"Do you want to tell me?"

"I don't mind." She scratched her belly. "Do you believe in magic?"

How to answer that truthfully, without offending her?

"Because I do. I don't believe the way everybody else does. I don't believe that all that matters—all that exists—is what you do and what you have. That we get born and then we die and in between all that counts is what we earn and where we live and what we drive ..." She ducked her head. "Sorry."

"No offense taken."

"But what's the point? We work brutal hours to make payments on the SUVs we buy so we can drive where? To *work!* So we can afford the big impressive mansions we don't live in because we live where? At *work!* So we can pay the day care where we send the children we never see because we're at *work*, so they can grow up and get a nice job and go to *work*. Why even bother? It's not like life is so much fun. Even when we get all that stuff. Do you see any deliriously happy CEOs?" She cringed. "Ho boy. I'm sorry."

"Go on."

"No, I'm getting myself into trouble."

"Not with me."

"Okay." She looked out the window, and a seagull scolded from a rail outside, as if to pick up where she left off so she could rest. When he finished, India spoke. "Roberta, you met Gil and Brenda?"

"Yes."

"You think they're happy?"

"Well … Gil seemed—"

"Driven. Not happy. And he drives Brenda, too. She left Russ for him, did she tell you that? I think he only wanted her because Russ had something he didn't, but she's not good enough for him. She's not young enough, or pretty enough. Did you see how her skin is stretched around her mouth and eyes? A face lift. Gil's idea. Because he doesn't want a real woman. He wants a fantasy."

She propped her elbow against the door and chewed her thumb. "He drives all that car, and builds all that house with all that view. But he'll never see it. He's too busy making more tanning parlors so women can get fake tans under a fake sun and get real skin cancer. And all the while he's trying to be Mr. Spiritual Nature, buying his hummus and carrot juice in plastic containers that get dumped in our landfills because he doesn't have time to look a real garbanzo bean in the face, to cook it himself, and mash it with a fork for crying out loud, instead of dumping it in that food processor he also doesn't use."

"India."

"What?"

"What do Gil and Brenda have to do with magic?"

"Nothing!" She lowered her voice. "Nothing at all."

"Then why are you talking about them?"

"Because I don't want to be like them. If all that matters is that your skin is tan, then it doesn't matter how it gets that way. But I think it does matter. When I get older I want to look wiser, not younger. I want to be gentle." She caught my glance. "Well I do. I don't want to be scared of my own skin like Brenda."

"You think she's scared?"

India rolled her eyes like I should know better. And of course I did. I'd seen.

"If all that matters is how we look, what everybody thinks of us, and how comfortable we are in our cubicles, then we can buy mass-produced gewgaws without asking who mass-produced them or under what circumstances. We can live in our big houses and drive fancy cars without stopping to think that there are people who have *nothing*. We can spray our bugs without bothering to meet their families first, we can put *Botox* in our *butt*-ocks—*ha!*—if nothing else really matters."

I blinked. "You don't want the car?"

"Didn't you say I could have it?"

"Yes."

"So it's mine." She scratched her belly and pulled her feet, first one and then the other, from the dashboard. "I just think things matter, things we don't see, and things we don't bother to look at." She wiped her arm under her nose, and shrugged. "Enough said."

"I doubt it. Go on."

"You'll think I'm nuts."

"Who, me? Saint Roberta?"

She turned in her seat to study me. "Maybe not. I want … I might be wrong, but I don't care. I want to believe."

"Believe what?"

"I want to believe in faeries." She snorted, and shrugged. "Or I don't know. I want to believe there's more. That if we could just see everything that goes on in the air that brushes our skin, in the light that shines from the sun and the moon, in the moisture down deep in the soil, in the water ..."

On cue, a wave dashed against the rock before us.

"If we knew what travels in the words we speak and the tears we cry, we'd see how much everything matters. We'd be dazzled by meanings we don't begin to ... I want to believe that every single step we take falls on holy ground."

She'd left me breathless. My heart fluttered like a bird in my throat.

"I want to believe that we're not stuck with things the way they are. That's why I go to the woods at night. I want to believe all the good wishes I have for the world, for Russ and for Brenda. And for you. Even for Gil." She wiped a tear, then placed the wet hand on her belly. "For this little baby. I want to believe I can make all those wishes come true. Just because I care." She frowned. "What? What did I say?"

She'd caught me crying. "Nothing, India. It's just ..." I shrugged. "Me, too."

CHAPTER 16

"Well, then," said India. "You, Roberta Denys, would make a very fine witch."

"A witch." I coughed.

"We're not so different. You light your candles and say your prayers. I light my candles and cast my spells."

"Prayers are not spells."

"What's the difference?"

"The difference is, when I pray, I'm talking to someone."

"So am I."

My cell phone rang. "Like who?" I flipped the phone open to check the ID. Suzanne, as I thought. I flipped it shut.

India lowered her brow and flashed an unholy smile. "You think I pray to the Devil, don't you?"

"Well …"

She laughed, and her smile was beautiful again.

I rubbed my neck. "I don't know what I think. But a spell seems more of a demand that the universe bend itself to your bidding."

"No, a spell is just …"

My phone rang, and I flipped it open. Suzanne *again*! I dropped it in my purse.

"Who's calling you?"

"Oh, it's not important. You were saying?"

"I was saying that a spell is using the power within and around you. Just knowing the natural way of things, and using it to bring about good."

Using "the natural way of things" seemed so unlike prayer, which was—ideally—more of a conversation, a close intimate conversation with God. But how could I say that to India? My own conversations in recent years had been one sided and far from intimate. "Are we ready to go home?"

She smiled like she'd just won the argument. She turned the key, checked behind us, and pulled out of the parking space.

"So, India, who do you talk to when you cast spells?"

"Diana."

The name she'd called out that first night.

"She's the moon goddess, the patron saint of childbirth."

"So you pray for your baby out there?"

"In a way. I'll tell you who should get to know Diana better: Brenda. Might help her stand up to Gil. She might even stop going under the knife over every new wrinkle that crops up."

"Why would Diana help her with that?"

"Because the moon has three phases: waxing, full, and waning."

I didn't get the connection.

"Diana is three goddesses in one," she said. "Like your God is three in one. Diana is the maiden, but she's also Selene, the mother, and Hecate, the crone. When I have this baby, I will become a mother. And when I get to be your age, past menopause"—she grinned—"I will be a crone."

"How very enlightening." I resisted the temptation to check in the mirror for warts.

"Or a hag."

"Bad to worse. Thank you."

"It's not so bad, is it? Here you have a new life—it's like you've been born for the third time."

"Uh huh, fresh out of the womb. Alone. With wrinkles."

"And wisdom. Isn't it better to accept the gift nature has given you, instead of groveling for something less? Brenda would be so much better off if she got that."

"Maybe."

When India pulled onto the highway, we found ourselves in a corridor between two towering banks of pine trees. We settled into a peaceful quiet. The car hummed along the pavement, and India ran a hand over the top of the leather steering wheel, like she was petting a cat.

I leaned my seat back and gazed out the sunroof at the clear blue sky. It really was a lovely car. But as much as I enjoyed lying there against the soft leather, I felt happy for the step I'd taken. I'd committed myself, stepped over a threshold, and there was peace in that.

By the time we reached the Black Road exit, I'd fallen asleep. I felt the car turn off the highway and opened my eyes.

My cell phone rang. Why check? I knew who it was. I let it alone.

"Whoever that is, they sure want to get a hold of you," said India. "Maybe it's important."

"With this person, everything is important." I sat up and raised the back of my seat.

India raised an eyebrow.

She drove a little fast for my taste. Especially on the narrow, winding mountain road. But it was her car now. And somehow, the step I'd taken made me feel, in a good way, that even my life was no longer my own. I was free.

India parked beside the Mountain Pantry behind her battered old truck and cut the ignition. "Would you like to come up for lunch?"

"Aren't you going to open the store?"

"Don't feel like it." She ran a hand through her hair in a motion that made me think that, for this moment at least, she felt independently wealthy.

"I'll have lunch at home, but I'd love some tea." I followed her up the stairs, past the hammock and the gazing ball, through the sliding glass doors to her apartment.

"Do you like Bengal Spice?" She whisked a cookie sheet of melted red candles from the coffee table.

Cotton, the white cat, brushed past my leg, then turned to brush again. A broom leaned on the wall by the door, next to the hook where she'd hung the keys. I remembered that first night in the forest, how she'd swept her way into the center of a large circle. With this broom?

I realized she'd asked what sort of tea I wanted, and was waiting for the answer. "Whatever you have."

"Yep, that's the broom."

"What?"

"Wasn't that what you were thinking?"

"No." But I could see she knew better. "Well, yes."

"It's not for flying." She grinned as she filled the kettle with water. "It's for cleaning, just like you'd think. For sweeping out the negative energy."

"What negative energy have you been sweeping out?"

"You want to know that, you'll have to give me something else. Like maybe your house."

"My house?"

"Not the one you're in now. The big one."

"My big one is gone. Burned down."

"Oh, right." She nodded to an open door across from the kitchen and sighed. "Then I guess that's going to be the baby's room."

I took a look.

"I'll clean it up."

She'd have to. The place was a mess of packing boxes, piles of laundry, and the smell of mildew.

My cell phone rang, and she shot me a look. "Are you sure you're not in trouble with someone?"

"No. I'm not in trouble."

"Because I could cast a spell on them." She winked.

"I'll pass; thanks, though."

The kettle whistled. She poured the water into a white china pot with red roses, then set a mismatched cobalt lid on top. She set the pot on a tray with two teacups and two saucers, no two patterns alike. "Shall we retire to the deck?"

We settled ourselves into two wooden chairs near the rail. The pads had been nicely warmed by the sun. Somewhere nearby I heard the waters of a brook.

India checked her watch. "You've missed your noon prayers."

"It won't be the first time. I haven't got this down yet."

"So." She leaned forward. "Really, why are you doing this?"

"It's a long, difficult story."

She leaned back in her chair and held the teacup with her fingertips. "It's a spiritual thing, right? Did you have an experience? Because I understand experiences."

I was sure she did.

"My granny. When she was young, she used to see things. She even saw the Virgin Mary once."

This made me uncomfortable, unsure as I was that the Virgin Mary even appeared to Protestants.

"You wouldn't know it to look at me"—she stroked a hand over her belly—"but I totally get the virgin thing. The goddess Diana is a perpetual virgin, you know."

"You said she was the patron saint of childbearing."

"Yeah, and your Virgin Mary gave birth to a son." She rolled her eyes. "Diana is the goddess of childbearing because when she was born, she turned right around and helped her mother deliver her twin sister."

I smiled.

"What? When you're a goddess, you can do these things."

"Okay. And when you're God, if you want a virgin to give birth, it can happen."

"I wasn't arguing with that. I totally respect that." She set her teacup down and leaned forward. "I was just saying, most people don't understand virginity. Most people think if you're a virgin then you're naive, and unsensual, and … weak or something. But no. A virgin is someone who belongs to herself." India drew her fists to her breast, like she was holding her own reigns. "It means you're autonomous. No one else owns you."

It hurt to think what it must have meant to this girl, to be owned by some boy for just a moment, and then what? Discarded perhaps? "It can be a beautiful thing, you know, to belong to someone. The right someone, under the right circumstances."

"I'm sure it can." She shrugged, and looked away.

"There's a book in the Bible, an unusual book, called the Song of Solomon. Did you ever read it? It's a love poem, about a man and a woman, and also, if you see it that way, about our relationship with God. It says, 'I am my beloved's and my beloved is mine.' How would it be, India, if life wasn't about using the natural order of things? What if it was more like being a bride, and a lover?"

"That could be a scary thing," she said.

"Hello?" The voice came from below, near the stairs. "India?"

"Who is it?" she called, though the furrow between her eyes told me she knew as well as I that it was Gil.

"Why aren't you open?"

"Didn't feel like it. Why aren't you at work?"

"I *am* at work. Technically. I've got a meeting in Palo Alto in about two hours. Brenda forgot my briefcase, so I had to come home."

"*Brenda* forgot *your* briefcase?"

"But I'm starved. I need a carrot juice and a Swiss cheese sandwich to eat on the run. Can you get it for me?"

"We can just take our tea in the store," I offered.

She picked up her cup, walked through the sliding glass doors, and returned with her keys. I followed her downstairs.

"Roberta!" Gil smiled. "Figure out that watch yet?"

"Not just yet."

India strolled by and we fell in behind her.

"I hope this won't take long," said Gil.

"I was just about to tell Roberta a story." She held her key ring up, and turned each key over, one by one. The last key was the right one, and I felt sure she'd known all along where it was. When Gil's face began to twitch, she let us in.

"I'm in a hurry," he said.

"Won't take a minute. I might as well finish the story while I make your sandwich. Just wait right there beside her, Gil. If you want, you can listen in." Ever so slowly, she opened the top of the deli case. She pulled out a sheet of waxed paper and lay it on the counter. "What kind of bread?"

"Wheat. Like always."

She retrieved two slices from under a linen cloth, and set them, one by one, on the paper.

"Is this going to take long?"

"It might. If you talk." She eyed him out the tops of her eyes.

"I meant the sandwich."

"So did I." She sliced open an avocado in the palm of her hand and pulled it apart. "Once, a long time ago …" She used a fork to mash the contents of one of the halves in its shell. "The goddess Diana decided she would bathe in a pool in the forest, and why wouldn't she? She had wandered there alone, and believed herself to be secure."

India paused in her avocado mashing to make the next point: "It should be understood, the goddess was young and beautiful. *And* she was also a virgin, sovereign to herself. No man possessed her. No man decided her destiny."

"She does this," Gil told me, rolling his eyes and then checking his watch.

She carefully spread the mashed avocado across the bread. "And, as I said, she was alone, or so she thought. Nothing and no one but the oaks and pines and ferns of the forest, and the small pool formed where the river swirled around great rocks. Diana stepped from her gown, and into the pool."

"Please, India." Gil tapped his foot.

She lifted a bunch of sprouts from a bowl, and arranged them on the bread like she was laying sod.

"But the goddess was not alone, for Actaeon, a hunter muscular and handsome, but of little"—she eyed Gil—"*valor*, had spied her as she walked through the forest. And loving her beauty only, he wanted to possess her for his own. So with the stealth of the cunning, he hunted the goddess.

"Diana stepped her foot into the pool, and she waded down the bank till the water met her thighs. Craftily, Actaeon hid among the ferns, and knavishly he gazed upon her nakedness, and raped Diana with his eyes.

"Diana began to feel unquiet. Why, she asked herself, did she suddenly wish to weep? At once she knew the answer, for she felt within her goddess heart that something sacred had gone out from her, wrenched, as it were, by the hand of a wicked soul. Quickly, she turned, and her eyes met Actaeon's.

"He recoiled from the force of her powerful gaze. He slid behind a fern and crawled behind a tree, afraid, because Diana pierced him with her eyes, and at that moment he knew profoundly that she was a goddess, and that her dominion would hold inviolate, for she would have her vengeance for his sin.

"'O Actaeon,'" India intoned Diana's words. "'You walk the earth strong and swarthy, thinking yourself higher than the gods, powerful to take that which is not your own and control the fate of a woman. But you will not have her. For even as you flee, Diana raises an arm and proclaims *your* fate. Presently, you find that you are a stag, and not a man. You find yourself on four legs, bounding, terrified, through the forest, but never, *never* fast enough. From this day *you* will be beautiful and frail, and men will lie in wait for *you*. They will steal what you hold precious, that they may possess what means little to them.'"

"India," said Gil. "I'll just go if you can't finish making the sandwich."

She leaned over the counter. "Actaeon was slain by men. And as he lay dying, the dogs came and chewed out his eyes." She lay a slice of bread over the sprouts and cheese, then folded the waxed paper around the sandwich, cut it in two, and skewered each half with a toothpick. "All done." She held it out.

He took the sandwich, slapped his money on the counter, and pushed past me to get to the door.

"What about your carrot juice?" She smiled politely.

The next moment we heard the rumble of his Lamborghini, and he was gone.

I turned to India, who stood behind her counter with a satisfied grin. "Why did you do that?"

"Because he is such a jerk." She passed a red cloth over the counter to wipe up the crumbs.

I rubbed my eyes.

"You're tired," said India.

"It's been a long day."

My cell phone sounded again, only this time it was just the plaintive little chirp that told me its battery was low. I'd plugged it into the car this morning, but it hadn't gotten a full charge.

"How did you plan to charge that thing?"

How *would* I charge it now, without even a car?

India sighed, and rummaged in a box under the counter. She came up with a used charger, then took my phone from me and plugged it into the socket behind her. "You can pick this up in the morning. You don't seem to get any calls you plan to answer anyway."

I smiled, swallowed the last of my tea, and handed her the cup. "That's a good idea. I'll see you tomorrow."

I walked the road toward home swinging my arms free, feeling a thousand pounds lighter. I climbed the stairs to my shed and found my horarium. It was time to begin my new life in earnest. I took my Bible and journal to the rock on the hill, to begin—and finish—my three o'clock prayers.

CHAPTER 17

On the sweetest mornings, you lie heavy against the warmth of your bed, luxuriantly aware that you are asleep, your hand curled around a soft fold of blanket, your face nestled into your pillow. You hear something like bells. And voices, soft and familiar, whisper your name in half-formed thoughts that waft by undisturbed.

The morning after my visit with Vernon, I found it was possible for a new widow, lying in darkness on a concrete floor, to have a morning like that. I never would have guessed.

I opened my eyes, stretched to reach the bottom corner of the door, pulled it wide to let in the light, and sat up to smile at the waking day.

To find myself so happy! Larry's memory was still there, twined into my soul the way he'd once wrapped his fingers in mine. Wouldn't his next letter come in another two days?

Perhaps I should write him back. I smiled at the thought, as though he were sitting right beside me sharing the joke.

My watch said it was five fifty-one, almost time for morning prayers. I got up and dressed, then took my Bible up the hill, to read aloud:

*My soul waits for the L*ORD
more than watchmen for the morning,
more than watchmen for the morning.

I pierced the canyon with the words like I was blowing a trumpet.

It was the start of a long, beautiful day. An ordered, and sunlit, and quiet day, full of the glory of new beginnings.

"Don't let anybody stop you," Larry had said. And I had no intention of stopping. I ate canned corn for breakfast and beans for lunch. Over the previous few days, I had already gotten used to washing my clothes, and myself, with a bar of soap and a bucket of cold water. That day, I prayed at six, at nine, at noon, and at six. They still felt like words spoken into the void, but at least no one came to disturb me.

At seven, I'd just set the can opener to my evening twelve ounces of tuna, when I heard the soft ringing of bells.

Not bells. A piano?

Music. Lovely music slipping through the pines like silk. Of course. India's party!

I finished opening my can, picked up my fork, and leaned against the door jamb. Ravenous.

Was that a violin I heard? A fiddle, more like it. The lilt in its music wore muddy boots, but it danced. Yes. A fiddle and ... an exotic sound, like a guitar, only sweeter.

India would have cooked something too. And her cinnamon rolls told me all I needed to know about the dark arts she practiced in her kitchen. Temptation lay that way, no mistake.

I forked a lump of tuna and lodged it in my mouth.

Besides, I'd said I wouldn't come. And I shouldn't. Parties didn't figure into a vow of solitude. Why spoil a perfect day?

A harmonica growled into the song like it was chasing a bear.

My stomach grumbled.

I swallowed the bite I was chewing. I actually felt it wedge its resistance all the way down my esophagus.

Had I ever really liked tuna straight from the can? I hadn't planned anything so fanatical as self-flagellation, but maybe choosing this as a main source of protein was the gastronomical equivalent of a hair shirt.

Still, whatever India had was sure to be the gastronomical equivalent of a Roman orgy.

But what was that beautiful sound? A flute. The mellow, drowsy song of a flute, coiling its way up the stairs to me like the smell of brownies warm from the oven.

Music was good for the soul, everybody knew that. How had I forgotten just how good? After a perfect day, it might be something of a celebration. It seemed appropriate.

I wouldn't eat anything, just enjoy the music.

I swallowed down the last of my tuna and put the can in the trash bag, then stood. I ran a hand through my hair to arrange it in some sort of style, though I had no makeup to freshen up with. I brushed the back of my pants off and looked down to inspect the front of my clothes.

Then I set off down the stairs, and up the road.

Yes, India had been cooking. I smelled cinnamon, Lord help me, and apples. Oh dear Father in heaven, the forbidden fruit on the tree in Eden *must* have been a baked apple with cinnamon and raisins and nuts. I was sure of it now.

I walked past my Lexus without a twitch of regret and climbed the stairs just as the song reached its final crescendo, swelling into a tantrum of guitar and drums and castanets. When I reached the top of the steps, I halted, because the tantrum had suddenly hushed, leaving a lone violin to keen out the voice of a gypsy, sorrowing for his lost youth.

Or something like that.

I heard cheers and clapping, more voices and more hands than I thought could fit in India's small apartment.

I stepped to the glass door and peeked in. The place was full of people, most of whom I hadn't seen before. A bearded man in torn jeans perched on the back of the couch. He took a swig of beer, spotted me, then rushed to open the door. I shook my head, trying to say I'd come back another time. But he grabbed my hand and shook it. "Hello. I'm Corbin. India!"

I could do this. Confident and competent, just like Suzanne.

I looked around. No ex-boyfriend with black hair and a pierced tongue, but a lot of people dressed in Silicon Valley Saturday slouch or bohemian dreadlocks, or anything in between. Which of them had flown in on brooms was hard to say.

"You came!" India maneuvered through the crowd with a tray loaded with more food than I would have imagined.

"It looks like you're crowded, India. I—"

"Have some baklava?"

Oooh, help. I loved baklava, and the honey was so rich I could smell it.

"No. Thank you. There's quite a crowd here. I could just—"

"I've still got your phone. It kept ringing, so I turned it off."

"Good idea."

"It was mostly just some real estate office. Probably some leach wanting to jump on your property. I had half a mind to answer it myself and tell them—"

"You didn't, did you?"

Grinning, she took my arm. "There's a chair for you. Back here." She wound her way through the crowd, pulling me along in her wake. She seated me near the food.

"How nice."

The musicians sat clustered nearby. A short man with a goatee held a round-bellied mandolin. He plucked a few strings to check the tone. Russ was there. He greeted me with a raised cup.

"What do you play?" I shouted above the chatter.

"A hurdy-gurdy."

"A what?"

He lifted what looked like a child's toy, a miniature accordion, the size of a coffee can.

"A squeeze box."

It was too noisy to talk. I nodded.

"Brenda's here." He motioned with his head, and I turned.

Brenda made her way toward me, pulling her chair behind. "Hello! Did you get something to eat?"

"Not hungry, thanks."

I smelled something spicy. Something German spicy, like my grandmother's sauerbraten. What had I been thinking, coming here?

Brenda lifted an hors d'oeuvre from her plate, a small brown cluster of something dark. She held it to my mouth, and without thinking, I opened up, and she popped it in.

And oh, oh my. It was some sort of rich meat, venison perhaps, with chopped bits of fruit, raisins, and caraway. Nothing had ever tasted so good. I swallowed the bite with a lump of guilt and opened my eyes to Brenda.

She looked pleased with herself. "My recipe. Or actually, it's Russ's. When we honeymooned in Baja, it rained one night, and we had to stay inside. But we were right on the ocean, so who cared? We'd gone to the *mercado*, and Russ came away with I don't know what all, a little spice, a little *carne*, some raisins, and mango. And that night with the rain pouring down on the beach outside, Russ set to work on our dinner. He has wonderful instincts in the kitchen. He just invented these little bite things so we could feed each other by the adobe fireplace. In the dark." She gave me a look, and I caught her drift.

But she was talking about her ex-husband! If my astonishment showed, she didn't notice. I turned to glance at Russ and caught him staring—not at me, but at Brenda. The way he looked at her made it clear he knew what story she was telling. And remembered it well.

And here I'd been worried about him hitting on me in his hot tub. Not a chance.

"We call them Baja Bites," shouted Brenda. "The name, at least, was my idea. Gil doesn't like them. He says they've got too much carne in them."

"Where is Gil?"

"He takes Friday nights and Saturday mornings to check on his stores around San Francisco, usually stays the night. And on those occasions, he doesn't need my help. So I have dinner with Dad, and

Dad watches TV on my big screen." She grinned. "Russ says I should cook what I want." She popped another Baja Bite in my mouth. "I thought it was a great idea."

Several members of the band took a long swig from whatever can or cup they were holding. They did a quick final tuning of the stringed instruments and then began to play again. I gave them my attention.

Is there anything lovelier than musicians at work? Russ set his eyes on some star beyond the ceiling. He lifted his elbows, and rocked side to side, playing his hurdy-gurdy. The guitar man played like he was riding a horse, swaying forward and back, his chin lifted like he was melting sonnets in his mouth.

I nestled back to listen. The music came in triple time, straight from the hills of Appalachia or County Tipperary, hard to say which. Within a moment I found myself in a place beyond illness and death, a place where angels waltz with the happy. The fiddle player stood to take his solo, and the tune he played came from some dark, firelit place, a place where people do die, where hearts do break, but in this place there was something else. This was the place where God danced with the joyful.

The song ended. Russ sidestepped through the crowd to squat beside me. "Roberta, tell me what you think of Brenda's nose. How's it look to you?"

I turned, but Brenda had hidden it in the cup of her hand. "Russ," she scolded. He leaned forward and brushed the hair from her forehead, then pulled her hand gently from her face.

"It's fine," I said. "Why?"

"I'm getting it fixed." She lay a finger along the bridge.

"No. Really? Why would you?"

"It's this." She pointed to the end of her nose.

"This what?"

"The tiny cleft at the tip," said Russ. "Endearing, if you ask me. But then it's not my opinion that counts."

"Gil's *not* making me do this, Russ. It was my idea."

"Did I bring him up? But I do recall a conversation that took place at your birthday party, something about your nose's length and shape. Which I always thought was elegant. But then it's not my opinion that—"

"Stop, Russ. I wouldn't do this if I didn't want to."

"No. I just don't understand why you want to."

"I can afford it."

"Ahhh." Russ nodded and looked away.

"Oh, Rusty. It's not like that." She turned to me. "Gil's got a good friend who's a plastic surgeon. He gives us a great discount."

"So you've …" I remembered my manners and refrained from asking if she was a frequent customer.

"Just a couple little things. Gil encourages me, is all. He's willing to cover the discounted cost, and he wants me to feel pretty."

"But, Brenda," I sat back to gaze at this lovely woman with brown eyes, and long chestnut hair. "Don't you?"

"Have a Baja Bite." She held one up, and I took it.

And then I took another.

The band continued playing. India made the rounds with another plate of baklava resting on the top of her belly. I helped myself.

"They're good for you," she said. "I made them myself from all the earthiest, roughest ingredients. Groats and gravel, that kind of thing. I call them Saint Roberta's Penance."

I looked at her.

"Just kidding."

The gravel didn't hurt them a bit. They tasted like God's abundance and mercy in all its sweetness and wisdom, baked up in a pan. I took another.

"India's quite the cook," said Brenda. "Sometimes I think she and Russ could get married and start a restaurant someplace. Everybody would come."

Did she not know this man still loved her? "You think he'd marry again?"

"Well, I hope so. I don't want him to be alone. Russ and I have always loved each other, and we've always wanted the best for each other. That's how we've managed to maintain such a close relationship after the divorce."

"You don't say."

"He and Gil are the best of friends. Have been for years, ever since they opened up a spa together. That's how Gil and I met. So Russ is like my big brother now. And he's teaching me how to handle Gil."

"How to what?"

"How to stand up to him."

Oh really? "How's that?" I asked.

"The other day, he told me the next time Gil complained that I didn't slice the tomatoes properly, I should just ask him to show me how to do it. And then once he started slicing, I should just leave the kitchen and let him make the dinner, since he knows so much."

"And you did that?"

"I did."

"And what did he do?"

"He set the knife down and came to tell me he'd turned the fire on under the wok."

"And then what?"

"Then I went in and finished making dinner."

"Well that certainly was a triumph."

———

It was midnight when I headed out toward my shed. Without my phone again. I acknowledged to myself the truth: that my "forgetting" to take it back was no accident, just a barely subconscious desire to leave it behind with the Lexus and, if I was truly honest, all the "friends" it kept me so in touch with.

It was, however, the only way Garrett could reach me, once he got home from Europe. But he wouldn't be back tonight. I'd get it in the morning.

Meanwhile I had serious repenting to do. I'd eaten at least nine or ten Baja Bites, and four or five baklava. Oh, and the source of that cinnamon smell was—you'll never guess—baked apples. With raisins and nuts. The witch gave me the forbidden fruit, and I did eat.

My stomach was as full and rounded as India's, and I felt pregnant with pleasure.

And remorse.

And bewilderment. Exactly what had Brenda found wanting in Russ, and what did she ever see in Gil? Was it only money? Money and plastic surgery?

I couldn't shake the image of Russ's tender hand molding a new concoction for his lady fair. And then, while the waves brushed the shore outside their window, feeding them to her before the dancing fire, kissing her, looking into her eyes the way Larry once looked in mine.

At the end of that perfect day, I missed my husband, and I wanted to cry.

The road to my shed was dark, shadowed by trees. My flashlight cast a bouncing circle of no help at all along the path before me.

Had I so quickly grown accustomed to the dark nights in this place? I didn't feel scared. I felt lost, invisible. If a woman walks in the darkness and nobody sees her, does she exist?

A few tears escaped down my cheeks, and I brushed them away. I'd come here to be with God.

But I still felt alone.

I slowed when I came to the rise in the road that told me my stairs were near. I ran my flashlight along the foot of the hill until I found them, then trudged upward.

I stopped when I reached the top, to listen to the sound of the wind I'd been so enamored of when I first came. It *was* beautiful, like the hushing breath of God ... almost.

Maybe all I ever did was imagine things.

I shook my head and opened the door. I squatted in the darkness to light the candle and turn off the flashlight, then rolled out my sleeping bag, and sat on it, too sorrowful, almost, to change into my night clothes.

Had I imagined things, years back, when I had my visions?

No. I was sure I had not.

Because if I had been imagining them, the visions would have made sense. Jesus would have made an appearance, or at least one of His angels. And He would have said something. Something useful.

Rose petals were a nice gesture. But what was I to make of the pomegranate? That particular vision had come to me the day my brother died. A day full of if-onlys.

If only I'd known what a bottle of Mom's best gin could do when coupled with the Mustang our father delivered when Jamie returned from Vietnam. If at sixteen I'd had the sense to tell Mom or the police or someone that he'd stormed home early from his job at the mechanic's shop, rifled through the liquor cabinet, and left, still crying over an argument he'd had with a customer who'd spotted dog tags—not his, but the tags of a lost friend—hanging around his neck. It seems the man, in all his enlightened wisdom, had called my brother a murderer.

But Jamie told me not to tell anyone. And I loved him. So I didn't.

The thing I had to absorb, that day and ever after, was that I could have prevented his death. So an exotic fruit that I'd only seen once or twice in my lifetime was just not the vision I would have made up.

CHAPTER 18

India had a new car. No, not my Lexus. Not my sleek, black, practically new Lexus. She turned up in a yellow 1979 Mercedes. It had electric windows, she told me. As if I should be impressed.

I'd just returned from my evening walk, when she pulled up at the foot of my stairs—the car's diesel engine rattling like a Model T—and honked.

"What's this?" I trundled down the steps. "Where's my Lexus?"

"*My* Lexus," she reminded me, hoisting her pregnant belly out of the drivers seat. "And I sold it."

Sold it? "Sold it? Why? It was barely two years old."

She grabbed me by both arms, and bounced where she stood. "I got fifty thousand dollars for it. *Fifty thousand!* I only paid three thousand for this one. And she's only ever had one owner, and she's beautiful—see?"

I peered inside. The car was well kept. There was a hairline crack on the dashboard, but the upholstery was still intact, and the carpet was clean.

"The guy said the color was 'mellow yellow,' so I'm going to call her Saffron. The air conditioner doesn't work, but I always say, if it's too hot to go out, you stay home."

My Lexus—gone!

"It's a diesel, Roberta! So it's cheap to run. But it's going to be even cheaper because I can run it on biofuel. I can make it run on vegetable oil! *Which* I can get free from this guy I know who runs a Chinese takeout. I'll smell like a traveling pot sticker, but you don't argue with free! Imagine driving on free—"

"But why did you sell it, India?"

"—fuel." She shut her mouth, and looked at me like she thought I should know the answer. And of course, before my words were out, I'd begun to catch on.

She walked to the back of the car and opened the trunk. It was full of shopping bags, a couple of large ones that read "Baby Super" on the side, and several pastel paper bags with jute handles, from boutiques I'd never heard of. A large box contained a stroller car seat. A baby monitor lay beside it, having slipped from one of the bags in transit. She retrieved a large bag from the back of the trunk, and pulled from it a quilt, matching sheets and curtains, all in a bright starlit pattern of periwinkle and butter yellow. She showed me an iridescent blue butterfly mobile, and a Moses basket lined with a purple quilt.

When I looked at her, she had tears in her eyes. She wiped them with the palm of her hand, and turned back to the trunk. "They're going to deliver the furniture tomorrow. A new crib, never used by anyone, a rocking chair, a dresser with a place to change diapers on top."

"Oh, India. Of course."

She hugged me. She leaned over her belly and wrapped her arms around my neck. "Thank you so much."

I went with her back to the store and helped her carry her purchases up the stairs.

When we finished and took our tea out to the deck, she excused herself and went inside, to return with a pale yellow bag from one of those boutiques. "I got all kinds of clothes at my baby shower, but no one gave me anything like this." With a flourish, she pulled out a christening gown and held it to her chest like she'd thought to wear it herself. She bobbed her knee. "It's chiffon, silk chiffon. I can't believe I found a blue one. I can't believe what I *paid* for it!"

"It's beautiful, India." And it was. It looked like she might have traded the whole Lexus for that one dress. It wasn't just blue, it was robin's egg blue, with a handkerchief hem at the sleeves and bottom, with creamy pearls sewn into the bodice.

"But what if the baby's a boy?"

"It's blue. Besides, it won't be a boy."

"The ultrasound?"

"Was inconclusive. But it's a girl. Her name's Estelle."

"And you're going to christen her?"

"Of course." She smiled. "In my way."

"It's getting late." I took my cup to the sink, then turned to go.

"Wait."

I turned again, and there she stood, holding out my cell phone.

"Whoever it is, just answer them once. Tell them not to call again or you'll sic your witch on them—and she'll turn them into ox guts and eat them with her toast and tea."

I hugged her once more, leaving her to the blue chiffon and butterflies.

She'd evidently turned the phone on for me, because it rang just as I crested the top of my stairs. Who else but Suzanne? What had India said to tell her? Was it ox guts, or—

"Bertie, just where have you been?"

"Right where you left me, mostly."

"Do you have any idea how many times I've called you?"

I did have an idea, but I didn't care to discuss it.

"I even drove up there last night. You were nowhere to be found."

"I was at a party."

"A party. Is that part of your ascetic lifestyle?"

I winced. "I'm sorry, Suzy. I've been busy."

"So I'm *given* to understand. I got a call from Vernon. Why do you need him to act as my contact? I don't understand."

I went inside, and squatted to light the candle. "It's not a big deal. There are complications with the property, an investigation to be finished before I can sell, and I just don't want to deal with it."

A glacial silence. Then, at last: "Don't you even want to know why I tried so hard to reach you?"

I stood, and braced myself against the wall.

"In the news this morning they said they found a body in the hills off of the 280, a young man in his twenties."

"Oh, God!" I sank to the floor.

"No, Bertie, it wasn't him. They announced the name an hour or so later—"

"Suzanne! Don't ever, *ever* do that to me!"

"I'm sorry, but they described the boy and it sounded just like Garrett, and I was scared to death and I couldn't reach you. Why didn't you answer?"

"I … My phone's battery ran down."

"Have the police contacted you?"

"No."

"You can't even listen to the news up there, can you? Well you can if you get in your car. Maybe you should take a drive once a day or so."

"Suzanne, why?"

"There was another fire last night. Just a mile a way."

"Another one! Anyone we know?"

"John and Becky Braxton. It started while they were at work, and here's the thing: The nanny had taken their little girl to the dentist's office, or they would have been in the house when the arsonist broke in."

"How do you know it was arson? Maybe the nanny left something on—"

"It was arson, Bertie. It was the *same* arsonist. At least that's what they're saying on the news. Did you call Lisbon?"

"No."

"Bertie."

The condescending way she said my name! I didn't want to answer. She'd long ago taught me the old sales trick: Once a challenge has been thrown down, the first one to talk, loses. I waited.

And so did she. I heard her breath, the pencil tapping on her desk. She sighed into the telephone.

"What?" I said.

"They found something else."

"What's that?"

"A Magic card. Becky found it in her mailbox. Specifically, the 'Fireshrieker' card."

"Stop it, Suzanne." My voice broke, just when I'd tried to sound strong. "You're making this whole thing into— After all, the cards only prove that whoever did this broke into our house and took Garrett's stuff. That's all it proves." I wiped at my tears.

"Are you crying?"

"No."

"Okay, maybe he's not setting the fires. But you don't know he's in Lisbon, either, not until you talk to him. Bertie, if Garrett were my son, I'd be worried. In fact, I am worried. I've known him since he was a little boy. I fully expected to be his mother-in-law."

"Suzanne, I don't want to worry about my son. I want to trust him. And I want you to stop calling and stirring me up. You know I'm not up to it now."

"I'm trying to help—"

"You're not helping, Suzanne. You're scaring me. And I want you to stop." I pushed the button to end the call, then dropped the cell phone back into my purse.

I pulled it out again. Should I call her back? Apologize?

No. Why should I? She certainly wouldn't apologize to me. Not the ever-sanctimonious Suzanne. I started to put the phone back, then grabbed my purse, sat in the umbrella chair, and struggled to calm myself. My hands trembled.

Where did she get off, thinking she knew more than the police? They hadn't contacted me about the Braxton fire, and that should have told her something. If she'd even heard me say it. Which she hadn't, because she wasn't listening. She was just so sure that my son was some kind of criminal. Probably because he didn't marry her precious Amber who might yet turn out just like her, and I shuddered to think what kind of marriage that would have been. Suzanne's certainly hadn't made it to the finish line.

Some better part of me marveled at the thoughts scorching through my mind. Suzanne was my friend.

"*Was* my friend!" I heaved my purse from my lap, then held my head and moaned. I wiped my tears, and knelt to gather the things that had scattered across the floor. My cell phone, my hairbrush, my wallet. A Magic the Gathering card. I leaned against the wall, and held it to the candlelight. This one was the "Dark Banishing" card. The picture was of a mermaid perhaps, with a fin on her back, clinging to something like a tree while water stormed around her. There was no handwriting on this one, but a quote from Shakespeare's *Romeo and Juliet*:

Hence "banished" is banished from the world,
And the world's exile is death.

I clutched my head, and beat my fist against it. Suzanne had poisoned my mind, and the only cure now was the truth. I found in my purse the phone number Eloise's mother had given me, retrieved my cell phone, and set off walking, back down the stairs again, down the road.

———

I was almost to Skyline Boulevard before I finally got around to dialing the phone. How could I possibly call my son, when I could hardly catch my breath, angry as I was?

I hated to think what time it was in Lisbon, but I had to talk to
Garrett. No need to mention about Larry, not till he got home, as I had
planned. I'd just hear his voice, reassure myself, and tell him I loved him.
Then I could call Suzanne and tell her with good authority that she was
not all knowing, and she was *not* my friend.

I smelled rain. The road before me began to speckle with the
tiniest of spots. I looked to the sky, caught four drops across my
cheeks, and settled onto a rock beneath a tree. It was starting to get
dark. I had to squint to read my watch.

It was seven thirty-one, or half past four in the morning in
Lisbon. Still, there was no putting it off. I steeled myself to sound
cheerfully ignorant of the time, and dialed.

It rang several times.

"Hello?"

"Eloise?"

"Who's this?"

"Honey, this is Garrett's mom. Oh dear, did I wake you? What
time is it there?"

"It's … four thirty in the morning."

"Oh, I'm so sorry, I didn't realize. I just wanted to call and tell
you how happy I am you're in Lisbon. Larry and I were there once,
and it's the most romantic place. Have you been to Saint Anthony's?
Did you try the Fado bars?"

"I'm sorry. This is who?"

"This is Garrett's mom, sweetie. Your mother—"

"Garrett's mom? Is something wrong? What's happened?"

"Nothing. Everything's fine." I forced a laugh. "I just didn't realize it was so early there. Is Garrett awake?"

"Awake? What are you talking about?"

"He is a sound sleeper. I can just call back in the morning, if—"

"Mrs. Denys, I don't understand."

I heard a voice behind her, a male voice—but not Garrett's. "Nobody," she whispered away from the phone. "I'll tell you later."

All at once I could hardly breathe. "Isn't Garrett there with you?"

"Here with me? No. Did he tell you that?"

"I was told he was … that you were in Lisbon with …"

"Just a minute." I heard a rustle, and then the wooden sound of a door. A wind gusted my direction, and carried with it a spatter of rain. "Mrs. Denys," Eloise said, "I haven't seen Garrett since February. I don't know what he's told you—"

"He hasn't told me anything. I haven't seen him either."

"Not since February?"

"No."

"Oh God."

"Eloise, what is it?"

"I should have said something. Oh God, I'm so sorry, I should have told you."

"What?"

"On Valentine's Day, we had a big argument. He'd been so strange, and we hadn't been getting along."

I felt nauseous. I got up and walked.

"We were supposed to go out. But he'd lost his job, you know? And I told him we could just go to the park. But he wouldn't get ready to go. He said …"

"Said what?"

"That he … didn't want to live anymore."

I came to a full stop in the road.

"Mrs. Denys, he said he wanted to die. When I asked if he meant that, he pushed me out of his apartment and locked the door. I didn't know what to do, so I called nine-one-one. And the police came and arrested him. I thought they'd just send a counselor or something. But they put handcuffs on him and took him away."

"Where? Where did they take him?" I was near panic.

"I don't know. Jail, I guess, or the hospital. Or I thought they'd take him to you. He was back home the next day. I saw him in front of his apartment, but he walked away from me and wouldn't talk. And he wouldn't answer my calls after that, nothing. I'm so sorry, I should have told you. But he was already so mad at me. I knew he didn't want me calling you, and anyway his dad was sick. I didn't want to—"

"His dad's dead, Eloise."

"Oh my God."

———

It was raining for real now. In less than a half hour it would be pitch dark, and I hadn't brought a flashlight or an umbrella. I tried to walk, but my throat had closed off. My breath came in heaves and coughs. I pressed my hand to my chest and struggled simply to stay upright.

Garrett could be dead. Oh God, oh dear God. Why hadn't I seen the signs? Was I so out of touch with my son? How could he want to die, and I not know?

I wrenched each breath from the air in shreds.

"Roberta?" I hadn't even heard India's car pull beside me. I turned to where she sat with her passenger window down, but I couldn't answer. I sobbed, rocking forward from the sheer effort it took to breathe.

She got out and ran to my side, then opened the passenger door and guided me in. "Slow down," she said, squatting beside me.

I couldn't.

"Slow."

I tried. My breath squeaked. I focused on drawing it out.

"That's good. Breathe slow."

"India, my son's in trouble."

"Shhh …"

"I don't know where he is, but he …"

"We'll find him. Just think about your breath. Slow down."

I took a long draft of air and coughed.

She smoothed the hair from my forehead. It was wet. "Inhale."

I did.

"Exhale."

A few of these and I had my breath back. She returned to the driver's side and got in. She drove me to the foot of my stairs. "You need to rest."

I trembled all over.

"Do you want to stay at my place?"

"I'll be fine in my hut."

"Let me walk you up there."

When we got inside, I lit the candle. "He's suicidal, India. I just found out that two months ago, he told his girlfriend that he wanted to die."

"That doesn't mean he wants to now, believe me. Breathe."

I took a breath.

"Do you want to lie down? I'll stay and talk if you want."

I settled into my sleeping bag and rested my head on my folded hands. "What if he's dead?"

"They would have told you. You would have known."

"I'm his mother. I should have sensed he was in trouble."

She sat on the floor. "How old is he?"

"Twenty-five."

"On his own?"

I nodded.

"If he wants to hide something from you ..." She shrugged.

"My husband was dying, and I was so caught up in caring for him."

"Big crime."

A tear coursed down the side of my face to my neck, and I wiped it away.

"I think twenty-five is old enough to understand what you were going through. Didn't he come to help care for his father?"

"No. Larry had an atypical Parkinson's syndrome. It was hard for Garrett, to see the deterioration."

India shook her head, silent a moment. "A lot of things are hard to see, but ..."

I remembered the look of Larry's eyes, when I would kneel before his chair to look into his downturned face. All but expressionless. Still, we had been married a long time, and I could read the slightest movement of his eyelids. I knew my husband, and he was beautiful. "It was hard for Garrett," I said.

She nodded and settled back against the wall. And stayed till I was asleep.

CHAPTER 19

"Suzy?" I sat the next morning in a dark corner, cocooned in my sleeping bag, holding my cell phone to my ear. "Did I wake you up?"

"No. I was just … what's wrong?"

"Garrett's not in Portugal," I almost whispered. "I called Eloise, and it's another boy she's with, not Garrett. And Suzy …" I swallowed. "When she last saw him, he was talking about suicide."

"Oh, Bertie."

"Are you sure the body they found was not Garrett's?"

"No. It wasn't him. I shouldn't have even told you. It was a Timothy somebody. Bertie, do you remember the summer Garrett and Amber taught swimming at the Y? They had to be fingerprinted, remember?"

"Yes."

"Well, if they found his body, even if he didn't have his wallet on him … And he would. But if he didn't, the police would know who he was by the fingerprints. If they found him, Bertie, you would know."

"Okay," I whined like a little girl. "That's good to know."

"I think the first thing is to fill out a missing-persons report. I've called around. We'll go to the police station in Santa Clara, closest to Garrett's apartment."

"Okay."

"We can do it when I go to lunch. Can you be at my office at eleven?"

"I don't think so."

"What? Why?"

"I don't have a car."

"What happened to your Lexus?"

"I gave it away."

"You what? You gave it away? To whom? Why?"

"To a young girl who lives down the road here. She's pregnant, and she needs a car."

"So do you. Bertie, that's—"

"It didn't seem crazy at the time."

"You can get it back, then. Just go tell her—"

"She sold the car. For baby supplies."

Silence.

"I didn't think I would need one, Suzy."

"Okay. I'll come get you. Besides, I've got other ideas. One of the realtors in my office hired this private detective when her sister went missing—just like you, it was a family thing—and the guy did a great job for her. She almost had to mortgage her life away to pay him, but he's the best.

"How much does he charge?"

"A lot. But not more than you can afford."

I pressed a hand to my forehead and shuddered.

"Why?"

"I don't have much money, Suzanne. Any ... any money."

Silence again.

Inhale. Exhale.

"Larry had insurance, right? Good medical insurance. Disability."

I nodded. "Yes."

"And your bills are paid?"

"Yes."

"And he had life insurance?"

"I gave the money away, Suzy. All but a few hundred a month to live on."

"You ... Oh, no. You can't, Bertie. What about Garrett?"

"Garrett's inheritance is safe. It's in a special fund, but I don't have access."

A very long silence. Then, slowly: "Bertie honey, who'd you give the money to? This girl?"

"No. I gave it to charities, I set up scholarship funds. But it's all out of my hands now. I talked to Vernon, and he took care of it all."

"But you need that money. You don't know what it's going to take to find Garrett—"

"I didn't think I would have to—"

"—you don't know what things will cost. You don't know what sort of help he might need when you find him. If he was involved in that fire, he'll need a lawyer—"

"He wasn't involved, Suzy!"

A long silence. "Bertie, are you ...?"

I tucked the sleeping bag under my chin and nestled into the corner.

"I'll come get you."

It took less than a half hour to report my son missing. The woman who asked the questions looked like she had less than fifteen minutes.

"Where was your son last seen?"

I didn't know. Eloise had seen him on Valentine's day, and I'd seen him just a few days before that.

"Known associates?"

Eloise. Christy before that. I didn't know if Garrett had any friends. I gave them the number for Vector Empowerment.

"Mental condition." The woman poised her pen above the form and glanced up, and for several endless moments, I cried. Finally I told her what Eloise had said. The young woman very carefully wrote "suicidal" on the paper.

I still had his Social Security number, thanks to an address book I kept in my purse. I didn't know his driver's license number. Suzanne produced a photograph she'd printed out before she came to pick me up.

"Scars, marks, tattoos?"

He had a tiny scar over his left eye where he'd fallen off his bicycle when he was nine. He'd just spent the day with Larry learning to ride, and we'd all gone for ice cream to celebrate. When we got home, we let him try one more solo ride to the end of the street and back, when he hit a sprinkler head. We took him to the hospital and got him stitched up, then took him back home to bed. Hours later, I found him crying into his pillow, afraid we'd take the bike away. "I'm sorry," he said. "I won't drop it again."

"Broken bones?"

He'd broken an arm in high school in a dog pile, trying out for, but not making, the football team. He was too slight, built too much like his father. Too much of a nerd, Garrett said, and when I told him that nerds were the heroes of the Silicon Valley, he shot me a look that said I didn't know anything.

Dental work?

He'd had braces in junior high. But why did they want to know that, or whether he'd ever broken a bone? How could they tell by looking at him?

"Skeletal X-rays? Dental X-rays?"

An appalling image crossed my mind, of steel tables on television forensics programs, of charred or decayed bodies identifiable only by their teeth. My copies of all his X-rays had been burned in the fire. And I didn't even know who his dentist and doctor were now. With failing hope, I offered the name of his pediatrician.

"Clothing?"

How would I know? He'd always liked T-shirts and jeans. Tennis shoes. He had sandy hair and blue eyes, never wore jewelry, never made any effort to stand out in a crowd. Quite the opposite.

"Car?"

Abandoned with his apartment, and repossessed by the bank.

And that quick, the woman at the police station was done with me.

"Wait! When will I hear from you next?"

The answer? They would keep the report on file, for purposes of comparison. If they made an arrest.

Or if they found a body.

———

"Bertie, take a breath." Suzanne and I sat in her car in a shadowed recess of the parking garage.

She handed me a tissue and I wiped my face. "Do you know any other detectives?"

"As a matter of fact, I've already hired one for you."

"Oh, Suzy. How much?"

"Does it matter?"

No. The truth was, it didn't, since I didn't have any money. She handed me a business card with a Sam Spade silhouette. The name on the card was Gordy Smith.

Suzanne rested her forehead on the steering wheel. "Now Bertie. I need to know about your state of mind."

"Oh, the usual, I guess. For a new widow with a missing son."

"No. Most widows, and most mothers of missing sons, don't give away all their worldly goods. That's not usual." She started the car and drove in silence till she pulled in front of her office. She pointed to the seasoned Honda Prelude parked in front of us, with the oxidized orange paint. "It runs."

"I don't understand."

"I bought it from one of our clients this morning. It's not much, but it'll get you around."

"Suzy, you do so much for me. Thank you." I pressed my hands to my eyes. The last time I had experienced this kind of shame I was a young mother, unable to pay the hospital bill for Garrett's birth. It had been that long since I'd felt this way. "How much did you pay?"

"Only a few hundred. It's not your Lexus, but it'll—"

"And how much for the detective?"

"Bertie. Just find your son."

———

The apartment complex didn't even have the same landlord. A young woman answered the phone, instead of the old man with the Australian accent I'd spoken with before. Further, the only two tenants who had even been in the complex long enough to know Garrett, didn't know him. This wasn't a place where neighbors stopped in to say hello.

I returned to Vector Empowerment and asked for Winton Tanaka. He didn't have time to talk to me—"Four hours of meetings to fit in between eleven and two. I've got a staff lunch to discuss a new push to ship more product, an ISO 9000 meeting, and a session to brainstorm ways to make the workplace more organic and human."

All this he said while walking down first one gray hallway, then another. I double-stepped to keep pace.

"I'm going to let you talk to Mark Proush; he used to work with Garrett." He placed a hand on the entry of a cubicle and swung his upper body through the door. "Mark, I've got someone I'd like you to give some time to. This is Garrett Denys's mother, Roberta."

I shook the hand of a young man with a blond buzz cut, jeans and a baggy T-shirt.

"Pleased to meet you."

"Mrs. Denys is looking for Garrett. She hasn't seen him in several months. And I gotta run."

Mark scratched the back of his neck.

Confident and competent, I told myself. "You worked with Garrett? Here?"

"Well, he had the cubicle next door. But I'm afraid I haven't seen him since he left."

"It's been longer since I've seen him. I don't know who any of his friends are. I was hoping you could tell me who he talked to, or who he talked about, so I could contact them, see if they know where he is."

"As far as I know, he didn't hang out with a lot of people, besides his girlfriend. He had some online friends, but I don't think he exactly … knew them … in person or anything."

"Online friends?"

"Yahoo! forums and stuff. He used to, like, chat with them on his lunch break."

⌢

"Eloise?"

"Mrs. Denys. What's up?"

I could hear by the noise behind her that she was in a Fado bar.

"Eloise, was Garrett part of an online group?"

"Yeah."

"Can you tell me which one?"

"Wait a sec." The music got louder, and then faded, and her voice came through more clearly. "I didn't snoop in his personal business.

But he used to check his e-mail and stuff at my place. I gave him trouble about his password. It was the same for everything, and it was the worst in the world: his initials, followed by his phone number."

———

Suzanne let me drop by her office and pick up her house key, so I could use her computer at home.

I opened a Firefox page, typed in the address Mark had given me, then logged in with Garrett's name, "GDenys," and his password.

I checked his list of groups. There was one for IP professionals, and one for people suffering from depression. The one I'd been looking for. I took a deep breath, and clicked into the forum.

"pamy u can make it girl," read the snippet from the latest, to answer Pamy's post, which began, "Is anybody out there?"

Nothing on the page from GDenys. I clicked on the link at the bottom for older messages. Nothing there, either. I went back eight pages, and three months, before I found not GDenys, but several posts addressed to him:

"GDenys, please post to let us know U R OK w ..."

"GDenys, you need friends and we are your fri ..."

"GDenys, are you still there? We're worried ab ..."

I clicked on that one. It read:

"GDenys, are you still there? We're worried about you. Please check in and tell us you're all right."

Directly below that one was a copy of Garrett's message that started it all:

"I hope someone wll answer me I cant remember why I should

get out of bed, why I should dress myself and go towork. Ive pulled myslf out from the darkness before but now I cant remember hwy I bothered. I hate everything about jmy life and I don't se how it will change I don't want to wake up tomorrow or anytime. If you're there please help."

I clicked the button to print off the message, then held my head in my hands.

Didn't anybody know Garrett? Didn't anybody know where he was?

Was this the last message I'd receive from my son?

CHAPTER 20

I picked up the private detective's business card that Suzanne had given me.

Gordy Smith. Somehow the name called to mind someone more ... what? More jovial than the levelheaded professional I needed. The card-stock felt thin, like the print-it-yourself stuff sold in the stationery aisle at the grocery store. I ran my finger along the edge and found a small tag where the perforations had failed to separate properly. And the navy blue silhouette of a trench-coated Humphrey Bogart did nothing to assure me that this Mr. Smith took his business seriously.

When I gave my money away, I'd anticipated the day would come when I would long for a lazy Saturday spent trolling the mall for one perfect new outfit, one lovely piece of pottery to fill with scented soaps and place on the bathroom counter I no longer owned. One fresh little bit of beauty to brighten my day. I knew I'd miss the money eventually. I was prepared for that.

I wasn't prepared to sit at Suzanne's computer wishing I could pay an investigator who had his business cards embossed on heavy stock, who charged a fortune because he could actually find my lost son.

But Suzanne had already paid Gordy his deposit, and he was what I had at the moment. I picked up the phone.

"Gordy Smith." The clipped voice was a woman's.

"May I speak with Mr. Smith, please?"

"I'm Gordy."

"Oh. This is the detective?"

"Yes it is. Gordania Smith. How may I help you?"

The complete lack of warmth in her voice put to rest any fears that she was too jovial, but somehow that failed to comfort me. "My name is Roberta Denys."

"Mrs. Denys, yes. You're looking for your son."

"That's right. He's been missing since February. He's—"

"Why do you want to find him?"

"*Why?*" I heard her breath against the receiver. "I don't understand the question."

"Before I take your case, I need to hear from you why you want to find your son. Sometimes adult children don't wish to be in contact with their parents."

How was this any of her business? "I want to *find* him," I paused to soften my voice, "because his father has died, and I haven't told him. He doesn't know."

"And Mrs. Denys, your son knew his father was dying?"

"Yes. He knew."

"Why didn't he stay in touch with you?"

"I don't know. You find him, and I'll ask." I softened my voice again. "I believe my friend paid you a retainer."

"The retainer can be refunded," she said. "But perhaps Mrs. Keyes failed to make clear, she paid my retainer because I'm licensed with fifteen years of experience, I keep my costs low and I get the job done. But I don't meddle in family disputes. If your son wants to be found, I have the resources to look for him." Her breath sounded against the receiver again, like a gust of wind in the void.

"Listen, Gordy. I don't know why my son hasn't stayed in touch with me, and it hardly matters why. If you can refund Suzanne's deposit, maybe you should do that."

"Certainly. If you'd like I can recommend an investigator you might find more personable."

I tapped my finger on the desk, unable to tell her, *Yes, I'd love a more personable investigator.* "Is he good?"

"Sure."

She was only telling me what I wanted to hear. I could feel through the phone line the roll of her eyes, the shrug of her shoulder. And what did I know? Maybe this was exactly the attitude a good detective ought to have: no nonsense, too efficient to bother with small talk. "I think Garrett may be in danger—"

"What kind of danger?"

I glanced at the printed discussion, still clutched in my hand. "I think he may be suicidal." I took a deep breath while I let that sink in. "I recently spoke with his ex-girlfriend, Eloise—"

"Eloise what?"

"Pavia. She works for Sun Microsystems."

"Eloise Pavia. Sun … Phone number?"

I gave her the cell phone number. "At the moment she's in Europe, but that number will reach her."

"And Eloise told you what?"

"She told me the last time she saw him she called the police because he said he didn't want to live. The police took him in and held him overnight, but I don't know what happened after that. Just now I found an online forum he was part of, a Yahoo! group for people suffering from depression. He quit all activity there about last February, and his last message …" Crying as I was, I couldn't read it aloud.

"What group? What password?"

I gave her the information she needed.

"I'll read it myself. Now Mrs. Denys, I have one more question, and it's not going to make you want to take me to dinner, but I need to know. In this arson case of yours, is Garrett a suspect?"

I should have known. Between Suzanne and the evening news, she already knew about the fire. "No. At least … I don't think so."

"Do you suspect him?"

"No." I held a hand against my mouth to quell the sob that had risen like floodwater. "Can you find him?"

"I'll see what I can do."

⌒

"What is that?" India stood in my door, pointing down the hill, where my orange Honda Prelude rested like a vagrant squatter in the place my Lexus had once occupied.

"That's my new car." I finished opening my can of tuna and offered it up. "Hungry?"

"No, thank you."

I shrugged and dug my fork in for a bite.

"Is that what you eat? Is that *all* you eat?"

"Tuna is good for you."

"Where did you go today? Were you looking for your son?"

"Something like that." I rubbed my forehead. "It's been a long day."

"I brought you something." She offered a closed fist. I held out my open palm, and she poured into it a dark string of beads that ended with a small silver medallion and a cross. "It's just a loan," she said. "It was my granny's rosary. She used to pray a lot, and she always used this—to count the prayers, I think."

I could hear my mother's voice: "You're not a Catholic; you're a Protestant." A distinction that obviously didn't concern India.

"It's beautiful," I said. And it was.

"That's Saint Theresa." She pointed to the small medallion.

The image stamped there was of Saint Thérèse of Lisieux. I shook my head at my own contradictions. Clearly my studies had also made little distinction between Catholic and Protestant. Saint Thérèse knew the God I tried to pray to, and that made her my teacher. "I'll take good care of it, India. Thank you."

"Oh! I almost forgot." She patted the back pockets of her jeans and retrieved a legal-sized envelope. "This came for you today. From a lawyer."

I took the letter from her, hoping. Yes, it was from my attorney, Bill Nolan. I felt through the paper and detected a smaller envelope inside, a letter from Larry.

"Probably probate business or something," she said.

"Something like that, I'm sure."

She leaned against the wall without speaking, evidently hoping I'd open it while she stood there.

"Thank you for coming by, India."

She took a step toward the door. "I should go."

"Thank you for delivering this. And for the rosary."

"If you need to talk or anything, you know where I am."

———

My Roberta,

You see? It's not so bad being a widow. No worse than one of my trips to Washington. You eat TV dinners and watch movies. You let the dusting and laundry go. You shop more.

And like always, you get these letters from me, to remind you I'm thinking of you.

I am thinking of you, Bertie, at the moment you read this. Rest assured that wherever I am, the thought of you makes me smile.

Do you remember the first letter I wrote you? It was two weeks before we were married, one month after you learned you were pregnant, and one week after the terrible day our pastor told us we were no longer eligible to be missionaries.

I don't think we ever talked properly about that day, perhaps afraid of where such a conversation would lead, once started. But I remember the atmosphere in the car after we drove away from the church office. Every breath saturated with fear, and remorse, and anger.

I have regrets, Bertie. I regret that I didn't tell you that I was not angry with you. If it wasn't strictly true at the time, I am so sorry that it wasn't.

*What did Adam say to Eve when they were expelled from
the garden? Did he reject her by his silence, leave her to deduce
for herself what his thoughts were toward her?*

*In gaining Garrett, I lost the thing I'd dreamed of. Your
pregnancy should have been the best news of my life, but it
precipitated the worst news, and I am ashamed to say I felt this
child had ruined everything. That you had ruined everything.*

*But Bertie, you didn't. I did it myself, and much later than
the day you and I made Garrett. I did it that day in the car,
when I failed to forgive and be forgiven, failed to trust, and look
forward with optimism, instead of resignation.*

*We did all right. I set to work supporting our son, and it
turned out to be something I did well. But how does one define
"doing well"?*

*We made a success. We built this house so big we found it
necessary to move into the guesthouse just to find each other.
We took our trips to Europe, and at the New Year's party last
December, you wore a dress that cost more than the price of our
first car.*

And it was money well spent. You were beautiful.

*Did you know, Bertie, that I loved you? Did you know that
your face was more than beautiful to me, that it was my home?
That the smell of your skin was safety and peace? That the longer we were married the more I saw in you, that your face held
the history we shared, the talks over books, the nights awake
with Garrett when he was small, the day I gashed my leg with
a pickax and you drove me to the hospital for stitches, as if you
were as comfortable with blood as with diapers.*

All these years I have seen you, seen the way you persevere, the way you do the things you are expected to do and pretend to be happy.

Bertie, I regret that I sit in this chair, while you clean the chicken soup I slopped on the floor at lunch. I watch you now, but you're too busy, too sad to notice. When you catch my eye, you smile for my benefit, but it does not cheer me. Tonight, of course, when you are less busy, you will look at me a different way, you will search my eyes, and I only pray you find me there.

You'll pull out your book and read to me the best parts—tonight it will be Teresa of Ávila—and we will be best friends again, leaning over the same book together.

Later, if I haven't spilt too much chicken soup, if I haven't been too much work, if you're not too tired, we will even be lovers. These days I am an awkward lover, but the love is true and good.

Till next week, my love.

Your Larry

CHAPTER 21

"Well, Love." I sighed to the empty space around me. "When you went to Washington, you always came back. That's the difference." I folded the letter and kissed it. The paper had an officey smell, of pine and ballpoint. I held it to my lips a moment before settling it into my lap.

How many widows, I wondered, stood right that moment in their closets, pressing old bathrobes and sweaters to their noses to breathe in the lingering smell of their husband's embrace? But Larry's clothes were all destroyed.

My husband had so little to regret; didn't he know? Things had gotten hectic sometime after the beginning of our marriage, and before the end. But yes, I did know he loved me. I knew that everything he did was for me, and for Garrett. Larry was a good, kind, brilliant man. If I'd known what went through his mind when he was alive …

A droplet fell from my eye to the letter, and I brushed it away with my hand, then brushed the welt left in the paper. I tilted my head back, and let the tears flow past my cheeks and down my neck.

The mission field was my dream too. We had planned to build a church and school in a forested village outside of Bogotá, Colombia,

near a plantation where they grew roses to be sold in American grocery stores. The villagers suffered a number of illnesses ranging from
headaches to asthma to congenital birth defects, due to exposure to
pesticides that are illegal in the United States. But without education, they had little choice. Larry and I were going to live in that
beautiful paradise gone wrong and bring hope to the mothers and
fathers, and new opportunities to their children

We both had endured loss and regret. In fact, I'd been the one
to initiate the liaison that led to my pregnancy, in an impulsive fit of
fear and desire, equal parts.

It happened after an argument over some aspect or other of the
wedding, I forget which. It was nerves, mostly, but the argument
grew to monstrous proportions, and when it was over, I felt shaken.
Did Larry really love me? Did he really want to go through with the
wedding?

I knew full well that it violated all we believed about waiting till
marriage. But on a Saturday trip to Capitola, on the beach beside
taffy-colored stucco apartments lined up like beads on a candy neck-
lace, I found a way to let him know: I wanted to take things to the
next level. Something more—not less—like marriage.

So Adam and Eve were expelled from the garden and sent to
the Silicon Valley. Larry would have found that funny. I cast a rueful
smile to the empty space.

"Roberta?"

It was Brenda's voice. I tucked Larry's letter into my purse, and
opened the door.

She stood with her arm around a carpet, rolled up and leaning
against her, slightly taller, like a lover. "I brought you this, and it's

heavy." She motioned me away from the door. I stepped aside, and she let it fall into my shed. "Gil had it in the waiting room of his Palo Alto shop, but he's redecorating. It's a lovely rug; he got it from a great little store in Newport."

"Oh, Brenda. Really, you— "

"Don't make me carry it home again." She pressed both hands into the small of her back. "I'll bet it's the right size to fill the space, and it will insulate you from the concrete floor a little, lend a little color."

We moved my belongings out and dragged the carpet to one end of the shed, then squatted, side by side, to roll it out.

"My word," I said. "It's beautiful." It was an Oriental, with one of those paisley patterns so intricately detailed that from a distance they look like no pattern at all. The colors were both muted and brilliant, clear colors like orange and magenta and chartreuse on lemon cream. Monet colors. I pressed my fingers into the soft nap. I couldn't find the weave at the bottom.

"I don't know if you should give this to me, Brenda. Did you talk to Gil?"

She gave it a good push, and when she did, the loose sleeve of her shirt inched up over her upper arm—revealing a small, dark bruise.

"Oh, he won't even miss it. We've got a warehouse full of these. He's remodeling several of his shops, going Zen with them all, you know? Teak and cedar and rice paper, copper waterfalls, that kind of thing. He wants his clients to feel like they're getting in touch with their souls."

"When they're lying in a tanning bed." I smiled.

"He says it'll up our profits. Pay for my nose job. But I don't know. He's putting in coffee bars, juice bars. He couldn't get venture capital, so he's taking out a loan."

"It sounds risky."

She gave another push. "That's what I thought."

We finished rolling out the carpet. It was so heavy, the ends didn't even curl. "Oh, Brenda. He must have taken out a good-sized loan for this rug."

"I'm giving it to you. It's my executive decision. My first in a long time."

"Why?"

"I don't know. Gil doesn't *like* executive decisions, at least not mine. But Russ reminded me the other night after the party that I used to have a mind of my own. I did. And I miss it. So last night I told him I cut tomatoes my way, and if he'd like to make dinner, he was free to cut them his own way."

"That's telling him. How did it go over?"

"Better than my calling in sick this morning. I was supposed to meet him at the office, but I was just not in the mood. Just tired. I got an extra two hours sleep, and a nice cup of coffee on the deck with my dad."

"Good for you."

"Let's move you back in."

The rug did look very nice. If I'd had a better day, I might have refused, and carried it back for her. But the dimming light from the doorway hit that yellow with all its dapples of color, and reflected on the walls in a way that was nearly celestial. We went outside to collect my things.

"By the way," she said. "Did you catch the news this afternoon?

There's been another fire. I didn't realize: They think your fire was an arson, and now they think the guy's still at it."

"No. No, I hadn't heard." I pressed a hand to my head as if that would stop the spinning sensation that had just come over me. When it didn't work, I collapsed to a sitting position on the ground.

"That's pretty hard news. I'm sorry." Brenda squatted to lift my stack of books, and when she did, I caught another glimpse of that bruise on her arm. Only now I saw several of them, five in fact, one on the inside, and four toward the outside—exactly as if someone had inked their fingerprints there.

"What happened to you?"

"What?"

"Your arm."

She looked, then turned away, snapping the sleeve down with a flick of her wrist. "I bumped into a door this morning." She offered a smile over her shoulder. "That's how tired I was."

———

I called Suzanne after she left.

"Bertie, this is getting scary. Did you hear whose house it was? The Gibsons'. And Rose Gibson was home at the time."

"Oh no!" Rose had lived in our neighborhood and had babysat both Garrett and Amber. She used to bake cookies for every child in the neighborhood. She drove herself to the Little League games every Saturday, till she lost her driver's license at eighty-three. That was five years ago. "Is she all right?"

"Yes and no. She's alive; thank God for alarms and sprinklers.

But she inhaled a lot of smoke before she got out of the house. She's in intensive care at Good Samaritan right now."

"Not Rosie."

"If she doesn't pull through this …"

She stopped herself and I was grateful. If she mentioned murder and Garrett's name in the same sentence, I was sure I'd fall apart, and I just might take her down with me.

"I've got a security guy coming tomorrow, to see how I can beef up my alarm system. How did it go with Gordy Smith?"

"She's a woman."

"I know."

"Well, I didn't know. And her bedside manner could use some work."

"I know."

"It went fine. And thank you for hiring her." I didn't tell Suzanne about the Yahoo! Group messages I'd found. This was Gordy's case now.

"Bertie, I'm worried about you."

"Don't worry."

"You've had a rough time. The past few years have been very hard. And now Larry's gone, and you're …"

"Acting crazy."

"Making serious life-changing decisions."

"It's not so strange what I'm doing. In the second century, Saint Anthony renounced his wealth and moved to the desert."

"In the second century. Had they even invented money back then?"

"Yes, they'd invented money."

"And wasn't he Catholic?"

"Jesus told the rich young ruler to give his money to the poor and follow Him."

"Follow Him? You weren't even in church on Sunday. How does it serve God for you to sit in the dirt and chant mantras or something? We've got the Businesswomen's Day Off coming up in a month. We still don't have cooks for the banquet, and our speaker has backed out due to some family thing. You and I used to do this together. I thought you'd get back into things eventually."

"Suzanne."

"What?"

"I don't chant mantras. I pray."

"Whatever. Anyway, I have some news."

"Only tell me if it's good."

"Two things. And they're both good. I'm going to be agency manager."

"Oh, Suzy. That's wonderful. When?"

"After our present manager leaves. That's in a month. I'm going to need the time, though, just to get used to the idea of making about half again my present pay."

"Oh, I know you. You're used to it already."

"But that's not even the best news."

"What else?"

"I'm going to need the extra money. To buy baby clothes."

"Baby clothes."

"Amber's pregnant. She's due just in time for Christmas. She waited two months to tell me."

"That's wonderful." I took a breath. "When did you find out?"

"Just about, let's see … about three hours ago. She came into the office to take me to Lisa's Tea Treasures to celebrate my promotion. And over scones and clotted cream, she let drop that she and Roger had news of their own. That's why—I didn't know this, but that's why she started doing her graphic arts from home last year. I thought she couldn't bear to leave her house in Santa Cruz to go to work. But no, she'd planned all along that she could be home with the baby, and still have her career. How very brilliant of her. And, Bertie, you know what I did? When she dropped me back at the office, I hopped right in the car and took off for Scotts Valley to talk to that guy Max about a cradle. Remember him? I just got back … Oh Bertie. I'm sorry."

I must have gasped at the reminder of Max, and the grandchild I never had. "I'm all right."

"That was thoughtless of me to bring him up."

"Not at all. I'm happy for you, for her."

I wanted off the phone. It wasn't just the memory of the lost baby. It hurt that Amber was doing so well, that she and Roger were so happy, that her career had progressed so steadily in the corporate world and hardly missed a beat when she took it home. It hurt that she was having that long-anticipated, long-planned for baby. It hurt that every dream we'd had for the two of them, Garrett and Amber, had come true. For Amber.

But not for Garrett.

———

I called Good Samaritan every day for half a week, checking in on Rose Gibson, the most recent fire victim and an old friend.

On Thursday, they moved her out of ICU to a regular room, and Friday afternoon I got in my Prelude and rattled all the way down the highway to the hospital.

She lay on the bed closest to the window, but the curtains were drawn, leaving the room grayish dark, except for the warm spot of light from the lamp over her head and the flicker from the television over mine. A machine clicked and hissed beside her bed, forcing oxygen through the transparent tubes that led to her nose.

It sounded like the whole last year of Larry's life.

"Mrs. Gibson?" The nurse spoke as though she were calling across a field. "You've got company!"

Slowly, Rose opened her eyes.

"It's Roberta." I approached the bed. "Garrett's mother."

"I know." She mouthed the words.

"How do you feel?"

She licked her lips. Her hands lay folded over her belly like a pile of birch kindling. The room smelled of beef broth and Lysol. I sat in the chair beside her and tried to think of something to say.

"Water."

"You want water?" I picked up the Styrofoam cup and held the straw to her lips. She drank.

"Drugs make me drowsy."

"That's okay. I can come back later."

"How are you?"

"Me? I'm fine."

"I'm so sorry …" She shook her head. "Your husband. Your house."

I took a long breath, and swallowed. "I'm so sorry for what's happened to *you*."

"It was only a corner of the house. Insurance." She shrugged. The oxygen tank kept its steady pace. "And you?"

"Me?"

"Will you rebuild?"

"Not sure." I smiled.

"How's little Garrett?"

"Not so little anymore. I don't see him as much as I'd like."

"I have a son. I know how it goes. But Garrett was a sweet boy. A caring child. He won't always be too busy for you."

"Rose, did you see the person who—"

"Set the fire? No. I was napping. I only heard the alarm."

CHAPTER 22

When a witch makes your breakfast, you wonder what's in it. All the more when it's a trail mix of organic matter in odd shapes and colors you fail to recognize.

"What's this?" I picked up a curved ruff that resembled the rim of some sort of mushroom.

"That's an eel's fin." She stood in my doorway with a flour-dusted apron still tented over her belly.

"Is that so?" I poked a finger into the clay pot she held in her hands. "I wasn't aware eels had fins."

"You have to catch them an hour before their death. Then they do."

I picked up a small seed and bit it.

"That's a gypsy's tooth. I know this dentist in Bucharest, who sends me all his surplus. And that's a possum's wart. You have no idea how long it took me to gather a half cup of those. You have to search through the hair, and sometimes the warts grow in places you just don't want to look."

"And I suppose this is a blood clot." I pointed to a shriveled bit of fruit. "From a slain convict, perhaps?"

She cackled. "Good guess. That's a pomegranate seed. From my own pomegranate tree."

"Where do you have a pomegranate tree?"

"Two miles down the road and over the hill. There's this grove of old fruit trees in a clearing."

"Then how is it your pomegranate tree?"

"Whoever the owner is, they don't come around. And they don't take care of the trees. I do, so as far as I'm concerned, they're all mine. I planted some vegetables and herbs there too. Those are rose petals, and those are rose hips, an excellent source of vitamin C. All organic, so don't worry."

"You don't have to bring me food, India. That's not my plan. Besides, I'm not sure I can eat gypsy's teeth."

She leaned in to cast a pointed glance toward the collection of cans and boxes I called my kitchen. "You can live this way, Roberta, but you can't be stupid about it. If you don't take care of yourself, you won't last. You could almost subsist on this trail mix alone, it's that good for you. Go ahead, eat."

I hesitated. "It looks like the potpourri I used to put out on Thanksgiving."

"Ever try it for breakfast?"

I took a handful and ate. It tasted earthy. Not entirely like mulch, though the word did come to mind. Still, it had a certain tang.

India tilted her head.

"Not bad. It's good."

She moved the towel from the basket on her arm. "I brought you something for lunch, too. Here's cheese, and apples—way better than the stuff you get at the supermarket. I made the bread myself. Tonight I'll bring your dinner, and your breakfast and lunch for tomorrow.

"No. Please, I appreciate all this, but my plan is to eat very simply."

"What's complicated about fruit, cheese, and bread? There's no cans to put in the landfill—or, by the way, in my Dumpster. There's no pesticides, no worries about dolphins." She nodded toward my tuna.

"All right. But not a lot. These things can last me two days."

"Okay."

"What shall I pay you?"

She rolled her eyes. "A Lexus."

"That was a gift, India."

"Then you can pray for me."

"*Pray* for you?"

"It's what you came here for. Put in a word for me."

"But you pray to ..."

"Some days it's anyone who'll listen. Even your patriarchal male God."

"Is this one of those days?

She turned away, and brushed off her apron. "Finish your breakfast, and I'll show you the nursery."

———

India had turned the baby's room into the sky at twilight, with a sunset blush spread across the lower walls, the sun dipping behind the crib's horizon. Stars appeared in the lavender blue at midheight, and a pearlescent full moon rested over the shoulder of the rocking chair. The ceiling was painted cobalt, festooned with washes of glitter and constellations of silver stars.

"This is amazing," I said. "Like sunset over Neverland."

"Or sunrise over Tír na nÓg, the Celtic Land of the Ever-Young. Did you ever hear anyone talk about 'thin places'?"

"Brenda's bound to bring them up sometime."

"Not fat farms." She laughed and collapsed into the rocker. "A thin place is a place or time that's two things at once, and neither one or the other. Like if you stand at the base of a mountain, right where it begins to slope upward, you're neither on the mountain nor on the plain. You're at the in-between place. Just as sunrise and sunset are neither day nor night, they're both and neither. The Celts called those 'thin places.' They are both magical and dangerous places, where the world we live in mingles with the world of angels." She passed a hand over her rounded middle. "I want my baby to live in the thin places."

"But you said they were dangerous."

"You never know what *kind* of angels you're going to encounter. But they're also wonderful. I think you can only find wonder in the dangerous places. It will be my job to help this child find the way through."

"Do you know the way?"

She pushed the hair from her face. "I'd better learn."

India pressed her fingertips together, and I was caught by the look of her hands. They were beautiful—muscular yet fragile, graceful, touching each other like folded wings.

"I have my granny's Bible," she said, "and I read it sometimes. There are thin places there, too. Like Jacob, between his home and the place he was going, waking up to find the angels climbing up and down their ladder to heaven. If Jesus was both God and man, then

He was a walking thin place, don't you think?" She cast me a knowing look and started rocking. "This time of your life is a thin place too, you know."

"How's that?"

"You're in menopause, aren't you? At least, at your age—"

"Go on."

"Remember what I said about the phases in a woman's life? Just as I'm midway between a maiden and a mother, you're midway between a mother and—"

I held my hand up, and she stopped, grinning. The words *crone* and *hag* wouldn't slip so easily from her lips when it was *her* time of life, I was sure.

"Not to mention your being a widow. Your husband's gone from your life, but not entirely, not if I'm as smart as I think I am."

She was every bit as smart, but I refused to say so.

"Anyway, both us *ladies* are in a time when magical things can happen. That's why you're here, Roberta. You're presenting yourself. You're being receptive."

Presenting myself. Being receptive. It sounded hopelessly irresponsible when my son was out there lost. I pressed my fingers to the bridge of my nose, and took a breath. "What kind of angels are you encountering, India?"

"A mix." She shook her head. "A real mix."

"The baby's father?"

"He's … an absentee angel."

"Is he going to pay child support?"

"I wouldn't trouble him."

"But you could get—"

"Roberta, the contact isn't worth it, believe me. You had a good husband, so you don't know. My dad used to tell my mom that as a Catholic wife she had to stay home and raise the children, all five of them—did I tell you? While he wrote all the checks and gave her thirty bucks a week. You know why he left her? Why he *said* he left her, why he said it had nothing to do with the neighbor's wife he ran off with? Because she snuck around and got her driver's license. And thank goodness for that."

All this she said with a voice so calm you could skip stones across it.

"I'm sorry," I said.

"I still call him on his birthday, and on Father's Day and stuff. I just wish he'd call on my birthday."

"Is that what you pray about, up there at night?"

Not a question I was supposed to ask; I already knew. She lifted her head and eyed me like a queen deciding the life or death of a supplicant. "Something like that," she said. "Would you like to see my garden?"

"The one up the road?"

"It's not so far."

⁀

It was far for a pregnant witch. We had to stop several times while she pressed her hands to her belly, grimacing. "Braxton Hicks contractions," she called them. I wasn't so sure.

"When are you due?" I asked, as we turned up the "thin place" at the slope of the hill.

"In three weeks."

She stopped to grip her belly.

"And you think these are false contractions because …?"

"Because I have three more weeks."

"Oh, you innocent dear."

She climbed, and I followed.

And there it was: India's garden, complete with a picket fence, painted blue. It was ringed by pink roses that tendriled along the fence. The garden was divided into four parts, by paths that led to a center ring, and between the paths grew lavender and sage, and young seedlings too small to identify, sprouting in neat little rows.

In the center of the garden, in the circle to which all four paths led, stood the pomegranate tree, wonderfully frilled out in flowers like orange hollyhocks.

"You have a marvelous talent, India."

"No. My ex-boyfriend was the gardener. Jack would have made it better than this. He'd have marigolds growing up through the squash or something. He was an artist."

Her voice had gone soft when she said his name.

"Where did you meet this Jack?"

"Oh, I used to belong to this coven. I don't go anymore. We both stopped."

"Oh?"

"Too much … Everyone thought that it was okay to just … be with whoever. Because it's natural, it's no big deal. But Jack and I … well, trumpeter swans are natural too, right? And they're monogamous; they mate for life. Jack and I wanted to be like that."

"So what happened?"

"I got pregnant. He didn't like that."

"Oh, India."

"So. That's it. When I cast my spells, they're all love spells. Not for Jack; I wouldn't impose. But for someone."

She pushed away from the tree trunk. "I'll bet you never saw where pomegranates came from."

She was right. I'd never seen a pomegranate tree. She showed me the waxy cases at the base of each blossom. "When the flower drops, these will bulge like giant rose hips, and the result will be your pomegranate. In ancient times, it used to represent both birth and death. Because when you pull open the fruit, it's full of blood."

She gripped her belly and leaned against the trunk, then tilted her head back to look up through the branches. "They used to paint pictures of the Virgin Mary, holding the pomegranate. It meant that the son she had given birth to had conquered death. Isn't that beautiful?"

I smiled.

"So I'll bet the tree in the garden of Eden was a pomegranate."

And I'd convinced myself it was a baked apple.

—

I escorted her home, half convinced she'd have the baby before we got there. Halfway up the stairs, she needed to rest.

"What if you get to the top and then go into labor?"

"I'll call my midwife. I'm going to have the baby here."

I helped her settle into her bed, then I headed across the hall to the bathroom, to collect a wet washcloth. On the way, I passed a low table with three candles: a white and a black one, and in the center, a red candle. Was this where she prayed, where she cast her spells? There was, of all things, a knife. And two bowls, one filled with water, and the other with something white—I leaned down to smell—it was salt. There was a twig with its bark removed, rubbed smooth to a shine.

Above the table hung a painting of a woman, lean and naked against an enormous full moon, her bow raised in one muscled arm while the other pulled the arrow. Her face was partially obscured by a swirl of moonlight. I leaned in for a better look.

It was India. Unmistakably, with her blue eyes and streaming black hair. With the formidable gaze of an archer whose aim is lethal.

I stepped back again, and imagined the scene:

India, kneeling at this table, lighting her candles, doing whatever she did with this knife and these bowls. Praying.

To India.

CHAPTER 23

Remember Teresa of Ávila, with her vision of Christ that lasted two years? Lest she seem too holy to be true, well, let me tell you a story:

Once, in the convent, a sister walked into the kitchen to find the great mystic hunkered over the wooden table, gripping a chicken carcass in two hands, shredding bits of meat off with her teeth. She was quite the spectacle, the sleeves of her habit rolled to the elbows, the chicken grease dripping from her chin. When Teresa noticed the sister gaping, she simply shrugged. She said, "When I pray, I pray. When I eat chicken, I eat chicken."

The story came to mind that night, as I swallowed down yet another can of tuna. I remembered the nightly dinners India had offered to bring me, and asked myself why, oh why I had turned her down.

But Garrett was missing, and I had forfeited everything I might have traded for his return in order to use this time to pray. "To present myself," as India had said. All I had was the mercy of God and the quality of my prayer. So I'd rolled up Brenda's carpet against the wall, folded Russ's umbrella chair, and opened my can of tuna.

After dinner, I took my Bible and set out on my sunset walk. Without caring where I went, I at last ended up in India's garden and paused to gaze at the pomegranate tree and think the first quiet thought of the afternoon:

The tree was beautiful.

India had suggested it was the tree in the garden of Eden. I tried to imagine. But which was it, the tree of life, or the one with the snake wrapped around it? If the fruit represented both life and death, it could be either. Or both.

I thought of the shoe-leather pomegranate in my second vision. As a young girl unschooled in the vocabulary of symbols, I'd accepted the fruit and pulled it open, and thought it was filled with rubies. But what did I know?

Maybe it was blood.

I wondered how Gordy's search was going. It was too soon to call. She'd asked me to wait ten days. I patted my pocket to make sure my phone was with me, just in case.

I walked beyond the garden, past India's small orchard, to a stand of madrones that crested the far side of the hill. A particularly expressive tree had split into two trunks, with one bent low enough that I could rest my elbows on the smooth caramel wood where the bark had peeled away. The wind ruffled the branches overhead.

I'd never been good at quieting my mind, once anxiety worked its way in. "All shall be well and all shall be well." I desperately wanted that kind of serenity.

Desperate for serenity. I could almost laugh at myself.

I opened my Bible, and there were the words again:

My soul waits for the LORD
more than watchmen for the morning,
more than watchmen for the morning.

But what was the good of waiting? I needed an answer now to my specific prayer. I needed my son.

I reached to the far side of the trunk and picked at the parchment bits of bark that still clung there. A breeze gusted by and flattened my hair to the side of my head. A crow cawed from a high branch, then flew away, its black wings clapping, its body too heavy, almost, for its wings to buoy it aloft.

———

When I returned to the hut and lit the candles, I spotted a brown bag leaning against the wall. I opened it and pulled out a plastic figure of a sweet-faced child with a crop of blond curls ... and an enormous red crown. A Catholic knickknack.

In one hand he held a blue ball, or rather something like an orb, with a gold cross on top. The other hand was lifted, with two fingers held as though he were taking the Boy Scout oath. He wore a white gown and red robe, like the vestment of a priest. Around his neck there hung a second gold cross, and—of all things—a string of pearls.

There was something else in the bag. I reached in and pulled out a bracelet, a rather old one. It consisted of two brown chains on which slid a number of medallions with color portraits of men and women, all with their golden halos. Saints.

It was a beautiful, quaint piece of jewelry. It had almost certainly belonged to India's grandmother, as had the Christ figurine. I would keep them safe, along with the rosary, for a respectful time, and then return them.

I put the rosary and bracelet in the bag, and started to put Jesus in as well. I pulled him out. If India didn't see her gifts here, she would think I didn't appreciate them. I set the figurine on the floor. But he seemed neglected there. I tried him on the ledge under my window, but the stone was slanted, and he toppled back into my hands.

Back to the floor. I fetched a linen towel, spread it out near the wall by my sleeping bag and arranged my candle and the Christ on top. I lay the rosary and bracelet across the front, placed my stack of books to the side, then stood back, satisfied with the effect.

And groaned, remembering India's little altar in the hallway.

But this was different. There was no knife here, and to me that seemed a great distinction. More important, I didn't worship the little doll, and even if I did, he at least wasn't me. My little shrine was very different from India's. I prayed to someone real.

Who I couldn't see, or hear.

Who had showered me with rose petals once, and then offered me a pomegranate. Marty Green once gave me a can of nuts when I was in fifth grade and I'd gotten over him quickly enough. And they were cashews.

I crawled into my sleeping bag and picked up the small book on top of the stack: *The Practice of the Presence of God.*

Just the title made me cry. I snatched up the little Christ Child, held him an arm's distance away, and told him I'd *been* practicing. To no effect.

"And let me point out," I continued. "I never had to practice the presence of Larry. He was just here, and when I talked to him, he answered back. Even dead, he still writes me letters. But *You*, You never write."

The figure maintained its beatific smile. I flipped it upside down and peered into the hole at the bottom of its feet that led to the hollow inside. I set it back in its place and talked to the dark ceiling overhead. "When I asked Larry for something, he gave it to me, no matter how unimportant. And I'm asking You for my son."

The walls echoed. I was talking to nobody.

Sighing, I picked up the bracelet and studied the medallions.

Saint Francis always made me think of Disney's Snow White, the way they invariably portrayed him with a bird on the tip of his fingers. Why not show him standing on his head? There was a story that had him meditating in exactly that posture, because, he said, God's way of seeing and doing is upside down to the ways of men.

"That much I'd believe." I complained to the echoing Nobody.

They'd given Thérèse of Lisieux a rose to hold, and I knew why. In her autobiography she wrote that she was content to be one of God's little flowers in the world. She'd live her simple life, and after death she would spend her heaven "doing good on earth." "I will let fall a shower of roses," she said.

Odd. I'd never connected her to my first vision. Did I suppose …?

No, I didn't suppose. I was a Protestant, and when you're a Protestant, Jesus drops the rose petals, not Saint Thérèse.

Still, He didn't seem to mind the sentiment. She was His little flower.

Why not me?

I didn't need to be canonized because I'd had visions. And I didn't think for a moment I was the first in history to have glimpsed the supernatural. From the beginning of the church and ever after, people have seen, and many—the Desert Fathers in their caves in Egypt, Brother Lawrence, Teresa of Ávila, and many more—wrote down their experiences. And what they wrote told me one thing: Each of them knew God, and He loved them, each one of them.

⌢

The day they released Rose Gibson from the hospital, Suzanne called to let me know. "She's at this elder care facility—a *very* posh one. Just during the day while her daughter is at work. The two of them are living at a Residence Inn till their new house is built."

"How's Amber?"

"Great. She just signed up at the gym, so she won't gain too much weight with the baby. You know how she's always been about her weight. I'd go with her if I didn't have this new position. I'm going to be working some long hours now."

"You were already working long hours."

"Longer hours, then."

Longer than twelve to fourteen hours was … what? I suggested she sell her house to someone who'd use it.

She laughed.

The next day I drove in to see Rose, and found her less drugged, more the Rose I knew.

"Hello, Roberta. You've met my manservant, Carter, I see." She nodded to the orderly from her wheelchair, where she sat by the sitting-room window, listening to a pink iPod.

Carter took his leave.

She took out her earbuds. "This thing's not half bad. Trish filled it up with Louis Armstrong and Ella Fitzgerald, even an audiobook. Something called *Oldest Living Confederate Widow Tells All*. I don't think I like the implication. Is my daughter *trying* to make me feel old?"

"How do you feel?"

"Old. Too many mirrors in this place."

"You look fine. You got your hair done."

"Yep. This morning, right downstairs." She touched a hand to the curls.

"You look ten years younger."

"That still makes me seventy-eight."

I looked around. There was indeed a large gold-framed beveled mirror on the opposite wall. "This is a nice place."

"Yes. Well. There's no place like home. As you would know. Whoever's starting all these fires paid you the distinction of making yours first. What did you *do* to get someone so mad?"

"I wish I knew."

She cast me a glance. "There was another one this morning, did you hear?"

I went dizzy and found myself a chair. "Whose? Anybody hurt?"

"Some family I don't know. No one hurt—they'd all gone to work. What are the police telling you?"

"Nothing much. You?"

"Nothing at all." She launched into a coughing fit.

"Is this your water?" I indicated a glass with a straw.

"It is. But just hand it to me, please. I don't need feeding, thank you."

I gave her the glass, and she drank.

"How are you finding widowhood?"

"I'm doing fine," I said. And cried.

"Everybody always says they're doing fine. And then they cry." She patted my hand.

"Really, it's fine. Larry was so sick." I pulled a tissue from the box on the table and wiped my nose. "And well, he writes me once a week."

"He *does?*" she raised an eyebrow above her glasses.

I explained the whole thing.

"Of all the nice things for him to do. You must have been soul mates, you and Larry."

"I think we were meant to be."

She coughed and motioned for the glass, and I handed it to her. "Meant to be," she repeated. "How's Garrett taking his father's death?"

I thought about how to answer. "I don't know," I said at last.

"He'll come around."

I hoped he would. "How's it going, staying at the Residence Inn?" I picked a piece of lint from the leg of my pants.

"Oh, it's lovely. We're enjoying the change of pace. I miss my old room, though. It had its own heater and thermostat. Now Trish and I have to set the temperature too hot for her and too cold for me. Still, we watch the History Channel at night. Trish probably thinks it takes me back to my youth."

I smiled.

"I hear you found a place to live too."

I looked her in the eye and again wondered how to answer.

"It sounds just wonderful, if you ask me," she said. "I used to want to do something like that. Back when I saw that photo of the kids putting posies in the soldiers' guns, I wanted to join right in, be a flower child—or a flower matron. Clive, who was *not* my soul mate, said I couldn't do it. Maybe I might have done it when he passed away, found myself a mountain man up in Big Sur, or a beach bum in Santa Cruz. But by then I was seventy-two, and Trish thought I should come live with her. If I'd been younger, I'd have done what you're doing. But not in black, Roberta. Go on out. Get you some love beads."

CHAPTER 24

When you spend your days alternately thinking and trying not to think, a hundred twenty square feet of living space can feel pretty cramped. By the end of the week I felt like a bullet shot inside a bowling ball: too much energy with no place to focus.

Everything hurt. I wasn't sleeping. The entire process, getting in and out of bed, had become an ordeal. At night I often stooped to pull back the top of the sleeping bag, then dropped to a kneeling position and collapsed to my bruised hips, to transfer the pain from my knees to my worn hands and wrists. In the morning I rolled to my belly and pushed up to all fours—all aching fours—and rocked back to a one-knee position, then stood as quickly as my tortured back would allow.

In between, I woke at night panicked for breath. It wasn't my dreams; I didn't have any. An imagined visit from Larry or Garrett would have been most welcome.

But no. I woke with the hot, vomitous dread of all I knew, and all I didn't know.

I couldn't read without crying. Days such as these were what television was made for. But I didn't have a television.

There was always the game of solitaire. Not the computer kind, the kind with real cards. When Larry was in the hospital that final time, when I knew he was dying and my job was to sit in his room and wait, I bought a pack of cards from the gift shop and played as though my own life depended on the rattle and clap of the cards, the snapping them out in nice neat rows, the moving and rearranging till they all were stacked in order, by suit. And then the rattle and clap again.

Two more days, and I would hear from Larry. Half a week, and I could call Gordy. Meantime? I walked to the Mountain Pantry and bought myself a pack of cards. My hut must have sounded like a production line for castanets.

When Monday finally came, I posted myself outside and watched for the mail truck. When it drove past I scuttled down the steps and up the road, then walked into the store like all I wanted was a tube of lotion—and my mail.

"I wondered when you were going to get something for those cuticles." India rubbed the sides of her belly. "I can sell you a tin of hand balm that would do better than the lotion."

"Sounds great." I put the Jergens back on the shelf. "Did the mailman—"

"How about a buffer? I can show you how to neaten up those nails and give them a polish with no harsh chemicals, no toxic waste."

"Not today. Thanks, India. Do you have any mail—"

"I'll even throw in a bottle of almond oil. You rub that into your cuticles, and you'll look like you spent the day in the salon."

"Okay, India. I'll take them." It would give me something to do, and if I bought them, she might shut up long enough for me to ask—

"You want to be my birthing coach?"

"What?"

"When I have my baby, do you want to coach me?"

"Don't you have a midwife?"

"Yep. She's a midwife, not a coach. I need someone to hold my hand, tell me to breathe, that sort of thing."

"But I haven't been through the classes with you."

"Well, no, and nobody else stepped forward to go with me, either. But you've had a baby, right? Marsha will give you a quick run-through when the time comes." India bit her nail.

"Of course. I'd be honored."

"In that case ..." She relaxed into a dazzling smile. "The buffer and the oil are on me. Now let me show you."

And right there in the middle of the store she oiled, shaped, and shined each of my nails, one by one, while filling me in on my duties. "I'll call your cell phone just after I call Marsha. You'll be closer, so you'll come and boil water till she gets here."

"Wait. What if the baby comes before she gets here?"

"It won't. And if it does, she'll talk you through it."

"Ooohh, India."

"But it won't. First babies never do. You've gotta get all stretched out down there before they just slip right out like that."

"Which you know from ..."

"Observation. My older brother took twelve hours. I took twelve minutes. Same with my cousins. How long did it take you to have your first child?"

"Nine hours and seventeen minutes. Garrett's my only child."

"There you go. You'll just help me stay calm, tell me I'm doing a good job, that kind of thing."

"If you are."

"I will. I'll do a great job. I won't yell at you for getting me in this condition, because of course, you didn't. How do they look?" She meant my nails.

"Lovely. And you're planning to do all this when?"

"Oh, Marsha says anywhere from ten days to two weeks."

"I boil water and hold your hand."

"And breathe with me."

"I can breathe."

"Good." And there was that smile again.

But I wasn't sure I could do this. I gathered my hand balm, oil, and buffer and headed for the door, trying to remember what all Larry had done in the way of coaching in those nine hours and seventeen minutes before they took Garrett by cesarean section. All I could remember was that he rubbed my arm like a windshield wiper in a heavy rain. Hardly comforting. I would try *not* to do that with India.

"Wait!" she said. "You got another letter from that lawyer."

———

I didn't even make it home. I found a tree to lean on at the side of the road and tore open first the outer, then the inner envelope, pulled out the letter, and shook it open.

And frowned.

It was barely legible. The writing took sharp jags to the left and right, so that it seemed almost a hieroglyphic made up of little arrows.

But if I held it at a distance, I could make out words.

Dear Bertie,

 As I begin this, you sit across from me, gazing at the television. The program runs a laugh track for Seinfeld's punch line, but you don't laugh. You're fearing for the future, and already it is hard for me to speak without lapsing into a paralyzing fatigue. I want to tell you that I will take care of everything, but the time for me to do that is running out.

 The skin on your face has the grim set that people develop when they're in pain. You hold your mouth like you have a toothache.

 Oh, Bertie.

 Yesterday I saw you at the laptop, the Quicken file open, with the checkbook laid out on the kitchen table, with one stack of bills, and another of statements and letters from our investments. You really do hate numbers, don't you?

 Tomorrow I will call a financial adviser. I can still make a short phone call. What do I have to offer you now, Bertie? What will be left for you to grieve?

 Remember I love you.

 Larry

I turned the letter over once, and then back again. I checked the envelope. Only one page?

He'd said so little, and I'd so looked forward to his letter. Of course, it must have taken a lot of time and effort to write it. But all he'd really said was that I was watching television and he was going to call Vernon in the morning.

And that there'd be nothing left for me to miss.

He was wrong.

⁓

Tuesday morning when India brought my trail mix, she found me chewing my freshly buffed fingernails.

"I can sell you some pepper oil to put on those," she said, "to remind you not to bite them. Actually I always thought it made them taste better. Gives them a little kick, you know? Here, nibble on bats' teeth, instead."

I picked a sunflower seed out of the mix and bit it in half. "I'm going to call my detective tomorrow."

"What do they do, anyway? Sit outside his friends' houses at night? Stand under the lamp post in trench coats?"

"As near as I can figure out, she makes phone calls and looks things up on the Internet. But she has special access, knows where to look." I found a pomegranate seed and put it between my teeth.

"I've been doing my bit, you know. Doing ... what I can to help you find him. Do you mind?"

I wasn't sure how I felt about it, if it had anything to do with that knife and the moon goddess. "No, not at all. It's very thoughtful. I'm praying for you, too, India."

That was true as far as it went. As far as my prayers went.

"My midwife is coming this afternoon. She'd like to meet you. You got anything going?"

"I have a few nails left to bite, but the way I feel, they won't last long. Sure. When should I come?"

⁓

Marsha Watts was a blue heron of a woman, all legs and nose with a short gray tuft of hair. She was lovely. She had that European way of talking with her hands, but the way hers moved brought to mind the neck of an egret in flight.

For instance: "India's going to know how to give birth to her baby; she's very attuned to her body. So we're just here to listen, and to help her do what she wants to do." And there would go Marsha's hands, gliding as though in flight.

India would feel pain but she wouldn't suffer. There'd be no rushing the birth, no drugs to speed or shorten labor. Our job at this time would be to comfort and encourage.

"She'll feel pain, but she won't suffer," I repeated, struggling to fathom the logic.

"Right. When you rub her back, I want you to use long, smooth strokes." Her hands glided into the action to demonstrate. "Very gentle, you see?"

As the final moment for the baby's birth approached, India's body would flood with endorphins, and she would shift into a trancelike state, a highly intuitive place, and then she herself would direct the birth process, and we would facilitate.

When I thought it over, back in my shed, I grunted. This was not the childbirth I remembered. The day I had Garrett, I'd grabbed my favorite postcard of a tranquil pond for a focal point, panted through a few practice Lamaze breaths, went to the hospital, and did what I was told. I don't remember any "intuitive" stage. I felt pain *and* I suffered. For nine hours I lay on my side, in a trance for certain, a pain-induced trance, while Larry ratchet-rubbed my arm as though his own velocity could speed my comfort.

It didn't.

Did I miss something? Something important? With Garrett?

There it was, the question I could eat with my nightly lump of tuna. I opened the can, sat on the floor, and held it in my lap.

Had I failed Garrett from the beginning? Maybe it really was important that a child be born in the time and way God designed. Maybe the first message I gave my child was that Mommy's intuitions were defective.

Well, that was the truth. I didn't remember ever letting my intuitions take over. All my knowledge of mothering came from lots and lots of books and magazine articles, a day planner with lists and checklists, every aspect of his growth, development, and schedule studied, managed, and double-checked.

How could I have missed whatever it was that might have told me he was in trouble?

Why was my son in trouble?

I thought back to the day I found him burning my picture in the bathroom sink. He'd skipped school and I'd run into him at the El Paseo Shopping Center, pitching pennies into the fountain. Did I even ask then why he found it necessary to get away? No. I assumed it was the same reason any child plays hooky, that he just didn't want to do the work. But what if it was more than that? All kinds of things can happen at school, and I never even asked.

What about the few months he woke with nightmares? I never took him to a doctor or psychologist. What if they were the sign of something terrible and I just didn't know?

My phone rang.

"Mrs. Denys?"

"Gordy! Did you—"

"No ma'am, nothing yet. I'm just checking in."

The tuna can fell from my hand to the floor.

"As near as I can tell, your son has left no paper trail at all. He hasn't rented an apartment or a motel room, he hasn't bought a house or a tank of gas. He doesn't seem to have done anything that would generate a record of any sort that identifies him. Except for one thing."

"Yes?"

"A week ago, it seems that Garrett, or someone, tried to make a purchase at a grocery store in Saratoga, using a credit card he canceled a year ago."

"So he's alive?"

"Mrs. Denys, I have no reason to think he's dead. No bodies have been found that match his description. It's more likely he doesn't want to be found, for whatever reason."

"Which grocery store?"

"Gene's Market on, uh ..."

"I know where it is."

"I'd like a little more time, just to check a few more sources, if you don't mind. "

"No, please keep looking. But will there be an extra charge?"

"Not more than Mrs. Keyes said she would be willing to pay."

And that was that. My long-anticipated talk with Gordy, over and out. Garrett had gone shopping at Gene's, where I'd gone every week for years. If I'd stayed where I was, I might have found him.

CHAPTER 25

Rose Gibson died the next morning. Trish found her, nestled in bed, with one hand between her cheek and the pillow. Gone. She was eighty-eight.

Soon after, I sat behind her family at the funeral, with the odd sense that I'd gone back in time and was burying my husband again. I didn't sit in front this time, and it was a different church, but the music, the coffin, the stunned, disconnected feeling were all the same.

In the mountains, everything was different from my life before, and in a way, that made things easier. I didn't look for my son's face, my husband's presence in places where I used to find them. But here in the valley where we'd lived ...

I'd driven in early to sit in the parking lot in front of Gene's Market, just in case my son stopped in for a carton of milk. The world empty of Larry looked much the same as ever. The same smiles on the same faces, the same warm sun, the same music on the radio in the car that pulled beside me. No one stopping to note the silence of his voice, the absence of his touch. Only me.

The drive to the church was like any other drive in Silicon Valley traffic. No one was stopped in their tracks by the absence of Garrett.

Even this funeral was business as usual. At the reception, a woman at the coffeepot asked Rose's daughter Trish about the reconstruction of her home. And Trish answered: "I can't rebuild until the case is closed you know, but I've picked out some gorgeous tile for the kitchen. I'm going green and taupe this time."

"All new appliances," said her friend. "You're going to have so much fun when you start building."

"Roberta lost her whole house," Trish said. "Same arsonist. Hers was the first, and can you believe? He set it during her husband's funeral."

I had to excuse myself. Everything was so … normal. When nothing was normal. But the moment I stepped out of the bathroom, there was Ronnie, Trish's son, who certainly seemed to grasp the situation.

"I think they should charge him with murder when they catch him." He wiped his nose with a wadded napkin. "Once somebody dies, it's murder, isn't it?"

"I'm not sure."

"Mom says she was old, she died of heart failure. But all that smoke. Maybe she'd have had another year."

I had to go. I found Trish to say good-bye, then rushed out the nearest door, which happened to land me half a parking lot away from my car.

"Roberta?" Trish called after me.

I pretended not to hear.

Thankfully, Suzanne had dropped the whole notion that Garrett was the culprit in these fires. At least she'd stopped talking about it. In fact, she'd been uncharacteristically quiet since hooking me up with Gordy. Probably working long hours because of her promotion. I stopped by the office to see if she was there. Of course she was.

She turned the key in the glass door and let me in. "Things have been crazy. I sent flowers to Rosie's funeral. Did she get them? White roses?"

"Yes, there was a big bouquet." I really had no idea.

I followed her to a large room in back. She didn't seem as happy as I expected, moving into the manager's desk. She lifted a box from a chair and ushered me to sit down, then poured two Styrofoam cups of coffee from a steel carafe.

"What's wrong, Suzanne?"

"It's just been …" She shrugged. "One of the realtors got upset that I got the promotion, and quit. One of our best."

"I'm sorry." But this didn't seem reason enough. Suzanne was crying.

"Amber's losing weight," she said. "Almost three months pregnant and she lost five pounds just last week."

"Morning sickness?"

"That's what she says. But when I'm with her, I'm not seeing morning sickness. What I'm seeing, is …" She sniffled. "Saturday I went by to take her shopping, and she was hyper, the way she gets sometimes. She couldn't leave because she was trying on outfits, just getting into one thing, then taking it off and putting on something else. I watched her change from her blue top to her yellow one and back again, three times. She said she'd eaten some cereal, but the only box of cereal she had was unopened, and there wasn't a box in the trash. At lunch I insisted she have a plate of toast. And when she went in the bathroom, I followed. And I *heard* her, Bertie. It wasn't morning sickness. I know what purging sounds like."

"But she can't. She's pregnant."

Suzanne shrugged, and started to weep.

I reached across the desk and took her hand. "Does the doctor know?"

"I went to his office after I dropped her off. If she finds out she'll hate me."

"What did he say?"

"That he'd take it under advisement." She rolled her eyes. "Amber hasn't done this—that I *know* of—since Charlie left. I swear that man was on her about her baby fat when she was three. He groomed her to be just the sort of neurotic he likes in a woman."

So much I didn't know about Suzanne's life, especially the past few years. "I'm so sorry I wasn't available to you, Suzy."

"You had your own problems."

"That you would have shouldered with me, if I'd let you."

"Yes. I would have."

"I can't explain why … If I had a choice about what I did, I didn't feel that I had one. I'm so sorry."

"It's past." She offered a sad smile. "Do you know who Charlie married? A chubby blonde kindergarten teacher, who comes home at one o'clock and bakes cookies, for heaven's sake! Whatever I am, Donna's not, and whatever I'm not, well, that's her specialty. I couldn't feel any more rejected." She ran a thumb around her Styrofoam cup. "And Amber. He spent his every spare moment with her, but he spent them telling her where she'd gone wrong here and what wasn't quite right there. To this day he doesn't understand why she doesn't jump at the chance to have dinner with him. I don't think she's told him yet that she's pregnant. It sounds terrible to say, but I swear he was actually happy when she miscarried that baby."

"He wasn't happy."

"You didn't see him at home."

"Oh, Suzy."

"It's past," she said a second time.

———

I slept entirely too well that night, almost like I was dead myself. It was my cell phone that finally brought me to the surface, but I opened my eyes on the last ring. I pulled the phone from my purse. The flashing red light told me I'd missed calls, and when I checked the list there were three, all from Trish. Something must be wrong. I called her.

"Roberta, thanks for calling back. I was so worried, the way you left. Are you all right?"

"Oh, certainly I'm all right. Just a little emotional."

"You've had a tough month. But tell me, did Ronnie upset you?"

"No." My voice broke. I wiped at my eyes, then tried again. "Rosie was a wonderful woman, and I'm sure Ronnie's just very sad."

"Thank you so much for understanding. We're both really hurting over Mom. Ronnie just can't feel bad without blaming someone. And this monster that's going around setting fires, I guess he's a fair-enough target. You have a son of your own. I know you understand."

I certainly did.

When Trish got off the phone, I crawled out of my bedroll and stood. A bowl of trail mix waited just inside the door. India had stopped by, probably called my name, obviously opened the door. And even that hadn't wakened me. I wanted to go back to sleep. I wanted all the thoughts in my head, the tension in my shoulders and neck and the palms of my hands, the loss of Larry and the fear, the terrible quaking fear, I wanted it all to go away.

I got in my car that day and drove back to Gene's Market to watch the people who didn't know or care that Larry was gone and that Garrett was missing.

———

"Roberta." A hand touched my shoulder.

I rolled over in my bedroll and opened my eyes. Someone squatted beside me with a flashlight pointed to the side.

I sprang upward and recoiled.

"It's okay, it's just me."

India. "What time is it? What's wrong?"

"Don't worry. I tried to call you, and you didn't answer."

"Oh! Is it time?"

"Marsha's on her way."

"You *walked* here?"

"I walked to the ridge. Then I came here."

"The ridge? How long have you known you were in labor?"

"I had to prepare."

I dressed in a hurry, and we set off.

"Did you blow out the candles on the ridge?" I asked on the way up the stairs to her apartment.

"I'm not stupid."

She paused and took a long breath, rubbing the underside of her belly with one hand, and bracing against the rail with the other. When she finished we continued to the top, where the white cat waited to be let in.

"Not tonight, Cotton." She left him outside and shut the door. Cotton gave a silent cry and pawed at the glass.

India washed her hands in the kitchen sink, then waddled down the hall to her bedroom. I followed. She immediately set about stripping the bed linens and stuffing them into a pillowcase. She pulled a black plastic bag from under her bed, lifted out a folded shower curtain, and spread it out on the mattress.

"Hospital corners," she said when I pitched in to help. "I don't want it slipping around."

After the shower curtain, she lifted the plastic bag and dumped perhaps a dozen old towels on the mattress. We spread them out to cover the whole bed.

"Now. There's a paper bag in the oven. Would you bring it here?"

"A paper bag?"

She pressed her hands to the sides of her belly and grimaced.

I did as I was told and returned with the hot bag in a cool roasting pan.

"Sheets," she explained, as she dumped the bag on the mattress. "That was to sterilize them."

When we finished making the bed with the warm linens, she left the room and returned with a white rag and a bucket of steaming water. She got on her hands and knees, then rolled to a sitting position and clutched her belly.

"India, what are you doing?"

"Contraction."

"No, honey, why are you on the floor?" I sat beside her.

"To clean."

"But ..." I looked around. "Everything looks very clean to me. I'll bet you did this already."

Her face crumpled and her eyes filled with tears. "I just want to be sure."

"Oh, sweetheart." I pulled her into my arms. "Are you scared?"

She nodded.

"Don't be. Marsha's told you everything to do, and she'll be here. And you're a very strong young woman. You're going to do a good job of this."

She snuffled into my sweater.

"Let's get you into that rocking chair. I'll wash the floor."

"I want to take a shower."

"Okay. Good. Will you be all right?"

She nodded. I helped her up, and watched her go into the bathroom and close the door. When I heard the water running, I got to work, and scrubbed every surface of the room. The water I poured down the drain from the bucket was barely distinguishable from what she'd brought me. The room was clean.

Marsha would be there any minute. I called through the bathroom door. "You okay?"

"Fine."

Sure enough, there came the knock at the sliding glass door. I went down the hall to let Marsha in. "She's in the shower."

"That's good." She stepped in, carrying a satchel that looked for all the world like Mary Poppins's carpetbag. She had the expression of serene efficiency to go with it. "I'm sure she needs to relax."

"That's the truth. I assure you, no hospital could be more sanitary than this apartment. The contractions are coming about seven minutes apart."

"We'll call them rushes tonight."

She almost made them sound like fun. "Okay …"

"Is the bed ready?"

"The sheets are cooked."

Marsha chuckled. "Enjoy this night, Roberta. Try to relax. Is there tea?"

"Oh! I forgot to boil water."

"Roberta."

"Yes?"

"We're likely to be here awhile. There's no hurry."

I slowed myself, filled the kettle, and put it on the burner, then found the tea arranged on a cupboard shelf—loose tea, in glass jars with no labels. I opened a jar and sniffed.

"Mint would be best," said Marsha. "I'm going to go check on India."

Mint at least was easy to identify.

When the two women returned, India wore a white cotton

nightshirt, her wet hair coiled into a chignon. I handed her a cup
of tea.

"I almost forgot." She walked to the refrigerator and pulled out
two platters, one piled with fruit and vegetables, and one with vari-
ous breadsticks, muffins, and cheeses. She'd catered her own party.

"Lovely," said Marsha.

I looked away and resolved to keep the dietary rules I'd set for
myself.

Marsha fetched a camera from her purse. "Here, Roberta, would
you be our photographer tonight? I'm going to go set up my things
in the bedroom." She exited down the hall with her carpetbag.

I lifted the camera.

"Wait." India grabbed a white pitcher from the fridge and a Mason
jar of wildflowers from the counter. She arranged them with the platters and a white cotton towel, then stood back to check the effect.

"Not yet," she said when I lifted the camera. She pulled a candle from the coffee table, set it off center in the arrangement, and
touched a flame to the wick. "There," she said, shaking out the
match. "All ready."

The first photo to go in the baby's scrapbook would rival any still
life Cezanne ever painted.

She waddled about, lighting more candles, starting a Spanish guitar album on the stereo. She pulled a Monopoly game from
another cupboard and set it on the table. "Marsha said it could take
awhile." She sat in a chair to brace for another contra—

Another rush.

"Cleansing breath," said Marsha, returning.

She took a long breath, and let it out, then bowed her head and closed her eyes. When it was over, Marsha asked, "How long since the last one?"

She checked her watch. "Five minutes this time."

We took a picture of India standing in a doorway. Her belly reached three quarters of the way across. I took one of her and Marsha, and Marsha took one of her and me. Then we set up the Monopoly game.

And I thought we were going to have a baby. I hate Monopoly. The game never ends, not unless everybody is out for blood. In our case, two of us were not. Guess who was?

The game would have been over sooner if India hadn't gotten up from time to time to walk circles around the living room, pacing, taking cleansing breaths, leaning her forehead on the wall. When at last she ended an especially long rush, she said, "I think I need to lie down."

"Can you go to the bathroom first?" asked Marsha. "You need to keep your bladder empty."

We all relocated to the bedroom. Marsha's open bag had released a cocktail of herbal and antiseptic smells reminiscent of a health-food store … or a hospital … or the two mixed together.

She checked India's cervix—dilation was at eight centimeters—and held a wooden horn-shaped object between her ear and India's belly.

"The baby's heart rate is strong." She smiled.

"Leave the game up," India said. "I want your Marvin Gardens." She winced.

"Breathe, India."

She took a cleansing breath and moaned.

When she finished, Marsha and I helped her to sit up and placed pillows behind her back.

"My granny was the best at Monopoly."

"Your granny," I said. "Your Catholic granny—"

"Was a financial barracuda. If the money was pink and blue. Ahhh …"

"Breathe, India. That's right."

"Breathe," I said, taking the cue from Marsha, rubbing her back a little too briskly. Marsha put a hand on my shoulder, and I slowed.

"Ride the wave, dearest. Each one of these is going to bring you closer to your baby."

India nodded, and a tear ran down her cheek.

When the rush was over, Marsha said, "You can talk to your baby now. Let her know it's okay to come out."

She began to cry in earnest now, and the keening sound she made took me back to that weeping girl on the mountain ridge.

"What's the matter?" Marsha brushed the tears from her cheeks.

"It's not okay. It's not."

"Why?"

"I can't take care of a baby."

"Oh darling, yes you can. You're going to make a wonderful mother."

"I'm only me."

"India," I said. "Marsha is right. Look at the beautiful room you made for your baby. Look at the little heaven you made."

"You gave me the money, Roberta. And I—"

"No, India. I gave you a car. You made it into a car and a nursery and layette. I never would have thought of that. You're going to do just fine."

She wrapped her arms around me, and I held her like she was my own child. "It's all right, sweetheart, I'm here." It felt so good, holding this girl who looked to me for nurture, that I began to cry as the two of us rocked together. For just an instant I wondered about my son, then I pushed the thought away. It would do India no good for me to fall to bits just now.

My eyes met Marsha's. She smiled and leaned across the bed to brush a tear from my face. Instantly I felt exposed, as though she'd seen that little image of Garrett that flashed through my mind, heard the sound of him yelling at his father in the garage. I turned my head.

India pulled away. "Owwwww!"

"Breathe, India!" I said.

She was breathing, too fast.

"Slow down, dearest." Marsha wiped India's brow. "Look at me." She made a show of taking a long breath. India locked eyes with her and followed.

"That's good."

"Good," I echoed.

We all breathed together till I thought I would fall over from so much air.

"Marsha," India said at last.

"I'm here."

"Maybe we should go to the hospital?"

"Why do you think so?"

"I'm so tired, and it hurts so bad. Is everything okay?"

"Let's have a look at your cervix."

India lay back and spread her legs.

"You're dilated to nine."

"Nine? Is nine good?"

"You're almost there."

"Okay."

Marsha pressed the wooden horn to India's belly. "Everything seems to be fine. You're doing fine. Very soon you're going to have your baby in your arms."

India nodded and groaned, and then we were all breathing together again.

As the contractions continued, the conversation wound to a close. India wrapped her arms around her stomach, rocking, the way I used to clutch a pillow when I had cramps. I remembered the lower back pain I'd endured when I was younger and moved my hands to the small of her back. Marsha put her hands over mine and showed me the right pressure and pace.

After an hour India said she wanted to take another shower. Marsha checked her cervix before she left, and again when she returned. She was still dilated to nine.

I brought some tea. India moved the pillows under her head and lay on her side. I resumed the back rub till she said, "No more, please."

"I'm here, India."

"Thank you." She took a long breath. "Could we turn the lights off?"

I did, and noticed for the first time the purple light from the window. It was five o'clock, and India had begun to sing to herself, in low animal moans that struck me as beautiful.

Hardly a sympathetic thought, I realized. Was this the meditative state Marsha had told me about? The midwife sat in the living room knitting a blanket. I studied India, to judge for myself. But I saw no evidence that her body had flooded with endorphins.

I sat in the rocking chair. After a time, the room got quiet, and I nodded off. I don't know how long I slept, but when my head finally dropped to my chest, I woke up. A pink shaft of light slanted through the window. I crept to the bed to check on India. She lay sleeping, her breath rising and falling in slow even waves.

I went to tell Marsha.

"I know. I've been listening."

"Then her contractions have stopped?"

"Yes. My guess is that she's finished dilating. Her body knows it's got some real work ahead, and it's getting its rest. It's amazing the wisdom we carry in our bodies. We're more competent than we know."

I wasn't so sure. If that was so, then why did Suzanne play music with subliminal messages to convince her? I turned my face from the plate of muffins and joined Marsha on the sofa.

"Do you have children?"

"Just one," I answered. "But he was born cesarean."

She nodded, as though waiting for more. But the birth I gave to Garrett was not the birth India was giving her baby. And I didn't want to think about him, not till I was back in my shed.

Marsha smiled. Against my better judgment, I continued.

"I never dilated. My water broke, and then we waited for hours, but nothing happened. So they induced labor, and we tried for nine hours more. But I just never dilated past five centimeters."

"That must have been painful."

"It was frightening. I kept asking the nurses if I was in hard labor. But they just said no, I wasn't even close. Of course, they were judging by my dilation, but I meant the pain. It was like the contractions were almost, but not quite, more than I could take. And then the nurses would turn the dial on the oxytocin drip another notch and the pains would get harder, and I got so scared. If I'd known the real labor wouldn't feel much worse, I'd never have given up." I'd started to cry.

Marsha put a hand on mine.

"I'm sorry."

"It's okay," she said.

"Just a long night, is all."

"You're being a good friend to India. You're doing a good job."

"Thank you." I dried my eyes.

"You had a healthy baby?"

"Yes."

"Then you are blessed. How is he now?"

"I'm not sure, Marsha. Maybe … maybe you could tell me why we call them rushes."

She smiled and returned to her knitting. "We find that the way a woman thinks about her birth process makes a great difference in her ability to deal with it. *Rush* is a word coined by a midwife named Ina May Gaskin. She didn't like to call them contractions because to contract means to pull in, and that's exactly what you don't want to do when you're having a baby. Think of a rush, a sudden rush of water, for instance. That's something you can go with, ride over it like you're riding waves."

"Riding waves," I repeated.

"Don't you find that true in life? Sometimes things are out of our control. But we don't have to drown in them. We can know that they won't last. We can trust that the pain is taking us somewhere, and if we just breathe through it, all will be well."

… and all will be well and all manner of things … I nodded and rolled the thought around in my mind.

"Roberta?" It was India, and she sounded afraid. I ran back to her room.

"Where'd you go?"

"I was just in the living room."

"Can you help me? I need to go to the bathroom. *Now.*"

"Wait a minute, maybe not," said Marsha, coming up behind us. She grabbed two gloves and put them on. "Do you mind if I have a look first?"

"Make it quick. I have to pee." She lay back. And let out a long howl.

"India, my darling," said Marsha. "Peeing's not what you have to do. I think you'd better stay right here and have this baby."

"Now? Am I ready?"

"Now. You are *completely* dilated." She almost shouted, a trumpet blast of an announcement.

The laughter started with India and rippled from Marsha to me and back to India again.

"Now keep breathing slow, but when the next rush comes, you just do what it tells you to do."

We didn't have long to wait. India's eyes grew wide. "I can push?"

"If you want."

She did want. She lifted her arms and grabbed the headboard, then growled through a tremendous push.

"Help me, Roberta," said Marsha. "The other side of the bed."

I became India's stirrups for the next push, and oh, oh my, I saw the top of the baby's head.

"India," Marsha said quietly. "Give me your hand." She obliged, and Marsha guided her so she could feel her child for the first time.

"Is that …?"

"Yes it is!"

"I feel hair!"

"*Lots* of hair!"

India grabbed the headboard again and gave another push, and … *Oh my Lord, oh my sweet beautiful Lord!* The baby's head emerged! I started to cry, but I couldn't wipe the tears because both of my hands were holding India's feet.

Marsha took the head and gently turned the baby so it faced upward. India pushed again. I braced against her, and the baby's shoulders emerged.

"Okay!" said Marsha. "Stop just a moment."

"*Why?*" India clearly couldn't think of a single reason, and neither could I.

Marsha flashed a beautiful smile. "India my dear, would you like to deliver your own baby?"

"What?"

"Give me both hands now."

She did, and Marsha positioned them under the baby's arms. "Just guide her out," she said.

"Can I?" I'd never heard India's voice so small.

"You can."

And she did. The baby slipped out, and India lifted her, and brought her to her chest. She gazed at her baby, and the baby looked directly into her eyes. India smiled her dazzling smile and whispered, "There you are."

And I touched my fingers to my lips. The room had become holy ground.

"A girl," I said.

"A girl," said Marsha.

"She's not crying." India frowned.

"She's not breathing—*yet*," said Marsha, and she was right: The baby's color was decidedly blue. Marsha slipped a short, narrow tube into the baby's nose and gave it a tiny puff. The baby sucked in a quick breath and then sighed and turned the color of a peach.

"There." Marsha suctioned the little nose with a bulb syringe, then clamped the umbilical cord in two places. I looked away, not eager to see what she did with the scissors in her hand. But it was quickly over.

"Roberta, come smell her," said India.

I did, and when I took in the sweet, soft smell, I wept. Only one other time had I breathed this fragrance, and I remembered it with a flood of emotion that almost sent me running from the room.

But I couldn't do that to India. This day was about little …

"Estelle." She smiled. "My little star."

Estelle was beautiful, with dark hair fluffed out like a baby bird, with large dark eyes and two rosebud lips drawn into a kiss.

"She still hasn't cried," said India.

"My dear, you delivered this baby so smoothly, she doesn't know she's been born. But I've got a few tricks up my sleeve."

She slipped the tip of a finger into the baby's mouth. The baby sucked on it, and Marsha pulled it out. "That didn't work," she cooed.

She ran a finger along the baby's foot, and the toes flexed upward. "That didn't work either."

She pulled the baby's arms outward. "Sooooo big!" She let go. Estelle pulled her arms tight into her body, and wailed.

Which delighted us all.

"You get a ten, little one. You passed the Apgar in flying colors. Let's see if we can't get her to nurse." And so we could, we three, with Marsha helping India to lift her nightgown out of the way, India guiding Estelle's head to her breast, and me stroking the baby's soft little back. Estelle latched on to the nipple like she'd done it lots of times before, and we all agreed that this was the way a baby was meant to be born.

It was ten o'clock in the morning before the pictures were all taken, the sheets changed, the notes logged, and the certificate signed. At last our little party broke up. India lay serenely in her bed with Estelle. Marsha packed up her bag, hugged us both, and went home.

And I returned to my shed and wept for the son I let them cut from my belly.

CHAPTER 26

The next morning, I found India up on the deck in the rocking chair, nursing Estelle.

"How's our little star?"

"She's perfect. Last night, she lay in the crook of my arm all night, only woke up a couple times, to nurse. I haven't opened the store yet."

"You just had this baby."

"I don't know when I'll ever bring myself to do it. But I have to. I have to support her, and I don't know. Maybe the store won't be enough."

"If it's not, you'll find something else."

"Would you like to hold her?" She pulled the baby from her breast. In her sleep Estelle made three last sucking motions with her mouth, then pursed her lips and sighed. And all the words that people always say around babies, "precious," and "beautiful," and "angel," all the words came to me with such force that they seemed entirely original to this baby, Estelle.

I held her to my shoulder and ran my hand along the back of her pajamas, the fine soft terry with her tiny spine beneath. I held her foot between my thumb and fingers, and through the fabric I found her toes, like little beans. My own grandchild would have felt like this. "Sweet, sweet darling." A life just beginning.

"I never even babysat when I was a kid, Roberta. I'm doing okay with the nursing and the diapers. But there's so much more, and I don't know ..."

Neither did I. I wanted to beg India to take care with this one. I wanted to tell her how easy it was to make a mistake with a child, how many years and how many ways there were to get it wrong, and when judgment day came, you wouldn't even know exactly how, only that you got it wrong somehow, very wrong.

I wanted to beg her to get rid of the knife on that low table in the hall.

"You're going to do just fine, India. She's a beautiful, beautiful baby, and you're the perfect one to care for her." Okay, I chose kindness over truth. Anyone would have said the same.

"By the way," she said. "You got a letter today. Another one from that lawyer."

Dear Bertie,

You try hard these days to keep things cheerful. You play my favorite music, bring flowers into the apartment, keep the curtains open to let the sunlight in. You talk in a voice that is more upbeat, I am sure, than you feel. I love you for making the effort, as I have loved you for everything you do. But I am so sorry it is you trying to make me happy, and not the other way around.

And I am sorry that your efforts are so futile.

Lately I can think of nothing but our son. I can't help feeling that my days as his father are over. He hardly comes around anymore. When he comes, he doesn't talk, and he doesn't stay long. How many times will I see him before I die?

I have tried to be a responsible father. I have worked hard to make his life a good one. I have tried to foresee every pitfall, tried to smooth the way.

I may not have always been right in my methods. I haven't always done the right thing.

When you see Garrett next, please tell him I meant the best.

Remember I love you.

Larry

⁓

I remembered my "upbeat" voice. I hated it, even at the time Larry spoke of, because it sounded so false.

Larry had been the best of fathers. And he had worked hard, through the worst of times.

I think the only book he and I ever fought over was the autobiography of a seventeenth-century woman named Madame Jeanne Guyon. I remember, because the stress of our financial situation made him act in a way that was so out of character. It was a Saturday morning when Garrett was small, perhaps a year before Larry and Charlie started ConjuTech, when I drove him to work because his car was in the garage with a bad transmission. It was the first time I ever loved a book that Larry didn't.

"She was demented," he said.

I heard a *thunk* on the floor behind me.

"It's not dementia, it's faith. Would you give Garrett back his bottle?"

"She thought God was her lover."

"She believed the church is the bride of Christ, yes."

"Nooo, she believed the Song of Solomon was written just for her."

"Not *just* for her." I heard another *thunk*.

"He's just going to keep dropping that bottle."

"Try the apple juice."

"And because God loves her so much, the guy she really does marry is a mama's boy who treats her like—"

"She believed God worked everything together for good. That's very Romans chapter 8."

"But He didn't work it for good. She lost her children, her wealth, her own brother turned her in, her own church sent her to prison."

"And all of it only drew her closer to Him."

"No. Closer to the edge."

"What's with you?"

"Am I supposed to say, 'Thank You, Jesus, my transmission's dead'?"

"Why not?"

"Thank You, Jesus, I have to spend our Saturday working overtime and it's still not enough? Thank You, Jesus, that everything we thought our lives would be just turned to …"

Not my favorite memory. But after that, Larry had put his whole heart into building a life for his family. He'd foreseen every pitfall and made the way smooth for us all.

When I returned to my shed, I picked up Madame Guyon's book again. And found on this second reading that I was more inclined toward Larry's opinion. Guyon was a nut. I put it aside and headed up the hill to pray.

The pain caused by my sleeping on concrete had made kneeling difficult, but I wanted to make the effort. It didn't have to be at the very top of the hill, where the ground was hard. I found a soft mat of leaves and got down on my knees.

Just when I began, a shaft of sunlight pierced the treetops to the little spot where I knelt. Quite theatrical it was, quite the divine nod of approval for some flash of spiritual perception I'd never actually had. An angel chorus would not have seemed out of place, except that this time God had shone His light on the wrong woman. I almost laughed.

Almost.

The bitter thought crossed my mind that my third vision had been something like this. It came the day after my mother's funeral.

Three days before that, a policeman had knocked on the classroom door and asked to speak to my world history teacher. She walked out into the hall and shut the door, and while she was gone, I joined right in with the whispered jokes over who he was going to arrest. Maybe it was the boy in front who wore the ugliest boots anybody ever saw. Or else the girl by the window who was eighteen already and hadn't yet gotten her driver's license. Somebody was going to get busted for criminal fashion misconduct or else for being just plain stupid.

"No, it's you, Bertie," said the girl across from me. "For having a boy's name."

And just that moment the teacher opened the door and said, "Roberta, would you please gather your things and come with me?"

Reality had only begun to tilt that moment.

The other kids snorted and said, "It's Ro*bert*a," till the teacher shot them a look. I tried to smile back at them, but I knew something was very wrong.

And it was. A neighbor had trailed an escaped dog around the block and through our back gate. She found my mother by the pool, on a lawn chair, dead from what would prove to be a complication of alcoholism.

My dad couldn't come till the next day, so I stayed that night with a family I didn't even know. I lay in bed and listened while they whispered about me in the living room. "If it hadn't been for that dog, she might have found the body herself."

Now wasn't that a thought?

Three days later Dad and I went back to my house to pack some things before we left that night for New Mexico, where I would finish out the second half of my senior year.

When I was ready to go, I looked out the window, and there was my father, out in the backyard where Mom had died, sitting on the lawn chair with his face in his hands. Exactly where I did not want to go. But it didn't seem right to just holler.

So I went out front and stood on the lawn, marveling at the still water my insides had become. Life had just struck its final, devastating blow to my family, and I couldn't muster a single emotion.

The sky was clouded over so heavy it seemed it would collapse from its own weight. There had to be at least four layers of clouds up there, laid one on top of the other, the way you pile blankets on cold winter nights.

No sunlight stood a chance with those clouds.

But a beam broke through and descended straight to my shoulders, bearing with it a scent like snow. It warmed me past skin and muscle, right into my soul, and I cried like a dam had burst inside me.

That's all I can say about my last vision. A sudden break in the clouds admitted a message that I heard loud and clear in the language of light, and though I shook with the force of my crying, I knew I would be okay. Crying was real at least, so much more alive than nothing at all. Moments later I dried my face and walked back inside, through the house to the backyard. I put my arm around the father I'd never forgiven and told him I was ready to live with him and the wife he'd chosen over me.

And now here I knelt in a solitary sunbeam in the forest. But there was no message in the language of light. It was only a stray bit of sun.

I whispered the Lord's Prayer by rote: "For thine is the kingdom, and the power, and the glory forever and ever, amen."

"Oh, wow!"

I spun around. There stood Brenda, her hands clasped before her like a penitent.

"What?"

"I'm sorry, I just never saw anyone do that before. It's really beautiful."

Painfully, I stood, stepped out of the sunbeam, and brushed off my knees.

"Are you done?"

"Yes."

"How's India's baby?"

"Fine. Both fine."

"Have you got a moment? Can I talk with you?"

"Hold on." I walked to the top of the ridge and sat on my rock.

She sat on the ground at my feet, like a disciple, which certainly made me feel odd, and smiled as if she were revving up to make an announcement. "I want to join you," she said at last.

"What?"

"I want to do what you're doing. I want to learn from you."

Learn what from me? How to set off on a foolish and failed quest for God while her child was lost and in trouble? I wanted to cry. I wanted Brenda to go away.

"I won't sleep in the shed, of course," she said. "But all the rest. The simplicity. The contemplation. The prayer. I can pray. If you teach me."

"You want me to teach you? What's Gil got to say about it?"

"As far as I'm concerned, Gil's not going to have much to say about what I do from now on. I've never had much to say about anything he did. Yesterday I found out he mortgaged our house—*my* property that Russ and I bought together—to help finance all those remodels he was doing on his tanning parlors."

"How? If it was your property?"

"Some fancy paperwork he had me sign. I didn't even read it. But when I found a past due notice in his drawer, when I'd only gone looking for a fresh checkbook, you know what he said? He said he hadn't authorized me to look through his desk drawers."

She sniffed. "Russ has been telling me I should stick up for myself. I'm a slow learner, but I'm finally starting to get it. I told him last night, I'm not getting that nose job, and I won't get a tummy tuck either. And this morning I called in and quit my job. I want to take care of my dad. Gil's the financial wizard. Let him get himself a secretary."

"And your wanting to join me? Did you tell him about that?"

"I don't guess it's any of his business. I don't guess I've authorized him to ask. I'll still live with him, of course, that's why I can't move into your shed."

I was certainly glad to hear that.

"I want my life to mean something. I want something real."

I placed a hand on top of her head, then realized how that looked like a benediction, with me on the rock and her at my feet. I pulled back. "Brenda, what about Russ?"

"Russ?"

"He's real, isn't he?"

She smiled. "Russ is the best friend I ever had, and always will be. But Gil has some indefinable *something*. Even with all his faults."

I glanced at her arm. The bruises had deepened to black in some places and lightened to yellow in others. It crossed my mind she had best define what exactly that something was that Gil had.

Meantime, what was I to do with her? "Let me get you a book," I said. If I started her off with someone difficult, like Madame Guyon, she might give up and leave me alone.

The dilemma was this: If I sat in Gene's parking lot, Garrett might not go to Gene's, he might stop in at Peet's Coffee instead, or Kinkos. But if I drove around everywhere else, he might stop in at Gene's. At least I knew for sure he'd come here once. I rolled down the window and unfastened my seat belt.

It made me laugh, the thought of Brenda coming to me to learn how to find God. The only real thing I'd found on the mountain was a beautiful baby born in a witch's bedroom, and the way she came into the world.

Maybe I should send Brenda to talk to India, with her candles and love spells. And her altar to a dark-haired goddess who—how could she fail to grasp this—was the spitting image of herself?

I reached into my purse to retrieve my lunch—another can of tuna—and found a box I hadn't put there. A little brown box with a blue ribbon, and a card:

Thank you for all you've done. —India

I pulled the ribbon and opened the box. And squinted, hardly able to process the thing I saw: It looked like a nun. Only … not a nun. It had multiple arms, like Vishnu. She only looked like a nun because she wore a white dress, with her black hair like a veil around her shoulders. This was a goddess.

My goddess.

The one India had found for me.

CHAPTER 27

I shook my head and groaned.

I set the goddess on my dashboard and gave her a good long look. If I thought she was India's little joke it would have helped, but I didn't. To her, it was a natural progression from the rosary to the saints bracelet to the Christ Child—to this! Christ wasn't even the pinnacle of the progression, and to India this did not present a disconnect.

I'd gotten something wrong, very wrong, and I struggled to put my finger on it.

I'd given her my car, for goodness sake! Didn't that tell her that I was … what? Protestant? I didn't know.

Despite her sharp little tongue, India was a kind person. She probably would have done the same for me.

But would she have given all her money to charity?

She certainly would have liked the option. And wasn't I pleased with myself the day I did it? I hardly even knew or cared which charities.

Was all of this, the books, the horarium, the black clothes, the cute little watch that never did chime correctly—was it all about me and my visions and how holy I was? So now I was to go home and pray to Saint Bertie of the Forest, and see if I answered?

What was I to make of this? What was I doing on that mountain in that terrible little shed?

I had to find something meaningful to occupy my time.

Suzanne would write my résumé up in a minute. But I wanted to be available, should Gordy Smith ever call with news. And I wasn't ready to jump into a job. A volunteer position would be the place to start, even Suzanne would say so. Something that would keep me busy.

When Garrett was in high school he did volunteer work to spruce up his résumé for scholarships and college. He picked up trash along the highway once. He said it gave him time to be alone and think.

Just what I needed.

For a time he worked at a soup kitchen in downtown San Jose. I used to drop him off and watch while he entered the building, to make sure he was safe. But it was in a decent enough area, not far from the courthouse. Maybe it was still there.

I stuffed Sister Vishnu back in my purse, then buckled my seat belt, turned the key in the ignition, and prepared to turn a new corner.

———

Louise let me know she didn't have time to train me, but I could stay if I could figure it out on my own.

"We'll get seventy-five tonight, maybe eighty if some of them are children, and then Bobby will turn the rest away. There are other places. Just none with my secret spaghetti sauce."

She trudged about, wiping the tables her husband hoisted into place, then led me behind the counter that separated the dining area from the kitchen. She handed me a pair of latex gloves, and two enormous steel bowls. "There are eight heads of lettuce in the refrigerator, and a bag of tomatoes."

No more to be said; this wasn't a difficult job. I set to work.

While I fetched the lettuce, I watched her open a huge can of tomato sauce and dump it into a pan over what looked like nothing more than cooked hamburger. How good could her secret spaghetti sauce possibly be?

"You won't believe it." Bobby dropped several loaves of French bread to the counter and pulled a knife from the drawer.

"Won't believe what?"

"Her spaghetti. I saw you looking."

"Don't you tell her." Louise pointed her spoon at him. "Not till she passes the test."

"What test?" I pulled some leaves from the lettuce and ripped them into quarters.

"This test." She gestured toward the dining room. "No one gets my recipe till they've stuck around awhile."

I never saw her put anything interesting into that sauce, just frozen chopped onions and the contents of a supersized can of mushrooms. I never smelled anything but tomato sauce and hamburger and chlorine bleach the whole night, not counting the smell of the homeless. Still, spaghetti sounded so, so very much better than tuna. And I hadn't gone home for dinner.

But there was work to be done. Dinner was at six. People started lining up outside at four. Two other volunteers, a young couple named Ben and Lily, showed up at five thirty.

For years I'd passed people with cardboard signs on highway medians and parking lot entrances. If Larry was with me I sometimes gave them money, but if I was alone …

After all, most of them seemed strong enough to work, so either they were lazy, and didn't need my help, or they were mentally ill. If Larry wasn't with me, I kept my doors locked, and studied something, anything in the other direction.

Now it seemed that every one of those people had laid down their cardboard signs, come to me, and held up their plates. There were more men than women, but there were women, and far too many children. An entire family—mom, dad, and four kids, aged one to eight. A tired black mother trailing her blonde little girl of four, all scrubbed and braided and cared for like she was the princess of the promised land.

"Adopted," Bobby whispered in my ear, reading my thoughts again.

"No salad, please," said the little girl.

"*Yes* salad, please," said her mother with an arched eyebrow.

"How's it goin', Vonna?"

"Just fine, Bobby. You got any ranch dressing for Fiona? Helps the medicine go down."

I gave Fiona lots of ranch dressing.

Directly behind her came a gaunt bearded man who wafted the odor of sweat and stale urine. He held his plate up like some sort of challenge.

"Ranch, French, or thousand?" I asked.

He said nothing.

"Paul doesn't like salad dressing," said Bobby.

I put greens on his plate and he moved along.

For two hours after that my hands did not stop moving. All I did was load salad onto plates, but I didn't have time to scratch my nose. Bobby served the spaghetti, Lily served bread and chocolate chip cookies, and Ben kept the tables clean.

Bobby had just started around the counter to shut the door and turn the remaining customers away, when I saw a man push to the front of the line, duck through the door, and skitter to the corner where Bobby didn't see. While Bobby pulled the keys from his belt and turned the lock, the man hustled to the line, and grabbed a plate. He held it up and grinned, flashing a gold-rimmed tooth. I glanced at Louise. She hadn't noticed. I scooped up some salad and put it on the plate.

"How's it going, Darnell?" Bobby changed into a new pair of gloves.

"Who's the new lady?"

"This is Roberta. Where'd you get that fine hat?"

I'd already noticed the felt joker's cap with bells on the tips of each point. We'd bought Garrett one just like it for his role in a play in junior high, where he'd played the narrator and stolen the show. The smile on his face when he got a standing ovation was one of my favorite memories. Later he said the applause was for the whole cast. A diplomatic thing to say, but he knew.

Everything, it seemed, reminded me of Garrett, or of Larry. An older man sat at the end of one table talking to Vonna, twirling the spaghetti around his fork in a spoon like a perfect gentleman—in a tie! His shirt was rumpled and his tennis shoes torn, but his tie was knotted up to his neck, and it was much like one Larry used to wear, blue, with a light brown paisley.

There was no getting away from my problems. Everywhere I looked, even in a soup kitchen, there were reminders.

And what I'd seen would do nothing to help me sleep at night. Most of these people were not insane, which put them, according to my former judgment, into the "lazy" category.

But they looked so tired. I thought of what they must survive every day, the lack of a proper bed and refrigerator—privations I knew all too well. The lack of privacy or protection. It was a difficult way to live.

During cleanup Bobby told me Fiona was the daughter of Vonna's best friend, who died of AIDS. But they weren't homeless, only poor. "They come here because nobody gets rough. I don't even allow bad language."

But the family with four children lived in a van which they moved on a daily basis, terrified of a visit from Child Protective Services. Paul, the quiet man who smelled of urine, talked through the entire meal—to himself. When Darnell strolled by and pocketed the cookie right off his plate, he didn't notice. Darnell slipped out the door, then turned to catch my eye through the plateglass window and let loose a stream of spit through the gap in his front teeth. I watched the saliva drip down the window, and wondered if I wouldn't rather pick litter off the highways. It was Ben and Lily's last night, and I hardly blamed them. Some things in life, you just don't want to know.

Still, all these people were getting fed, including the children. It was a better way to spend a day than bowing down to Saint Bertie.

When I got home, I stopped to check on India and the baby. I heard Estelle crying before I crested the top of the stairs. When I knocked on the glass door, India let me in, with tears in her eyes. "Just where have you been?"

"Why? What's wrong?"

She thrust the baby into my arms. Estelle took a long breath, and launched into a fresh wail.

"She's been doing that all afternoon. I don't know what to do."

I began pacing, stroking her little back. "This happens, India. It's not unusual."

"That's what Marsha said. She also said I should call the doctor."

"And did you?"

"I made an appointment for tomorrow. I've been feeding her, and rocking her. Her diaper's clean. I don't know what she wants."

I picked a blanket up from the couch, and wrapped it tight around the baby.

"It's warm enough in here."

"Babies have a low body mass. It doesn't take much to get them cold."

"Oh."

"Besides, they're used to a confined space. They like to be wrapped up snug like this."

"It's not working."

It wasn't. Estelle was still crying. I sat in the rocking chair, and set the baby into motion.

"I tried that."

"Well, my dear, you just keep trying things."

"I *have* been trying things."

Estelle caught her breath, then let out a shriek that could break glass. I laid her, stomach down, over my two knees, and patted her bottom. She took another breath, and let out a long belch that would have done justice to any truck driver you could name.

The baby quieted.

And so did India.

"Gas," I said.

"Gas."

"I'm sure you've got some mint oil."

I followed her to the kitchen where she found a little brown bottle. I washed one hand under the faucet, then touched a bit of the oil to the tip of my finger, and offered it to Estelle. She latched on and I felt the hard ridges of her palate, the strong muscles of her mouth. When I withdrew, her tongue rolled to a little cup, followed my departure, and gave two sucks more. She closed her eyes, and I held her to my shoulder. She burped once more, and in a moment, she slept.

"I can't believe it was that simple."

"It's often simple, but not always. Sometimes babies just cry, and no one, not even the doctor, knows why. When that happens, you have to just relax into it, like it's a rush."

"But I've got a store to run. What will I do if she—"

"One day at a time, India. You'll handle things as they come, and some days will be tough. But not impossible."

Only when Estelle was older would things get impossible.

India wiped a tear from her face. "I don't think I can do this, Roberta."

"You can do it."

"You don't know the things I've failed at. I didn't even finish high school. I messed up a job as a file clerk, and another as a cook at Taco

Bell. I used my inheritance from my granny to take over this store, because at least here no one could fire me."

"You cooked at Taco Bell?"

She wasn't laughing.

"Why did they fire you? You've got a very good head on your shoulders."

"And a very big mouth. I couldn't even make it as a greeter at Wal-Mart. I tried."

"You can raise this baby, India. You're going to do fine."

She shrugged her shoulders.

"Maybe she'd go in her cradle now."

"It's back in my room."

I walked down the hall and found in India's bedroom a cradle made of wood carved into lace, with angel wings to serve as rockers. I knelt and tucked the baby in under the flannel quilt, and passed my hand over the rounded cove that shielded her head.

"The cradle was bought from a gypsy in Romania." India stood in the doorway. "That's what the lady at the yard sale told me."

"So beautiful." I rested back on my heels.

"Did you get your gift?"

I forced a smile.

"I found her at a yard sale, too. I thought she was so perfect, so beautiful."

"She's lovely. Thank you." I stood and crept from the room, and paused to examine her little altar in the hall. The moon goddess was there. The candles, the incense. A small, wilting nosegay of wildflowers.

But no knife. It was gone.

CHAPTER 2 8

"Roberta? Is that you?"

I'd only just climbed to the top of my steps. "Brenda! What are you doing here?"

The light from her flashlight bobbed its way down the hill. "I'm sorry. I didn't want to disturb you if you were doing something important."

"No. I'm just turning in. Does Gil know you're here?"

"He's working late. And he's really unhappy with me."

Oh dear.

"I wanted to tell you, I read the book you gave me."

"You finished it?" I walked through my door and lit the candle.

"I'm only partway done. But Madame Guyon is amazing. You were so wise to suggest her book first. She makes me see everything different. Because she had a husband she could never please. Just like me!"

I rubbed my forehead.

"But it was all God's gift to her, so that she could learn to be humble and submissive."

"Submissive."

"Everything she suffered, the death of her children and the loss of her position, the sickness, and the scarring on her face, all of it was a gift from God. It's so hard to see it that way, but once you do it changes everything."

What had I started? "What kind of everything?"

"By accepting her husband's cruelty, she was able to … to let go, to die to herself, and that made it possible for her to see God."

"Brenda, I don't think she meant to say … You're not thinking of getting that nose job are you?"

"Well, I don't know. Maybe. Or maybe it's just vanity after all."

"Maybe it is."

———

The next day, I learned the names of the four children who lived in the van: Daniel, Gabriel, Glory, and baby Jean. The parents were Jake and Lauren, and I started to greet them by name. Of course, Bobby told me that very likely none of those names were real. "That way when CPS comes asking, you've never heard of them." But still, it was something to call them.

When Darnell turned up, I told him if I saw him sneaking or stealing again I would tell Bobby, and if he ever even thought of spitting anywhere near this place I'd call the police.

He winked and jingled his hat and behaved for the rest of the night.

I brought Fiona her own bottle of ranch dressing to take home as a gift.

A woman I hadn't seen showed up at the door that night, a bottle redhead with a face full of pimples. Bobby took one look and headed for the dining hall. Louise leaned my way. "Lolly's on meth so bad she's working street corners to buy it. She and Margo are rivals, but it's Lolly who starts all the fights."

"I won't," Lolly protested at the door. "I'm just hungry."

Bobby let her in and she got in line.

Once again, everywhere I looked I saw memories. A man with a ponytail sat with his back to me, and from behind, that homeless man looked just like my husband. Another man arrived in a pullover like one Larry used to wear.

It was a trick of the mind. Like when I was carrying Garrett and all of a sudden it seemed that every other woman I met was pregnant. When something is on your mind, everywhere you look, you see it.

———

That night, deeply tired, I lay in my sleeping bag and closed my eyes. My cell phone rang.

"He hit me, Roberta." Brenda almost whispered the words.

"What?"

"Only once. He didn't mean to. But I'm so confused."

He may have only hit her once, but I'd seen the bruises from five fingers on her arm when she brought me the carpet. "Don't be confused, Brenda. Listen to me. This is simple. You've got to—"

"I know. I know what Madame Guyon said in her book. I finished it this morning, but—"

"No! No. Brenda, I'm not talking about the book. You can't let this man hit you."

"You really think that? Because nobody has ever hit me before, not my parents, not anyone."

Certainly not Russ.

"Sweetie, look. I never meant to give you the message that you should let Gil abuse you. Do you want me to come over?"

"No."

"Do you want to stay with me tonight?"

"I don't want you to see me." Her voice peaked at the end and she started to cry.

"Oh, Brenda. Is he there with you now?"

"No. He went into San Francisco. I don't think he'll be back tonight."

"I don't care. You've got to get out of that house. What about Russ? He's your best friend. He loves you."

"He might let me stay with him."

"Good. That's good."

It was a long night. I called Russ and made very sure he knew what had happened and would keep Brenda safe. Might even see to it that it was Gil who needed the nose job should he ever show his face again.

Then I lit my candle and pulled my Bible into my lap. I prayed the words of the first psalm I found, then closed the book, took a deep breath, and said a prayer of my own:

"What is it, God, that you find so attractive about suffering? Why does India have to raise her child alone? I know, she did the wrong thing and she prays to someone else, but can't you pull some strings? You're God.

"Why was Brenda so foolish as to leave Russ and marry Gil?

"Why do people have to be homeless? Why do women sell themselves on street corners?

"Why did Amber lose her baby, *my grandchild*, and why does she vomit the food that should feed the child she carries now?"

That last question could have ended with a *selah*, the Hebrew word that meant you could ponder it for eternity and never plumb the depths.

But I'd wound my way at last to the questions that had wedged so long between my heart and my lungs:

"Why did Larry have to die the way he did? A heart attack would have been kinder.

"Where is my son? Why does he want to die? And why, *why* can't I find him?"

Not a prayer for the records. But it was my prayer, and it felt, at least, real.

CHAPTER 29

At the last company New Year's party before Larry's diagnosis, I wore a blue dress. Alice blue, that pale gray blue that Teddy Roosevelt's daughter, Alice, wore because it matched her eyes.

It matched mine, too.

I'd never spent as much on anything I'd ever worn before, not even my wedding dress. But I never looked as good in my wedding dress either, and I'd been the better part of thirty years younger.

The dress was tea-length, an exquisite silk georgette, sleeveless with a surplice bodice that made me look curvy and a skirt that started narrow at the waist, then blossomed like a lily just starting to bloom. Between the bodice and the skirt, it had a cummerbund of kimono silk, a stylized floral in blue and taupe and silver.

Very distinctive, the floral pattern on the cummerbund.

I special-ordered the shoes to go with it, silver sandals, with one strap each of taupe and Alice blue. I actually had them made in those colors, just to match the dress.

And the reason I mention this is that the next time I saw Lolly, she turned up at the door of Louise's soup kitchen, collected her dinner, adjusted the dingy bra strap that slipped from her shoulder, then swished across the dining hall to wrangle herself a place on the bench directly across from Margo …

In that dress. And—I was certain I saw them—those sandals.

It didn't make sense. Everything had been destroyed in the fire. My dress was gone. Of course, it wasn't a one-off. But how could it possibly be a coincidence, Lolly putting that dress together with those shoes, custom made? At that cost.

"You okay?" Bobby took from my hand the roll I'd held poised over someone's plate.

"Fine, yes." I turned my attention back to the serving line. I served Vonna and Fiona, and the man with the pullover like Larry's, and then, a man who wore a jacket like the one Larry used to wear when we went camping.

I had to stop thinking this way. It was just an ordinary jacket, a blue fleece windbreaker that happened to be Larry's favorite. Not even an expensive one. There had to be hundreds like it all over town. I gave the man his roll and told myself I was losing my mind.

I tried to catch another glimpse of Lolly's sandals, but there were too many tables, too many people between us. The dress sagged against her body so badly I wondered if it was even the same dress. Or if I'd looked as good in it as I thought I did. She probably wore ordinary silver sandals. She couldn't be wearing mine.

But didn't I see the taupe and blue straps? Was I going that crazy that I was hallucinating now?

I remembered something about Larry's fleece jacket. He'd torn it on a trip to Yosemite, catching his arm on the broken branch of a tree. I said he should throw it away, but he loved that jacket and asked if I would mend the tear. I didn't want to go shopping just for a spool of blue thread, so I found some leftover embroidery floss in a slightly lighter shade and whipstitched the tear shut. Then, as a joke, I embroidered the tiniest blue daisy at the end of the tear, just under his arm, where no one but Larry would be likely to see.

I kept my eye on the man with the fleece jacket, hoping to catch him with his arm lifted, but he just bent over his dinner and ate. The four children held their plates up for a roll, and I forced a smile for each of them, still watching over the tops of their heads. Darnell stepped into my line of vision, in a talkative mood this time.

"Didn't spit last night."

"That's good, Darnell. I'm proud of you."

"And I won't spit tonight. In fact, I'm shooting for a spit-free week. I've done it before, gone a whole week, a month even, without spitting."

"Well keep up the good work, then."

A commotion in the corner caught our attention.

"Just shut up, Mar." Lolly shoved a plate across the table and stood.

"Don't you call me Mar. You're not my friend."

"Nobody's your friend. Everybody knows you're a …"

"She's swearing. Bobby, I heard her swear!" It was the man in the fleece jacket, and he'd raised his arm to point. I took my chance and leaned across the counter to catch a glimpse of his sleeve.

And I saw the daisy.

"Witch! I said witch!" Lolly recoiled to the wall, but Bobby already had her by the arm.

I heard a low chuckle, and turned back to Darnell just as he spat a stream through his teeth, directly to the side of my face.

"Oops."

Before I had time to react he was out the door, ahead of Bobby and Lolly, who screamed, "You hurt my arm!" I took one last look at her sandals in the evening light—too small, with her heels extended over the edge, but there were the colored straps, taupe and Alice blue.

Bobby locked the door, then turned back to all the stunned faces in the dining hall. He straightened his apron. "We're just going to give her time to calm down and go away." He started back toward the kitchen, then leaned down and came up with a bent and soiled photograph. "Anybody lose a picture?" He held it up so everyone in the dining hall could see, but he got no takers. He looked at the photo, then turned to me. "Roberta?" Still wiping furiously at my face with a napkin, I gave it a tired glance. And clapped a hand to my mouth.

It was my wedding picture. From the second wedding. The snapshot the priest took by that lake in Alaska.

Louise got me a chair to sit in. Bobby unlocked the door and did his best to encourage people to eat up and clear out, so we could talk.

I clutched that photograph in two hands and stared past it to each moment of the previous two hours. I waited for Bobby and Louise to tell me I should call the police. That I wasn't crazy. To tell me what to do.

Nearly everyone was gone when a young bearded man in grimy clothes, with a large, overstuffed backpack, trudged out of the night, through the door.

"We're just closing up," said Bobby. "No more food."

"Do you have maybe just a piece of bread? I'll wash dishes."

Oh God. I knew the voice.

CHAPTER 30

"We have some leftover rolls, and a couple of apples," said Louise. "You can just take them."

"Thank you. Very much."

The kitchen and dining hall rocked around me, five degrees to the right, back to the left and right again. Because this was the voice of my son.

I stood to look, to make sure, and just that moment his eyes caught mine. His blue eyes under that filthy mop of hair.

He held my gaze for a moment, and then turned, and simply left.

"Garrett!" I screamed after him. I dropped the photograph and dashed around the counter to the dining hall and out the door.

"Garrett!" He turned and looked at me, then turned again and ran.

But he ran slowly, his backpack flopping back and forth behind him like it was loaded with rocks. I half caught up with him and cried, "Please, Garrett, please."

He halted under a street lamp. His head dropped and his shoulders folded toward his chest. I stopped running and walked the final ten feet to stand before him. "How are you?" I felt stupid asking.

He shrugged, and nodded, and shook his head.

"Would you like something to eat?"

Another stupid question, but to my relief, he said, "Please."

"I don't have much money, Garrett. Is Kentucky Fried Chicken okay?"

I bought him two half-chicken meals, two little bucket parfaits, and a large Coke and sat across from him, steeled against the odor of sweat. He seemed to want to eat in silence, and I was fine with that. For the moment, I just wanted to search out his face under the beard and blackened pores, and fill his stomach.

When he finished, he kept his head down a long moment, then without looking up, finally asked. "How's Dad?"

The place was fluorescent lit and crowded with people. "He's gone, Garrett. We have to talk."

"We can go to the park."

So we walked down Alum Rock Avenue and wrapped around the block, past the limousines in the shimmering valet drive-through of the Fairmont Hotel. We crossed the street to César Chávez park, and made our way past the ground-lit vertical fountains, past the brown snake statue of Quetzalcoatl, "coiled like excrement," just as D. H. Lawrence once described the Aztec god, till finally we found a shadowed park bench with no one around.

We sat side by side, each with our hands folded between our knees, and I waited, afraid to begin the conversation.

Garrett drew in a long, tired breath, and I knew that he was crying. "He's dead?"

I nodded and mewled out a long "Yesss." We both wept, a strangled, high-pitched duet. But he kept his arms folded across his chest, and I held my hands clasped in my lap, the distance between us inviolate.

"Where were you, Garrett? I couldn't even tell you about the funeral!" The words came out louder than I'd intended.

He didn't move, but the chasm between us widened.

"I'm sorry. Sorry. I've just been so …"

I wiped my eyes and set my hand down on the bench between us. He snuffled, and waited, but at last he put his hand on mine. It was our first touch, and hungry for him, I turned my hand and wove my fingers into his.

"What happened, sweetheart?"

He shrugged. "I lost my job." As if that explained all of it.

"You could have come to us—"

"I didn't want to."

"Okay. But you have an inheritance, now. You can—"

"I don't want your money."

"There are worse things."

He didn't answer.

"At least tonight I can give you a place to sleep. Do you think you can handle that?"

No answer.

"Probably not much better than where you've been, but … Our house is gone, Garrett."

"Gone? What happened?"

"A fire. It burned to the ground."

That got his attention. "Mom. Are you okay?"

"Fine. Just fine."

"So where are you staying?"

"I found a little place in the mountains."

"What caused the fire?"

"You haven't been watching the news at all, have you?"

"No. I don't get cable where I live, so I figure, why bother with a TV at all, you know?"

"Very funny."

"What happened?"

"It was arson."

He turned his shoulders my way and stared hard into my eyes.

"Someone started it while I was at your dad's funeral. The first of several. The arsonist is still out there, still starting fires. Do you remember Rose Gibson? She was hospitalized for smoke inhalation."

"Mom." He pulled his hand from mine.

"She died not long after."

He gripped his hands to the sides of his head, like he couldn't stand another minute of this. "Mom!"

"What?"

"Go home. Go home now."

"You're coming with me."

He breathed hard, like he was out of air, and I thought he'd refuse. At last he said, "Then let's go."

We walked in silence, back to my car. I unlocked the doors, and got in, while he walked to the other side. He opened the passenger side door and leaned in.

"I'll see you later."

"Garrett, get in the car."

"No."

"I won't leave you here."

"I … I'll talk to you tomorrow, Mom. I'll meet you at that soup kitchen, okay? Just go home."

"Why? Why not now?"

"I'll tell you tomorrow."

"You promise you'll be there."

"Just go."

He shut the car door, turned, and crossed the street. And in a moment, he was gone.

———

Gordy had been afraid of this, she said when I called on the way back. "Homeless people don't leave a paper trail. Makes them hard to find." How much had she charged for that pearl of wisdom?

Suzanne said not to worry about the cost. "I just can't believe you let him go. Are you okay?"

"Sure, fine." I pinched the bridge of my nose. "It's just he's a little bit bigger than I am. Anyway, he said he'd be there tomorrow."

"Thank heaven you found him, today of all days."

"Why today of all days?"

"There was another fire this morning. No one we knew, but it was only two blocks away. And this time, Bertie, there was a fatality. A little boy, nine years old. His name was Marcus somebody. Devlin, I think. He ditched school and came home to watch television upstairs. The fire was set downstairs, and …"

I pulled over to catch my breath. *Inhale, exhale.* If the fire was that morning, and I saw Garrett after dark, then was it possible …? But he'd said he knew nothing about the fires. And I believed him. He'd looked so stricken. I was certain I could trust him. Couldn't I?

"Bertie, are you sure you're okay?"

"Yes. I'm sure." Best to change the subject. "How's Amber?"

"Thin. She *says* the doctor tells her she's doing fine. I'm calling him in the morning."

By the time I got home, my mental checklist was set to go. I didn't have time for ridiculous speculations. I had only one day to get ready for Garrett. Tomorrow we'd have dinner, and then he'd tell me everything. Meanwhile I'd call Russ to check on Brenda, just as soon as I'd looked in on the new mother and child. She might even lend me some extra blankets and pillows. Then tomorrow I'd clean my shed from corner to corner. Figure out something better for dinner than canned tuna fish. I didn't want Garrett to think he was still homeless.

I collected my flashlight, then hurried down the road and up the wooden stairs to India's. When I got there, I saw through the glass door that her lights were off. It was nearly ten o'clock; she must be in bed. I started back down the stairs. It was probably too late to call Russ as well—

"Roberta?"

The voice came from nowhere. I jumped.

"Sorry." A flashlight clicked on no more than ten feet away.

"Russ! You scared me. I was just checking on India."

"She's not—"

"I know. I didn't wake her. I'll try again in—"

"Roberta, listen. She's not asleep. She's gone."

"Gone? Where?"

"I don't know where, but it looks like Gil's the father of that baby. India's left with him."

CHAPTER 31

"Oh no!" I braced against the stair rail. "With Estelle? But he's violent."

"Would you mind sitting with Brenda? She's pretty upset."

"Russ, he beats her."

"I took her in for stitches today. She says he only hit her once. But it was more than once." He sounded so tired.

I found Brenda in Gil's office, rifling through his desk drawers and slamming them shut. "He can't possibly be the father of that baby." She blew her nose and fingered the bandage on her forehead. "Because see, we got married eight and a half months ago. He would have had to have had this little tryst, what? While I picked out my wedding dress? Can you imagine?"

Yes. I could imagine.

She swiped an arm across her eyes. "Did India tell you she was after him, or did she just keep her little secret to herself?"

"Brenda, I never heard her say a kind word to or about Gil. She thought he was mean to you. She thought he was shallow, and frankly, I—"

"It's the money then. But she's going to find out, as I did this afternoon, that he has a lot less money than he pretends to have.

Come to think of it, so do I." She kicked the open door of his cre-
denza, then stood and held her arms out. I hugged her. She pressed
her face into my shoulder, and sobbed.

"Oh, sweetie." I patted her back. "Shhh …"

"I can't believe I was so stupid."

"Anyone can be taken in. You trusted—"

I started to say "him," but Brenda jumped right in and said, "I
did trust her! I should have seen what she was doing. We'd hardly
been married a week, and she already knew exactly how he likes his
sandwiches, how many sprouts, how much mustard. She's a pagan
you know. Did she tell you that?"

Something about this woman sapped the compassion right out
of me. I endured two hours of this, then checked my watch. It was
past midnight.

"Would you stay here? Would you sleep on the couch? I don't
want to be alone."

Her couch would feel like the caress of angels after weeks on a
concrete floor, but I wanted out of her house. I wanted to pray out
my own gratitude for Garrett, and anguish for India and Estelle. I
wanted to go home.

"Can't your dad stay with you?"

"I can't be around him right now. He says India did me a favor.
He's just mad about this." She touched her bandage.

"What about Russ? Maybe you could stay with him—"

"I want to be here. In case Gil comes back."

CHAPTER 3 2

I stayed till two in the morning, then made my escape.

As soon as I lit the candles in my hut, I spotted an envelope from Bill Nolan's office, laying on my pillow.

A yellow note was stuck to the outside:

Roberta,

> *Estelle and I have gone to live with her father. The story will be all over the mountain in the morning. Please understand.*

> *India*

I removed the note and wiped the tears from my eyes, then tore open the outer and inner envelopes and pulled out Larry's letter.

And squinted. I aimed the flashlight directly on the paper. Larry's handwriting was jagged and fitful, like it had printed off a heart monitor. I stared until some of the scratches began to resemble words.

Dear Bertie,

> *… days … quiet …*

Oh yes, the days did grow quiet, with a kind of drudgery, and a guilt-soaked boredom that made me behave as though he were furniture, sometimes. Larry! I had regrets of my own.

I tried to read further.

... secret ... something ...

What was the next word? *Exercise?* I held the page closer, then further away.

... forgiveness ... CEO ... GOD ... forgive me ... I would
tell you ... Bertie, forgive.... would have ... comforted ...
Larry

One, two, three *forgives* in the letter—that I could make out. Of course, it would be like him to ask forgiveness for getting sick and causing me trouble. Still, it was a letter from my husband—and I couldn't read it! And what I could decipher left me shaking.

I didn't sleep that night. I sat in my shed and waited for morning. As soon as it was eight o'clock, I dialed Bill Nolan's number and asked for his secretary.

"Mrs. Denys. How are you?"

"Judy, are you the one who has been mailing Larry's letters to me?"

"I am. He asked Bill to see that you got them, and Bill gave them to me."

"Was there anything legal about it? I mean, if I had a good reason to ask for them all at once, could you give them to me?"

"I'd ask Bill, but I've already sent you the last one. I mailed it the day before yesterday."

"No, there had to be more. He said he was going to send them every week for a year. I need to see the rest, because the last one was illegible, and it had some things ... I just need clarification, and I thought if I saw the rest of the letters ... He said there'd be fifty-two. Would you ask Bill?"

She put me on hold, and a moment later, returned. "Mrs.

Denys, maybe he couldn't finish. Maybe he meant to, but couldn't, because of his illness. I talked to Bill, and we're sure there are no more."

I whispered a thank you and flipped the phone shut.

No more letters.

I wrapped my arms around my knees and began to rock. Larry was gone, really and truly gone now. There would never be a touch, never a smile, and now never a word from him. I tried to read the letter again, but my tears made it quite impossible.

I rolled to the floor, unable to think. For hours I lay on the concrete, till some inner clock told me it was time to get up, go find my son, and bring him home.

———

At Louise's suggestion, I didn't work the line that night. "You have enough on your mind without trying to manage a serving spoon. Here, I saved your picture for you. Just stand over there, and watch for your boy."

By "stand over there," I knew she meant I should stay out of the way. I'd become a nuisance, a failure even in the soup kitchen. But this night I would see Garrett. What else mattered?

The previous night's disturbance had evidently run people off. There was no Lolly or Margo, no Darnell, no Vonna and Fiona, no family with four children. Just a lot of men. Just the hungriest.

But Garrett wasn't one of them.

After a time I went outside to stand on the sidewalk. I waited till the sun went down, and longer, till I heard Bobby set the metal folding chairs on the tables so Louise could mop the floors. When he finished, he came out and set a hand on my shoulder. "Why don't you come inside?"

"I'm going to take a walk."

"Not by yourself, you're not." He took his apron off and tossed it in the door.

I'd been looking up and down the street—I don't know—for sleeping bags in the gutters, I guess, trying to fathom where the homeless would go after dark. I turned to Bobby. "Do you know where he sleeps?"

"I don't know *him*, Roberta. Never saw him before. He could be any number of places. There are shelters in town, but I'll tell you, he might not give them his real name. Some of them are canny that way. How about I take you around tonight … we can both look for him."

Bobby took me to check the nearby shelters, and as he had warned, none of them had heard of Garrett.

"They move around, you know. Someone gives them a BART or a Caltrain ticket, a little cash, and they're as mobile as anybody else."

We checked the overpasses and walked along the thicket that lined the Guadalupe River. We found men there, and some seemed to want to help, but if they told the truth, they didn't know Garrett. Quite a few seemed hungry for conversation. One man explained in copious detail who all he *did* know, he knew several young men just newly homeless, good boys all of them, too, but no, he'd never heard of anyone named Garrett.

And so on.

One man with a New York Yankees baseball cap stared at us as if he didn't understand a word we said.

When I was nearly frantic, I spotted the man who had Larry's jacket, up the street, going into Starbucks. I darted off to catch him, leaving Bobby behind.

"Excuse me," I yelled. "Excuse me," I called when I got inside. And everyone turned to look except the man with the jacket. I got in line behind him, and touched his back.

"I'm the lady down at …" I pointed over my shoulder. "May I ask a question? It's important."

He only stared at me.

"Would you please tell me where you got that jacket?"

He stared so long I thought he was like the quiet man with the Yankee's cap, unable or unwilling to answer. I wasn't far from the truth.

"It … it was a gift."

"From who?"

He chewed his lip and ran his tongue across it. "I have a Starbucks card."

"What?"

"I can be here like anyone else."

"Please, Mr. … I don't know your name."

"I can be here like anyone else, without being bothered."

"Please, stop yelling; don't get upset; I don't want to bother you. It's just very important. I need to know—"

"If you need this coat more than an old veteran with nothing to call his own except asthma, well …" He hustled it off and stuffed it in my hands. "Take it. Just don't bother me."

He turned and rushed past Bobby, who stood at the door.

And left me standing with Larry's jacket in my hand. I caught Bobby's gaze, and waited for him to tell me what to do.

———

He drove me home, with Louise bringing my car behind us. "Where do you live?" He pulled to the side of the road.

"Just up the hill there."

He leaned forward, as though by doing so he could see to the top. It was a dark, moonless night. "You live alone?"

I nodded, too numb to speak. The next moment, I thought of going back to that shed without my son, with no idea how to find him—*again*—and I began to choke.

"We're going to breathe now, Roberta. Slowly. A long breath."

I tried.

"Come on. A *long* breath."

I made a concerted effort, and succeeded to a degree. Then, just when I thought I was under control, I began to tremble. The panic started again, and I pushed my fingers into my hair and balled them into fists, whimpering, pulling, and rocking.

"What's going on, Bobby?" Louise stood at the driver's side window.

"She's in trouble. I could take her back to a hospital, but the traffic …"

"Does she have neighbors?"

I nodded, pointing up the road.

"Then let's go."

Bobby talked to Russ in the driveway while Louise sat in the back holding onto my shoulder.

The next moment Russ squatted by my open door, and took my hand. "What's wrong here?"

I began to sob. "My son's gone, Russ. I found him. But then I let him go because … he said he would meet me. But he didn't. A little boy is dead. And I don't know if … Larry is gone … and India and Estelle. Now Garrett. And if he doesn't want me to find him … then I just won't, will I?"

Russ ran his hand across my forehead, then stepped away from the door. "Come inside."

"I need to go home." I got out of the car.

He took my arm. "Later. Soon. But—"

"Maybe he'll come here. I need to get ready." I broke away.

"Roberta!"

"Bobby!" Louise commanded him to stop me, but I ran around the bushes, past the trees. It was so dark. I groped my way in the dwindling porch light. Someone came behind me through the bushes. I ran faster.

And slipped on the layers of leaves and needles. I slid downhill into complete darkness, unable to see the rocks I skidded over, the tree limbs that snatched as I scraped by, the bramble that finally broke my descent. My yelps caught, strangled in a throat that would not open, and I cried, I'm certain, like a soul in perdition. For what else was I?

After several moments something rustled nearby. "It's me, Roberta."

Russ settled beside me. He put one hand on my arm, and the other around my shoulder. I turned and clung to him, weeping and gasping. He made a soft blowing sound, and slipped a hand between us to press my abdomen. "With me," he whispered, and I felt his chest expand.

I inhaled, and pressed against his hand with a slow, full breath of air.

"Hold a moment." Together, we held our breath.

He blew softly, as his chest released. I exhaled with him and shuddered.

"Shhh. With me." Together, we took another breath.

When I was quiet, a faint beam of light appeared beside us, lighting the shadowed outlines of leaves and pinecones. I glanced up to its source, a flashlight held at the top of the hill.

"Russ?" Bobby jiggled the light. "You can come up this way."

"Are you hurt?" Russ whispered the question.

"No."

"Will you come with me?"

I nodded, and he helped me up.

⸺

When Russ had invited me for a soak in his hot tub, I had this notion of his house, all black leather, wide screen, and bedroom. What I found was a paneled great room with a stone floor. Four cushioned oak chairs before the fireplace, clustered around an old kitchen table. A clay teapot filled with ginger tea, a half loaf of bread.

He broke a piece off and held it out. "When did you last eat?"

"I ... don't know."

"Take this."

I held it in my lap, staring. It smelled like yeast and butter. The crust was firm, and the bread inside was light and soft. I didn't know what to do with it

"Roberta, tonight you have to heal. Eat the bread."

I took a bite. The taste spread its warmth down my middle and across my shoulders, and I wept, both from the pleasure and the defeat of everything I had tried to do.

Russ brought a cushion for the hearth, so I could put my feet up.

"More bread?"

"No."

"Lay your head back."

I did, and he stood behind my chair and slipped his fingers under my neck, then gently pressed upward, directly into the pain that had grown from weeks of sleeping on the floor and years of lifting my husband into and out of his wheelchair. I let my tears flow down the sides of my face. He brushed them away, then pressed his fingertips over my temples and into my hair.

In a moment, I slept, an agitated, troubled sleep, but the chair was so soft and the fire so warm. I woke to a sound like small bells and opened my eyes as Russ finished laying silver on the table beside me. He set down a plate with a slice of beef, a salad, and two red potatoes.

I stared at the food, a feast compared to what I'd allowed myself. Was I really giving up? I pressed a finger to my lips.

Russ reached over and touched my other hand. "You need to eat."

I lifted the fork, and began with the potato. "It's so good."

"You're hungry. These are just leftovers."

"Your home is peaceful."

"It's sparse, you mean, but thanks for putting it that way. Boyd and I like it. Brenda took most of the furniture. Which is fine. I didn't want it."

"Where is Boyd?"

"When Gil's away, it's movie night with Brenda. And well, he's away tonight. I helped Dad pick the movies this time: *First Wives Club* or *Sleeping with the Enemy*. She can watch either, or both."

He'd made me smile. "You're putting ideas in her head."

"It's a pretty thick head."

Russ looked beautiful to me, that moment. The smile in parentheses, the lines around his eyes. His thick hands cradled around his cup. I remembered his touch on my abdomen, the way he'd shown me how to breathe. His fingers against my neck, and the kindness, such wonderful kindness.

I looked into my cup, ashamed of the feeling that had risen in me at this of all moments. I knew the shape I was in. I was so lonely, so frightened. This was no time to think how it would feel, if he were to touch me again. And when I looked up I saw he didn't want me getting the wrong idea.

He rubbed his nose and shifted in his chair. "When you moved up here, your friend stopped by to give me her phone number. Just in case."

"Oh."

"I called while you slept. I … thought she might be of help. She said she had some work to finish up. She'll probably be … another hour, maybe. I've got some things to tend to here, some bookwork, but if you'd like to take a soak outside, it always makes me feel better. I've still got an old suit of Brenda's."

So I wound up in his hot tub at last—alone—in a suit that would have fit Brenda with several extra pounds, and me with one or two less. The air was brisk and the water was warm. When I stepped in, the scrapes on my hands and legs from the slide down the hill all prickled and stung, then quieted into a tired languor. I propped my arms on the ledge, laid my head back, and let my legs float free.

Russ brought a fresh cup of tea, then went back inside, leaving the door open, turning off the light.

His deck extended to the ridge over the canyon, with the tree-tops well below. When the lights went dark, all they left in the world was me and the stars and this womb of warm water.

When Suzanne came, I knew she would ask me, as gently as her nature would allow, to stop this nonsense. I wondered what I would say. And then I didn't wonder.

"I'm sorry," I whispered skyward, and the stars gazed back as though they'd known all along what I would decide. I gripped the rim of the hot tub and allowed myself to slip deeper into the water, and submerge. When I came up again, I wiped my face, took a deep breath, and waited for Suzanne to fetch me home.

CHAPTER 33

Sometime in the years since Larry's diagnosis, Suzanne had painted her dining room the color of dark chocolate. I'd only just noticed. With the silver and crystal, the mirrors, and the zebra print rug, the room was all of Suzanne and none of Charlie, who had liked steel better than silver, black better than brown. Above all, he liked his home to give the impression that he lived, breathed, and slept in the future, and in his mind, I have to say, the future was a cold place.

Once, before the divorce, Suzanne found a stray pair of panties in her drawer. "Not my color, not my size, not my style, not mine," she said. The housekeeper had found them in her bed and thrown them in the laundry.

When Suzanne showed them to Charlie, he took them from her and said, "I'm sure they're Marlee's; I'll see she gets them back."

A very cold place, Charlie's world.

I wish I'd known at the time it happened. Suzanne had only just told me the previous night, after she brought me home from Russ's. I followed her to the linen closet where she stopped to get some sheets so we could make up the guest bed. On top of a stack of storage boxes, I glimpsed the rim of a large frame and recognized the silver and ebony design. I pulled it out. It was Suzanne and Charlie, Larry and me, celebrating at the Good Earth Restaurant in Los Gatos, the night we signed the papers to incorporate ConjuTech. Two handsome men, and two hopeful young women.

"What happened to you and Charlie?"

Knowing the day I'd had and the shape I was in, she skipped the details and just told me this story of the final deathblow to her marriage.

"I wish you'd told me," I said. "I was just across the street."

"You were half a world away."

I bowed my head.

She put a hand on my arm. "You don't defend yourself very well."

"What?"

"Stand up for yourself. Ask why I wasn't a better friend to you when Larry got sick."

"I didn't let you in, Suzy. We both know I pushed you away—"

"Skip the clichés. We also know very well that I can push right back when I want to. Bertie, we were both losing our husbands at the same moment. We each did the best we could do."

I hugged her and whispered, "I'm so sorry."

"You're my friend, my very dear friend. I won't let you down this time."

So here I was, in her home again. The sheers she'd hung in her dining room were the color of steamed milk, and the morning light shining through did nice things to the room.

I pushed them apart and gazed across the street at the remains of my home. Everything looked the same as when I'd seen it last. But it felt infinitely more sinister, and I was infinitely sadder, even than I'd been as a widow just back from the funeral.

To think that I'd stood there watching my house burn that day, telling myself, "All shall be well, and all shall be well."

Perhaps the sentiment was only Julian of Norwich's levee against the despair of life in plague-torn Europe. But my levees had all broken, and the despair had flooded in and found its level. Strange how it can shine like still water sometimes. I felt calm as the dead.

"Do you want to walk over to your place?" Suzanne padded up behind me and held out a cup of coffee.

"No. Wainwright will start barking, and Carroll will call the troops. Really, I'm done there. I want to move on. I'll look through the want ads this morning, see what I can do about a résumé—"

"Why not work for me?"

"As a realtor?"

"Well, eventually. But you could start out as my assistant."

Dear friend or not, that sounded like a fate worse than canned tuna. I gave her a look meant to say as much.

"It would give you something to put *on* your résumé should you ever decide to leave, and I could help you get your realtor's license—"

"You don't need an assistant."

"Actually, I do."

"What happened to Cammie?"

"Quit. Walked out. Said she'd rather die than work for me."

"Oh, Suzanne. When was this?"

"Just last night. Minutes before I left to pick you up."

"But you picked me up at … it must have been eleven o'clock, which means if you came right from work … Cammie was working that late?"

"Well, I *needed* her."

I suppressed a smile. Suzanne chuckled, and I put my arm around her shoulders.

"Am I really such a—"

"Sometimes. You can be."

She shrugged. "I'm also a very good friend to have when the chips are down."

"It's true."

"The best, in fact."

"The very best."

"Because not only did I arrange, however unintentionally, for a job to open up just the moment you happened to need one—and I can mellow out. I can do anything I set my mind to. But I also have an apartment, well within range of the salary I'm going to pay you."

"Really."

"One of my clients, Mrs. Jorgen. The nicest old lady you ever met. She's owned this wonderful old Snow White cottage in Willow Glen, since the plans were drawn up, I'm sure. She's got a guesthouse out back, one bedroom, one bath—"

"I can look at it today, if—"

"No, she's out of town till Monday. But trust me on this." Suzanne always did love being right, and she obviously felt like the Empress of Perfection this morning. She smiled, and sipped her coffee.

Still in her pajamas.

"Don't you need to get ready for work? You go on, I'll decant the hot water in the processed oatmeal; I haven't forgotten how to cook."

"Not going."

"No?"

"Consider it part of my new mellow-out program. I thought since you don't have to look for a job or an apartment, we might as well do lunch today. I'll ask Amber to join us. How long since you've been to the ocean?"

"Not that long. I was there the day I gave my car away."

"And your money?"

I nodded.

"I see. *But.* Did you have lunch at the Acapulco?"

"No." I shook my head, then sank into the chair by the window and focused on my folded hands.

"What, Bertie?"

"There is something I have to do. I decided this morning. I have to talk to the police."

She took the other chair.

I told her what had happened at the soup kitchen besides my finding, and losing, my son. All the things I'd thought had been lost in the fire, that now turned up among the homeless. Larry's jacket. My dress. That photograph. "The day of the Devlin fire, I didn't find Garrett till nighttime—"

"Bertie."

"—so it's possible he—"

"Bertie, stop. I was out of line to accuse Garrett. I jumped to conclusions. We don't know—"

I put my hand up. "I can't think too much about this, Suzy, or I won't be able to do it. The fires have to stop. So I have to do what is right and let the truth take care of itself."

"I'll go with you."

"Suzy …" I looked at her and tried the kind of smile that said I was fine, really. "I think I can do this myself."

"I meant drive. I'll drive you."

"Okay."

———

It was a simple matter telling the police what had happened. As simple as it had been to file the missing person's report. The policeman took down my information, and thanked me for my time.

It was much too simple. Even when I told them I had found Garrett, and how he behaved, they simply noted it and thanked me.

I wanted to ask if anything I'd said implicated Garrett, but I didn't want to put the idea in their heads if it hadn't. "If you do hear from him, will you please ask him to call me?"

"I'll make a note in the file."

And that was that.

When I stepped outside and looked for Suzanne's car, it was gone.

Perhaps she'd driven around the block. I waited. But she didn't come. I called her cell phone.

"I'm on my way. I've hit a little traffic."

"Where'd you go?"

"Just on an errand. Sit tight. I'm getting off the highway now."

When I got in her car, she handed me a large box from Ann Taylor.

"What's this?" I pulled the ribbon, lifted the lid, then pushed the tissue aside, and caught the smell of new clothes. It was a pantsuit, in a warm shade of dove gray I'd always loved, in a style that was as far from my black "habit" as she could have found in the short time she had. It was another step away from my mountain.

"I thought you'd like to dress up for lunch. The Acapulco has the best fish tacos ever. We'll stop at my place to change. I got you some shoes, too." She reached behind my seat and retrieved the bag.

Gray mules with just a bit of heel, to match the suit.

———

As we walked down Pacific Avenue toward the Acapulco, Suzanne started the game we used to play with our kids during road trips. "On the sidewalk in Santa Cruz I saw a man reading tarot cards."

I resigned myself and joined in. "On the sidewalk in Santa Cruz I saw a man reading tarot cards and ... a woman singing a terrible Joni Mitchell."

"On the sidewalk in Santa Cruz, I saw a man reading tarot cards, a woman singing Joni Mitchell, and a man on the corner playing Chopin on the piano. Not bad, either."

Suzanne was the only one I knew who found it necessary to dress up for Santa Cruz. As for me, I'd grown accustomed to my Stuart Weitzmans, and these new shoes had already become a problem. They clopped and slapped with every step, and I felt I had to grip them with my toes to keep them from flying off my feet.

I looked up the street and spotted the second person in the world who would dress up for Santa Cruz.

"Your turn." Suzanne nudged me.

"On the sidewalk in Santa Cruz, I saw a man reading tarot cards, a woman singing Joni Mitchell, a piano player playing Chopin, and a man doing a meditation walk, dressed all in pink with a parasol and a feather boa."

"I let you say the pink guy, I'm so good to you. On the sidewalk in Santa Cruz, I saw a man reading tarot, a woman absolutely ruining Joni Mitchell—I can still hear her—a man playing the piano, a pink guy doing a Zen walk, and a bumper sticker that says 'Keep Santa Cruz Weird.' You gotta love this place!"

We dined outside, where the warmth of the sun mixed with the cool of the ocean breeze. A guitar man played flamenco not twenty feet from our table, between us and the Art Deco sign of the Del Mar Theater.

"Boy, did I need a day off." Suzanne squeezed a lemon slice into her water glass and pushed it down with a straw. "I left a mountain of stuff to do, but you'll help me catch up."

"I'm not sure my working for you would be good for our friendship."

"It would be the best for our friendship. You'd save my life."

"Where's Amber? Isn't she going to join us?"

"No. I talked to the doctor, and sure enough, he's worried. Wants her to eat. And to rest, and Amber says dining out doesn't fit his definition of rest."

"Maybe it doesn't."

"Maybe. But I'll bet she's not resting or eating, either one. I'm going to order her a lunch and bring it to her after we eat. Do you mind?"

"Of course not. But do you think she'll eat it?"

"She will if I sit there and watch."

"But what's to stop her from purging after we leave?"

She sighed. "Like you, Bertie, I do what I have to do. Roger's doing everything he can. He made an appointment with that counselor she saw when Charlie left, but she canceled it. The doctor says she could miscarry …" Suzanne pressed her lips together and wiped her eyes. "Listen, I'm going to go freshen up. When the waiter comes, tell him dos Fish Tacos, two orders. You'll love them." She made her escape.

I shouldn't have brought up Amber, not here. Suzanne wouldn't mind crying in front of me, but in front of a street full of people?

As for myself, if, as she said, I was doing what I had to do, why did I feel so wrong sitting here? The smells drifting from the restaurant launched me into ecstasies of remorse. And after weeks of woodland silence, Santa Cruz seemed a pandemonium. I noted every singer, guitar, piano, accordion, and horn, the sizzle of a grill someplace, the drone of cars going by. I heard the tinkling silver of a dozen outdoor cafés and the seven or eight conversations in each. Somewhere, someone had a persistent cough, and someone else had a persistent horse laugh.

It didn't bother anyone else, and it didn't used to bother me. I'd get over this. It was what I had to do.

That distant cough drew nearer. Behind me, someone hacked and grumbled to clear a throat that must have been clotted with mucous. I knew the feeling. I'd suffered those kinds of colds since I was a child, the kind that make you feel that a thick bubble has formed like a diaphragm over your windpipe.

The poor soul gave a final hawk and trudged past, with a backpack that looked like the weight … wait. Garrett!

"Garrett!"

He turned and looked at me, then turned again and resumed walking as though our eyes had not just met. I pushed away from the table, grabbed my purse and ran as fast as I could in those shoes. "Garrett!"

He jostled between the pink-umbrella man and a couple holding hands, and I did the same. "Don't you walk away from me. Don't you dare."

He stopped, chuckling, half crying, like this was all just too much. "Mom. Go back to your place in the mountains."

"You're coming home with me."

"I can't."

"Why not?"

"It's not that I don't … I love you. But just believe me, I can't."

"Well. That's just not good enough, young man. I think you owe me an explanation. A lot of explanations."

He shook his head, and began to walk.

I followed. "Just anytime. I can wait."

He didn't answer. The two of us walked side by side for a block or two, he in his torn sneakers, me in my flapping mules, till he turned and said, "Mom, look, here's the situation. I won't go with you, and you won't like where I go. I know your cell phone number."

"Yes. Well, I guess you've known all these past months how to reach me but you didn't—"

"I'll call you."

"—did you? And as to your promise, if you can't be where you say you'll be, how can I expect that you'll call when you say you will? I think I'll just stay with you. I don't have to like where you go."

He coughed. "It's not that you won't like it. You won't make it."

I took stock. My past few weeks had been a crash course in survival living. I had my purse. I had my cute little gray mules. Not a perfect setup, but all in all … I squared my shoulders. "Just watch me."

He turned and walked, coughing. I straightened my purse on my shoulder, and kept up. We'd almost got to Beach Street when my cell phone rang. I cringed and answered. "Hi, Suzanne."

"Where'd you go?"

"I'm so sorry. I found Garrett. And I just followed. There wasn't time to tell you."

"Is he all right?"

"He's got a really bad cough. Other than that—Garrett, slow down." But he wouldn't.

"Where are you now? I'll come get you."

"We're almost to the wharf. Garrett."

He waved me off. "Tell her to come pick you up."

"Good," said Suzanne. "Stay at the wharf. I'll be there."

"She's picking us both up."

"No." He crossed a parking lot, and I followed.

"Suzy, hold on. Garrett, wait."

He walked onto the sandy beach beside the wharf and kept going. When I got to the sand, the heels of my shoes sank in. I stepped out of them, snapped them up and put them in my purse, then ran slow motion through the sand to catch up. "We're on the beach, Suzy. I don't know where to tell you to meet us."

"Bertie, sweetie, if he won't come, you need to come with me."

"No."

"You haven't even eaten. Okay, that was stupid. But, Bertie, you're not up to this. What are you going to do, go homeless?"

Did she think I wouldn't? "I'll call you later." I flipped the phone shut.

We trudged past beach blankets and umbrellas. He walked between two sunbathers who lay so close together that I had to fall back or step over them. I fell back, then hustled up beside him. We made our way to the parking lot of the Dream Inn, and I brushed my feet off and stepped back into my mules. This cost me several yards, and I hobbled to keep up. My phone rang.

"Answer the call, Mom. Tell her to pick you up at the Surfer Memorial."

There was no point in answering him or the phone. I walked. He led me to the memorial, the bronze statue of a young surfer as toned and confident as Garrett had been himself, once.

"Call her."

"I'll only get in the car if you get in first."

"Will you just believe me? I can't."

The phone rang, and I answered.

"What's going on? Where are you?"

"I'm going to need some time, Suzy."

"How long? Do I come back in an hour?"

"No. Give me—"

Garrett leaned over. "She's at the—"

I clapped a hand over his mouth. "—till morning. I'll call in the morning."

"Do you have a place to stay?"

"Yes. We've talked. It'll be fine."

I made a show of turning the phone off, then dropped it back in my purse.

CHAPTER 34

Without a word, he turned and started walking, and as best as I could, I kept up with him. He led me down Cliff Drive to the lighthouse, then, as though he were pacing, turned back the other direction and kept moving.

Coughing all the way. He had a terrible cold. Other than that he was silent.

I might have started a conversation myself, if I could have caught my breath. I certainly had plenty of questions. But I knew what he was trying to do: He thought if he could just walk far enough and fast enough he could shake me off. It wasn't going to work. With every step I had to grip my mules, and my feet were cramping. But I stayed with him.

We walked that way for more than a mile, past the Neary Lagoon Park to Mission street, where at last I could see some sense in all this motion. I followed him to Taco Bell, and finally, he broke his silence. "Do you have any money?"

"No, Garrett, I'm sorry. I don't."

"I think they take cards."

"I don't have any cards."

"Oh, that's great." He coughed, and set his hands on his hips.

"Are you complaining? I can't believe this. Where's your money? Where are your cards?"

"I must have left them at home. Wait here."

"I'm not leaving you."

"Then follow, but stay back and be quiet."

A young father emerged from a Volvo with his three children, and headed for the restaurant. Garrett fell in behind them, and mumbled something in his ear. The man glanced from Garrett to his children, who watched, looking from their daddy to the poor man asking for help. "Just a minute," said the father, and entered the restaurant. Garrett waited beside the door, while I watched from a distance, fighting the urge to hide myself, to pretend I didn't know this homeless man. My son.

When the young father came out and handed him a large bag of food, Garrett walked back, sat on the curb and motioned for me to join him. When I sat down, he handed me a burrito and I ate.

He coughed, and I could hear that he was struggling to clear his lungs.

"You should see a doctor about that," I said.

"I'm fine."

I felt his forehead. He had a fever. "Sweetie, I could just call a walk-in clinic right now. I have my cell phone."

"Mom." He wadded his wrapper up and tossed it in the bin. "I'll be fine." He got to his feet and started moving. I hurried to catch up.

We walked up along the old houses of High Street, further up the hill into the university, then back down again. Finally, when we'd seen most of Santa Cruz and it was getting dark, Garrett slowed his pace.

My feet hurt terribly. I hadn't worn a coat, and it was getting cold. He pulled a blanket from his backpack and draped it around my shoulders.

"Where do we sleep?" I asked. He scratched his head and looked around.

I'd hoped against hope he might know a friend in town with a nice floor we could sleep on. Even an indoor shelter would do. Either option would be humiliating, but still better than sleeping in the doorway of some shop where people would step over us in the morning. I was hungry. A shelter might offer us some food, so we wouldn't have to go begging again.

But Garrett changed direction and headed out of town, where there was no dinner, and no place to sleep that I could see.

As night fell, we found ourselves on a patch of road near the Cabrillo Highway that was almost completely dark. I kept pace with Garrett by sound, and the light of an occasional passing car.

"Where are we going?"

He coughed. "Almost there."

After a time I heard him fumble around his jacket, and the light of a small penlight appeared. He scanned it to the side of the road, and led me to a stand of trees. We walked a distance in, and, keeping his light very low to the ground, he stomped the bed of leaves softly with his foot, then squatted to touch them with his fingers.

"This is good." He turned his pen light off. I heard the zipper of his backpack. "Give me the blanket."

I held it up, and he took it, then replaced it with something thicker.

"A sleeping bag. Just spread it out."

"Do you have something to sleep in?"

"Yes."

I laid the sleeping bag on the ground and crawled in. It smelled of mildew and sweat. I heard a rustle of leaves, and felt certain that all he had done was to wrap himself up in that blanket.

"Garrett."

He didn't answer.

I reached out in the dark till I found him. "Garrett, you're not well. You take the sleeping bag."

Still no answer, and in a moment, he began to snore.

———

I woke early, having hardly slept at all. The old ache in my back, the smell of eucalyptus mixed with the odor of the sleeping bag, the feel of a loosened bra under a new gabardine pantsuit and damp leaves beneath my hair, the darkness, the sound of the distant ocean and the near highway, all worked against any inclination to sleep. Finally, at some early hour, I closed my eyes to the stars and the swaying trees overhead and drifted into a fitful rest.

And then awoke in a gray light, beside an open pack covered with a damp blanket. I was alone.

"Garrett?"

I scrambled out of the sleeping bag and stood. "Garrett? *Garrett?*"

"Shhh!" His voice came behind me. "We can still get caught."

"Where were you?"

He sat on the ground and rolled his eyes. "Running errands." He motioned for me to join him. I sat on the sleeping bag.

"First, a gift." He reached into his jacket and pulled out a pair of tennis shoes. "Size seven, right?"

"Where did you get these?"

He didn't answer. The shoes were well used, dingy pink, with their soles worn smooth, and the distinct imprint of someone's foot inside. Only the day before Garrett had said I couldn't take his way of life, and I had answered, "Just watch." He waited for me to put the shoes on, and I did. They were warm, snug, and well broken in, and they would be good to walk in. Much better than the mules.

"Now, breakfast." He waited out a short coughing fit, then slipped his hand back into his jacket and pulled out a rumpled bag from McDonald's. He reached into the bag, and handed me a sausage biscuit. He retrieved one for himself, and when he unwrapped it, I noticed his was partially eaten.

"I don't guess anyone threw away any orange juice."

"The more liquid you drink, the more you have to pee."

I nodded. It wasn't so hard to find toilets in Santa Cruz, but out here ... Once in the night I had gotten up to creep as far from our little camp as I dared and used only the darkness for privacy.

"What do we do now?"

"We walk up the coast a ways."

I decided to venture into my questions. "Did you hear there's been another fire?"

"No."

"A little boy, nine years old was killed. He lived just two blocks from us."

Garrett snuffled, wiped his eyes with one hand, and nodded. And said nothing.

"Sweetie, if you know anything about this, please tell me."

"I'm sorry, Mom. I didn't mean to do anything wrong."

I swallowed back tears and put my hand on his arm. "Whatever you did, we'll work it out. We can get a lawyer. I mean, we have to do the right thing, but we can … I'll never leave you, Garrett."

"Why a lawyer?"

I looked at him.

"I don't need a lawyer. Do you think I started the fires?"

"No." I searched his eyes.

"Because I didn't."

"Fine. But—"

"You think I did it."

"I think I deserve to understand what's going on."

He ran a hand over his head, then nodded. "Did you meet a man at the soup kitchen with a gold cap on his tooth?"

"Darnell."

"The first night I spent at a shelter, he was there. He spent the next few days, helping me out. Showing me how to find a place to sleep, how to …" He shrugged. "How to find the best food in the trash. But one night, I just needed a shower and a bed. I knew you and Dad weren't in the main house. I let Darnell come with me, to thank him or something. I guess he …" Garrett cupped a hand over his forehead and began to rock forward and back. "I guess he read the security code over my shoulder. I didn't think. Mom, I'm so sorry."

I took his hand, but he pulled it away. "He was stealing everything, all kinds of things. I saw him with Dad's Nikon, with the strap

I made in school. He sold what he could. Clothes and stuff he traded for favors."

"Okay, so he stole things—"

"When I saw the camera, I told him if he didn't stop, I'd call the police. A week later, he had your wedding ring. He was on something, out of it, so I managed to get it back, and I told him I was going to call the cops. He said the cops couldn't catch him and he could prove it. That was the night before ..." He sighed. "The night before your fire."

Garrett reached in his pocket and pulled out the diamond ring Larry had removed that day in Alaska.

I took it and ran my finger over the diamond.

"You can put it on."

"It was your father who took it off, to replace it with something better." I slipped it into my purse. "Anyway, none of that means Darnell set the fire."

"He bragged about it. He's proud of it. The night you told me about the fire, I went to him and asked. He was in the crowd, watching. He didn't know about Dad's funeral till someone told him. He said you didn't cry, you just stood with a dark haired lady who took charge of everything. Suzanne, right? That's why we're in Santa Cruz, Mom. That's why we can't sleep in the shelters; we have to stay low. I told the police. If they don't find him and he finds out they're looking for him, he'll start looking for me." He coughed.

"But he won't find you here. He's in San Jose."

"So was I." Coughed again. "Why are you crying?"

"I'm just ... happy to see you."

"Okay ... You really thought I set those fires."

"No." I grimaced. "I didn't know, Garrett. How could I? And don't look so offended. Nothing you do makes any sense these days. I don't understand why you won't come home. I don't understand why you disappeared when your father ... Garrett, your father was dying! How could you just—"

He burst to his feet and then bent over to brace against a long coughing fit. When he finished, he snatched his backpack and started walking.

"Wait!" I grabbed the sleeping bag and followed.

CHAPTER 35

I'd never known or thought to ask how long it would take me to walk from Santa Cruz to Davenport. That day I found out. It took about four hours, the first two a lot faster than the last. Happily, when I asked if we could take a rest, he collapsed to a patch of grass near the CEMEX plant, across the highway from the New Davenport Inn.

I sat next to him. "Remind me to ask Suzanne how a cement factory ever got built on prime oceanfront property."

"It's been here a long time. Maybe they didn't care so much back then." He took the sleeping bag from me and stuffed it in his pack.

"Tell me, are we going someplace? Because I'm tired, and it's a long way to the next town."

"We're going someplace."

No other explanation. I still had my cell phone if I needed an ambulance for him or a sanatorium for myself. I sighed, and pointed to the inn. "Your dad and I came here one anniversary and stayed in one of the rooms upstairs."

Garrett showed no sign that he'd heard me.

"After dinner," I continued, "we took a walk up the street. The moon was full and the church there at the end was lit with amber lights. The lights were on inside one of those tiny houses, and maybe a window was open, but someone, a child I guess, was playing a scratchy record of 'Mary Had a Little Lamb,' of all things. When the song got over, they just played it again and again. We walked behind the church and found our way by moonlight to sit beside a little creek. Down there the stars shone like fire, and the frogs and crickets outsang the ocean. It was a strange, mystical, romantic night. One of my best memories, and here, I just gave it to you."

Garrett looked at me and almost smiled. Then he leaned back on his elbows against the grass.

"Once, Amber and I drove out to Monterey. We never told you or Dad or her folks, because it was Monday and we skipped classes. But Amber said she had something important to tell me, and I just had a feeling about it. So I told her to wait. We left at ten so there'd be no traffic, and we made good time. But then on Monterey Road, we got behind this white-haired old farmer with a big hat, in a little truck going twenty miles an hour. There was no passing, so we were stuck. I was going crazy, but Amber started laughing. We started talking to this old man. He couldn't hear us, but we'd pass an asparagus stand and say, 'Wouldn't you *please* like to pull over for some asparagus? Apricots? Maybe some strawberries?' Finally the road widened and I got around him. I took Amber to the Bay Aquarium. I paid a lot of money for those tickets, but she wouldn't look at the kelp forest, she wouldn't touch the bat ray in the little pond. She wouldn't do anything till she'd said what she wanted to say. So I took her out to the other side, to that big deck area where you can see the whole Monterey Bay. And she told me. She was pregnant." He wiped the tears from his eyes, and looked away. "That's my best memory."

Finally we were getting somewhere. I laid both hands on his arm. "What a beautiful memory. And how wonderful you were to her. I'm so sorry, sweetheart, that she lost that baby."

He shook his head. "She didn't."

"Didn't what?"

"She didn't lose it, Mom. She had an abortion."

He stood, and I meant to follow, but I couldn't move.

"Wait here," he said. "I'm going to get us some food." He let a car pass, then crossed the road.

I felt my mind detach and drop straight into limbo.

An abortion. Suzanne and I had practically named that baby. It was real; it *mattered* to us! And not just to us, but to Amber as well. At least, she seemed happy. She took Suzanne and me to lunch in Los Gatos, she positively *glowed* when she gave us the news. And when it was over, when she returned early from her trip to Hawaii and fell into her mother's arms, she looked pale and bewildered, like a young woman who'd miscarried her baby. No one was surprised that she and Garrett broke up. Terribly sad, but tragedies do things to couples, especially young ones.

An abortion.

Garrett returned with a loaf of stale bread he'd begged from the back door of the restaurant.

"No, thank you," I said.

He tore off a piece and stuffed the rest in his pack. I stood, and we started to walk.

"Did you know, Garrett?"

"Not till after."

"But why did she do it?"

"Because her father told her … what were his words? Only a slut would have a baby out of wedlock. We told him we'd get married, but he just kept at it. He said she'd be like people who did nothing with their lives, she'd be like people with no money. People like me, maybe, right?"

"Charlie." I went dizzy at the realization. "I don't know why I'm surprised. You should hear how he treated Suzanne."

"I know how he treated Suzanne. It's not news."

"Was I really that stupid? Anyway, I am so glad your father didn't know—"

"He *did* know, Mom!" Garrett erupted. "Who do you think paid for it?"

"No, he did not! He'd never—"

"He did."

"In the first place, Charlie would have—"

"No. He said Amber was on her own. She got herself into this mess, and she could …" He hit his head with a fist and wept. "It wasn't a mess. It was our baby."

I staggered further off the road and collapsed. Garrett followed.

"Breathe, Mom."

I tried.

"*Breathe.*"

I put my hand on my abdomen the way Russ had done and pushed a breath slow against it, then held for a few counts. After several moments, when I was all right, I dropped my head to my hands. "Why would he, Garrett?"

"He said he was thinking of me and Amber. Our futures.

"Your futures?"

"He wanted us to be free to live our own lives. The logic sucks, I know. He didn't want us making the same mistake the two of you ... The mistake you made when you had me."

CHAPTER 36

I don't remember walking. I don't know how far we went, or how long, or what went through my mind. I don't even know if we spoke to each other. At some point it was evening. A fading sun lay near the rim of a colorless sky. We turned off the road and climbed our way down the rocks to the beach.

I stared out to sea and wondered if I'd ever understood my life at all.

"Joseph!" Garrett cupped a hand and called again. "Joe!"

I turned and looked. "There's no one out there."

"He'll be here."

"Who?"

"A friend I met a few months ago."

He dropped his pack and crossed the beach to a pile of driftwood. I found a rock and sat down to rest. The water brushed ashore in white ripples that traced fine little trees in the sand when they receded.

I remembered Larry's last letter, the word *forgive* once, twice, and again, and began to guess at the parts I couldn't read. But the very word made me feel too tired to live.

"Mom!" Garrett called. "Come here!"

I took a deep breath, and forced my legs to stand, then trudged across the beach. "What is it?"

He didn't have to answer. When I drew near I saw that the pile of driftwood was not a pile, but a small structure, arranged something like a log cabin, with weathered branches stacked first one way, and then another to form a square, with longer pieces laid side by side on top for a roof. One end was left open with a metal oil lamp hung to the side. Shells and bits of glass had been threaded on twine and hung from the crossbeam to form a sort of curtain over the door.

"Your Joseph did this?"

"Look inside."

"Maybe I shouldn't."

"No, look."

I knelt, and moved the curtain aside. The interior was lined, floor, ceiling, and walls, with a canvas that admitted the yellow light of the sunset but little wind. A small mattress was made up with a blue cover, and a book lay open, pages down, on the floor. I leaned in to see what he was reading: Henri Nouwen, *The Way of the Heart.*

I sat back on my heels.

"What?" Garrett smiled.

"Nothing." I moved forward for another look. A lemon crate served as a low table, with a beer bottle holding wildflowers. Old silver, cast-off plates.

I stood and brushed the sand from my knees.

"Wait till you meet Joseph."

I glimpsed in Garrett's eyes a look of esteem that his father had only wept for in his last days, and if I could possibly feel sadder, I did in that moment.

We walked together to the ocean. I slipped my shoes off to let the advancing water rush over my feet, then retreat to leave me sinking in sand. "This Joseph is homeless?"

"He'd tell you he's not." Garrett pulled off his shoes and rolled up his pant legs. His feet were dark with grime like coal dust, but when he stepped in beside me, they washed white and bony as they'd been when he was a child.

"You weren't a mistake." I spoke the words out to sea.

"I shouldn't even have told you."

"You must have been so tired of keeping it to yourself."

He nodded.

"There are reasons to preserve sex for marriage, Garrett, and I won't say they aren't good reasons. The promise you make has to do with honoring a person for being more than just a piece of merchandise you can choose or discard. It was part of your dad's beliefs, and mine, and when we failed ... Well. We no longer qualified to go on the mission field, which was our dream. But you ..." I wept. "You did matter. You were *not* a mistake."

I pressed a hand to my throat. Every breath hurt.

A rush of water wrapped itself around our ankles and pulled back to leave a scatter of bubbles at our feet. A flock of sandpipers rushed in a distance away, then turned as one to scuttle inland when we started to walk.

"It's like the prodigal son. When he came back, he thought his father would punish him, but instead he put a ring on his finger, and threw a party. You were grace, Garrett. You were the ring on my finger."

He launched into a spate of coughing so violent it bent him double.

"You're getting so sick."

"Don't worry."

"I can't help worrying. Garrett ..." I took a breath and made myself ask the question: "Did you ... When you disappeared, did you want to die?"

He gave me a long look. I felt sure he was putting together some of what I'd done to find that out, but I forced myself not to flinch. I held his gaze.

"No," he said at last. "I felt pretty bad then. I felt terrible. But I'll be okay, Mom. I want to live."

"Hey! Ho!" The call came from overhead. I looked, and there on a high rock, silhouetted against the red sky, stood the figure of a man with one arm raised.

"Barnacle Joe!" Garrett called out to him.

The man waved both arms, rushed down the trail, and ran barefoot across the sand. He must have been sixty at least, or older. He had a thick, long nose, and behind it gathered what seemed like a large face hung from small bones. Tobacco-gray whiskers curled over his lip and around his chin, stone gray hair curled out from his watch cap and up over the sockets of his eyes.

"Garrett? Is that you?"

Garrett opened his arms, and Joseph ran into them, rocked into the hug, then backed away. "Cripes, kid, you stink!"

Garrett coughed.

"Are you sick? What's wrong with you?"

He continued to cough, and pointed my direction. "Joseph, this is my mother."

The man turned to me and clapped his knobby fingers over his heart. "I'm so sorry. I'm going blind. My name is Joseph."

"Roberta." I held out a hand.

He took it in both of his and almost bowed. "I'm honored. Have you been waiting long?"

I shook my head. "Garrett showed me your little house. I hope you don't mind. It's a work of art."

He smiled, and two of the folds in his face turned to dimples. "You must stay for dinner."

Garrett needed to eat, but I didn't know how to answer. I'd seen a plastic jug of water in his hut but no food.

He pulled a woven shoulder bag from around his neck, and began to relate to Garrett his good fortune in short, emphatic phrases. "Since you saw me last, I've found a church that will let me in. And that church has a lady who owns a health-food store. She's thirty-four, and she's beautiful, married, but I think she likes me, because she gives me food. Good food. Except that she's a vegetarian. But her husband is not, and when she's not looking, he slips me things, like hamburger and hot dogs and …" He pulled a package from his bag. "The occasional slab of beef. I've got an Italian stew in my bag that just needs that little extra umph, and it won't take any time. Garrett, why don't you help me start the fire?"

He dropped to his knees, crawled into his hovel, and returned with a skillet and a knife. Before long he'd propped the skillet over the fire with stones, and sliced the steak into stew meat.

While it cooked, he turned to Garrett. "Tell me."

"Just a little cough."

"Nooo. It might have been just a little cough yesterday. You've got your mother with you, who must have nursed you through a thousand coughs big and little. Have you done all that she told you to do?"

Garrett didn't answer.

"And I'll bet you didn't drive her out to see me in your car, did you? What are you doing to your mother?"

"She invited herself."

Joseph glowered at him, and Garrett started to cough.

"And have you asked the God in whom you live and breathe to make you well?"

"You're the preacher, Joseph. You pray."

"You've got an attitude. He doesn't mind an honest attitude, but He hates a cheap shot." Joseph stood, and placed his hands on Garrett's shoulders. He lifted his head as if he were going to pray, but only stood with his eyes closed for an endless time. And swayed like kelp.

At last he spoke, so quietly I almost didn't hear it over the sound of the surf.

"God in heaven, You know."

CHAPTER 37

Joseph insisted Garrett sleep in the hut, but he also insisted he bathe himself before he laid one toe on his nice clean bed. So this is how it worked: Joseph heated a pot of water over the fire, then handed Garrett a washcloth and a bar of soap. Then he and I stood with our backs to the ocean and held Garrett's blanket up to give him privacy and to shield him, as much as possible, from the wind. Then Garrett stood near the fire and washed.

Once he went to bed, Joseph handed me a cup of coffee and sat with me by the fire. He pulled out a tin whistle, a child's toy, and began to play—a hymn, I think. A song I couldn't place. When my cup was empty, he stopped playing. Something about his smile made me feel that I must be transparent. I needed to make conversation. "You read Henri Nouwen."

"Yes. Have you read him?"

"Some. My husband and I used to read together, books like from Thomas Merton."

He nodded. "A good writer. There's a new fellow named Brennan Manning I like very much too. Ever read *Ruthless Trust?*"

"You're quite the reader."

"I used to teach seminary."

I nearly dropped my cup. He took it from me and filled it with coffee.

"You did?"

"Place nearby named Bethel Theological."

"But why? I mean, there are programs, you don't have to be—"

"No, I don't have to be. I have Social Security, and a small retirement. This is something I chose to do."

"Why? It must be miserable sometimes. Not so much on a night like this. But if it rains, or if a storm kicks up. What would happen to your hut?"

"Even a little storm can blow it apart. Once the tide came in higher than I expected, and my house washed out to sea."

"Joseph! If you'd been sleeping—"

"I was sleeping."

"What did you do?"

"I moved very fast." He pointed up the hill.

"But what about your house?"

"I built another."

"That can't be good for your health."

"Health is not all that counts, Roberta. People talk all the time about living longer, but they never talk about living wider. This is my calling."

Living wider. I liked that. In an odd way, I began to feel proud of my son for liking Joseph so much.

"When I started getting old," he continued, "I left the seminary to lead a small church. They asked, and I said yes. I wanted to pastor a sweet group of people, sort of my reward for a life well lived. I'd spent years telling students how to do a good job at preaching and

ministering, and I was ready. I jumped in and got a little youth group
going, some social events for the seniors. Did some nice things for
the ladies' group, sent them off to tea once a month, and the men
had pancakes. My sermons were good too, you can be sure. But the
best thing I did for that church, the very best thing was to start a
Wednesday-night workshop on how to build a wonderful marriage.
This was something I really knew about, because Sherry and I had
been married for thirty-five years. Sherry taught the class with me,
and the young couples were all coming. We were changing lives, we
two.

"And then one night—it was a Tuesday night—Sherry told me
she wanted a divorce." He sipped his coffee. "Seems a fellow she'd
had an affair with six years prior had finally left his wife. I'd never
known he existed."

"Oh, Joseph." I downed the last of my coffee, unsure I wanted
any more of his story. I had my own sorrows to process that night.

"Furthermore, I learned that the church finances were not so
well off as I'd thought—some decisions she'd made without my
knowledge—and my congregation did not love me so well as I
believed it did, once word got around about the mess I'd made
of things. Of course, I paid the deficit out of my own resources,
which was no easy matter when you consider the divorce settle-
ment divided my resources in half. But the damage was done."

He poured me another cup of coffee.

"All this to explain how I found myself with no wife, no money,
and no reputation. Suddenly I didn't know who I was. Which was
strange because all those years I had taught that we are beloved children of God, and nothing else. But when I wasn't a professor or a

pastor, when I wasn't happily married and financially secure, I found
I no longer felt like God's little boy. I felt like highway litter, wind-
slapped against some bit of God's creation, where I didn't belong. All
my props—well, almost all my props were gone. I did have two left.
I had a house, and a television, and I liked to watch Oprah, and I
didn't mind David Letterman.

"All my adult life I'd prayed the erudite kinds of prayers that
reflect study and depth of understanding. But the kind of prayers
that start down where it's just me, not my education or my job or
my accomplishments, but the broken, scared, real me that can't even
speak in God's presence, can barely even breathe. That kind of prayer
was always devilish hard to pray."

Joseph took the lid off the coffeepot and lifted out the inner basket to dump the grounds in the fire. Was he going to make another
pot? Already I doubted I would sleep at all that night.

"So what do you think, Roberta? What does a man do when he's
down to his last two props?" Joseph leaned forward, lifted his eyebrows, and grinned. "He kicks them out, and has done with them."
He reached his arm toward something behind me and indicated I
should give it to him. I looked, then handed him the plastic con-
tainer of Folgers. "No," he said. "I think we've had enough coffee
for tonight. The blanket, please. Now tell me, how close are you to
your son?"

What to say? "Um, p-pretty close. Until just recently. When he
was younger—"

"Because that bed in there is small, but you'd be better off inside
the hut. Can you …?"

"Oh. Yes. I think that will be fine. But what about you?"

He held up the corner of the blanket. "My house has blown away many times, Roberta."

When I crawled in beside Garrett, he rolled in his sleep to make room. His body temperature was as warm as a furnace, and before long I slipped my leg out from the covers into the cool air.

The labored sound of his breathing and the pounding of the surf throbbed into my mind like tremors and canceled all but wordless images: Garrett, homeless at the soup kitchen door, begging for a piece of bread. Amber's stunned expression when she returned from Hawaii. Larry and me in that photograph, strangely young and just starting anew.

⁓

I didn't want to wake up. I buried my face in the pillow and caught the foreign scent that must have been Joseph's. His voice, and Garrett's, carried in from outside. The canvas filtered a white light that suggested midmorning. At some point I would have to join the two men.

In a dream, I'd sat across a table from Amber, while Larry stood, disregarded, in the darkness behind.

"Was it a boy or a girl?" I asked.

"I don't know." Amber stared at the table.

"A girl," Larry pled from the shadows. "Angeline."

Amber lifted a skeletal arm to push the hair from her face. "They didn't say."

I wanted to go back and sit Larry down at that table. I wanted to ask him why. But it doesn't work that way. You never can plan your dreams. I sat up and straightened my clothes, neatened the bed, then crawled out through the shell curtain. And looked into the face of my son. Clean shaven, bare chested, and halfway through his haircut.

"Garrett!" I sat in the sand and looked up at him, as though he were an apparition.

"Good morning!" Joseph moved the scissors to the side in classic barber style, and smiled over Garrett's shoulder.

"You look beautiful," I said. "Really beautiful."

"You mean him, or me?" asked Joseph.

"Thanks. I think." Garrett smiled.

"How do you feel?"

"Better." And to prove it, he took a full breath and let it out.

"Hold still." Joseph snipped a pinch of hair and stuffed it in a plastic bag that hung from his belt loop.

"I just haven't seen your face in so long. It's just ..." *Beautiful* was the word, but he wouldn't want to hear it a third time. "I'm so glad you're better."

"You slept?"

I shrugged. It had taken me hours, long, tormented hours to drift off. "You?"

He nodded.

Joseph pulled the scissors away. "Maybe you two would like to talk and we'll just finish the haircut later."

I almost laughed. Garrett's hair had grown long and bushy, and Joseph had cut it short up the back and over the ears. "He looks like a poodle."

Joseph touched Garrett's chin, gave it a lift, and continued cutting. Garrett grew shy under my scrutiny, but I absorbed every twitch of his lip, every lift of his brow, and marveled at the transfiguration. The angel Gabriel would have looked less … beautiful.

When he finished the haircut, Joseph served up coffee and pulled a foil bundle from the campfire. He unwrapped a loaf of bread, and the smell of hot cinnamon burst out with the steam.

Garrett nudged his arm. "Your girlfriend's a baker?"

Joseph tore off a piece and handed it to him. "You've never tasted cinnamon bread like this."

Oh, but I'd smelled it. I quelled the sudden thought of my witch and her baby, but not without tears.

After breakfast, Joseph stood and picked up his shoulder pouch. "I've got some errands to run. Will you two be all right here?" We nodded, and he left.

"Where's he going?" I asked. "Is there a town nearby?"

"Not really, but people know him. He hitches rides. You all right?"

I nodded.

"What do you think that is out there?" Garrett pointed out to sea.

I squinted till I saw what he meant: A distance out, the swells had turned an odd silty color. "I don't know. Kelp maybe."

⌣

Joseph returned bearing gifts. A pair of linen pants and a silk-blend sweater for me. Jeans and a cotton sweater for Garrett. All used, but clean and comfortable and not too precious for the homeless life. I crawled into the hut to change out of my gray suit, which had not lived the life it was promised at the mall. When I reemerged, Garrett had already added his old clothes to the campfire. Where had he gone? I glanced up and down the beach.

"He's behind that rock, exploring the tide pools. Thinking, probably. Maybe even praying."

"Praying, well." I rubbed my neck. "His dad and I always took him to church, but I don't think he's been in a while. And, well, he may have trouble swallowing anything we ever told him."

"He may."

"He's talked to you?"

"We've talked."

I sat beside Joseph near the fire.

"I brought you one more thing. In case you get cold." He pulled from his pouch a wool shawl in an intricate cream and charcoal paisley. Exquisite.

"Joseph. How could a wife ever leave you?"

Each fold of his face flushed the color of refined abashment. "Well. She taught me that clothes can make a woman feel better."

I wrapped the shawl around my shoulders. "We're not as different as you may think. I've lived the past few months in a gardener's shed. By choice."

"Tell me."

I told him everything, without ever meaning to. I started with Larry's illness and our second wedding, the fire after the funeral and the subsequent fires. I related my trial and failure at the consecrated life in my mountain hovel. I told how I'd lost and then found Garrett—twice.

I meant to leave it there, but as I spoke, the tension in my back began to release, and something less nameable went with it. I told him about India and baby Estelle, off someplace with a man who was not good for his wife, and definitely not good for them.

I told him about my husband, who I'd thought was so good for me. I certainly didn't mean to tell him that.

I told him about my visions, and the times in which they occurred.

"They were silly things, Joseph. I have no idea what they meant. But when they happened, the thing is that I felt … I felt that someone was there with me, someone more amazing than I can describe. And in that presence, I felt such comfort. Like everything was all right, really. Really all right. And I felt that I was called to something." I ducked my head. "Stupid."

Joseph poked a stick in the fire. "You are called."

I looked up.

"The proof is not in the visions. Those may have been just the little presents you bring to a hospital bed. The proof of your calling is in the pain."

"The pain."

"There's something holy about sorrow, Roberta. That's why no one wants to read a story that has none. If your story is one of unbroken happiness and success, then it's all about you. But if it involves suffering and anguish and wrestling with angels, then it's everyone's story, and it's God's story. The holy ground Moses walked on was the place of the burning bush. Jesus' resurrection came only after He was crucified and dead, and He said up front that you have to lose your life to save it. Blessed are the broken and poor, blessed are they that mourn. Your greatest gift, the greatest proof of His love, is in your pain."

Oh, now how I regretted ever talking so much to this stranger. I cringed to cry in front of him, but the flood broke through before I could stop it. "I don't want this gift. I don't know what to do with it."

Joseph took my hand in his. "Use it for a path." He smiled as if he'd just told me the greatest secret of all time. "The next time you pray I want you to follow that pain down to the part of your soul that hurts, where it is only you, with no props, just your fears and mixed motives and shame, where it's only Roberta. That's where you'll find that presence you felt. He's been there waiting all along. He's given you a way in to Himself."

CHAPTER 38

They never warn you before you have a child how much you will love him.

The first hour I ever spent alone with Garrett, after he was born, came later than I'd imagined it would. Larry's parents took the sleeper couch, and friends dropped by with gifts. Even Larry's barber, Mark Goldstein, came and raised his voice over the baby's cries, to relate a Jewish tradition, that an angel enters the womb and whispers into a baby's ear all the wisdom there is in the universe. But then, just before the baby is born, the angel touches him between his nose and lip to leave a tiny groove, and when the angel does this, the baby forgets all he has learned.

"Why would he do that?" someone demanded.

"Lovely story," said someone else.

"Well, snookums," cooed Larry's mother, "I see some wisdom slipping out right now." She dabbed Garrett's nose with the corner of his blanket.

It was maybe four or five days before the chatter and advice, the baby talk in grown-up voices, the casseroles and the cases of Cokes and endless pots of coffee all went away and left me in a quiet living room, on the sofa with my baby.

I can still hear the moment. The dripping of the faucet in the kitchen. The gossamer sound of his milk-scented breath. I still see the shimmer of his eyelids like petals, the worried crease in his downy brow, the tiny peak his lip formed just under that groove where the wisdom slipped out. Could it be that the peak had kept some of it in? He certainly looked wise in that moment.

It struck me exactly then—the wonder and the fearsome power of all the love I had for this child. All I would do to protect him.

The very next moment, terror set in. Because I realized how much there was to protect him from. I saw it all in a flash: the ill-intentioned strangers. The well-intentioned but stupid strangers. The day he would walk out of my reach. The day he would go to school. The day he would go away. I knew with what fierce primordial fury I would protect my son. But I didn't know if it would be enough. It's a terrifying thing, loving a child. No one ever tells you.

But neither do they tell you the peace he can bring, just by a touch, by the scent of his hair, just by being near, and well.

I spent the day on Joseph's beach with my boy. Any stray thoughts of Larry or anyone else, I pushed aside. There were tide pools to explore. There was a Frisbee to throw back and forth. There were meaningless conversations about the business practices of Wal-Mart and Starbucks Coffee. If a question arose in my mind as to Garrett's future or the state of his soul, I tabled it for another day.

Only once did things threaten to turn serious.

"Look at that water," I said, and pointed out to the murky patch we'd noticed that morning. It had spread and turned darker, almost a red color. "Are there sharks here or something?"

"Dun-ta dun-ta …"

"No, really. It looks like blood. Maybe some animal …?"

"It would have to be a whale. It's pretty big."

"I guess we'd know if a whale were in trouble. Wouldn't we?"

"I'm sure. Maybe some prophet has laid his staff on the water like Moses. You think?"

"I'm sure that's it."

Dinner was flax potato chowder with tofu, and gas-station hot dogs—compliments of guess who, and guess who. Could this marriage be saved?

"How do they get along?" I asked.

Joseph shrugged. "What do I know about marriage?"

What did I know about anything? My son sat across from me, enjoying his meal. It had been a good day, and for the moment, that was all I wanted to know.

I gazed out at the ocean. "I've never seen it more beautiful," I whispered. And truly, in all my life, I hadn't. The sky was a wild persimmon red and the sun spilled its light across the water like molten gold.

But it was the surf that caught my eye. Near shore it still glistened a gemlike blue that played games with the sunlight when the water swelled and curled over to poured glass.

Garrett barely gave it a glance. Joseph smiled at me, then bit into his hot dog.

The last bit of sun sank beneath the horizon as we drank our coffee, and the ocean began to draw my attention in earnest. Because the evening had grown quite dark. But the water had not.

A large wave crested and collapsed, and when it broke, I saw—I *thought* I saw—a blue shimmer in the foam.

"Joseph."

"Hmm?"

"Out there."

Garrett had started to look now, and a trio of waves, one behind the other, now glowed with a distinct blue light.

"What is that?" Garrett pointed. Only then did I know I wasn't seeing things.

"It's a red tide." Joseph sipped his coffee.

"It's blue," said Garrett.

Something clicked in my mind. "Is that the blood we saw?"

"Not blood. It's an algal bloom, luminescent algae that multiplies under the right conditions. It looks kind of red in daylight, but when it's disturbed, it glows. You only see the glow at night. Some kinds of algae are poisonous, but this kind is fairly harmless. I've been hearing about it for days, on the radio when I hitch rides. I wanted it to be a surprise."

Much more than a surprise, it was magical. I stared for timeless minutes before it crossed my mind to draw close. I got up, and we walked within twenty feet of the breakers. For long quiet moments we stood there, reverent before a great luminous mystery.

Garrett was the first to step closer, and when he set foot on the sand left wet by the surf, a broad disk of light spread under his foot. "Whoa," he said, and I laughed.

He took a second step, and another disk of light appeared. I tried it myself. Each step I took got the same star attention. Garrett skipped an awkward, wide-legged dance step, and Joseph began to laugh, and the next moment, the two of them joined hands and did a circle swing, kicking up their feet, spraying sparks of light behind them.

Joseph produced his tin whistle, and we all danced together for maybe half an hour. All the steps were lively flicks of the feet, meant to scatter stars in our wake. We danced our own versions of the tarantella, the flamenco, the boogaloo, the bunny hop. We grabbed fistfuls of sand and tossed them in the air to throw stars back into the sky.

When we grew tired, I approached the water and dipped my hand in, to pour it out like … well, liquid light.

I turned back to the two men, and found that Joseph had splashed water in his beard, and both of them had run wet hands through their hair.

You can imagine. For just a moment, they were angels and clowns and twinkling faces of wonder.

———

That night while Garrett slept, I lifted the corner of the tarp that hung on the wall to peer at the continuing miracle just outside. I couldn't close my eyes.

The campfire had dimmed, which must mean that Joseph was asleep. It crossed my mind that I didn't have to sleep just yet. I wasn't tired. I slipped from the bed and crawled outside.

When I reached the shore, I strolled along the waves, noting the striations of lambent blue that stretched far out to sea. Moses may have turned water to blood, but he'd never turned it to light. An "algal bloom." Was this a miracle, or biology? And wouldn't that have made for a fine discussion with—ooh—my husband?

Something tumbled in my mind, and every sorrow I'd postponed throughout the day came upon me and demanded its due.

I missed him. I felt so terribly lonely.

And he had paid to have them kill Garrett's child. Not a tragic miscarriage, but an abortion, a tragedy of his own making. Our *grandchild.*

Angeline, perhaps? A guess was better than nothing; a name better than no name.

But I couldn't call Larry back to that table in my dream and ask him why. I couldn't tell him that I hated him for doing it. And he couldn't pull me into his arms and tell me it didn't really happen the way I thought, that he would never do such a thing. He couldn't wipe it all away, so we could go back to the way we were. There was no going back. And now I couldn't even grieve my husband with a heart of unmingled love.

My breath came slow and steady. This was not the panic of sudden shock. This was the eternal ache of slow realization. Which was infinitely worse.

Joseph said that my pain was a gift, a path. In desperation, I closed my eyes, and tried to follow. But it did burn. I balked at the pain.

Nothing but me, Joseph had said. The real me, the broken me, the part that hurts.

I tried again, and this time it seemed that something grew quiet, and then quieter. I found myself in a dark place, but it was a warm darkness, like a tented blanket, like a conversation in bed. I found it easy to present myself, not as the happy wife, the good mother. Not as a nun or even a devout. I was not and never would be confident and competent. I was only me.

None of this happened in words. It was something I knew by touch.

And someone was there. A peace settled over me, and I came to understand that all was truly well. Not that everything would change at once. In the morning I would both rage at my husband and miss his touch. I would worry what would become of Garrett and everyone else I loved. In the morning, nothing would be solved. Not yet. Not for a long time.

But that was all right.

"I love You." I think I whispered the words. I opened my eyes, and looked out at the miracle before me. "I love You, love You," I said, and the luminous water seemed to murmur in reply.

I stepped closer and watched the waves break into blue light. I glanced back toward the hovel, where the fire glowed in red embers, and wondered. If I stepped just a little further around the rock, the embers disappeared from view.

The water was cold. It was a stupid idea. And an irresistible one. I stripped off my clothes and waded in.

The first few steps were agony. If I was to do this, I would have to move quickly, quicker than I'd thought. I ran several steps, dove in, and turned rigid from the shock. But I was immersed in this miracle, floating, rising, and falling with the rush of it. I lifted my hand before my eyes, and it trailed light like the hand of an angel.

I needed air, and I was ice cold. I found the sand with my feet and stood. The water streamed from me, and when I walked ashore, quaking, I looked down to see that I twinkled, over every constricted pore, with blue stars.

I used my hands to brush the water from my skin, then patted dry with my shawl, pulled my clothes on, returned to the hut, and crawled in.

Garrett's mouth was open, I could tell the by sound of his breathing. I crawled in beside him. He lay curled to his side, with his head tilted back against the pillow, the way he'd slept as a child. He smelled like my son, since his bath and haircut. I turned to my side and hovered over him as I'd so often done, to brush the hair from his face, to kiss his forehead, to shield him from harm. He sighed, and I laid my head next to his, and slept.

CHAPTER 39

A noise woke me. I didn't know if it was real or part of my dream. I opened my eyes.

And heard nothing. I rolled over and raised the tarp. It was the violet hour of dawn, but the light was still there in the water, though so dim it could almost have been my imagination. My newly baptized imagination. Comforted, I dropped the tarp.

I heard another noise, like a footstep. Joseph? I took in a breath to whisper, but stopped when I heard a liquid sound close to my ear.

And smelled gasoline.

"Garrett!"

He stirred, but that was not good enough. *"Garrett!"*

He sprang forward to sitting. "What?"

Outside I heard Joseph's voice in a long bellow.

I crawled backward out the door. "Fire, Garrett, get out!"

He started to crawl for the door, and I heard a whoosh sound. A red flame cut a hole in the tarp behind him. I fell back out of Garrett's way, just in time to see the entire hovel flare up like a bonfire.

Something moved to my left and I turned. Joseph knelt astraddle another man. I saw two legs and a pair of boots. The man bent one knee and pushed to send Joseph tumbling, then scrambled to his feet.

"Darnell!" Garrett rushed him like a quarterback. Darnell beat with his arms but Garrett grabbed his wrists. The two pressed into each other like bucks with locked horns.

Joseph stood and plowed into Darnell's side, and he went down, kicking and twisting. I got to my feet and ran to join the pile. I lay over the top of our attacker, and the three of us spread ourselves like cords to hold him still.

Joseph reached an arm and snagged his blanket with the tips of his fingers. Somehow, by benefit of arm twisting and rolling, and the sheer weight of three people, we rolled Darnell up in that blanket. Then while Garrett and Joseph continued to hold him, I retrieved my purse from Garrett's pack and found my cell phone.

When the police arrived, the hovel lay in embers, and the waves washed in with a last glimmer of light.

CHAPTER 40

My cell phone said I had twenty-seven missed calls. All from Suzanne. I braced for the worst and dialed.

"Bertie! What happened? I've been trying and trying to call. I'm watching the news right now, and they've caught the arsonist—"

"I know."

"—in Santa Cruz! Do you know how worried I've been? You said you'd call."

"I'm sorry. I've been preoccupied with—"

"It's not Garrett, Bertie."

"Well, yes, with Garrett. We had some things to talk about—"

"No, I mean the arsonist. It's not Garrett."

"I know it's not Garrett."

"Of course it isn't. But still, I've been so—where are you? You said you'd call."

"I'm sorry. Garrett and I had to talk through some things, and I didn't want …" Her interference was what I didn't want, but there was no good in saying so now.

She sighed. "Anyway, I've been calling all the motels. I even called the homeless shelters, I was that crazy. Where did you stay?"

"We found a little place by the beach."

"Good for you. Where is it? Can I pick you up?"

"Oh, Suzy, are you sure you want to drive out here?"

"I'm already out here. Still at Amber's."

"Still? Since I saw you last? I thought you were swamped at work."

"I am. I made some calls. The agents are going to cover for me where they can, and I hate to think what will be left of my job when I get back, but ... Well. She's my little girl. You know?"

Yes. I knew. "Why not come for dinner? We'll cook."

"That sounds like heaven. But I'm bringing her with me."

"Oh. Do you think she'll want to see Garrett?" Did I think Garrett would want to see her?

"I think we both need to get out. Roger is just beside himself. She'll look you in the eye, crying, saying she wants this baby, but ... Bertie, I bring her just an apple, and I sit with her to make her eat it. I stand at the door when she goes to the bathroom. Once Roger goes to work, I don't dare leave her for a second."

"Oh, Suzy. Of course, bring her. But it's a bit of a drive. Are you up for one?"

"Dying for one. But what drive? You were on foot."

"I'll need you to pick us up some things."

"Let me grab a pen."

I asked her to bring some steaks, some cherry tomatoes and bell peppers, a pound of coffee ... and a mattress.

"A mattress?"

"Just a top mattress, twin size. We'll pay you back. Get some sheets and a pillow and blanket. Oh, something like a fruit crate, maybe a plastic bin? And some canvas tarps, and some twine. And some used plates and bowls. They'll all fit in the back of your Escalade, won't they?"

"Yes …"

"Can you stop at the bookstore? Pick up a Bible. And *The Way of the Heart* by Henri Nouwen. In fact, pick up two of those."

———

You build a beach hovel around the mattress so you don't have to fit it through the door. Just one of many shards of wisdom I gleaned from Joseph during our stay. When the ordeal was over he cheerfully set to work as though he'd rebuilt his home a thousand times before. He showed us where to pile the debris for later removal, how to choose the best driftwood for building.

Garrett was beside himself, pacing the beach like he had someplace to go. "You could have been killed, both of you!"

"All three of us," said Joseph. "But we weren't."

"And what if the police come and tell you to move on?"

"If they evict me from my home?" Joseph clutched his chest, then grinned. "I'll think of something."

"It was my fault. I should have warned you. Did you tell someone in town we were here?"

"What's it matter? That kid's not going to set any more fires. If that's your doing, then you're a hero."

"They'll want me to testify. They'll find out I gave him the security code!" He kicked the charred remains of Joseph's bed.

"You'll recall, yours wasn't the only house he burned, and you didn't give him all the codes. And as to your dire revelation, there's no law against stupidity. Now, why don't you help me carry that mat-tress up to the trash. Put yourself to use."

Later, he took Garrett for a walk along the beach, to talk a bit more sense into him. I watched them go and thought again how Larry would have longed to have been the man beside his son right now.

I fetched his last letter from my purse, and climbed to the top of a high rock. The red tide was still out there, perhaps even bigger than before. The miracle wasn't over yet.

I felt so tired. It had been quite the morning. Quite the life.

When the police led Darnell up the hill to their car, he had on Garrett's denim jacket, I'd noticed. Actually it was Larry's jacket, one he'd worn while we were dating. But Garrett had dressed as a hippie one Halloween, so Larry had donated the coat, and I'd stitched a peace sign on the back.

Darnell was hardly older than my son, and he was in serious trouble. And somewhere, he had a mother. The poor woman.

Larry and I once thought we'd make the world a better place, a safer, more beautiful place. At least for someone. We finally settled for making a lovely little fortress for ourselves, complete with an alarm system and a security code. Which didn't hold, in the end.

I opened Larry's letter. I still couldn't make out most of it, but there it was. There was the word, right in the middle of the page, plain as if he'd typed it out for me:

Abortion.

I clenched my eyes, to shut it out. How many things had I cho-sen not to see?

I heard a noise beside me and turned to find Garrett just cresting the rock. I slapped the letter facedown on my lap.

"What are you doing?" he asked.

"I'm reading a letter."

"Oh. Something personal?" He stepped away, like he might climb back down the way he came.

"Ah, Garrett. Personal to us both." I turned the paper over, and patted the space beside me, motioning for him to sit. "Your father wrote letters while he was sick, and gave them to his lawyer to send to me, one per week after he died. So I wouldn't miss him ..." I looked skyward and took a deep breath to calm the tears. "So I wouldn't miss him so much. He was only able to write a few."

Garrett took the letter from my hands.

"This is his last," I said. "I can't make out most of it but he's writing about Amber's abortion."

Garrett choked, and brushed a tear from his face. "This is his handwriting?"

"He had tremors." I shrugged.

"How bad did it get?"

"Bad. He couldn't do anything for himself. He had to have a colostomy, and a feeding tube. He got terribly thin. He had a lot of mucous, so I would suction him out at night ... and ... maybe I didn't do it well enough." I choked on the words. "He got pneumonia, and he was too weak to fight."

Garrett passed a hand across his eyes. "I should have been there. But I couldn't look at him. What would I say? I was so ..." He clutched at his hair. "I wanted to scream at him, but it was too late for that. And I didn't want it to be too late. I couldn't watch him die, Mom. I'm so sorry."

"Oh, Garrett. Oh, sweetie." I wrapped my arms around him and pressed the bones of his shoulders to my lips. After a moment, I mumbled my own confession.

"I hardly talked to him myself, toward the end. He couldn't open his eyes, and he always looked like he was asleep. Maybe he was, half the time. But I knew he was in there, listening. So I'd say, 'Nice day today, honey. Would you like the curtain open? Let some sunshine in.' I must've sounded so patronizing, like one of those nurses who see a dozen like him every day. Not the woman who ... not like his wife." I pulled away and bit my thumbnail. "I thought there might be something in the letter, if I could read it."

Garrett held the paper up, and squinted. "'*Dear Bertie. Our days ... have ...*'" He peered closer. "Forgiveness. '*I need to ask forgiveness ... as many letters in CEO as in GOD.*'" Garrett grunted. "Sounds like Dad. This says '*executive decision,*' and this ..." For a moment he couldn't finish the sentence. "This says you would have loved your grandchild; it would have been five years old." He folded the letter and gave it to me. "He wants us to forgive him."

What could I say to that?

After a moment, Garrett looked away. "When I went to Darnell about the fire, he said, well, a lot of stupid stuff. But he called me a 'poor little rich homeless boy.' Because I have a choice. I can just go home. I mean, I could, before—"

"Garrett, I don't think it's any of Darnell's business why you're doing this."

"It's just, I can't see taking Dad's money, not when I know what he used it for."

"For heaven's sake! Consider it my money, then. I helped along the way, and I was in on the decision to set it up for you."

He didn't answer.

"Garrett?"

"I don't want to spend my life so angry. I don't want to hate him. I don't know what to do."

"Neither do I. I wish I did."

He nodded. We gazed out at the red water that would shimmer like angels after dark. I remembered my prayer of the night before. "We don't have to figure it out today," I said.

"Yeah. That's what Joseph says."

Joseph again. How many parents was this man going to replace? I might be next, when I told Garrett that something *would* have to be faced, and within a few hours. "Garrett, I did something you might not like. Amber's coming to dinner tonight."

"Amber! Here? Why?"

"I invited Suzanne, not knowing she'd want to bring her along. She's pregnant, Garrett."

"Pregnant." He shook his head. "Well, good for her."

"Yeah, only there's a problem. She's not eating, and it's very serious. She could lose the baby."

Garrett ran both hands over his head. "I haven't seen her in a long time, Mom."

"It was stupid of me. I can call it off."

"She'll think I'm a homeless guy."

"You'll think she's anorexic."

"I'll think a lot of things. Why'd you and Suzanne have to stay friends?"

"Well. Because …"

"That was a joke."

I nudged him. "They're bringing a bed for Joseph."

"Ah, well, he needs a bed. Will you go home with Suzanne?"

"I don't know. Is that what you want?"

No answer.

"What will you do?"

"Help Joseph build his house."

"That will take a few hours."

"Do you think he …" Garrett swallowed. "Do you think Joseph's a good influence?"

"Of course, he's a fine man. But …" But what? I brushed tears from my eyes. "He doesn't have a phone."

"I could get a phone."

"How would you charge it?"

"They make a little hand-crank generator for cell phones. I'll use that."

"Really. So. Do you plan to use your inheritance to pay the bills, or are you going back to Vector?"

"At Vector they wanted me to be Larry Denys Junior. I'll think of something else, Mom. For now, I'll use a little of my inheritance to pay the phone bill."

"I have another confession. When I asked Suzanne to pick up some things for Joseph and for our dinner, I told her you'd pay her back."

"*I'd* pay her back?" He pushed my shoulder. "Why me?"

"Because I don't have much money."

"Neither do I."

"No, I mean I don't have any. I gave most of my investments away."

"Away?"

"To charity. I left myself a small pension."

"Why?"

"Because when I was young, I thought I'd be poor and devout, like Saint Francis of Assisi, or Teresa of Ávila."

"No kidding. Bertie of Saratoga."

"Santa Cruz."

"Right, Santa Cruz."

"After your father died, I thought I'd give it a try."

"A try. You gave your money away, that's not a try."

"It changes everything."

"It would."

"Do you remember our property in the mountains? There was a little shed."

He grimaced, like he was getting a headache.

"Some neighbors helped me put a new roof on, so it's fine now. It's where I live."

"You're going back there?"

"Yes."

He shook his head.

"I don't think I've ever surprised you before, Garrett. It's kind of fun."

"You surprised me when you slept on the ground in my sleeping bag."

"The ground was better than a concrete floor."

"You've been sleeping on concrete?"

"I wouldn't recommend it."

"What if I buy you a mattress too?"

"I might just let you."

"Tell me this. What's so different about your life, and the homeless life?"

"Well. For one, I have a phone."

"I'll get a phone."

"And I'm fifty. I don't have my whole life ahead—"

"You don't?"

"Not as much."

"If I ..." He rubbed his chin. "If I let most of the money sit for now, and if I stay with Joseph, living like you, for at least a few months, wouldn't I still have a lot of my life left over?"

"Like me." I smiled. "Would you be a devout?"

"Maybe. I might be a devout."

"You'll call sometimes?"

"Yes. I will call."

"And take baths."

"Once in a while."

"Because the water's right there."

"It is."

"And would it be too much for you to own a car?"

"I think it would be too much."

"Okay. Fine. But you'll come to my place for dinner. I plan to cook wonderful dinners. I'll pick you up."

"Next Friday?"

"Deal. Now, tell me about this windup charger."

⌒

"So," said Suzanne. "Where are you staying?" Her voice cheery, modulated. So tight it squeaked.

We stood beside her car looking down on Joseph's beach. The wind whistled through a hole in a rock someplace. She scanned right and left; we could see for miles. Garrett and Amber at the water's edge. Joseph starting a camp fire. Not a single house. A burnt pile of rubble by the road.

"Here," I answered.

She stood silent a long moment, then raised an eyebrow. "Camping?"

"That's right."

"And the mattress is for …?"

It took a little explanation. I did my best.

"Something tells me you're not going to come work for me."

"Call Cammie back. Say please. Tell her about your mellow-out program."

"Are you planning to live here now?"

"Oh, no. I'll go back home."

"Home?"

"Home." I smiled.

"What about Garrett? Is he going to move into that shed with you?"

"No. He's going to live here."

"Oh, Bertie! I don't get it! You can pray in Mrs. Jorgen's guest-house as well as you can in a shed; in fact she's got a darling little rose garden out back and I know she'd let you have your quiet time right there by the meditation pond. If you work for me I'll let you keep your Bible at your desk; you know I've always been fine with that. They're going to have this seminar at church next month on 'Fulfilling Your Greatness.'" She caught my look and held a hand up. "Okay."

"How can I explain, Suzy? I want more than a quiet time in the morning and a Bible in my desk drawer. I don't want to fulfill my greatness. There's something deeper than that, I've glimpsed it, and I can't just look the other way and get on with my life. Not again."

I'd raised my voice to rival her own, and that pleased me. But I could see she didn't get it. I shrugged.

"Look at them," she said, nodding toward our children.

I'd been looking. Garrett and Amber stood on the shore like rocks, rigid and quiet, some twenty feet apart. Their awkwardness visible even from a distance.

"I wonder if they would have been happy," said Suzanne. "If they'd gotten married."

"They certainly seemed to be in love, back then."

"Do you ever think about that baby they lost?"

"All the time. I think about her all the time."

"Her?"

"Angeline."

She smiled.

"What about Roger? Is he good to her?"

"Roger is wonderful. I don't think that kid—*man*—will ever give up on her. It's Amber I worry about." She shook her head.

It had been a shock to see Amber. Her belly looked more distended than pregnant. When I hugged her, my fingers settled between her vertebrae. Desperate not to say the wrong thing, I grabbed for something neutral: "I hope you like shish kebab," I said. And cringed, to have said it to a girl who didn't eat.

Down on the beach, Garrett turned to say something to her, and without moving, she shrugged her shoulders. Garrett turned away.

"Shall we rescue them?" I asked.

"Angeline is a nice name."

———

We pitched in to help Joseph rebuild his hovel, and that helped all of us to relax. Suzanne, Amber, and I used sand to rub soot from the shells and bits of glass from Joseph's curtain. Amber grumbled that some of the soot just wouldn't come off no matter how she tried. Garrett leaned down to see, and said the damage actually made them look better. "Like they have a history."

And for the first time I'd seen that day, Amber smiled.

We spread a tarp on the sand and laid the mattress on top. According to Joseph's directions, we built the walls up with driftwood, and then the roof. We strung the shells and glass onto new twine.

"Amazing," pronounced Amber when we got it done.

"A good wind would blow it away," said Suzanne.

"Has, many times," said Joseph.

"He just builds another," I explained.

While Joseph finished setting things up inside, the rest of us set to work on dinner.

"Garrett," said Amber. "I remember the first time you ate a shish

kebab when we were kids, do you? Your dad looked at your plate after
dinner and the skewer was eaten clear away, all but the pointy end."

"At least I ate," he said. "Remember prom night, when you
fainted because you'd only had celery all day?"

"That was embarrassing. Since I landed in Krista Tan's lap. But!
The dress fit!"

"You'll eat tonight." He pointed with a half-loaded skewer.

"Yeah, yeah. Eating for two. Celery *and* carrots."

"No, I mean it. You could lose the baby."

"I know right where the baby is. Poking out the front of my blue
jeans. No way I could lose it, trust me."

"Get serious."

"I'm serious about fitting into those jeans when this is over. I
probably *will* lose the baby in a closet someplace, as hopeless as I am,
but at least I can fit into a size two."

"Amber, stop," said Suzanne.

"Maybe you and I can try again, Garrett, if I fail as a mother and
Roger doesn't want me."

"I don't want to try again," he said.

"Oh, right. You hate me. I forgot."

"I don't hate you."

Amber looked up and quieted.

He had tears in his eyes. "I want you to be well. I want you to
feed this baby, and be a great mother. I want you to be happy with
Roger. I don't hate you, Amber. Just please eat. Please."

I was standing on holy ground, watching my boy, and I knew
it. Maybe Amber knew as well. She brushed her own tears away and
nodded.

⌣

The magic happened just at dinnertime, the same as the night before. Only this night, it seemed that fifty galaxies had sprinkled their starlight in the water.

I noticed. Garrett and Joseph noticed, and we all exchanged glances. Suzanne was oblivious. She listened, frowning, to Joseph's story of how he lost everything, and came to build his hovel by the sea. Amber ate a full plate of food and asked for more, but she stared at the fire, hardly speaking, the whole time.

Would no one notice the water?

"Did you consider legal action?" Suzanne picked a tomato off her skewer.

"Legal action?" asked Joseph.

"Depending, of course, on how exactly she absconded with the money. But it seems you shouldn't have been the one to pay it back."

"How would legal action help?"

"How? If you recovered the money, it might help you start over, for one."

"I did start over."

"No, I mean …"

"Hellooo!" Someone called from on top of the rock, up near the road.

"Roger!" Amber got to her feet.

Joseph used his lamp to help him find the way down. Amber ran to meet him, and the two walked, arm in arm, back to the fire. Amber talked the whole way, her eyes fixed on her husband's face.

"You guys didn't tell me you were this far out," he said. "I almost didn't see your car."

"I didn't think you'd really join us," said Suzanne. "Are you hungry?"

"I ate most everything; you're barely in time," said Amber.

"Really?" He smiled and leaned down to kiss her.

Suzanne averted her eyes … then focused on a point, a luminous point beyond my shoulder. "Bertie," she breathed. "Look."

Amber turned to see. "What is that?"

Joseph chuckled.

"It's the red tide," said Roger. "I've been hearing about it all day."

"They said something about it on the news," said Suzanne. "But I was all caught up in the arson thing. I didn't know it was so … it's magical."

There were dances again, jitterbugs and tangos and the hava nagila. There were fireworks and water fights and one great sparkling beard.

But I didn't join in. I was happy to sit by the fire, to listen to the tin whistle and the surf and the singing, to watch my son, and know he would be all right.

The air felt like cool silk on my arms. I wrapped my shawl around them and closed my eyes, eager to make my way down that path to the ravishing place where I was only me: Bertie the broken, Bertie the unsure, Bertie who bled with fresh wounds every day. Bertie the beloved.

Something in me began to sway to the music of Joseph's whistle, and I found myself caught up in a long, slow dance with the One I'd always hoped to find. *Spread out your arms.* I heard the thought, not the words. I reached out, and someone on each side laced their fingers with mine. I found myself in a circle of joined hands, and knew I was surrounded by every soul I'd ever loved.

Can I tell you who? Thérèse of Lisieux was there with her roses. Francis of Assisi standing on his head, Teresa of Ávila eating her chicken, and Julian of Norwich smiling her knowing smile. Thomas Merton, and Henri Nouwen and others, many others I didn't know. We began a winding dance on the sands of creation, and each step we took flashed with light. When I grew dizzy with the dancing, we slowed, and stopped, smiling together.

I had to try this: "Is he here?"

And out through the crowd, shyly, stepped my husband. I clapped a hand to my mouth and wept.

I suppose I could have asked him all the questions I'd wished to ask, but in this place none of them crossed my mind. He reached out a hand, and I held it, not with understanding, but with a love deeper than the best we'd ever known. There was time enough to grow into the answers. For now, this was enough. This would do just fine.

I heard my son laughing on the shore and opened my eyes, and caught the scent of something sweetly transcendent, while out at sea there shone the magic light of all the stars in heaven.

EPILOGUE

I rise from my communion supper and slip another bite of the cinnamon roll into my mouth. Raisins cooked till they swell in the bread and pop between your teeth. Liquid spice and toasted walnuts. If love has a taste, this is it.

A knock sounds at the door, and I pull it open.

"Russ!"

He steps in. "I think we have it, this time."

India's wedding invitations. We've gone through seven tries with Russ's client, the calligrapher.

"If she doesn't like them, I'll have to offer him two free massages."

India was clear about her opinions: She didn't like the sketched hearts—too sweet, she said. She didn't like the calligraphy with no sketches—too plain. When he sketched in the woodland flowers and a bird's nest, she rolled her eyes. Even the moon and the stars were "a bit too new-age-ish."

"Really." I raised an eyebrow.

"I read The Song of Solomon like you said. And I think it's okay to be a lover, and a bride."

"Do you still believe in magic, then?"

A slow smile was all the answer I would get. For the time.

But a bride she will be, and in only three months. "Let's see what he's come up with." I hold out a hand, and Russ pulls the paper from a manila envelope.

"Oh, Russ." I touch one hand to the paper, and another to my lips. It's a sketch of India, wrapped in Garrett's arms.

"I took the photo a couple of months ago, out on my deck. I thought maybe he could draw from that."

The smiles are perfect, and the warmth in their eyes.

I remember the day Gil dropped India and the baby back at the store and sped off in his Lamborghini, to continue his life with someone else. He couldn't have given me a better gift.

Four days later, Garrett came for Friday night dinner, just like always.

A new hot plate and a small refrigerator fueled by a new power line—thanks to Russ and Boyd—and I'd cooked quite a lovely beef stew. I found some flowers to put on my small wooden table, made a salad. And India brought a loaf of her fresh wholegrain bread.

Later, she offered to show Garrett her garden. I held the baby on my shoulder and watched them walk down the road, side by side. And I thought, *of course!*

Before long, they thought the same thing. India taught Garrett how to bake bread, and Garrett had some ideas for improvements to the store.

And now we have a wedding to plan.

I sit on the edge of the bed Garrett bought me and run my finger over the sketch once again. This is my son, and the girl who wants to be my daughter. "It's beautiful, Russ."

He pulls up the umbrella chair. "Boyd and I were talking. This place wouldn't be so dark if you had a larger window. It wouldn't take any time to put one in."

"That sounds wonderful. Thank you. Thank you for everything."

"Boyd thought of it."

"Do you hear from Brenda?"

"Of course. She says I'm her best friend. She has a new beau."

"Oh, Russ."

"He doesn't sound so bad. Doesn't like her clothes, though. Says she wears too many bright colors."

"She's stupid, that's all. Why doesn't she come back to you?"

"Maybe one day. We'll see how this Malcolm lasts."

"Anybody home?" We hear India's voice outside. I cross the room in two strides and open the door. And lower my eyes to look for someone just over two feet tall. There stands the small girl, in orange pajamas and red tennis shoes.

"My little star!"

Estelle holds her mother by one hand. "Gamma," she says, and totters into my shed on wobbling feet. I lift her to my hip and kiss her cheek. She wraps one soft arm around my neck, lays her head on my shoulder, and sucks her thumb.

"I bought a dress," India says, holding up a box. "*The* dress! I found it at a little vintage clothing shop, so there's no waste of resources. I looked at some new ones, organic fabrics, but hemp silk is so expensive! But this one. It's from the nineteen twenties!"

"It sounds lovely. Russ has a new design for the invitation." I hold it out. "Wait till you—"

"I found a lady who will make the bouquet from flowers that grow in my—" She stops, finally looking at the paper. "That's … us!"

"Do you like it?" Russ moves forward in the chair.

"It's perfect. Oh, it's beautiful." She wipes her eyes.

"I can't tell you how glad I am to hear that." Russ brushes his knees off, and stands. "Now, you're going to want to try on that dress, so I'll leave you two ladies to your business."

When he leaves, she pulls off her shirt and jeans, pulls the dress from the box, and slips it over her shoulders. She lifts her hair to the top of her head, and strikes a pose.

She could have modeled for Erté. In that nineteen-twenties drop-waist sheath, with her body curved as though swaying in some gentle wind.

"Have you ever been so beautiful?" I ask.

"I don't think so," she says.

Estelle lifts her head, rubs her nose, and lies on my other shoulder. India sits beside me on the bed.

"You know," she says, "I stopped believing in magic, for just a few days."

"When was that?"

"Right after I left with Gil. It didn't take me long to know what a mistake I'd made. He got upset over everything: when I talked about his pretentious, gas-hungry car. When Estelle spit up on his clothes. When she cried—*ho!*—when she cried. Everything I'd asked for, cast all those spells for, I'd gotten. And as soon as I did, it all just went gray. And I thought, there was no holy ground, no magic. There was only getting by. But wasn't that better than not getting by? So I shut up about everything, just did what he said to do. Only I couldn't make Estelle stop crying.

"Then one night we were driving to his shop in Aptos, and he was yelling at me again—yelling at me still. I just tuned him out and stared out the window at the ocean. Then, all of a sudden, I saw something, like there were faeries in the water. When the waves crashed into themselves, there was this light. I told Gil to look, but he hardly did. He said, "It's just algae," and went on with his lecture. But I knew when I saw that. There was still magic."

"Yes. Every step we take falls on holy ground."

"Oh! I almost forgot. Would it be okay? Can I borrow back my grandma's rosary, and the bracelet? I'd like to have them for the wedding."

"You know? I think I'll return them to you."

"Return them?"

"As a wedding present. And anyway, the rosary was just a loan, right?" I take her hand. "They'll be even more special now, and you'll want to keep them. And one day, you'll give them to Estelle."

India wipes her eyes. "I'm so happy you came to this mountain and moved into this shed."

Me too. I'm happy too.

Estelle raises her head. "Cannos," she says, then blows a little puff.

"Later, little star. You can blow them out later."

"Hello?"

It's Garrett's voice outside the door.

"No, wait!" India cries. "He can't see me in this dress."

She hurries back into her jeans and shirt, then folds the dress back into the box and opens the door.

And kisses my son. And kisses him again.

Then turns to me. "Are you sure it's okay about Estelle? I can come back early if you don't want her the whole night."

"If I don't want her?" I press Estelle to my shoulder and hug them both. "Joseph likes cinnamon bread. Tell him if he does the wedding, you'll make him some of these rolls."

I watch them leave in Saffron, the yellow Mercedes, then I carry Estelle back into the shed. I tear off a small piece of the cinnamon roll, pick out the walnuts, and tuck it in her cheek.

"Gamma," she reminds me. "Cannos."

"Yes. Let's blow them out."

We kneel on the floor. She blows out the first, and then the second, third, and fourth. Finally, she fills her cheeks with a big puff of air, leans over, and blows out the last.

We crawl into bed, and lie side by side in the darkness. I kiss her forehead, hold her hand, and start down that path, where I am only me, and she is little Estelle, and the two of us are deeply loved.

... a little more ...

When a delightful concert comes to an end,

the orchestra might offer an encore.

When a fine meal comes to an end,

it's always nice to savor a bit of dessert.

When a great story comes to an end,

we think you may want to linger.

And so, we offer ...

AfterWords—just a little something more after you

have finished a David C. Cook novel.

We invite you to stay awhile in the story.

Thanks for reading!

Turn the page for ...

- **A Conversation with Kathleen Popa**
- **Reader's Guide**
- **India's Cinnamon Rolls (recipe)**

A CONVERSATION WITH

KATHLEEN POPA

What inspired you to write a novel about a woman seeking a life of solitude and poverty?

I started life as a Catholic, so maybe that had something to do with it. I've always had a spiritual bent, and as a girl I used to wonder if I might not become a nun someday. My fantasy did not survive adolescence, but I nevertheless am fascinated by the ancients who really did renounce wealth and position in order to gain a sumptuous, costly, deep relationship with God. When I started to write *The Feast of Saint Bertie*, I asked myself how that impulse might play out in the life of a modern-day Protestant, middle-aged woman who is used to shopping at Nordstrom, who is as attached to her cell phone as I am.

Which character is most like who you—Bertie, who pursues the devout life; India the witch; or Suzanne, who seeks fulfillment in her career?

There have been times in my life when I have wanted—*badly*—to be Suzanne, the one who always knows what to do and how to get it done, who always has the very thing you need right in the back of her car.

I never really adopted that nature, and I'm grateful for that. The times when I've come closest to the "confident and competent" ideal have not been great times for me, spiritually. The sheer rush and effort to get life under control and keep it that way hinders my ability to watch and listen for the presence and the direction of God.

In some secret corner of my soul, I am a lot like India. I tend to look for meaning and wonder behind and beneath things. But though I sympathize with the impulse, I think that any attempts at casting spells would only be another try at wresting control away from God. In fact, I think some of my own prayers have been uttered in a spirit of arrogance and self-will, and as such have hardly been better than spells.

For me, the way Bertie learns seems better: to come to God, not as a goddess, not with my thin veneer of confidence and competence, but simply as myself. I'm learning to trust that He can manage things fine, and if I'm very good and promise to be careful, He'll let me help from time to time.

India has some hard things to say about our cultural values, or what she would probably call our lack of values. Do you share her convictions?

I speak more gently than India, simply because I'm old enough to know how often I need to hear my own sermons. But yes, I think most people are living driven lives, with too little unstructured silence in which to rest, to listen and pray. My mother and I have taken up the habit of walking around a nearby lake several days a week, and that has been deeply good for us on many levels. I'm not saying our lives should be all about quiet and not about action, but I think the quiet would help us to choose the wiser actions, the better use of our lives.

Where did you get the idea for Joseph's hovel?

Years ago I found a hovel exactly like it on a beach near Pescadero, California. From a distance it looked like a pile of driftwood, but when I got closer I saw that it was a tiny house. I bent to look through the small opening and saw that someone had set up housekeeping in there, with a bed and a nice little table. The occupant wasn't around, and I felt like an intruder, so I didn't take any pictures; I just backed away and left it there. But I never forgot, and I never stopped wondering who lived there, and what was their story.

Two scenes in your novel, the childbirth scene and the red tide scene, are richly detailed. Have you witnessed a red tide? Have you given birth at home or witnessed a home birth?

I've never seen a red tide (or an aurora borealis, or even a firefly, and I really, really want to). It was at the party my husband threw for me when I sold *To Dance in the Desert*, that some friends, Dave Koon and his wife, Jill Jones, started talking about this amazing thing they'd once witnessed, when the proliferation of a certain type of algae had made the water luminescent. Everything they said just enchanted me, and I knew I had to find a place for the red tide in my next book.

The one time I gave birth, it was a C-section much like Bertie's, except that Bertie, in her distress, remembers it as a less joyful experience than mine was. Still, I knew that India would have her baby at home, so I called my friend Peggy Durfey, who is a doula, and asked her to describe for me how such a birth might play out. Again, I was enchanted. But there was Bertie, anguishing over her son, watching this beautiful birth. I knew she felt that by having the C-section, she had failed Garrett from the beginning.

What were you trying to say when you wrote Bertie's prayer scene on the beach in the final chapter?

A lot more than I can put into words. But here are some thoughts:

So much of the way we live is about appearances. We aren't often conscious of this, but our subconscious minds are a windstorm of anxieties about how we come across, whether we are productive enough, intelligent, beautiful, smart enough. And since we all know that we aren't enough of any of these things, we try at least to look as though we are.

You can't pray that way. If you do, the person you send into the Holy of Holies will be an impostor who leaves you sitting outside, wondering what's going on inside. If you want to enter in yourself, you have to make sure it's the real you. And one good way I know to be sure is to find that weak, or ashamed, or confused person you never show anyone. That one, you can bet, is real.

It's hard to write well about prayer, because prayer goes beyond words. So I get fanciful. Have I ever found myself dancing with Brother Lawrence or Julian of Norwich? I'd love that, but no. Still, when I read their works, I recognize the God they loved so passionately as the same God I spoke with this morning. How beautiful that is.

When Bertie first looks inside Joseph's hovel, she discovers the book he is currently reading: *The Way of the Heart* by Henri Nouwen. Later Joseph recommends to her *Ruthless Trust* by Brennan Manning. Should the reader interpret this as a thinly veiled "recommended reading" list?

Oh dear, I've been caught.

If you visited me in my home you would stand a good chance of getting read to, out of whatever book I was most enthralled with at the moment. These were two books I read while I was writing *The Feast of Saint Bertie*, and I think ten years from now I will still consider them two of the most important books I've ever read.

The Way of the Heart is Nouwen's exploration into the origins of Christian monasticism and the disciplines of solitude, silence and prayer. He writes about these in a way that is deeply relevant to us in our ordinary, twenty-first-century lives.

In *Ruthless Trust*, Manning talks about a faith that rests in quiet trust when we have no control, when things don't make sense, when life hurts.

What are you reading now?

I'm reading *The Sacred Way* by Tony Jones, a very good book about the sorts of spiritual disciplines Bertie might find herself practicing as she grows into her new way of life. I don't plan to move into a shed— *I don't think*—but I'd like to grow into these practices myself.

I'm also several pages into *Fatal Deduction*, the latest of Gayle Roper's wonderful suspense novels, and I think it may be her best yet. On my iPod I'm listening to *The Cure*, a novel by Athol Dickson, having recently finished his *River Rising*. Dickson is the newest on my short list of favorite authors.

What are you writing now?

I'm writing a novel about a reverse-prodigal situation: an aging hippie who thinks he has failed as a father because his son became a stockbroker, and his daughter became a pastor's wife. Now he is sick, and he wants to love just one person well before he dies.

READER'S GUIDE

1. In the novel, Bertie regrets that as her family gained in wealth and position, her marriage lost the intimacy of its early years. Have you had or do you know anyone who has had a similar experience? Do you think that such losses are an inevitable part of life, or can they be prevented?

2. Why do you think the author set this story in and around the Silicon Valley?

3. What was your first impression of Suzanne? Did your feelings toward her change in the course of the novel? If so, how?

4. Did you empathize with Bertie's desire for a cloistered, devout life? Why or why not?

5. If you moved into a shed in the mountains as Bertie did, what would you take with you?

6. How was Bertie's approach to the spiritual life similar to and different from India's? From Suzanne's? How did Bertie's approach to God change over the course of the story?

7. Why was Bertie so upset when India gave her the little statue of "Sister Vishnu"? How might you have felt?

8. Were you surprised to learn that Garrett was homeless? What were your feelings when Bertie joined him in his lifestyle? Would you have done the same?

9. What was your response when you learned that Larry had paid for Amber's abortion? Do you feel that Garrett and Bertie had cause to be upset?

10. At the beginning of chapter 38, Bertie tells us, "They never warn you before you have a child how much you will love him." Do you agree? What has been your experience, either as a parent, or as someone who loves a child who is not your own?

11. In chapter 37, Joseph says, "There's something holy about sorrow." Do you agree with him? In the same conversation, he says, "Your greatest gift, the greatest proof of [God's] love, is in your pain." What does he mean by that?

12. When Garrett reveals that he intends to remain homeless for a time, but under the mentorship of Joseph, Bertie seems content. Would you be as comfortable with Garrett's decision if you were his parent? Why or why not?

13. What meaning do you attach to the word *magic*? How does that word play into the theme of the story?

14. The appearance of the red tide comes as a special message to both Bertie and India. What is that message? Have you ever seen something that affected you in a similar way? What did you see, and how did it change your perception?

15. Were you satisfied with the way the story ended? How would you have liked it to end?

INDIA'S CINNAMON ROLLS

Note from India:

It's up to me to keep the author honest. When Kathleen tried this recipe, I shamed her into using free-range eggs—just look up how they treat the chickens that lay the eggs you eat in the morning and ask yourself if any of God's creatures deserve such cruelty. But Kathleen wrote "organic" all over the place just so I'd shut up. Still, it's true, you can even find organic shortening if you look for it, and it's better for you. I make cinnamon rolls with organic white flour to keep my customers happy, but it wouldn't hurt you to make them whole wheat. Kathleen did, and even she admits they were delicious.

Grease enough muffin pans to hold twelve cinnamon rolls.

½ C hormone-free milk
½ pkg. yeast
3 T organic shortening
1 T organic butter
⅓ C organic sugar
½ t salt
1 free-range egg yolk, beaten
1½ C sifted whole wheat flour, or, alternately, white flour
Melted organic butter
¼ C organic brown sugar, packed
2 t cinnamon
⅓ C organic raisins
⅓ C organic walnuts

Syrup:
½ C organic corn syrup
½ C organic brown sugar, firmly packed
⅛ C butter

Heat the milk to boiling, and allow to cool till it's just warm. Sprinkle yeast over top. Cream shortening plus 1 tablespoon of the butter; stir in ⅓ cup sugar and ½ teaspoon salt. Beat together till light and fluffy. Add the egg yolk, the yeast/milk mixture and enough flour to make a soft dough. Knead on a lightly floured board. Roll the dough into a square about ¼ inch thick. Brush the square with butter. Mix together the ¼ cup of brown sugar and the cinnamon. Sprinkle the square of dough with this mixture, plus the raisins and walnuts. Roll the square of dough up like you're rolling a rug. Cut the roll into 12 slices.

Make the syrup by heating in a small pan ½ cup of corn syrup, ½ cup of brown sugar, and ⅛ cup of butter, till all are melted together. Pour a little of this mixture into each cup of your muffin pans. Place the slices in the muffin pans. Cover and let sit for an hour, or if you used white flour, till the dough rises to twice its size.

Bake in a hot oven at 400 degrees for 12–15 minutes. Remove from oven, flip over the pans, and loosen the rolls. Then while the rolls are still upside down, lay the pan back over the tops of them, so the syrup will ooze into the rolls.

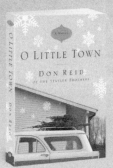

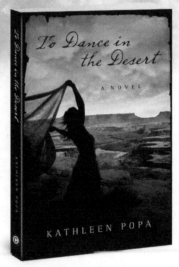